Polar Axis

Winter's Verse Part II

Nicole Hayes

Iona Print

Library of Congress Control Number: 2023921250
ISBN (Hardcover Edition): 979-8-9894105-1-4
ISBN (Softcover Edition): 979-8-9894105-2-1
ISBN (Ebook Edition): 979-8-9894105-3-8

Printed in the USA
Iona Print
nicolehayesauthor@gmail.com

WINTER'S VERSE

Copper & Snow

Polar Axis

The Vast Collective Series

The Burning Cinder Trilogy
Last of Daylight
By the Pale Moonlight
Asylum in Firelight
Nox's Verse
The Warding Gait Trilogy
Glass Chains
Pyrite Prison
Restraining Silver
Korac's Verse
The Drowning Enki Trilogy
Thirst
Levee
Flood
Xelan's Verse
Cascading Light

To those of us who confront what we fear to face.

CONTENTS

Acknowledgments...ix

01   Winter's Royalty...01

02   Pure Deception...31

03   Black Heart...64

04   Lost Time..85

05   Dazzling Snow...109

06   Thawing Frost...137

07   Burning Flame...159

08   Tarnished Love..184

09   Diamond Truth...208

10   Founding Day...232

11   Golden Butterfly...259

12   Copper Union...284

13   Little Death...306

14   Platinum Winter..333

Epilogue..358

Author's Note...364

Acknowledgments

Batman, your reception of this conclusion encouraged me to keep writing, but also to take a break. It's time that I enjoy spending time with you without a story running wild through my mind. We can bask together now that I've finished this duology, and I am looking forward to it.

Firefly, I know the final act of *Copper & Snow* wasn't to your liking, which makes your love for *Polar Axis* even more special. Thank you for trusting me to always have a happy ending. Here's to fifteen of them <3

Thank you again, Destiny, for loving my story enough to edit it.

Rebeca Covers, thank you for all of your excellent illustrations and for bringing my worlds to life in full color.

ONE

Winter's Royalty

"But, and I can't believe I'm saying this, Snow *did* help me with one thing. Lexia Tempest, will you spend the rest.of your time on this planet with me?"

"My time belongs to us."

"Well, what kind of father would I be if I didn't warn my son of his fiance's indiscretions?"

"You rank, abusive bastard. Come for my inheritance, but don't you dare come near Lexia again. I don't care what 'indiscretions' you'll claim to protect me from. She's as much an angel as her mother, and you know it. Leave my engagement alone."

"Do you know what happens when a cigar meets flesh?"

Snow claimed Winter and all/

Even the Diamond who came to call/

But the Heiress escaped in time/

Before the Count committed his crime/

And now they both await/

Judgment at the copper gate/

Who will end up in the Wall?/

"Axis, it wasn't Gauge's fault. It was mine."

"Master Flicker. Count Snow. Let's listen to reason and talk as civilized people—"

"Fuck you, Leon. You've sided with my son after everything I've done for you. And Snow. Don't think for one second I don't see how you benefit from this."

"I think it's transparent how I benefit from this. The factory, the mines, and the crops make for a symbiotic relationship. You're the only one who was ever too foolish to never see it that way."

"Father. Father, breathe. Take a breath—"

"You killed him."

"You're in shock."

"Those fucking cigars. You may as well have killed him yourself."

"Just make sure Prince Axis knows if he needs anything, he shouldn't hesitate to call on me."

"Son, stay with us. I'll act as chaperon, so you won't violate the pre-marital laws. I don't like the idea of you alone in that apartment tonight."

"If Valve hadn't fought for Winter, none of us would be here, today. And that counts for something. So, in respect to his love for the future, I dedicate this in Valve's name."

"But today, I want to introduce you to the dawn of that dark night. Last Founding Season, the late Master Flicker and I developed something extraordinary. And while we all recover from the shock, I think Valve would want us to embrace the good with the bad. So, I present you with a new sport designed entirely by Master Flicker. Ice skating."

"Prince Axis, I challenge you to a race."

"You can't expect me to race on my first day against someone who's had at least a few months' practice."

"Oh, please, Axis! I'm sure you can win. You're already moving about with ease."

"What're the stakes?"

"The same as our fencing match. A dinner with Ms. Tempest, and I'll keep my good faith measure of extending the invitation to you."

"You're on."

"Hm? Forgive me. I must've drifted off."

"Are we not stimulating enough for you?"

"You're both plenty stimulating for me. Now, tell me what I've missed."

"It's about Ms. Cloud. I wish to revoke her exile and have her return to my factories, if you deem it so."

"Well, *Master* Flicker, your wish is mine to fulfill. Are there any other wishes you would make of me tonight?"

"To Ms. Tempest for bringing us together tonight."

"Here, here."

"To a new beginning."

"To a new beginning."

"What is it you want me to get out of your father? Because I will do anything to ease your troubles."

"Is the friction that obvious?"

"Painfully so."

"I think father is hiding something about mother from me."

"I'll do what I can."

"My daughter is so intelligent and capable, but she doesn't always think of the consequences ahead of her actions. Consider Winter's dueling law, for example. It needs refinement, of course, but to revise it completely in one beautiful act is reckless. Yes, that's how I'd describe Lexia. Especially of late."

"Is there something wrong with Lexia?"

"Son, what do you know of Lya's death?"

"Nothing, sir. I was shocked to hear the news. She never seemed ill, but I know there are plenty of ailments which strike the healthy to the quick. I always figured it was like that."

"Axis, what I am about to tell you can never leave this room. Do you understand? Lexia can never know the truth."

"Lexia, I'm moving back to my apartments, and I think we should reconsider some aspects of our engagement."

"What do you mean? Why?"

"I am unfit as your partner. More to the point, your father has enlightened me of some health matters which make me unfit as a father. And I would never ask you to accept a life without children—"

"We can adopt. Orphans aren't common anymore, but there are still plenty of children in need of parents. We can adopt."

"Forgive me if I find this difficult to move beyond. I ask for a few days to think on it."

"Of course. Yes. Please give the idea some thought. I could go forever without children, but please don't ask me to go a lifetime without you."

"Son,

"I know you're upset with me, but I want us to put our differences aside. We share a common threat to my daughter, and I fear we may already be too late. Lexia confronted me last night, and when I proved too cowardly to confess my sins, she ran.

"Axis—Lexia fled to the Cathedral.

"Avoid the papers. Don't believe the headlines."

"I'm close friends with several people who staff the Cathedral, and I can say she only stayed the night in a guest room. There was nothing inappropriate about her visit aside from the lack of a chaperon, much to her reputation's detriment. Do you understand me?"

"Prince Axis, tell us your thoughts on Ms. Tempest's betrayal?"

"Is the wedding off? Or postponed until you can include Count Snow?"

"Be gentle with Lexia, and please don't fault our Count for the natural progression of things."

"Prince Axis and I are here to see Ms. Tempest."

"Now"

"I'm afraid Ms. Tempest is indisposed, and the Count isn't taking visitors today."

"Lexia! Lexia! Forgive me! Lexia! Please! I need to see you!"

"Is it over?"

"Has the Heiress left you for the Count?"

Indisposed.

The natural progression of things.

Was it over…

No.

AXIS FLICKER, THE PEOPLE'S PRINCE, OPENED HIS EYES TO FIND HIMSELF STARING BACK. He blinked soft green eyes into a reflection cast from the canopy above. His short burgundy hair was a mess around his topaz-complected features. Brows, cheekbones, and jaw were all angular, sharpening his face aside from one full bottom lip which the love of his life enjoyed teasing. With his white button-down gaped open, he could see the small circular mounds of scar tissue marring his skin all the way down his chest, ribs, and stomach before they disappeared into his black slacks.

The bed was a rich mahogany mammoth covered in lush soft gray linens. Strangely, the color reminded Axis of familiar irises belonging to—

"Son."

On edge, Axis startled and turned to face Dr. Leon Tempest. The good doctor looked as if he'd been asleep in the chair beside the bed. He set aside the newspaper in his lap, stood, and reached out a hand for Axis' forehead.

For one shining moment—a second of peace—Axis rested back against the pillow and closed his eyes expecting the cooling hand to relieve his flushed skin. Then he remembered.

Everything.

"No!"

Axis bolted upright in the bed out of Leon's reach, glaring at his fiance's father. Former fiance? Oh, why was everything so irreversibly damaged?

The gentle paternal figure of Axis' childhood tilted his head to the side, lending a glare to his thin wire-framed glasses and pitching his expression into mystery. He repeated with a questioning lilt, "Son?"

Axis climbed out of the bed on the other side and buttoned his shirt, saying, "You were right in your missive. I *am* upset with you, but for her sake not mine. How can you go on lying to your daughter, Leon? You drove her to the Copper Cathedral into..."

Gauge Snow's waiting arms.

While Axis tried to swallow the bitter taste in his mouth, he knew the sourness showed in his expression.

Still cast in the floor-to-ceiling window's glare, Leon said, "Well, I think we can both take some responsibility in that. No one told you to end your engagement and ignore her for three days. We both know how headstrong our butterfly can be. How impulsive. For instance, I knew she would break into my study to uncover the secret. Perhaps, I also predicted she would run out—But to you. Not to Snow. I thought it would sort itself out that way, and maybe I didn't see her until the wedding. Sadly maybe even years longer, but one day I knew she would forgive me for keeping the secret. Forgive us both. But with Snow in the mix… Nothing is predictable now."

At the end of his unfortunately accurate speech, Lexia's father tossed the newspaper onto the bed between him and Axis. In bold print, the headlines condemned them all:

Heiress Slave to Count's Every Whim

Prince Down for the Count

Royal Throuple Theory Reduced to Ruins in Wake of Butterfly's Destruction

Heat and Pressure: Winter's Diamond to Carbon

Every single article was about them.

The room spun, dizzying in the mirror's reflection as Axis' knees went weak. He clutched a bedpost, closed his eyes, and rested his head against it. It took him two tries to say, "How long have I been out?"

Leon's voice was filled with concern and an ounce of pity. "Only a day, but all of Winter is on fire with this scandal. And my daughter is at the heart of it. I hurt for Lexia. She even sent for some of her things delivered to Snow Plaza."

What was happening…

Sniffles and gentle sobbing had awakened Axis from his nap in Tempest Manor. He let Lexia and the other children sleep before walking out of Lexia's room on the fifth floor and down the stairs to the room below. It was a library, and there he found Lexia's mother alone. He rubbed the sleep from his eyes as he asked, "Mrs. Tempest, why are you crying?"

Lya startled, but relaxed instantly when she saw it was Axis. She held out her arms, and he went into them without hesitation. In a mother's

embrace of which he'd never known, Axis squeezed Lya to show her how much he loved her.

After some time of her rocking him, Lya confessed, "I miss my family."

"But we're your family."

"Oh, sweet Axis. There is so much you don't understand."

Axis still didn't understand. Not completely. But he had at least one piece of the tragic puzzle. He said, "Please, Leon. Tell Lexia the truth."

"My boy, you assume the Copper Count already hasn't, and that she doesn't continue to dwell in that place to punish me."

Axis shook his head. "Dwelling isn't really in Lexia's nature. The moment Gau—Snow tells her the truth, she'll walk down Tempest Boulevard and tear into you for keeping it from her. Seeing as that's not the case, I'll be off now."

With a cursory glance around the room, Axis spotted his coat. As he slipped into it, Leon asked, "Will you bring Lexia home, Axis?"

Home.

Would Tempest Manor ever be home to Axis again? Or to Lexia? It made the People's Prince heartsick to consider it. At the door, with his back to Leon, Axis said, "If she'll listen—if she'll have me—I'll salvage us. But I'm only armed with the truth and the pervading desire to make this right. That doesn't look good for you, Dr. Tempest."

"Whatever it takes, son."

Whatever it takes.

The bubbles sudsed over the edge of the tub and splashed onto the black granite floor in a magnificent wave as Lexia rose above Gauge Snow in the water. She rode him slowly, giving him a show of her perfect alabaster breasts, slim waist, the swell of her hips, and those long, long legs.

Eternity, Gauge loved Lexia's legs. Right now, they straddled him in ecstasy.

Again.

For the hundredth time in thirty-six hours.

And sweet Lexia was a quick study for someone with only one prior lover. For instance, she knew how much Gauge enjoyed the silkiness of her white hair between his fingers, sans gloves. Without the usual protection, his overly sensitive fingertips drank in the softness eagerly and almost painfully. The knowledge of it shone in her black eyes as she let her hair down for him to touch the long waves.

Gauge enjoyed when Lexia explored herself. Her soapy hands glided over her breasts and below the waterline in a display he devoured. He appreciated when she arched her back for him, and she always did so just perfectly for him to nibble her breasts. And of course, he reveled in the way she said his name at the height of pleasure.

But aside from foundation-rattling sex, what did Lexia get out of this?

Gauge wrapped his fist in her hair and pulled Lexia down to him for an aggressive kiss. She moaned into it, and he felt her pull away until it surely hurt. All the while, their fucking intensified.

Not yet, little butterfly.

Gauge released Lexia's hair to grip her by the waist, lift her off him, and rise from the water. She stared at him as the soapy liquid poured down them both, with her panting from exertion and flushed yellow from desire. He grabbed her wrists, and she struggled, fighting against him.

Lexia was a robust and healthy young woman of twenty-three years without illness or malady. Gauge was heading into his thirtieth year of coping with a lifelong affliction. If not for his regular physical therapy and workouts with his butler, Jan, Gauge wouldn't stand a chance overpowering Lexia. But fortunately…

With considerable effort, Gauge pinned Lexia's hands to the edge of the tub, bent her over, and bit into her shoulder as he fucked her— quite literally—like an animal. Her orgasm wrenched them both to completion.

They sank back into the water and soaked for a moment in silence, giving Gauge's agonized bones time to recover. Lexia stared at him with dark bruises under her eyes from all the kinky strangulation and lack of sleep. More bruises in the shape of his fingerprints and teeth marred her perfect skin at the neck and wrists.

Without his spectacles covering his weak corneas, Gauge wondered what he looked like to Lexia. Bleeding from scratches all over his body and messy braids tangled to his shoulders. Was she as proud of their disaster as he was?

Two days.

They'd gone at it non-stop for two days. Well, minus the earliest hours of the morning. Lexia had requested to sleep alone, reminders of the last vestiges of her promises to Axis. She adhered to the pre-martial laws—No staying the night with a partner until marriage. At least, in this, she'd remained faithful.

But as the hours ran into days, Gauge thought himself decent enough a man to notice that Lexia was not handling anything. She was not facing or confronting or even dealing with her issues.

Did Lexia believe the headlines? That she'd betrayed Axis mere days after he'd abruptly broken off their engagement? Or did Lexia recognize she'd sought solace in Gauge when she'd realized there was nowhere else to go? Perhaps she felt bad for using him.

Well, Gauge certainly didn't.

"When was the last time you've eaten?"

Lexia countered, "I can't remember the last time I saw you eat anything, either."

Touche.

Perhaps even a little too close to home. Gauge asked, "Would you care to join me for..." Was this morning? Evening? "A meal?"

There.

Lexia gave Gauge the smile again. It was warm and full of so much light. Even too much. There was hope and kindness in it. Longing... It meant more to Gauge than he'd like to admit. She said, "I believe it's some time in the afternoon. An early dinner then?"

"Let's."

The smile faded quick as it came, breaking Gauge's heart. So much darkness plagued Lexia like a shadow. Once a butterfly entangled in a net, she was now subdued after days of capture in a jar. Soon, the light would snuff out completely if someone didn't give her some air.

When Lexia stood, the lost look on her face was so much that Gauge couldn't appreciate the water sluicing down her body. She stepped out of the tub with those long legs and went into the shower. This time, he wouldn't follow.

Soon.

Very soon.

The Heiress would need to face her demons, and while the Count wanted to be there for her, he was one of the monsters who'd put the lid on the jar. Gauge had tried to tell Lexia the truth in the beginning, but she'd made her demands clear. Sex, first. Destroying the security of her entire world, later. Who was he to deny her?

Damn it.

Gauge got out of the tub and joined Lexia in the shower. Surely, he was going to hell for this. And poor Axis. News was, the People's Prince had yet to awaken from his fainting spell in the Plaza. At least, that was as of Gauge's last update an hour ago. Any minute now, he expected the valiant young boy scout to march his twenty-four-year-old and mightily fit ass back to the Copper Cathedral demanding admittance.

Was Gauge of half a mind to let Axis in? Oh, yes.

Did Gauge dread the ass kicking which would surely ensue thereafter? How could he not?

If not for Lexia's brave and frankly reckless declaration to ban duels to the death, Gauge would certainly face his end on Axis's sword. It wasn't very wise to sleep with the former fiance of a man with unfortunately impressive swordsman skills.

Even with all this in mind, Gauge and Lexia sated themselves twice more in the shower. Once on the floor and once against the wall. She *really* enjoyed sex, and it was about time for Gauge to dose himself with more adrenaline to keep up.

With a voice soft from fresh strangulation, Lexia said, "I'll see you downstairs," before quitting the room in nothing but a robe. The silk clung to her assets in such a way as to invite another fresh bout of rousing exercising, but Gauge had to steer control of himself at some point.

Right.

Clothes.

Gloves.

Glasses.

Food—

Shit.

Gauge glanced at the kit on his bistro set. Lexia was a clever young woman. She'd surely take notice of her partner not eating at their first meal in thirty-eight hours.

A knock sounded at the door.

"Come in, Jan."

The 'butler' proceeded into the room with a tray—Bless him. Jan said, "I took the liberty, sir."

Gauge sat down to eat, smiling for his considerate companion. "You're a lifesaver, old friend." He poured a bit of blue powder onto the fish and dropped a bit of black liquid into his drink. When neither reacted, he ate greedily of the metallic-tasting fare. With this current predicament in mind, he asked, "How long do you think before she notices?"

Jan didn't hesitate. "Ms. Tempest will notice immediately, sir, but not to worry. We are serving her in the guest room as we speak. It seems the dining room and kitchens are in need of a cleaning to prepare for Founding Day."

Gauge couldn't contain his grin. The old spy was beyond reliable. Gauge said, "Thank you, Jan, but I can't keep it from her forever."

"Nor should you, sir. But perhaps, for a few more meals until Ms. Tempest is ready to know the truth."

Wise.

And so very well-informed.

Gauge nodded for his butler who left the room to serve his new favorite ward. They were all getting attached, rather too quickly. Lexia's time here slipped out of Gauge's gloved fingers even though she slept here and ordered some of her things delivered in order to stay longer. This situation was far too precarious.

Reckless, even.

But this was Founding Season, and Gauge would be damned if he let anything get in the way of enjoying it.

While it lasted.

———————————

Lexia stared down at her plate of food and couldn't find her appetite. Couldn't find her will. Nor her mind. She wanted to be numb, and only feel the exhilaration of the physical acts between her and Gauge. All the while, her heart shattered into smaller and smaller pieces.

Axis.

While Lexia had avoided the papers, and the servants here at the Copper Cathedral seemed to avoid her, she'd heard their whispers and the shouts from the streets. The People's Prince had come to the Cathedral to claim his Heiress, and the Count's butler had turned him away. Whether Axis came to tell Lexia the truth or to warn her away from Gauge, she'd been too 'indisposed' to address him.

Should Lexia thank Jan for that? She'd come to the Copper Cathedral three nights ago seeking sanctuary in Gauge's arms, and like a gentleman, he'd given her a night and a morning to deliberate the consequences of her actions. But wasn't that what all of this was about?

Consequences.

Lexia's father and her fiance knew a secret. A most devastating secret about her mother and possibly about Gauge. Perhaps it pertained to Lya Tempest's death, something Leon never divulged much on. Or perhaps there was something even more sinister woven through the threads of Lexia's entire existence.

White hair.

Black eyes.

White skin.

Blue freckles.

Yellow blood.

Never sick.

No broken bones.

What was Lexia, and how were she and her mother different from everyone else left on Winter? Why did this conspiracy feel more monumental than even the details of Founding Season?

"Mommy, why do you hug me so tight?"

"Because you smell of home, my darling. You smell of home."

Shattered.

But that's not who Lexia was or the stock from which she was made. Alone in the guest room across the hall from Gauge on the highest floor of the Copper Cathedral, Lexia took in her surroundings and sorted the pieces together. White walls cleared the mind. The plush black rug over the pale gray parquet floors resembled her current situation. Neither right nor wrong, but gray hovered over by a black storm. The enormous bed with its sturdy black posts and white linens had kept Lexia safe the last three nights she'd slept alone. From the opened stained glass balcony door, Lexia could hear the pulsing beat of Winter carrying on in its afternoon traffic, waiting for news of her infidelity.

Or not infidelity, depending on the publication.

Gauge and Axis were so different. While Lexia reveled in Gauge's powerful grips and bruising teeth, she longed for Axis' deliberate and thorough exploration. His stamina. Without the glasses, Lexia could see how tired Gauge was by the faint lines surrounding his otherwise penetrating blue eyes. How much he hid the weakness in his limbs of which she refused to pry.

Everyone deserved their privacy, and Lexia valued that more than ever given her current circumstances as Winter's flawed Diamond.

No.

Shattered just wouldn't do.

Lexia blew the bangs out of her face and got to work. First, clothes. She dressed in her signature colors: a gold silk blouse cinched with a black leather corset. The soft leather Axis liked. Then she slipped her long legs into skin-tight leather pants, the black ones Gauge liked. She tossed her long waves into a loose ponytail and made up her face with black eyeshadow, kohl, and lipstick.

The last accessory Lexia fastened to her wrist. Axis' timepiece was made of burgundy leather with silver metallic accents. She stared at the embossed seal of a flame without a single doubt he would still want her to wear it.

They could work this out. Between the two of them, they'd done some damage to one another over the course of the last week. But they'd been together since they were children. Best friends, then lovers. Axis keeping her father's secret, and her sleeping with Gauge to cope would not drive so much a wedge between them as to end this kind of love.

With that, Lexia quit the room and headed down the stairs. Servants scattered ahead of her entry into every room as she made her way to the conservatory with her stationery in hand. Black envelopes and paper with gold ink. She would seal the letter with the gilded butterfly, her trademark. Was it wrong of her to compose the missive on the fallboard of the very piano which started her affair with Gauge? Or was it right to bring everything full circle?

Gray.

It was gray, and Lexia felt the color in her marrow as she wrote.

Dearest love,

Yes, you are still the dearest to me, and you are still my love for you will always come first. I know you're hurting, and I know I'm responsible for some of your pain. I won't make excuses, but I'm not sure I should have to apologize either. Let's be frank with one another. Let's be clear.

We are in love, and we are engaged. Nothing will change that for me. Has it changed for you? Because I don't believe it has. You and I will not let this conspiracy drive us apart. Not any further.

I want to mend what is broken. Please tell me you feel the same way—

"Lexia?"

She peered up from the missive to see Gauge standing in the entryway of the glass room. He'd also gotten dressed and smartly so in a double-breasted three-piece. It was the same burgundy as Axis' hair. A black silk button-down and tie completed the ensemble. He accessorized it with a black cane and black lenses in his copper-framed spectacles. It was the first time either of them had worn clothes in the last two days.

Gauge's eyes fell on the timepiece on Lexia's wrist. She'd gotten better at reading him even with the glasses, and to his credit, he didn't look offended or hurt by the accessory. More curious. Relieved even. He said, "The Prince is never far from our thoughts, is he?"

Lexia shook her head, unable to speak just yet.

With a slight gait to his step, Gauge walked across the room and sat beside her on the piano bench. He continued, "No matter how hard we tried to lose ourselves in each other, it never felt quite right. Not without..." His words trailed off as he glanced down at the letter.

"It can be." Lexia raised her chin a little higher and straightened her shoulders. When Gauge met her eyes, she said, "I believe we can clear the air, now. I'm ready, but only if Axis is with us."

Gauge searched her eyes for a moment. Whatever he found there made him smile in resignation. He said, "As it so happens, the Prince is on his way over to storm the Wall of Pain once again. Shall I let him in this time?"

Relief washed over Lexia without a trace of dread. That should speak to her optimism. She breathed, "Yes."

Gauge's smile crooked into a mischievous smirk. "Well, this should prove interesting."

<hr>

"Prince Axis! Are you heading back to Snow Plaza?"

"Do you think the Heiress will see you this time?"

"Can you tell us—Is it over?"

Axis' head swam. If not for Bolt and Tija on either side, he would've fallen over again. They discretely held him up with their arms looped through his on their way to the car parked alongside the cobbled street. As his chest became tighter, Axis looked to the skies of Winter above. The dome, so far up, glinted with the light beyond.

Could the perpetual snow storms battering the capital city match the gray in the depths of Axis' conscience? He'd lied to protect Lexia, but hurt her in the process. Then he'd refused to face her in his cowardice— No, that wasn't fair. With the recent death of his father and the constant publicity, Axis had bowed under the stress. With friends like Tija and Bolt, he wouldn't break completely.

And that's what kept Axis' resolve steady on the drive up Tempest Boulevard. He could face Lexia, tell her the truth, and let her decide how it affects their relationship. Even if she and Gauge...

Axis swallowed his heart back down his throat and prepared for the consequences of lying to his fiance.

"Are you nervous, Prince Axis?" Tija asked from across him in the car's backseat. Dressed smart as ever, her peacoat hid the short length of her tight dress. Black tights and thigh-high boots gave her legs some length despite her petite stature. She'd plaited her straight black hair into one long braid and tossed it to the side. Thick kohl around her eyes made the blue of her irises pop brightly. Right now, they were shining with intelligence as she searched Axis for his courage.

The People's Prince said, "I am resolute. Resigned, even."

Would Lexia forgive him?

Tija nodded with something close to admiration in her expression.

From the driver's seat, Bolt said, "We're here for you, sir."

It was enough to make Axis smile—Something he hadn't done freely in almost a week.

Would Lexia understand his position?

The intrusive thoughts swirled around Axis as the car pulled up to the Copper Cathedral. There, the press crushed around the vehicle to see inside. There was no hiding his wince.

Tija reached forward and squeezed his hand, offering her strength from delicate fingers.

Bolt said, "I'll keep them at bay as best I can, Prince Flicker." He held up a steam cannon.

Axis waved him off. "Don't hurt anyone. I'll get through this—"

A whistle from outside the car made them all turn toward the Cathedral's steps.

Jan.

At his signal, a small battalion of sizable men marched down the stairs and pressed their weight through the crowd until they formed a barrier. It allowed Bolt, Axis, and Tija to exit the car and freed them to walk up the steps in formation. His friends supported him through the onslaught of insensitive shouting which meshed together in a senseless din.

One voice rose above the others: "Did you know the Count pinned the Heiress, naked, to the conservatory's wall?"

It was probably for the best Axis grind his teeth and ignore the rest.

Jan gestured for them to follow him through the copper gates peppered with faces cast in perpetual screams. Axis ignored the chill down his spine and let the man he was certain wasn't a simple butler lead them into the multi-storied foyer. A pair of grand staircases swept high up, forming the Cathedral's backbone. Their boots clunked along the polished parquet flooring. The delicious aroma of roasting meats implied dinner wasn't far off.

Axis' stomach growled. He hadn't eaten in a day. Before that, he hadn't eaten much at all. But that was something to think about later. Now, he looked at Jan and asked, "Were we expected?"

Tija waved at the butler with which she was so deftly acquainted.

Jan smiled kindly at Tija before nodding at Axis. "Yes, Prince Flicker. Although, Ms. Cloud and Mr…?"

Axis' companion said, "It's just Bolt."

Jan said, "Ms. Cloud and Mr. Bolt can wait here. Ms. Tempest and Count Snow have asked for your presence alone."

Snow.

Axis clenched his jaw as he tried to keep his imagination from running wild in territory he'd rather not venture. But he would face Lexia under any terms. He said, "Please. Lead the way."

Tija squeezed Axis' arm before letting it go.

Bolt saluted him.

Jan led Axis to the familiar entryway for the conservatory's glass rotunda. Lexia, a vision in that ensemble, sat on top of the conference table with her feet in a chair. Her beauty struck Axis to the quick, compounding the ache in his chest. He barely glimpsed Gauge at the head of the table with his hands laced together pressed to his lips—

Wait.

Was the Count wearing a burgundy suit? He'd left his braids down, and their length surprised Axis.

The pair looked solemn, grave, but also... Open? Was that the right word? They stared at Axis with the peculiar expression on their faces—bright in Lexia's black eyes and deep beyond the black lenses of Gauge's glasses.

Axis stood and waited. Lexia and Gauge had forged a private and safe space between them which Axis needed an invitation to enter. Three days. It had taken only three days for this bond to form.

No, that was wrong.

It had been building all this time. Ever since the first moment Lexia and Gauge had laid eyes on each other at the Founding Ball. Mutual curiosity of each other. Infatuation. Then friendship and now respect.

Was Axis an intruder after breaking Lexia's heart—

"I'm glad you're here," Lexia said. "It's fate, I think. I was just writing you a letter when Gauge told me you were on the way." She stepped those long legs out of the chair and crossed the conservatory in two graceful strides.

The timepiece.

Lexia was still wearing Axis' timepiece. Close enough to touch, she asked, "Are you ready, Axis? No more secrets."

Gauge settled back in the chair, propped his feet with his ankles crossed on the tabletop, and rested his hands on his lap. Waiting...

Axis swallowed. His answer here and now would determine if they'd invite him inside. This was momentous. Could they resolve the tension between them and rebuild? Could they resume leading Winter despite the media storm? As friends.

Axis would take Lexia's friendship. He glanced down at the timepiece on her wrist before saying, "I'm ready."

Lexia reached out her hand, and Axis noticed the bruises on her wrists. Fingerprints. He clenched his jaw again and took her hand in his, accepting everything which came with it.

Gauge sat up, grabbed his cane, and stood. "Let's have it then. Follow me."

Axis asked, "Where are we going?"

Gauge stopped in the entryway to the library and answered over his shoulder, "To the truth. We're going to the vault."

Hand-in-hand, Lexia and Axis followed Gauge into the dark.

————————————————————————

As Gauge led Winter's Royal Couple up the spiral staircase in the library, he wondered if Axis had noticed the bruises under Lexia's eyes yet. The Prince had seen the ones on her wrist. Gauge was sure of that, but perhaps Lexia's makeup hid the rest.

It was frightening and thrilling to let someone inside the vault. Adrenaline coursed through Gauge as he slid back the fake books which concealed the combination lock. When the chambers released the hinges on a hiss of air, the hair on the back of his neck stood on end.

Were they truly prepared for this? What would they think of Gauge after seeing how much dirt he'd gathered on their families over the years? Would Lexia survive the reality-shattering truth her father had kept from her all her life?

Gauge entered the vault, a mausoleum of secrets, and took comfort in the familiar aroma of leather and blackmail. Each copper slot in the wall represented dirt under which he'd buried many souls to lay the foundation for Winter. That was the true story of Founding Season.

Warm fingers slid into Gauge's gloved hands, and he closed his weak eyes to soak in Lexia's kindness. Perhaps for the last time. He felt a tug, and he opened his eyes to see her take Axis' hand. For all his credit, the boy scout was handling this with grace and magnanimity. Axis had suffered a great many shocks in the last few weeks, and it showed in the width of his soft green eyes and how they darted about, seeking refuge from the thoughts no doubt plaguing his mind. This venture into the vault would surely worsen the spiral.

Downward they went.

Gauge led them into his most inner sanctum, more sacred than his bedroom, and let them take in the private space. Tufted leather couch, mini bar, low lighting to accommodate Gauge's weak corneas, and the three walls of slotted avarice.

Lexia, quick as she was, immediately zeroed-in on the two tallest collections labeled 'Tempest' and 'Flicker.' Consumed with her search for the truth, she went to them without a word. Axis followed, silent for the shock on his face and less for his curiosity, for certain. Gauge stepped aside and let them have it all.

With nimble fingers, Lexia opened all the slots pertaining to her family and sorted through the documents. Deeds, trade deals, certificates of all kinds—Any and everything Gauge had collected on the Tempests since before the Founding of Winter. He'd started evidence collection at a young age, beginning with his own father.

"Can you repeat the lecture verbatim, Ms. Cloud?"

"Yes, Prof. Snow."

"Do so and don't let my instruction interrupt you."

"But, sir—"

"Scholarships come at a cost, Ms. Cloud. Now. From the beginning…"

Tija's swallow was audible from the hallway where Gauge—only sixteen years old—listened at the door. She said, "There are other worlds, yes. Beyond our sky. We were once a galaxy united under rulership of the mighty. Now we are but scattered experiments of life gone awry. Not all the planets were equal—Professor, please!"

"Sh… Carry on."

Gauge thought he understood what he heard beyond, and no, his father wasn't above it. It was just as Jan had said. The recording went on. One more protest...

"Uhm... Each world advanced at their own pace, and ours gained momentum in technology exponentially compared to the others—Stop!"

That was it.

Gauge burst into the room to see Prof. Snow with his hand up Tija's pleated skirt. He'd forced her to sit on the edge of his desk while he sat across from her and...

"Bastard. I knew it!" Gauge growled.

Tija startled out of the way as the son took the father by the lapels and slammed him into a holo-bookcase. Oh, the professor did enjoy decorating in some bygone idea of vintage age. The fake books tumbled around them as Gauge slammed him again.

Tija didn't scream. Somewhere behind Gauge, she closed the door, hopefully with her on the other side to leave him and his father alone. He snarled, "How could you be so despicable?!"

Prof. Snow grunted with each slam, but kept his cold eyes steady on Gauge. It chilled the son to his weakened bones. Father said, "She agreed to this in the contract for her scholarship."

Gauge kept his voice down when all he really wanted to do was scream. "Liar!"

"He's not lying."

Still pinning his father to the shelves, Gauge spun on Tija. She flinched and took a step back, but said, "I didn't know it, but it's written so in my contract."

Incredulous, Gauge cried, "That you agree to molestation?!"

"That I agree to do whatever it takes to maintain the assistantship with Dr. Snow." Tears spilled down Tija's reddened cheeks.

"See, Little Bones—"

"Do you really think it's in your best interest to call me that at this moment?" The icy rage in Gauge's voice surprised even him. He thawed it some for Tija. "Ms. Cloud, I'm associated with Dr. Tempest. There is no way he'd allow this misconduct as a stipulation of any contract in his university. As a matter of fact, there is a strict no fraternization policy on this campus."

Defeated, Tija sobbed. "But there's no proof. Only my word against his." She sounded as if she'd headed down this spiral many times before, and it was enough to set Gauge's teeth on edge.

Prof. Snow said, "She's right, and you know it, Gauge." He possessed enough intelligence not to smile smugly or celebrate victory prematurely.

Which was just as well because… "Oh, but there is," Gauge said as he let up on the pressure on his father's chest. At the fear widening Prof. Snow's eyes, Gauge nodded. "That's right." He held up his hand and displayed the footage stored in his palm device. "I've backed this up onto two physical hard drives for safekeeping as well. You'll never be rid of the evidence."

Prof. Snow wet his lips and glanced at the marble column near the entrance to his desk. Atop it was a small, almost invisible device.

Yes.

Gauge had smiled as he stored the camera on one of his father's precious pieces of 'otherworldly' architecture. "You're finished, old man."

Tija's hands went to her mouth as realization dawned behind her bloodshot blue eyes. "Is it true?"

While he watched his father fall to ruins, Gauge said, "Ms. Cloud, how would you like to come work for me? I can see that Dr. Tempest secures you with a research grant on the Winter Project. Best of all, you'll never have to endure my father again."

Only a few years older than him, Tija sounded far younger than her years as she sobbed, "Yes, please."

"Enjoy what remains of your career, old man, because if I hear even a whisper of you assaulting anyone else, I'll publish this campus-wide."

Lexia held up a certificate written by her father and read it aloud, "Research funding dedicated to terrestrial shield technology granted to Tija Cloud." She and Axis glanced over at Gauge as Lexia asked, "Is that how you met her?"

Axis flinched. So Tija had told him the entire story. Well, as much as Gauge wanted to clear the air, he didn't feel as though Tija's experience was his to tell. He settled on, "More or less."

Respect, begrudging and cool, passed through Axis' eyes before he turned away to pilfer through his family's slots. Valve Flicker had been much less complicated to corner. Debts, massive ones, required regular loans and favors from Gauge's mining coffers. In fact, if he wanted to pass along the Flicker legacy to the son, it would crush Axis under the weight of benefits burden.

Yet...

No matter how this turned out, barring Axis didn't murder Gauge, the Count would be charitable toward the Prince. Even if there was no friendship for the three of them, the very notion of harming Axis unduly turned Gauge's stomach.

Then there was Leon.

Lexia's fingers sifted through a sophisticated structure of carefully composed statuary. That is… the good doctor's life was made of stone. Every facade contained its own chip, and it had taken the better part of two decades for Gauge to sink into the cracks for anything concrete.

Then about ten years ago, a wrecking ball arrived on Gauge's doorstep.

Perhaps, it's why even now he couldn't spot the bruises on Lexia's neck. Because they'd healed, hadn't they?

Just like Lya Tempest.

As if she'd heard Gauge's thoughts, Lexia asked, "Why aren't there any files about my mother?"

Gauge shoved his hands in his pockets and tried to look elsewhere. Not at Axis—He'd find no mercy there. Eventually, he cleared his throat and said, "They're here." He tapped his head with a gloved finger. "You say you're ready to know the truth, Lexia. This is your last chance." *Please don't make me break your heart.*

Lexia reached out blindly, and Axis took her hand. True to the legends of their love, the physical contact seemed to strengthen them both, and Gauge wanted so badly for them to let him in.

Lexia swallowed her fears and said, "Please, Gauge. Tell me everything."

Gauge took off his glasses and rubbed his eyes, mostly to avoid facing her. "It starts with the electromagnetic pulse, years before the Founding of Winter…"

And then Gauge held out his palm to bare his soul.

TWO

Pure Deception

Lexia clung to Axis as a projection, the likes of which she hadn't seen since her early teen years, illuminated in the palm of Gauge's hand. She opened her mouth to ask, 'But how?' Yet no words came out. She merely gaped at the improbable image.

The gentle tug on Lexia's hand brought her around to Axis, who stared, wide-eyed, at the active device in Gauge's palm.

Squinting at it, the Count slipped his glasses back on and said, "You'll understand it all soon enough. First, let's start with the night Leon, Lya, and my father met."

As if summoned by Gauge's memory, a scene played in the projection.

"Lya, this is our new hire, Prof. Cam Snow."

Gauge's attention lifted from the dessert cart to the doctor with the soft gray eyes. It was one of the rare occasions when father had let his son, thin and weak as he was, out of the house to socialize. He'd been promised other kids would be at this party.

So far, not the case.

Instead, Gauge would indulge his weak appetite with a sweet if his step-mother could convince father it wouldn't set back the maintenance of his delicate sugar levels. He needed food to grow his bones, right? Right?

Then an apparition, a ghost, or a mirage—call it whatever—entered Gauge's field of vision. An ethereal angel of white hair, white skin, and deep black eyes appeared at the kind doctor's side. She wore a white dress which draped off of her like wings, and this close, she smelled of vanilla and brighter things.

Despite the lovely, wonderful, and exceptionally amazing Tilly Snow at his side, father did a double-take and practically drooled over the new arrival.

The woman held out her hand, and Cam Snow kissed her knuckles as she said, "Lya Tempest. I'm actually the one who recommended you for hire, Prof. Snow. I'm a fan of your lectures. Other worlds are out there, I can assure you."

Oh boy.

Not this again.

Gauge went back to eyeballing the dessert cart while clinging to his step-mother's skirt to keep him upright. Though, by her trembling, not much was keeping her up now that father had let her go to fawn over Mrs. Tempest—

"And who is this? Little Snow?"

Gauge peered up to find the beautiful woman waving at him.

Nuh uh.

Gauge hid his face against his step-mother's thigh. The pretty lady would get no drooling from him.

Well, that was until Lya said, "Let me introduce you to my daughter, Lexia."

Lexia blinked away from the image as Gauge paused in his retelling. Even from behind the glasses, he wouldn't meet her eyes, and he avoided Axis altogether. Eventually, he cleared his throat and said, "Lexia, you were only three at the time, and as you do now, you looked just like your mother. A vision."

Lexia's cheeks warmed before she noticed the tension in Axis' hand. She respected how he was coping with all of this, and later, she planned to thank him properly. But for now, she nodded for Gauge to continue.

A miniature Lya toddled between her parents' legs, saying, "Mommy, will Axis come to play tonight?"

Leon and Lya smiled at their daughter before her father said, "No, honey. Mr. Flicker wasn't invited tonight after the last projection screening."

The adults chuckled.

Valve Flicker's exploits were infamous and loud even to someone as young as Gauge at the time. At nine years old, he'd overheard many stories of the athlete-turned-king pin's antics. But he'd heard of the son only in passing. That he was strong and brave at four years old, and Gauge desperately wanted to meet him.

Lya knelt to hug her daughter, and from his step-mother's side, Gauge heard Lya say, "But you can play with Little Snow. His name is Gauge, and he would like to make you his friend."

Tiny Lexia met Gauge's eyes and broke into a radiant beam. "Hello. Will you play with me?"

The image of Gauge as a child blushing and hiding his face in his step-mother's skirt warmed Lexia's heart. It loosened the tension in Axis' grip, and all around softened the atmosphere in the icy vault. But this surely wasn't why they were watching the projection.

While Lexia in Gauge's memory took him by the hand and dragged him to the dessert cart, the adults continued with their chat.

Prof. Snow said, "Mr. Flicker has his place, of course."

At his side, Tilly Snow looked less than convinced this was true. The frail woman let her eyes follow the children, at the ready should Gauge collapse like at the last function they'd let him attend.

At the look Lya gave the Professor, Leon said, "Yes, well. We hope to enjoy many years of your fantastical research, Cam."

Cam Snow winked at Lya indiscreetly. "Well, perhaps you can show me evidence of your research sometime, Lya."

Gauge listened and glanced back even as Lexia shoved a piece of squishy cake in his hand. No one ever believed father's stories or thought of his research as credible. So why were these people interested in his work?

Lya smiled and said, "I will, Prof. Snow. I will." But there was something dead in her eyes as she said it. Like a shark scenting blood in the water.

Lexia felt the walls shrink in around her, and the room spun. She dropped Axis' hand to hug herself out of a defensive reflex.

Axis sounded incredulous. "Leon never mentioned an affair."

Gauge shook his head, quick to say, "No. Nothing like that. It's only that a few months later, father 'discovered' the meteor site which supported his work almost unquestioningly. And only later did I learn it was all connected. I ask that you please listen to the entire story. If you interrupt at every outlandish instance, we'll be here until next Founding Season."

With a calming breath, the room expanded to its original size, and Lexia needed to cut the tension. "I want to hear all of it. Please, Axis. Gauge. I know I'm asking much of you both, but let's get through this and then decide how to move forward." Knees weak, she sank down on the tufted leather couch.

On a sigh, Gauge said, "Thank goodness," before collapsing into the matching armchair across from her as if his bones could no longer support him. The cane could only go so far.

Lexia peered up at Axis, wondering how he would decide. Her fiance, or maybe not her fiance, glanced between her and Gauge before sitting on the couch and nodding for the Count to continue.

"Let's skip forward. Shall we?"

———————————————————————

Despite the close quarters and the nature of the vault, Axis felt the opposite of claustrophobic here. Unlike outside, with the press of the hounding paparazzi, here... He felt safe. Gauge and Lexia wouldn't hurt him or shame him—Not how Axis' father had, anyway. Instead, they stole glances at one another which spoke volumes of a connection Axis had yet to join. Lexia trusted Gauge's method of storytelling, impossible as it was, and this encouraged Axis to trust it as well. Insofar, anyway.

The memories played on.

"Little Bones, I want you to see this."

Gauge needed a wheelchair today. His head felt airy, and his tendons could barely pull his muscles along. The terrain his father wished to traverse wouldn't allow for such an accommodation, so Jan carried the boy in his arms. Despite his love for the butler, the arrangement had shamed Gauge into a foul mood.

He let the venom into his voice. "What is it, father? I was close to a breakthrough in the lab." Always close. Never quite there. Something about his malady continued to elude his attempts for a cure or even a treatment. Anything but more of that foul tonic.

If only Tilly were still around. For the year she and Cam were married, she would dash the tonic away and tell Gauge to lie about drinking it. She'd left for the continent last month with not so much as a goodbye for Gauge.

Jan knew about Tilly and the tonic, but said nothing to father about it.

Prof. Snow led the small party of three across an empty field the likes of which Gauge had never seen before. Here, butterflies stole nectar from pale flowers with black throats. The grass was a green so deep, if he looked at a blade a certain way, it would shift to purple. Massive oaks—no, not oaks. Some other form of hardwood—silver in color—provided shade for the wildlife which seemed unafraid of the bipedal trespassers. Off in the distance, some manner of bird walloped.

They walked a long way from the hovercar with the professor never once answering his son, and Jan providing no clue as to their destination. Gauge huffed most of the way and sulked in Jan's arms. He wanted to climb one of those magnificent trees, but had only heard of one boy capable of doing so.

At this point in the story, Axis tried to meet Gauge's eyes behind his glasses. The older man refused to look at him, hindered by shame and fear. Both emotions tightened the lines around his eyes and flattened his otherwise full lips. Their pasts were almost as complicated as their present, but did their futures have to be so?

As Gauge fast-forwarded the long journey, Axis kept his bewilderment at the electronic relic to himself. For now.

Far from the technological center of the main island, Cam Snow led his son to a geological marvel. Grown over, Gauge had almost mistaken the crater for a valley aside from the igneous mountain in its center. It glittered with ore veins of varying colors and richness.

The professor stood on the precipice and declared, "This is it, Little Bones. This is all the proof I need."

Gauge blinked down at the sight, certain his eyes were playing tricks on him. How could such a mineral-rich meteorite go unnoticed by their geological scanners? Or the atmospheric censors miss the gasses fuming from its core? Gauge swallowed and asked the third question which came to mind. "Will you lead the excavation?" Truly, this would make the man's career.

"No, Little Bones. We'll strip it for all its worth, and I'll never tell how I discovered it."

"How *did* you discover it, father?"

Prof. Snow smiled and said, "An angel told me. Now, let's begin with the copper, shall we?"

Axis kept his eyes on Lexia to measure her response. She watched intently, and only the slight hitch in her breath indicated she understood the revelation. This wasn't at all what Leon Tempest had told Axis, but it made sense as pieces to the puzzle fell into place.

Lexia said, "But your father didn't build Winter's capital on the Ignis crater. You did, right, Gauge?"

Gauge wet his lips and nodded. His hands shook as he poured himself a drink. Then he did something strange. Gauge took out a vial and squeezed out a drop of blue liquid into the tumbler. He peered at it as he said, "Yes. Half a decade later when I learned of the electromagnetic pulse, but before I tell you more about that, I need to make a confession." He swallowed the drink in one gulp and glanced between Axis and Lexia, finally meeting their eyes.

There was a world of secrets buried in this tomb, and Gauge wanted to share it with them.

As always, Lexia dove in headfirst, asking, "Is this about the tonic?"

Axis frowned at her question, and it deepened as Gauge nodded slowly.

"Yes, it is."

Gauge stared at himself in a mirror. He was sixteen here and dressed in a dapper tuxedo, but that wouldn't distract people from the crutches he leaned on for support. Once, the university had offered to fashion him a hover disc, but Gauge knew it would only make him weaker and complacent with his malady. No. That wouldn't do. Despite the ache in his legs, there was no way he'd miss this social function. So, he straightened his bow tie and put on his top hat.

Show time.

The convention center did the best it could for Prof. Snow's retirement party, but given the circumstances of his forced resignation, there was no need to go all out. Most of the guests attended as much for the scandal as for the open bar and free food. Some came to whisper about the graduate students, and others, like Gauge, came to gloat at the man's abject failure to convince anyone of his 'other worlds' theory.

Anyone but one guest.

Lya Tempest walked into the convention center wearing the most extraordinary gown. Truly, it took Gauge's breath away as he paused during his lurch down the stairs. It was black with nebulous clouds floating all throughout. Diamonds twinkled among the velvet night. Rubies, sapphires, and emeralds formed large clusters around brilliant stars. The night sky danced along her breasts, waist, and hips in a stunning display of solidarity.

Other worlds were out there. Lya believed this completely, and she had funded most of Prof. Snow's research until he found the wellspring at the Ignis crater. Then he didn't care what people thought of his reputation, and Gauge's leverage over the man's behavior waned as much as the son's health. But even so… One couldn't keep a lid on several sexual assault charges from various graduate students across the years.

Tija among them.

Gauge wouldn't find her at the party, but she promised to sneak into his room later tonight. Something to look forward to more so than his father's disgrace.

The old man didn't show for his own party, and Gauge couldn't conceal his smug smirk as he made his way to the nearest balcony for fresh air. Two hours of mingling on his bones had proved exhausting. He needed more practice. Jan followed Gauge out onto the terrace as if he knew it wouldn't be long before his ward collapsed and he had to return to his father's custody. But until then, he was free.

Skyscrapers soared into the clouds, threatening to touch the stratosphere. Projections loomed everywhere, adjusted to each individual's commercial needs as designed by the implants inserted into their palms. Hover cars darted by in boring programmed traffic jams. It smelled of ozone and a slight trace of neuron decay. The noise would deafen a being from another world, should one ever dare to visit.

Sometimes, Gauge liked to close his eyes and imagine it quieter. Less bright. The constant neon assault bore down on the adjustable lenses over his corneas. The sound left an echo in the chamber of his heart. And he wanted to save time with more organized transportation, instead of people wasting half their lives in pre-determined queues.

Instead, Gauge imagined it like one period in time his father had lectured about from another planet called—

"It's nights like this that I wish all the lights would go out, and I could see the stars again."

Lya's voice from behind startled Gauge, and he whirled on her.

She glided up to the banister beside him and carried on as if she hadn't noticed his anxiety. "They're more beautiful than this dress, you know? True stars."

Gauge had visited a holo-planetarium once. It'd been the closest he'd come to a real night sky. Even being out by the crater couldn't shield against this level of light pollution. Well-versed by now in polite charm, Gauge said, "I don't believe such a thing is possible, Mrs. Tempest. You look lovely tonight."

Lya bowed with her head, beaming in delight, before she searched the sky once again. This time, the facade slipped. It was a moment, a brief glimpse. But Gauge saw into a well of sadness so deep it threatened to draw him in for the warmth. She said, "I miss my family."

Gauge wanted to say, 'They're inside,' but he realized she didn't mean the doctor and their friends. Also, he felt something kindred to the sentiment. And in a rare moment of emotional vulnerability, he confessed, "I miss my mother."

In response, Lya said the strangest thing. "Iron, Little Snow. You only need more iron."

"What—"

"There you are, dear. Oh, hello, Gauge." Leon stepped out onto the balcony. "This is a nice event, but we'd better get back to Lexia."

The good doctor always did the one thing Gauge wanted people to do. He held out his hand for Gauge to shake it. After letting one crutch take all his weight, the younger man accepted the warm gesture. Gauge had been so taken with the moment that he'd almost missed the reassembly of Lya's mask.

Leon held out his arm for Lya to take, asking, "Shall we, darling?" A beacon from an overhead advertisement drone shone onto Dr. Tempest's glasses and masked his eyes.

Lya stiffened, but accepted his arm. "Good night, Little Snow. Remember what I said."

At Gauge's pause in the story, Axis found himself grinding his teeth. He was impatient for the Count to unveil all his secrets, and so far, all he'd implied was that Lya had helped the professor locate the meteor. Oh, and the iron.

Lexia frowned, puzzled as well, but far more patient.

Gauge took a vial from beside the bourbon decanter and said, "Will both of you please hold out your hands?"

Trust.

The Count asked for trust from the Heiress and the Prince. They glanced at each other before offering their hands. He sprinkled a black powder into their palms, saying, "Taste it. Smell it. It won't hurt you."

Axis cautiously sniffed to find a metallic tang.

Lexia, reckless and impulsive, licked the powder up immediately and exaggerated tasting it as if it were a vintage wine.

Together, they both said, "Iron."

Gauge took out a utensil from the bar and sprinkled the iron compound onto it. A tiny plume of smoke fumed from the spoon. "It's the key ingredient in a kit I designed specifically to detect traces of other heavy metals such as lithium, zinc, and—"

"Copper," Lexia finished with a flash of her black eyes.

Axis recognized her brand of anger, but she only reserved it for men like his father. She couldn't tolerate abuse. Axis was beginning to understand. "The tonic…"

Gauge nodded. "The tonic."

"Air it all out in the open, then spend a few days with the three of you in bed together."

Again, Tija could make Gauge laugh like no other. It was downright wholesome, and Eternity did he need it. Incredulous, he asked, "All of it? Even the secrets I keep from you? And you would be fine with this?"

Tija's feminine laughter implied she knew Gauge better than he knew himself. "Yes. Everything. The gloves. The glasses. And the domes over

Winter. Everything, love. It's the only way you'll ever truly find happiness. Trust someone completely."

As Gauge assessed their reactions, something passed through Axis' soft green eyes. Anger, pity, and precious above all, understanding. Commiseration. They shared something in common other than their affection for Lexia. Unfortunately, Gauge wished it was anything other than a history of child abuse.

Gauge said, "Now, you may wonder what this has to do with Lya, other than her observation granting me this epiphany. My confession isn't over yet." He glanced between the two, but in the depth of Lexia's eyes, he saw a knowledge there which she shouldn't have.

Ah.

She'd guessed about Valve. Then the next wouldn't be a surprise to her.

It took some time, but eventually Jan confessed to suspecting. He helped Gauge conceal the test kit, and everything from the food Gauge ate to the water he drank popped hot of copper tampering.

It was systemic. To think of all the charities held in Gauge's name—in his mother's name—to support his father in research for a cure. The funds went to enormous telescopes and the mining project. All the while, he'd been poisoning them.

Rank bastard.

Lexia interrupted the projection to ask, "But if this was before Winter, you didn't have servants. Why was Jan there?"

Sharp. She didn't miss a thing. Unfortunately, that was also a tale which wasn't Gauge's story to tell. He wasn't entirely certain of the details himself. "You'll have to ask Jan, and fair warning, I'll be well and truly jealous if you get more out of him than I ever did."

That got a smile out of Axis and a blush out of Lexia.

"Good, hold on to those happy thoughts as we move into the next bit. It gets murkier from here out. Lexia, do you remember that your mother came to visit my father more in the days after his banishment from the university?"

Frustrated, Lexia blew the bangs out of her eyes. "No. I must admit, I have been oblivious to most of what you've shown me." Then she frowned, and the sadness in it made Gauge regret this entire confessional. She said, "But lately . . . I've been remembering arguments between my parents I'd long forgotten—I wish I couldn't remember."

Out of what Gauge assumed was a reflex, Axis put an arm around his fiance/not fiance and tucked her against his side. Comfortable in the gesture, Lexia allowed him to do it, and they snuggled together across from Gauge. Axis said to her, "You had similar issues right after your mother died. I just assumed you couldn't accept her loss. I'm sorry I didn't listen to you then."

The Heiress stared into the Prince's eyes, and the Count took lonely comfort in the rekindling of their relationship. It might mean pushing him out again, but at least he hadn't aided in any irreparable damage to the Royal Couple's bond.

"Moving on."

Confronted with the knowledge of copper poison, Gauge sought his father out. Although they'd amassed quite a mountain of wealth from the meteorite's resources, the only help living in the house was Jan. It was likely to keep the poisoning under wraps, and the details of Cam's affairs discrete.

When Jan left for his only day off, Gauge stormed his father's office. As much as someone on crutches could, anyway; however, he found the door especially hard to open. In the few days since the retirement party, people expected the professor to surface, but truth be told, Gauge couldn't remember the last time he'd heard his father's voice, let alone had seen his face.

So when Gauge pushed with all the effort his bones could afford, the expression which met him was a surprise. Ghastly, hollowed out.

Cam Snow had been dead for at least two days.

With the heavy door open, the foul stench of the decaying body sent Gauge recoiling back into the hallway. He tripped on his crutches and fell to the floor panting for fresher air. Dizzy, he shook his head, trying to clear it. Someone—Cam, presumably—had barred the door with a sofa and beyond that, father sat at his desk with a bottle of gin and a note on his blotter. Projections of his theorized galaxy swirled about the room in a colorful display antithesis to the grim scene.

Alone in the house, Gauge forced himself back onto his feet with his crutches. Could he make it over the couch on his own? Or should he wait for Jan to come home? There was no calling the authorities until Gauge could talk to Jan.

No.

Gauge waited. He sat back down on the floor, staring at his dead father until the kitchen door opened. Finally, he could scream.

"Jan! Jan!! It's father!"

As if he'd teleported, the butler appeared at Gauge's side. Or maybe Gauge was losing time in his shock. Either way, the older man went to the door and forced it open with a strength Gauge couldn't help but envy.

Jan didn't bother checking for a pulse. Cam hadn't blinked the entire time Gauge stared at his sunken eyes. Instead, the butler sealed the lid on the bottle of gin, set it where it went on the minibar, and checked the note on the desk. He glanced over at Gauge, asking, "Do you care to read it?"

Gauge had to swallow twice to answer. "Please."

Jan said, "It says four words. 'Lya is the truth.'"

"Burn it." Gauge didn't hesitate to get the words out this time. "I don't want evidence showing a correlation between those two. Can you arrange the body to make it look like an accident? A medical event?"

Jan examined the corpse and the surrounding space. With a shrug, he said, "There's nothing here which suggests it wasn't. I can't find a cause of death."

Eerie, but useless for now. Gauge cursed. "I can't believe he died before I got the chance to kill him myself."

The butler waved his finger. "No more talk like that, young man. We'll still need to call the authorities before this night is over, and you'll keep your motives to yourself. There's plenty of reason Prof. Snow would kill himself, but there's also a mysterious malady hanging over your family. A medical event is just as likely."

Gauge almost spat at the word, 'malady.' Poison. He said, "It's just as well. What do you suppose the note means, Jan?"

"I suppose it's best not to know, sir."

"We let the rumors spread. People gossiped over the cause of the death, but everyone agreed it was best he bowed out without pomp or circumstance. You two were barely teenagers when the old man died, so you likely don't remember, but the funeral was the cheapest and simplest I could spare."

Gauge had stared at the old bottle of gin on his mini bar for most of the story. It startled him when a warm hand took his gloved fingers. Lexia, still snuggled with Axis, had reached out to Gauge. She peered through the black lenses, and her deep eyes pierced his soul with too much kindness. It was painful to accept.

The sentiment softened her voice as Lexia said, "I'm sorry your father was horrible to you."

Even with all this secrecy surrounding her mother, Lexia still found it in her to care for Gauge. He was falling in love with her, and soon, he would lose her for certain.

Gauge stared down at their hands, gave hers a squeeze, and said, "Don't. Not until you know everything."

Axis said, "We're listening, Gauge. We're here."

It was all the Count had ever wanted to hear. He only hoped the next didn't frighten them away.

Lexia wanted the story to stop. It was already taking a dangerous turn. She felt it, and the tension in Axis' hard body said he sensed the same. There was too much sorrow in Gauge as he approached what could only be the climax.

The electromagnetic pulse.

Lexia had heard the rumors, of course. That the Count had set off some global device and struck Winter into electronic darkness to play out his own steampunk fantasy. Between the active projection in his palm and the direction of his story, these rumors seemed supported by some modicum of evidence.

But, no.

Despite everything of late—including her father's intentional deception—Lexia could believe in someone. She believed in Axis and Gauge. Tija, Bolt, and Jan. She wasn't alone.

"Please continue, Gauge."

The Count sighed and took his glasses off to clean them with his pocket square. He was adamant not to meet their eyes as he said, "Of course, if I couldn't confront my father, I would confront your mother. At my father's funeral, no less."

People ate up the mystery of Cam Snow's death and drank heavily at the funeral, steeped in gossip. Gauge encouraged the talk at Jan's recommendation. It steered any potential accusations away from patricide. Instead, he mingled, remaining both entertaining and mysterious. The groundwork of his persona began in tragedy, but he knew this presence would carry him far from the shadow of Prof. Snow's disgrace and the research into the falsified malady. After a week without copper in everything Gauge ate or drank, he felt stronger, surer.

Gauge was free.

Free to pursue interests aside from what ailed him, and free to network connections outside of his father's circle of 'other worlders.'

After a few hours of this, Gauge went outside for some 'fresh' air, once again wishing for a quieter setting. Lya found him alone as before. He said, "I knew you'd make an appearance, Mrs. Tempest."

Lya's smile was like no other. Radiant and cold. Youthful and ancient. Wisdom shown in her eyes, while lust lingered on her lips.

Captivated, Gauge caught himself staring, which made his cheeks redden.

Apparently accustomed to this response, Lya said nothing to further his embarrassment. Instead, she said, "I see the iron is doing you some good."

Here they went on this carousel of secrets. "Yes, Mrs. Tempest. May I ask how you knew I was *deficient*?" This among other questions had plagued him since his father's retirement party.

"It's all in the eyes, Little Snow, but don't worry. I saw to the rest."

The rest.

The rest . . .

On a soft sigh, Lya added, "After all. Your father needed a dose of his own medicine."

Gauge swallowed, hoping that would unclog his ears. Had he heard her right? Was his brain processing what she meant, or was he imagining the confession?

"What do you think of all this noise, Little Snow?" Lya asked as she gestured to the city beyond.

The change in subject gave Gauge whiplash, eliciting an honest answer without hesitation. "I detest it. The lights, the constant barrage of consumerism, and the misalignment of values. We're all searching for another world because we're tired of this one."

Something… changed.

Lya turned her back on Gauge. Over her shoulder, she said, "In a year, come to me. You'll know when," and left him alone to solve her mystery.

Lexia felt her heart sink. A year. From the Founding Play, she knew a year after Cam Snow's death, Gauge discovered the recurring pattern of the solar electromagnetic pulse. But how…

"Are you saying Mrs. Tempest knew about the pulse?" Axis asked the question on Lexia's mind.

When Gauge took off his glasses and pegged Lexia with a hard stare, she nearly gasped at the intensity. "It's more than that. I've never solved it, not completely. But the Ignis crater and your mother shared an undeniable connection. I wasn't studying astronomy or astrophysics when I discovered the EMP. I was researching the history of the meteorite. Scarring in the sedimentary stratification of the crater corresponded with a geological event which switched the planetary poles. The magnetic force attracted the meteor to the planet now known as Winter, and I discovered we were due for another."

"I need to speak with Galactic Leader Yed. This is Gauge Snow, and don't waste time. This is an emergency."

The fool barely listened to the emergency, and then laughed loud enough in Gauge's device to vibrate his palm. "A solar EMP our scientists have missed? Boy, you're as mad as your father."

"If you won't take action, I will."

Lexia said, "We saw this in the Founding Play." It was reassuring to see how close it stuck to the truth.

Gauge slipped his glasses back on before saying, "Well, it didn't show who I called next."

"Lya," Axis guessed.

Gauge nodded, and the projection continued.

"You are expected, Little Snow."

Gauge wasn't so much shocked that Lya had predicted the call as overcome. "How did you know about the EMP?"

Lya shook her head. "That's the wrong question. The correct question is, 'How do we survive it?' The moment the pulse deactivates the atmospheric controls on the planet, we'll understand the true meaning of winter."

Gauge wanted to pull his hair out. How could Lya be so calm about this? He nearly screamed at the projection as he asked, "What do we do?!"

"Soothe, Little Snow. I've had a long time to prepare, and together, we can accomplish the impossible with copper and bone. When you call Leon to tell him, don't mention my involvement. He will agree to your terms without question because your connections and charisma are the key, young man. This is what we'll do..."

Lexia stared at Gauge as he lifted her hand and kissed her knuckles all while his eyes stayed on Axis' timepiece. Against her fingers, he said, "I didn't build Winter. Lya did." He brought her hand to his face and leaned into Lexia's warmth as if comforting himself from the truth as he confessed it. "The domes, the underground tracks—All of it was already constructed and prepared for launch at the meteor site. The Ignis crater was designed for it. Once, she'd asked me, 'How many cities do you want?'"

Axis held Lexia tighter as Gauge kissed her palm, refusing to look at them. The Count said, "She gave me a choice. I was only a teenager laughed into infamy—A doomsday cult leader. A joke. Between all the bitterness from my affliction and my wrath for the exile, I chose to limit Winter's foundation to only three cities. Simply enough to protect those already loyal to our belief with some room to spare for growth. That was it."

That was it.

The rest of the world died under a blanket of snow. But Gauge had been so young and—

"You weren't certain you believed her." Axis surprised both Lexia and Gauge with his pronouncement. Gauge's brows went high above the frames of his glasses as Axis continued, "You were seventeen, Gauge, and looking for a compass. A way out of calamity and validation for your theory. Not unlike your father, I must say."

By the wince on Gauge's face, Lexia could tell Axis' words had stung, but rung no less true. As much as she felt for the Count, all these confessions raised more questions than answers for the Heiress regarding Winter's enigmatic Diamond.

Lexia asked, "Is there more? Did you ever learn how she knew? Or how my mother could ever prepare for it—I can't even fathom it enough to ask the right questions. But are we all in agreement? We think my mother knew Winter's future, and somehow possessed the technology to develop these arrangements?"

Even thinking it made Lexia blink. Once. Twice. She knew she was staring at the far wall of slots, and if she focused hard enough, she could make out the one which said, 'Tempest.' Her skin felt cool, and her body felt light.

Floating.

Fuzzy.

Gone.

Axis held Lexia as her eyes went vacant.

"There she goes," Gauge said before he helped Axis lower her onto the couch. "Lexia, can you hear us?"

Once, not that long ago, Axis would wrench Lexia from Gauge's touch and push the Count away from her. But now, because of Lexia's choice, Axis would mind his peace. He asked, "Do you have a—"

Gauge hand Axis a cool cloth. He swept aside Lexia's bangs to place the compress on her brows and gave her some space. Neither man looked at each other. It didn't take any stretch of Axis' imagination to wonder what had occurred between Lexia and Gauge over the last few days. Even so, it twisted some part of Axis' insides to see them so intimate together with so much ease in front of him. It was the kind of public affection Lexia deserved, but which Axis could never give her.

"Will you kill me?"

Axis blinked before turning around and finding Gauge peering at him from over the rim of his glasses. He stood there leaning on his cane with both hands, looking uncertain.

Frustrated, Axis swept his jacket back to place one hand on his hip and used the other to pinch the bridge of his nose. Almost on a groan, he said, "No, Gauge. Not today."

But what exactly would Axis do about all this? He'd broken Lexia's heart and turned her away into Gauge's arms. The sweetness in her black eyes when Axis had held her only moments earlier flashed, and he remembered the relief he'd felt when he saw her wearing his timepiece. Yet just minutes ago, Gauge had kissed her hand, and Axis had felt Lexia's blood quicken at the older man's touch.

Was Lexia in the middle? And was she happy there? Did any of it matter if they could all be happy—

"Axis?"

Lexia stirred on the couch, and Axis went to her side. Gauge took a step closer, but only went to her when she held out her hands to them both. They helped her sit up, and Lexia peered between the two of them. "Please tell me I didn't miss anything."

That...

Smirk.

Lexia's beautiful lips twitched at the corners with mischief and… hunger.

Bewildered, Axis blinked at her. It startled him when Gauge barked out a laugh. Far more familiar than Axis was ready for, Gauge said, "You're never satisfied, butterfly."

A tiny voice in Axis, which sounded suspiciously a lot like his father, told him to be jealous. But truly, as yellow flushed Lexia's cheeks, he could only shake his head to hide his smile. Utterly incorrigible. He killed the mood when he asked, "Shall we get back to it?" After all, there was still the matter of Lya's death to uncover.

Lexia would have things her way. "Both of you sit with me."

Without question, they hiked up their trousers and sat on the couch with Lexia between them. And as if coordinated, they both crossed the opposite leg over a knee, framing her in the mirror image. Gauge in his burgundy three-piece, and Axis in his blue button-down and black blazer. They made for quite the picture with their black and gold butterfly between them.

"I'll tell you the same thing I told Gauge. Air it all out in the open and throw yourselves at each other."

Tija's words came back to Axis, and he lingered on them far longer than he'd intended when Gauge held his palm out once more. While the images played, and they experienced his emotions, Gauge said, "You know by now, we fashioned Winter after my favorite of father's lectures, but what you don't know is how our Diamond lost her brilliance over time."

Perhaps to spare Axis, Gauge fast-forwarded through Valve's involvement in the Winter project, including all those embarrassing instances the Count eventually used to blackmail the Factory Master. This was finally leading to the piece of the puzzle Axis knew. The one Leon told him about a few days earlier, and the quickly passing images made it more obvious to Axis than he'd ever seen in real time.

Lya smiled less and less until not a scene passed where she looked happy.

Lexia frowned as if she'd noticed it as well, and Gauge returned to hiding his eyes from them. He said, "Here. At the Founding Ball, two years ago. It wasn't the first time I'd noticed something was wrong, but it was the first time I did something about it."

Gauge followed Lya up the sweeping stairs in the Copper Cathedral's foyer. It was filled to the brim with dazzling dresses and dapper suits. They twirled about in a dizzying miasma of prismatic elegance. Despite the air of jubilance from the guests, sorrow gathered in Lya's wake. She'd frowned all evening, and this time Gauge would catch her alone and ask.

"What brings you outside on this chilly but gorgeous evening, Mrs. Tempest?"

Winter's Diamond didn't startle or whirl. She kept her dark gaze on the starless dome above. It was only when her shoulders shook, that Gauge approached her. He asked, "Mrs. Tempest—"

"Don't call me by that name again, Little Snow." When Lya peered over her shoulder at him, a yellow tear rolled down her cheek.

Gauge went to the balustrade beside her and tried for levity. "Well, if you'd reconsider your endearment for me, I'll do the same. As you can see, *Lya*, I am no longer little." Since his father's death ten years ago—eight years since the first Founding Day—Gauge had honed his body to make lovers sigh and enemies think twice before engaging him.

Endearment warmed Lya's voice as she assured, "You'll always be small to me, child." They both stared out over Winter in silence for a long stretch before she asked, "Was this everything you wanted?"

Gauge looked down at his cane which he barely leaned on for support. He wanted to smile, but then he noticed the absence of a timepiece on his wrist. His voice came out soft. "No. Not everything." Melancholy didn't suit the evening, so Gauge bumped Lya with his side and said, "I never thanked you for it all, Lya. You'd been right about everything, and you saw to Winter's survival while I took all the credit."

Lya shook her head. "You took all the scrutiny with it. The last thing I want is more eyes on me."

Gauge peered over at her, saying, "I am ever in your debt. Should you need anything, please just ask." He meant it sincerely. With all this power, he could afford to repay this enigmatic woman whatever she might ask.

Axis felt a chill when Gauge met Lexia's eyes for the next.

"Little Snow, I need you to help end my suffering."

Gauge recoiled as if she'd slapped him. He couldn't speak for his mouth hanging open. The words kept choking in his throat.

Why? What?! No!

But Lya trembled with determination, and the resolve in her eyes gave her the strength to press further. "I can't stay here! Free me."

The tall ethereal beauty took a step toward the Count, and he backed away until he bumped against the balustrade. He warded her off with his gloved hands, saying, "Absolutely not, Lya. No. How could you— Why would you even—"

Lya stopped her approach and hugged herself, her willowy form shrinking. On half a breath, she said, "I can't stay here a moment longer, and Leon won't understand."

Gauge shook himself out of his shock. "Mrs. Tempest, I worry you're not thinking clearly."

"The next inferior man to say that to me will come to understand how hard a diamond can be." There was nothing willowy or small about Lya now. She stood to her full height, spine tall and shoulders straight. She even raised her delicate chin for good measure. "Child, I have looked after you for some time now, and you will make good on your debts to me."

Chilled to the bone, Gauge couldn't fathom the angry angel before him. "Why are you coming to me for help, Lya?"

As if the answer were obvious, she said, "Because you're the only one with enough power to free me now."

So much flashed before Gauge's eyes. Leon's handshake, Lexia's chubby cheeks, and Lya's yellow tear. He said, "You talk as if you hate your husband—your family."

"I only hate that which keeps me here."

Perhaps…

Perhaps there was a way Gauge could salvage this. He would play along to appease Lya, all the while talking some sense into her. Maybe Tija would know what to do. Feigning his defeat, Gauge sagged his shoulders and asked, "What do you need from me?"

"Tomorrow, I need you to arrive at this location at this exact hour and minute. Do not be late. The rest of the instructions are disclosed here. I ask that you don't open it until after the deed is done. This is my last gift. Do not waste it."

Lya handed Gauge a silver envelope sealed with wax pressed in the shape of a diamond. He wasn't sure what disturbed him more. The level of preparation she'd already committed to, or her presumptuousness that he'd be willing to help.

While none of this was the story Leon had told Axis, all of it was making sense. He remembered glimpsing tears on Lya's face more than once, but he'd never realized—

"My mother was unhappy."

While Axis curved his arm around Lexia's waist and pulled her against his side, Gauge took her hand and held it in his lap. She blinked away tears as she said, "Please go on."

Gauge didn't find the opportunity to consult Tija for advice as the hour descended quickly. After a day of sending his spies out to gather information on the Tempests, he'd learned from several reliable sources of Lya's waning happiness. Of her growing detachment since Prof.

Snow's death. Since Founding Day. And since Lexia had become an adult. Not that Gauge had seen the Tempests' daughter since he was nine.

So instead, Gauge resolved to arrive early and talk some sense into Lya before she gave up on everything in her life. Divorce wasn't pretty, but he'd help her re-establish in another sector. Lexia could choose which parent she wanted to live with, and it could all be settled with as much discretion as the Count could afford.

Determined, Gauge had Jan drive him to Tempest Cemetery. Unlike the boneyards of old, this place boasted some of the most beautiful trees in Winter. An orchard of the dead.

Truth be told, Gauge had never visited this place. He attended all the weddings, but few of the funerals since Winter's Founding. He didn't expect to find so many trees, and some were silver—

"Leon, I promised to stay until Lexia was old enough to be on her own. You can't keep me here! Ow! You're hurting me!"

"You promised to spend the rest of your life with me!"

"The Wrong Side of Eternity would be more bearable! Let go—"

There was a soft cry.

A loud thud.

And then nothing.

Gauge and Jan turned the corner, and even the butler stopped cold at what they'd found. Lya lay still on the stone path. Leon knelt at her side with his hand on her throat, the light refracting off his glasses. He peered up to find Gauge and Jan standing there. The light changed, and when their eyes met, Gauge knew.

Leon cried, "Help! Lya's fallen, and she doesn't have a pulse!" He rolled her over onto her back, tilted her chin back, and began chest compressions.

Gauge muttered to Jan, "Go to him. Don't let him out of your sight."

"Yes, sir."

Meanwhile, Gauge opened Lya's letter.

Axis held Lexia as Gauge let go of her hand and walked over to the slots. He opened the only one without a name and took out an envelope and a fold of silver cloth. He handed the envelope to Lexia, who opened it in such a way to let Axis read it at her side.

Little Snow,

By now I am gone, my suffering ended. Please ensure Leon never hears the end of this, but don't let my daughter endure this burden. I trust you know what to do.

Find enclosed the instructions for my remains. There will be no trees for me. Only copper and bone.

Thank you, Little Snow.

Lya.

Axis remembered them burying a tree for Lya's funeral in the cemetery, but this wasn't the secret. Leon had said Lya killed herself, and that Gauge helped stage it as an accident or heart failure.

Axis' throat constricted, and incredulous tears burned his eyes.

Lexia's voice came out thick with emotion as she asked, "Gauge, the instructions?"

Gauge held out the cloth and unfolded it before their eyes. Copper and leather were woven in an intricate pattern centered with an amber jewel cut like a brilliant diamond. He said, "Lexia, your mother had me construct a special furnace in the heart of the meteor. This was forged there. It's made of her bones."

It was Gauge's timepiece.

THREE

Black Heart

GAUGE STARED AT LEXIA AND AXIS, WATCHING THEM PROCESS EVERYTHING. As expected, toward the end of the memories, the couple changed color. Lexia, a sickly shade of green, let the tears roll down her cheeks. Axis, nearly gray compared to his usual topaz complexion, swallowed bile and winced.

Yes.

Gauge figured this would be a revelation for them, but whether they accepted the truth, as much of it as the Count knew, was another story.

Finally, Axis said, "This isn't what Leon told me. Lexia, I—"

Lexia reached out a shaky hand and touched the amber stone with her slender fingers. Her black-polished nails tapped on her mother's remains. She inhaled a broken sob.

Gauge wanted to cry for her, but there was too much work ahead of them. If they wanted to dig to the bottom of this mess, they'd need to organize. Air out everything they knew, and come together for a united front. The appearance of one anyway.

Axis unclenched his jaw to say, "Leon told me your mother killed herself. That she'd been unhappy for some time, and he kept it from you to prevent breaking your heart."

Lexia looked away from the timepiece and faced Axis, raw and unbridled in her anguish as much as in her lovemaking. She said, "If you'd known this much—what Gauge showed us just now—I know you wouldn't have kept this a secret from me."

Axis shook his head, bewildered. "Absolutely not. I had no way of knowing your father was implicated in your mother's death. But there's more to it, isn't there? We must all be thinking the same thing."

"How could Lya know?"

The three of them blurted it out at once.

Gauge set aside the timepiece and ticked the points off on his gloved fingers. "Not only did she know I'd show for certain, she knew I'd arrive early. She knew Leon would…" Gauge couldn't bring himself to accuse the doctor of outright murder. Instead, he said, "That she would meet her demise that night. That I would use it to blackmail Leon to my ends."

Lexia and Axis stopped looking at each other to gaze up at Gauge at the last. He swallowed before adding, "I'm not proud of it. You can't imagine what it's like making two older men do as you say even when it's for the betterment of everyone in Winter." Gauge ran a hand through his braids and gestured frustratingly. "It's been like pulling teeth around here to get anything done. Without Lya's future preparations, I never would've finished sector twelve. Not with those two codgers in the way."

"Gauge." Both men looked at Lexia as she said, "Thank you for honoring my mother's last wishes."

Axis' mouth fell open just a touch. It was a funny thing to think a man could look attractive on the edge of exhausted insanity, but here they were. Axis with his chiseled jaw and carved cheekbones covered in 'haven't bothered to shave for two whole days,' and Lexia with the tip of her nose flushed yellow, making her periwinkle freckles pop.

Fuck it.

Gauge pinched Lexia by the chin and pecked a kiss on her lips. "You're welcome." He caressed Axis' stubble and gave the younger man's face a pat. "*You'll* thank me later." Before Axis could recover from looking absolutely stunned, Gauge turned on his heel and headed out of the vault he, for once, considered dreary. "Come along, you two. There's work to be done."

On his way down the spiral staircase in the library, Gauge called, "Jan?"

"Sir?" The butler appeared out of the shadows, as one does.

Gauge smirked at the old spy. "I *do* love when you do that. Please, we'll need refreshments to prepare for battle. And water. Lots of water." He hadn't hydrated for days.

Jan bowed at the waist before gesturing out toward the conservatory, saying, "And Ms. Cloud and Mr. Bolt?"

"Oh, Axis brought them along? How wonderful. Please see them in. We'll make use of them yet, and don't worry, old friend. I haven't forgotten our guests in the basement. I think you'll soon have one other to entertain."

Jan.

Beamed.

It was enough to steal an incredulous chuckle out of Gauge as the old butler left and the Royal Couple finally made their way downstairs. There was a distance between them since Axis' arrival. It was one Gauge hoped to bridge before they all left for their assigned duties today.

When Jan brought Lexia a glass of water, Gauge was proud of how greedily she drank from it. Before Tija and Bolt came into the library, Gauge ran a quick iron test on his food and drink.

Axis watched with sharp eyes during the process. He said, "I don't suppose Ms. Cloud knows."

"Only you and Lexia, and I thank you to keep it that way. For now."

The People's Prince surprised the Count by saying, "Only if you promise to eat a meal I prepare without testing it first."

Gauge blinked at Axis, and Lexia held her breath beside them, peering at one then the other. Twelve years had passed since Gauge last ate something without the metallic tang of his test kit coating his tongue. And now Axis asked him to trust food prepared by his hand, the hand of the man whose fiance Gauge had just spent the last three days in bed with. Of course, Axis had said he didn't plan to kill Gauge.

Not today, anyway.

"Trust someone completely."

Tija and Bolt arrived in time to see Gauge nod his acquiescence to the arrangement. The Count was either a dead man walking or one meal shy of tasting actual food. Either way, Axis cooking for Gauge would change his life forever.

The four guests to the Copper Cathedral, the butler, and the Count gathered in the library. They all waited for Gauge to speak. He looked them each in the eye before saying, "It's finally time to solve the mystery of Winter, and we'll need to work together to uncover this. Only then can we truly move forward into this new sector without the shadow of the past looming over us. Lexia. Axis. I know this is asking a great deal from both of you after everything you've gone through, but please. Keep your faith in me a little while longer."

When Lexia had sent for her things two days ago, she'd asked for clothes, her hairbrush, and a picture of her family at a picnic in a grove on Tempest Grounds. As she repacked her things, she picked up the picture and stared at it. The memory was so vivid, she could almost feel the artificial sunlight warm on her back. She could smell the marigolds on the fresh spring breeze.

"Don't wander off too far, sweetheart."

"Let her play, Leon. She'll only be four once."

Lexia would need scissors, but who would she cut from the frame? Her father? Or herself? If Lya had known Leon would kill her, does that mean she'd provoked him? Or was there something more prescient at play here—

"Lexia."

She looked up to find Axis leaning casually in the doorway. With his arms crossed, the threshold framed him perfectly against the backdrop of Gauge's door beyond. A servant peered in from the floor below as Axis straightened and slowly closed the door, locking him and Lexia in the room together.

It was time for the talk.

Lexia turned back to her luggage and said, "It's funny. For how high up I am at the Cathedral, I felt less like a caged bird here than I did in my own home. Gauge let me move around the house freely at all hours without asking me to check in with an itinerary for my every step. In some ways, I feel more like an employee to my father than a daughter."

From closer behind, Axis asked, "Does that mean Gauge makes you feel free? Was that part of the appeal for you?"

Lexia paused in her work to consider his question, staring out over the balcony where Winter waited for her to resurface. She said, "I suppose it is. You make me feel safe, protected. Father approves of you—mother did, too. Our relationship is rich with so much warmth. I could drink from this fountain forever and never feel it drain."

When Axis said nothing, Lexia continued, "I know you've already forgiven me, and I won't take it for granted. But I won't ever forgive myself until you make it fair. Make it right."

Warmth suffused Lexia's back, and Axis' lips brushed her ear as he purred, "Are you asking me to punish you, Lexia?"

There was something to the edge of Axis' voice. Something Lexia had never heard from him before. A slight growl with a touch of... danger... to it.

Lexia wanted Axis to take out his hurt and anguish on her. To get lost in her after weeks of shock and confusion. When she answered, it came out breathy for the hike in her pulse. "Yes. Please."

With his hard front pressed to her back, Axis slipped out a pair of panties from Lexia's luggage and methodically tied the lingerie around her wrists. Lexia's heart skipped a beat, and she couldn't control her shallow breathing. The anticipation mounted as Axis led her to the balcony door.

Still from behind, Axis walked them up to the banister. The height, thirteen stories up, was dizzying. She could hear the clock tower tick with the beat of her heart as the city pulsed and writhed below in afternoon routines. It was broad daylight, and people would see them from down there. What was Axis thinking?

Axis kissed Lexia's sensitive skin on her neck below her ear. Then her jaw. Cheek. The freckles on her temple. He whispered, "Are you afraid? I can feel your heart beating like a butterfly in a net. Do you want to feel free, Lexia?"

Lexia closed her eyes against the swirling sight below and tilted her neck to let Axis have more of her. "I always feel free with you, Axis."

"No. You said 'warm' and 'safe.' Right now is about feeling free." Axis slipped his hand into the waistband of Lexia's pants. The leather gave way to his long familiar fingers and warm palm. All the while, he said, "You want a release, and I plan to give it to you. *My* way."

Lexia threw her head back against his shoulder and let out a soft cry as Axis teased her. He slid his free hand into her blouse and found no barrier between them. Just skin.

The publicity of it. The adrenaline from this high up. Bound by her own panties—Lexia's moans grew louder the more Axis' practiced fingers brought her to the edge. Down. To the edge again.

This was Axis' way.

Gauge brought Lexia's walls down like a battering ram. Axis preferred to fashion himself a key which unlocked one long, slow release. Painfully slow.

And Axis loved every second of it. As he kissed Lexia along the shoulders and neck, she felt him smirking with pride in his work. He leaned her forward and said, "Open your eyes. Look down at them. They can see us if they look up, and I can't bother to care anymore, Lexia. Let them watch me make love to you on top of the Copper Cathedral."

Lexia wasn't sure how it happened, but her pants fell down around her boots and Axis was inside her in the work of a moment. Her scream tore through Snow Plaza, and some people definitely looked up. Axis gripped Lexia's hips and thrust again with enough force to bow her spine against him. With her wrists tied, she threw her arms up behind her to lock them around the back of his neck. To hold on from falling.

Axis was speaking, but Lexia made out only some of the words. "You promised it would be us forever. Did you let him in, Lexia? Did Gauge have you every way?"

Oh.

Lexia had to swallow her next climactic scream to say, "No." She understood what Axis meant, and she understood why he asked. "You can have all of me, Axis."

Axis stopped taking Lexia one way and began another. There was no need for him to say anything. This would hurt without practice, but he tried his best to ease her into it. Lexia knew, deep down, Axis claimed something from the pain it caused her. She understood it, embraced it, and ground back against it.

Let him have her pain.

The height, the publicity, and the first time with Lexia this way left Axis intoxicated with endorphins, adrenaline, and anxiety. A heady cocktail at the pinnacle of climax. He lost himself in Lexia in ways he never had before, and she cried out loud enough to alert all of Winter to their escapade.

Gauge was right.

Axis *would* thank him later.

Lexia's long legs shook as Axis eased her onto the balustrade. In a dizzying display of awesome beauty and terrifying wiles, she sat thirteen stories up, poised on the edge with her hair in a sexy mess and her cheeks flushed bright yellow. But when Lexia's lips quivered, and a tear plumped over her lashes, Axis stepped between her thighs and wrapped his arms around her.

"Sh. I know why. I don't hate you, so please don't hate yourself. We've been together far too long for three nights with Gauge to come between us."

Lexia squeezed back and muttered against Axis' shoulder, "You can have three nights with anyone you want. We'll make this fair."

Axis barked out a laugh in the wild waves of her hair. "Hah! I think it would only be fair if it was three nights with Gauge, seeing how much it changed your life."

To separate them, Lexia leaned so far back that Axis worried she might fall. She searched his eyes before gasping, "Really?!"

Again, Axis laughed and enjoyed not answering Lexia's question entirely too much. Torturing her by changing the subject was simply what she deserved. He headed inside, left her gaping on the banister, and said, "Let's finish packing your things. It'll be dinnertime before too long and I, for one, look forward to our missions."

"I didn't sleep with Gauge," Lexia confessed as she hopped off the balustrade.

Axis turned back and peered at her with his brows high.

She said, "We slept in separate rooms. I promised that to you, and I didn't break that promise. When we spend our wedding night together, that will be the first time I've slept in someone's arms."

Trust.

It'd been a long few weeks. This Founding Season had changed Axis' life, but he was starting to see he'd come out the other side of it for the better. He reached out, fluffed Lexia's bangs out of her eyes, and smiled at her. "Once this is all over..."

She leaned into his hand and nodded.

But 'this' would take time, finesse. Careful and thorough effort from all involved. The magnum opus. Once this was all over, Winter would have its epic.

They finished packing Lexia's things and headed down to the foyer where Jan, Bolt, Tija, and Gauge waited. The Count had found the time to change clothes and shave. It amused Axis to think of the man across the hall from Lexia's room while the reclamation took place—

"I'm happy you two have made up," Tija blurted. She fidgeted with her hands as if she'd tried to hold back her remark.

Axis and Lexia stopped on the last step and blinked at her.

Bolt mumbled, "Loudly, I might add."

Gauge glanced between Axis and Lexia as he said, "Yes. We were inspecting the crater when we received the… announcement."

Axis took comfort in Lexia slipping her hand into his and giving him a squeeze. She knew. She always knew. He closed his eyes to fight the initial dizziness and tried to swallow through the emerging panic.

Who cared if all of Winter knew the Prince and the Heiress were together again? That was the point, wasn't it?

Axis opened his eyes and cleared his throat to say, "Is everyone ready for their assignments?"

Gauge's lips quirked into an amused smirk with a dash of refined sadism. So it was true. He *did* tease Axis on purpose.

The Count looked away and faced the others. "Our tasks aren't simple. There's a risk to everyone involved. If at any point you feel like backing out, come to us, and we'll see you safely ashore. There are no martyrs on my watch. Are we all clear?"

Nods all around.

With a flare of his coattails, Gauge turned back and held out his gloved hand to Lexia. "My dear."

She took what he offered and let him lead her down that last step to the copper doors. Everyone avoided looking at the Wall of Pain. Which reminded Axis…

"Don't forget our conversation about the mercenaries and rehabilitation."

Jan coughed into his fist as Gauge spared Axis a glance. Axis couldn't see Gauge's blue eyes, but even behind the purple lenses, Axis knew they sparkled.

Gauge said, "I'd never forget a conversation with you, dear Prince."

The room took a collective breath and stared at the two men. Axis let his eyes fall over Gauge. He remembered the smallness of him as a boy, considered the strength it took to recover from a lifetime of poisoning, and found himself appreciating the man in front of him today. He let the admiration show in his eyes.

Between the glasses and the decade of schooling himself for diplomacy and politics, Gauge's reaction was inscrutable. But Axis detected a hint of a… challenge. In the silence which stretched between them, Gauge dared Axis to do something about the growing tension. The curiosity of each other.

Should Axis ask Lexia what Gauge was like as a lover? Or would Axis soon find out for himself?

Bolt cleared his throat, and, just like that, the moment ended.

Axis and Gauge glanced over at the valet.

Lexia and Tija groaned and rolled their eyes, simultaneously complaining, "Aw, come on." "You wrecked it."

When Jan coughed into his fist this time, Axis could hear the laughter in it.

Gauge let out a hearty laugh, and Axis shook his head to hide the incredulous smile he couldn't contain.

What a band of fellows. What a family.

Gauge walked Lexia through the Wall of Pain. The copper monument screamed silently at them on the way out. Neither looked at it. They stopped at the steps leading down to the cobbled street, and he took a moment to admire the young woman beside him.

Lexia stood tall with her chin high, so like her mother in some ways, and carried her suitcase as if it weighed less than the burden in her eyes. Despite the sadness in those black depths, resolve set her shoulders back and straight. She would survive this.

Gauge said, "Remember. If it becomes too much—"

"Ask for help. Thank you, Gauge." Lexia didn't need to climb on her tiptoes to kiss him.

Gauge tasted Axis on Lexia—woodsy and warm married with the taste of rain in the summer. The Count parted his lips to explore her further. Too soon, she separated them with a sweet smile.

Lexia said, "Wait for my signal."

"Good luck." Gauge leaned on his cane as he watched his childhood crush take one long walk of shame down Tempest Boulevard. All in all, Lexia had handled the truth about her mother's death with grace beyond her years, but Gauge suspected more toiled beneath the surface of their reckless sprite. The storm of her fury was yet on the horizon. He only hoped she could contain it until the optimum moment.

Back to work.

Gauge returned to the foyer to find Axis sprawled in an armchair. He slouched in the seat, his hands were laced across his button-down, and his legs were spread out until their full length threatened to trip the next passerby. Sporting two days' worth of stubble, he made quite the picture staring up at the ceiling with bloodshot soft green eyes. Who knew exhaustion could look so enticing?

"Young Master Flicker."

Axis' eyes shifted until he glared down the length of his body at Gauge.

Tija snickered, Bolt humphed, and Jan looked ready to scoop them all out to have his home back in order. For good reason. Gauge needed about three days and nights of uninterrupted sleep. Lexia had drained the life out of him with mind-blowing sex, but also with more than a little danger.

Gauge needed a drama-nap. He nudged Axis' boot with his loafer, saying, "On your feet, your highness. We have work to do."

Axis straightened up, sat forward, and stared up at Gauge for a heartbeat. After a tense staring contest, he said, "I could get used to that."

"What?" Gauge asked.

Axis broke into a fantastic grin. "'Your highness.'"

"Now, boys," Tija said as she stepped between the two with her hands out. "Like you said, Gauge. We all have work to do, and we can't leave Lexia out there doing her part alone."

Bolt grumbled something about "Not getting anything done with all this flirting."

Gauge kissed Tija on the cheek. "You're absolutely right." He held out a hand to Axis. "Truce?"

Axis took it and let Gauge help him stand even as the Count held onto his cane for support. "Truce."

The People's Prince was far too tall. Gauge cleared his throat before gesturing toward the door. "After you. Tija, I expect a full report tomorrow."

The gorgeous brunette beamed. "I look forward to our brunch." She gave a graceful bow with her head and said, "Gentlemen," before escorting herself out.

Bolt threw an arm around Axis and squeezed his ward's shoulder. "Are you ready, sir?"

Axis said, "I'm as ready as one can be." Then he stared down at Gauge another moment before holding out his hand. "I'll hold you to that meal."

Gauge shook Axis' hand, filling to the brim with the healthier man's warmth. Gauge said, "I look forward to it… Your highness."

With an incredulous shake of his head, Axis left while Bolt groaned alongside him.

What a week.

"Sir."

Gauge turned away from the frozen shrieks of pain in the door to face Jan. The butler stared the Count down through furrowed brows and asked, "Permission to speak freely?"

Gauge couldn't help but smile. "You know? I think I'll expect it from hereon. There's no need to ask for permission, old friend. I value your wisdom."

Jan's chest swelled, but then deflated as he remembered why he'd asked in the first place. He said, "You must know I don't approve of the risk to yourself."

With a turn of his heel, Gauge headed back toward the vault. "Of course. What is there to like?" He wished he could climb the spiral stairs two at a time as Axis had done, but alas, his bones could barely haul up this sack of heavy muscle.

Jan lingered outside as Gauge collected the assets necessary to complete his mission. Gauge said, "Carry on, soldier. I know you're not finished."

Gauge could hear the old spy's furrow deepen from behind him as Jan said, "Ms. Tempest is worth some sacrifice, but I'm uncertain of the Flicker boy. How do you know he won't turn on you to support the doctor and avenge this slight?"

A slight.

What a polite way to refer to Gauge and Lexia's affair.

Gauge said, "I trust the People's Prince to do the right thing as much as I trust Lexia to lose sight of our goal and act with her heart at the most inconvenient moment."

Could one hear 'boggled' in someone's voice? Because Gauge thought he did as Jan said, "But-but... Sir?"

"You know as well as I do that we need contingencies." Upon contingencies. Their task was no simple one. Gauge held up his 'contingency' in the palm of his hand.

"Because you're the only one with enough power to free me now."

Gauge returned to the library with a medical kit and the parcel of silver cloth. He held out the former to Jan, who took it with an exaggerated sigh and a roll of his old brown eyes.

The butler said, "The things I do for you."

With a grin, despite the very serious pain he would soon endure, Gauge grinned and patted Jan on the arm. "To new adventures, old friend."

People crowded Lexia at first, mobbing her with a battery of questions regarding her personal life. She'd lived a lifetime under scrutiny, but never at this level. Someone had even asked her to compare orgasms between Gauge and Axis. Since the same thought had occurred to her within the last hour, Lexia couldn't really blame them for wondering. But she almost did.

Unlike Gauge, Lexia didn't invite the attention. It was simply there, and she coexisted with it. However, over the last few weeks, she really gave thought to marrying Axis and having children under this shadow. Maybe some of Axis' public phobia was chafing off on Lexia.

Eventually, Lexia's silence discouraged the squawkers, or they found some decency to stop following her down the Boulevard. She arrived at the gates of Tempest Manor carrying her own luggage. The gate guard, whose tone-deaf child Lexia had tutored on the tuba, couldn't meet her eyes as he opened the wrought-iron threshold.

Lexia felt no shame as she walked down the drive to her childhood home. She felt purpose. A grown woman with a mission. Lexia only hoped she could keep this calm when she met her father's eyes for the first time since...

"The Wrong Side of Eternity would be more bearable! Let go—"

A soft cry.

A loud thud.

And then nothing.

Mother.

Winter's Diamond and Snow's Angel.

Lya had left quite the mystery for Lexia to solve.

As if summoned by her thoughts, Leon waited on the portico. He stood there with his arms at his sides in a neutral stance. His expression was remote, but as Lexia walked closer, she could see the fear behind his clear glasses in his soft gray eyes.

Leon should be afraid, and Lexia found herself regretting her recent decree on duels to the death. She stopped on the drive just shy of crossing onto the stone entrance. Chin high. Spine straight.

"Hello, father."

"Hello, daughter." He sounded… resigned.

Lexia shored all her strength for what would come next. With a strangled sob, she ran to Leon and threw her arms around him. He didn't hesitate to hold her as Lexia cried against his collar, and his body loosened against her like it was letting out a sigh of relief.

The voice of her childhood sounded so soothing as Leon said, "Sh. You're home now. Everything will be forgotten soon enough, and we can get back to our lives."

Lexia said nothing. She held onto this familiar embrace and let it lull her into a peace she couldn't know without it. Mother hadn't died of some mysterious physical ailment. Instead, she'd chosen to leave Lexia with a man Lya had despised enough to implicate in her death.

Without Gauge, Axis, Tija, Jan, and Bolt, Lexia wouldn't know what to do with this. But that wasn't the case.

"Father?"

Leon kissed her hair and soothed, "Yes, my dear?"

Lexia swallowed a half sob to ask, "Is it all right if I take my meals in my room for the next few days? I don't want any messages or visitors. Unless…"

"Unless?" Her father chafed her arms before separating them and peering down at her.

Lexia let tears well in her eyes. "Axis…"

With gentle force, her father embraced her again and rubbed a circle in her back. "Of course, darling. Anything for you. No messages. No visitors. Just Axis." He sounded so relieved that it made Lexia's stomach twist into knots.

The butterfly once again captured in the jar. The bird in the gilded cage.

Rhyme appeared with his face schooled, but Lexia could see the censure in his usually warm brown eyes. They'd turned to ice as he took Lexia's luggage and carried it inside without a word, kind or otherwise. It was probably for the best. She wasn't much happy with him either.

Unfortunately, as Lexia crossed the threshold into the Manor, the reception from even her most familiar companions wasn't very warm either. No one looked at her, and things went about as if she weren't there. She felt like another piece of the furniture for as much attention as they paid her.

Leon escorted Lexia up to her room, and her heart pounded like she was headed to the gallows. He would lock her in there, as she'd asked, and Lexia would spend days, possibly weeks, trapped inside her room. Trapped inside her head with these thoughts and conspiracies and little relief from them.

Axis would come.

Axis would come.

Lexia repeated her new mantra to save her sanity and stave the tears, no longer forced for her father's benefit. Once again among the black floors and white walls of her room, Lexia turned and faced her father in the doorway.

Leon asked, "What of the Founding events?"

"I shall attend as per my family's name and reputation."

Her father nodded with approval, paused, and peered at her over the rim of his glasses. "And Count Snow?"

Lexia clenched her jaw, but had to look away to say, "I want nothing more to do with him. I will engage him on professional matters only and conduct myself as a Tempest on official business only."

Again, the nod of approval. "Very well, dear. I will arrange everything, and when Axis calls, I'll let him straight up to see you. Things can return to as they were. You'll be surprised at how they fall back into place."

Like after mother's death.

As a chill claimed Lexia, she fought not to shiver in front of her father. Leon offered a weak and timid smile before turning, walking through the door, and closing it behind him.

There'd been love in the doctor's eyes. He was happy to see Lexia safe and sound, home and trapped, under his domain again. With her safe fiance and her certain future.

Is this how Lya had felt? Cherished but suffocated.

Lexia opened the suitcase on the bed and peered down at the picture nestled in with her clothes. Leon was trying to hold the squirming four-year-old Lexia still for the snapshot, but Lya...

She stared off in the distance with the breeze in her hair. There was something haunting about the black and white image now. A cloud over Lya's head.

Cherished but suffocated.

"Is that why you wanted to leave us so badly, mother?"

Lya didn't answer, but Lexia was determined to find out.

Lost Time

{One Week Later}

FINALLY.

The day had come.

Axis left his apartment to the sound of birds chirping, and they were the only ones squawking. The press had stopped hounding the families a few days ago. Winter had become bored with Axis' workout regimen, Gauge's outings with Tija, and Lexia's silence. Now people milled about their mornings without fresh gossip to occupy them from the lulling of Founding Season. Soon, work would resume, and routines could return.

Thank Eternity. Axis could hardly wait.

Bolt pulled up to the curb with his driving gloves wrapped tightly around the steering wheel. The People's Prince slipped into the backseat and patted his friend on the shoulder.

Things were in motion, and progress would be made. Even so, Axis clenched his jaw the entire way down Flicker Avenue to where it ended at Tempest Boulevard. The myrtles lining the cobbled street budded with fresh growth, and Axis found he would welcome this year's spring.

They arrived at the gate, and the guard let them through without hesitation. Almost as if they were expected. Bolt gripped the wheel even tighter as they drove through, and Axis could swear he heard the other man's teeth grind.

Gauge didn't show Bolt and Tija the projection. He'd wanted to keep the technology a secret, deciding the fewer people who knew about it the better. But both the young brunette woman and the valet with his salt and pepper hair had trusted Axis and Lexia's faith in Gauge. It was quite the leap to believe Dr. Tempest was culpable in Lya's death. That was all they knew. Nothing about the domes or Snow's Angel or any of that distracting nonsense.

This was about discovering the truth of Lya's death. The rest was up to Gauge.

Rhyme waited for the car to pull up to the portico before opening Axis' door. The Prince normally didn't care for such service, but in the bodyguard's case, he'd make an exception. Axis glided out of the car, buttoned his black blazer with the gold brocade, and masked his eyes from Rhyme's careful scrutiny.

This was about rescuing Lexia. Not about teaching her bodyguard some manners. Oh, sure. Rhyme made all the right moves and said all the right words. But there was something… darker about the man's presence over Lexia now. Overbearing. More like a warden than a protector. He'd been with her since Lya's death, and reported on Lexia's actions directly to Dr. Tempest.

Rhyme couldn't be trusted.

"Good afternoon, Rhyme."

"Prince Flicker."

Axis detected a hint of suspicion from the old bodyguard and chose to ignore it. "Is the doctor in?"

Rhyme nodded at Bolt as the driver came around and said, "Dr. Tempest is waiting in his study. Bolt can come with me. Sami's been looking for another taste tester in the kitchen."

Bolt mused. "Not one for the salt, are you, Rhyme?"

Rhyme humphed, and Axis was happy to leave his company. Although, perhaps it was better than facing his next ordeal: looking Dr. Tempest in the eyes.

Once in the foyer, Axis couldn't help but glance up the five stories to Lexia's bedroom door. Seven days trapped inside. Word was she hadn't even come out to interact with the Manor's children. She was such a social creature. How had she endured this forced introversion?

Axis hoped Lexia's spirit was intact.

"Hello, son."

That voice saying that word had meant the world to Axis his entire life. But now...

"Good afternoon, Dr. Tempest."

Axis shored himself and faced Leon, forcing sincerity and concern in his eyes. When all he wanted to do was curse the man whom Axis had considered a father figure. When he turned, he saw Lexia's only living parent standing in the doorway to his study. The soft gray of his linen suit brought out the steel in his eyes and draped a bit off his lean figure as if Leon had lost some weight. Dark circles under his eyes indicated he'd lost sleep at the very least, and the smile lines around his mouth seemed more prominent than the last time Axis had seen him.

The Prince gestured toward the study and asked, "May we step inside? I have some matters I'd like to discuss with you."

Leon waved him in. "Of course. Have a seat."

The last time Axis had sat in this chair across from Leon had been unequivocal. The older man had stared into the younger one's eyes and lied to him, nearly ruining Axis' relationship with Lexia forever. But as they sat down, Axis understood they both desired the same outcome: Lexia and Axis happily wed forever after.

Could this be salvaged?

Leon stretched out his hands until his sleeves shifted back and then folded his arms across the table. He oozed genuine concern as he said, "Tell me what's on your mind."

"Lexia." Axis told the truth. "After considerable deliberation, I've decided I don't give a damn what happened at the Cathedral. I'd like to carry on with our wedding as if the entire..." He let the word 'affair' fill itself in the blank space. "*Incident* had never occurred. I'm here today to ask if you believe that could be possible."

Leon nodded his approval, saying, "Absolutely. I'm not just saying that for the sake of my daughter's happiness. I believe it's in your best interest as well. You two have the strongest bond of any couple in all of Winter." Not in part due to grooming from their parents. "Even now,

Lexia awaits your correspondence. There is regret—remorse, even—living in her heart. You know how impulsive and reckless she is. I won't claim no small amount of responsibility for what transpired. After all, I frightened her off. You of all people know how protective I am of her happiness. She hasn't asked about her mother or any of that business since before…" The 'affair.' "I think we can all put it behind us."

Axis almost missed it, but Leon's eyes flicked to the covered portrait of Lya on the wall over Axis' shoulder. So… The good doctor wasn't totally convinced. How nerve-racking it must be to live with this kind of secret hanging over one's head day in and day out. Especially knowing someone like Gauge held the truth in the palm of his hand.

"I agree with you completely, sir. I miss Lexia. Every day, it became harder to breathe without her smile." Also, the truth. "May I go up and see her?"

Leon beamed. "Please do. I'll let Rhyme know to let you up. Excuse me." He stood and held out his hand.

Axis hated himself a little as he shook it. Hated himself even more when the father of the bride glowed before he left to find Rhyme. With a heavy heart, Axis spared Lya's covered portrait a glance.

A promise.

A silent vow.

Axis wouldn't fail Lexia again.

"So, tell me, Gauge. What surprises are in store for this year's Founding Day? If you've been playing it this close to your chest, it must be something extra spectacular."

Tija smiled into her mimosa over their third brunch this week. Later, Gauge would take her to the theater for a cabaret show after dinner. They'd have fantastic sex loudly in their private theater box before excusing themselves early for a night of raucous exercise somewhere else public in Winter. Perhaps a civilian train car.

The show must go on.

Not that Gauge was complaining. Tija's company was a balm on his nerves. He soaked in her reassuring presence and the familiar scent of cinnamon and lust.

However, Gauge couldn't keep his mind from wandering to Lexia. How had she fared this last week without contact from the outside world? Even though their paths had only crossed in recent weeks, he knew her to be a radiant extrovert. After seven days of her silence locked in that tower, Gauge wanted to sidle up on a trusty steed and rescue the butterfly from captivity.

But that wasn't in the cards, now was it?

Even with all this between them, Tija still wasn't getting Gauge's secrets out of him. He smirked over his gloved fingers laced under his chin and said, "You'll have to wait and see like everyone else, my dear."

Tija moved a piece on the board, saying, "Now that the Prince is in play, I expect to hear from the good doctor."

Gauge idly nudged his piece. "Yes. The union agreements will resume to appease the Heiress' wounded spirit. In this position, you can provide our wild card some guidance."

After downing her morning champagne, Tija arranged three more pieces in place. She peered at the board as if considering Gauge's next move before asking, "Are you aware of the risks? Truly?"

If Tija had to ask, then Gauge's strategy evaded even her thorough understanding of him. This was optimal, leaning toward obtuse to the doctor. No one could guess the surprise before the end.

"I am." Gauge smiled and laid down the center piece.

A knock sounded from the bedroom door. Tija called, "Come in, Jan." She'd been the lady of the Cathedral in all but name for some time now, so the butler was used to it.

Jan entered with the mail in hand. "Sir." The sparkle in the man's deep brown eyes implied he'd recently finished with the mercenaries downstairs. There was even a little extra pep in his step. Gauge would need to resolve the rehabilitation situation with Axis, soon.

But not today.

"Thank you, Jan." He filed through the many invitations to grand openings for new shops and entertainment venues. Any requests for benefit reconsideration he handed straight to Tija for her purview. However, one invitation interested him immensely.

To our lauded Count Snow,

We humbly invite you to attend the premiere of our newest opera, *Tarnished Love*. As our special guest, we guarantee the finest amenities at your request. Whatever you should desire.

The playhouse eagerly awaits your correspondence.

Gauge tapped the card against the frame of his glasses as he considered the contents of the opera. Surely it would take longer to prepare an opus on the past month's drama? At Tija's raised brow, Gauge handed it over.

She took one second to glance at it before she let out an incredulous laugh. "They can't be serious?"

The nonplussed look on Tija's face elicited a chuckle out of Gauge. He said, "I'm afraid so. Would you like to attend? It's in three days."

"Oh, I wouldn't miss it for the world." Tija beamed and warmed his heart.

Gauge held out his gloved hand to her and tried not to wince when she took it. When her face fell, he knew Tija had seen it and changed the subject to distract her. "How do you think our Prince is faring with the good doctor?"

Tija allowed the subject to change. "I think he's heartsick, and I hope he finds comfort in Lexia. That they find comfort in each other."

"As do I."

While leading Tija out the door to the convertible, Gauge ruminated a bit, wondering if Leon would make it so easy for the Royal Couple to reunite. It was a chilly afternoon, but the early signs of spring sang all around them. Birds chirped, rodents chittered, and there was the faint scent of rain to chase away the frost. Not as warm as the summer showers of Lexia's skin with the promise of sun afterward, but more the promise of renewal.

The cane let Gauge pull himself up onto the back of the seat, and he helped Tija sit beside him. She covered them with a blanket and beamed. By the glitter in her brilliant blue eyes and the glow of her fair skin, all this extra attention suited her. Could he ask for a better Lady of Winter? A Countess—

Lexia's black eyes flashed, and Gauge's fingers longed for the silk of her hair. He wanted to kiss the freckles on her temples and bite the white skin of taut stomach. Her long legs wrapped around his hips—

Tija smirked.

After a blink, Gauge realized he'd been staring.

"You think of her often," Tija observed. She knew him entirely too well.

Caught, there wasn't a damned thing Gauge could do about the reddening of his cheeks. He could only hope his dark complexion disguised it, but as Tija's smirk spread into a grin, he ordered, "Driver. To the restaurant."

Tija's laughter held an edge of teasing, but Gauge knew it was all in the name of friendship. Even so, he struggled with his attachment to the diverting Heiress.

"Gauge, you feel too good to be wrong."

"But even now I'm keeping secrets from you."

"I don't care. Just don't take your hands off me."

There was something about the reckless abandon in Lexia's eyes when she offered her throat to Gauge's grip.

Intoxicating.

That was the word.

Tija was safe and close. Gauge's attraction to Lexia was dangerous and precarious, poised on a ledge between her loyalty to the Prince and her desire for the Count.

Yes, it would make for engaging opera material.

Tija asked, "Where are we having dinner tonight?"

"Before the cabaret, I thought I'd take us to this quaint place on the corner of Tempest Boulevard and Flicker Avenue. I rarely frequent it, so this will be a treat for us both."

Of course, they'd pass Tempest Manor on the way. Gauge would spare it nothing more than a casual glance because to look away from it completely would provide more fodder to the press. This was a delicate tightrope they were walking, and tonight, Gauge would test the others.

The Count only hoped the Prince and the Heiress could handle it.

When a knock sounded on the door, Lexia looked up from the mass of papers on her desk. Wadded balls of dispersed ink spilled onto the black floors, and she'd drawn a visual diagram on her white wall in eye kohl and lipstick. Quickly, she pinned a sheet over it and swiped her desk clear, shoveling all the papers into the drawers.

Lexia glanced at the mirror off to the side and considered her appearance. Every day for the last week, she'd gone through her hygiene routine: fixed her hair in a braid or a wavy bun, applied a moderate amount of signature makeup, and dressed for Winter's spring weather. Slacks with layered belts, oversized shirts, and straps to tie in the waist. Today, she'd chosen purple as the primary color.

Because today might be the day Lexia was freed. Or so she'd thought every day of this mission. Hopefully, it was finally today.

"Come in."

Rhyme opened the door, and Lexia tried to school her face not to show her disappointment. As if he'd seen it, the bodyguard gave a cruel half chuckle before stepping to the side. With him out of the way, the doorway framed the most beautiful sight Lexia had seen in seven days.

"Axis!"

Lexia didn't wait. With everything in her, she ran across the room and leapt into her fiance's arms. When Axis accepted her with a tight embrace, she wrapped her legs around him.

Was she crying?

She didn't want anyone to see her cry. To see how desperate she'd been for affection or attention over the last week. For a kind word or a warm glance. From anyone… Anyone…

Axis said against her hair, "I've got you. Sh… Everything will be all right."

Eternity, but Lexia needed to hear it from someone. "I love you, Axis. I'm so sorry."

At the last, Rhyme gave another chuckle before excusing himself. "Enjoy, you two."

The second the door closed, Lexia pulled back enough to face Axis. Reminding her of Gauge, Axis winked. The whimsy and confidence of it suited him, and she beamed.

They were in play.

Axis pressed his forehead to Lexia's and said, "You are amazing, but truly, how are you doing?"

Lexia took a shaky inhale and let it out on a sigh. "I'm in desperate need of you." It was too soon to mention Gauge in the same breath as sex with Axis, but in truth, she'd thought of the Count's forceful grip as much as Axis' patient persistence over the last week.

It was a discussion for later. Right now, Lexia wanted to get lost in Axis, and he obliged.

By the time they surfaced from the sheets, it was time for dinner. Lexia was determined to go out, and it was expected of her. Leon lingered near the foyer with Rhyme as if they'd waited for the Royal Couple to emerge.

When she glimpsed them below, Lexia froze at the top of the stairs. How far did this go? Had her father's spies listened at the door while she and Axis made love? Or had they waited all this time to catch her on the way out?

Sensing her reticence, Axis took Lexia's hand and led her down the stairs before Leon could notice her hesitation.

"Axis. Lexia. Are you on your way to dinner?"

How could Leon sound so casual—

No.

Lexia needed to focus. "Yes, father."

Axis held out his elbow, and Lexia firmly hooked her arm through it. A unified front.

The good doctor beamed and said, "Splendid. My kitchen staff have recruited Bolt for dinner preparations. Rhyme, please escort Axis and Lexia."

"Yes, sir."

This was suffocating. Lexia couldn't see Rhyme's stubbled smiles or frowns without seeing a double meaning behind them. She'd always known he reported her actions to Leon, but never truly appreciated the lens from which he observed. The loose cannon daughter to remain forever at the father's side. Potential trouble requiring a bridle.

Lexia smiled and held out her hand to Rhyme. "Won't you walk with us, Rhyme? You can tell me all about how you and Sami are getting along."

Rhyme let her loop her arm around his elbow as well. They would walk down the street together. Eyes on each other. Lexia preened, and Axis coughed to disguise a smirk.

Something about the way the light cast on Leon's gray eyes shone with a glare from his glasses. He wasn't one so easily fooled, but he beamed like a proud papa. Everything was back in its place.

Leon said, "You three enjoy your evening," as they made their way down the drive.

Once through the gate and out of sight of the Manor, Rhyme separated from the couple. With the snow melted, he took to the dried cobbles easily. No more tripping over his steam-powered prosthetic.

He said, "Well, well. The Heiress finds the will to live among Winter once again. Thank goodness you came along, Prince Axis."

Unconvinced.

That's how Rhyme sounded.

Axis stuck to the script. "It took time for the vultures to stop circling. I never intended to leave Lexia for so long."

Lexia strolled between them, feeling the tension ebb and flow like she was tethered to a buoy during high tide.

Rhyme shoved his hands into his pockets, clucked his tongue in disapproval, and shook his head. "You two couldn't survive a week apart. That doesn't exactly seem healthy."

This was a test, and Lexia wouldn't fail. She said, "It was the most turbulent week of my life. Not since mother… I haven't felt such a loss in the last two years."

Axis lifted her knuckles to his lips and kissed them, staring into her eyes. The soft green of his flickered with the flame of his admiration.

Rhyme groaned and swiped his hand down his face. "My apologies, Heiress. I didn't mean to upset you."

Unlikely.

Rhyme insisted, "I mean it. As an act of contrition, I'll stay outside the restaurant and leave you to your date."

Axis squeezed Lexia's hand, and she took the hint. She said, "That won't be necessary, Rhyme. I feel… safer with you around. Please join us in the bistro."

Something flashed in the bodyguard's brown eyes. Acceptance. It was working. "Very well, Heiress. Here we are."

The normally quiet restaurant bustled with a flurry of activity. More than Lexia had seen in over a week in her own home, let alone at the small establishment. She was a little apprehensive, but as Axis tugged her along, she knew she could face anything.

Except for what waited inside.

Sat at the table in the restaurant's center—Lexia and Axis' usual spot—was Tija and...

"Gauge."

When the Count's name left Lexia's lips on a breath, she knew they were in trouble.

———————————

Axis fought not to tense when Lexia said Gauge's name aloud. The emotion behind it didn't hurt him so much as alert Rhyme to their charade. The Count wasn't making it any easier. The Prince ground his teeth as Gauge glimpsed the Royal Couple in the entryway, locked eyes with the Heiress, and toasted a wineglass to her. Lexia melted against Axis.

There was no other word for it.

Gauge had reduced Lexia to a puddle with a mere smirk.

Axis knew his part to play. He and Lexia would resume their relationship as if her stay at the Copper Cathedral was the satiation of a natural curiosity. One that after which Gauge, the dark knight, discarded Lexia for Tija. Then the white knight arrived to pick up the Heiress' shattered pieces. Leon could carry on living in his carefully constructed paradise.

And Axis believed it was working until now. What was the Count playing at?

Lexia stared at Gauge with hunger reflected in her black gaze. All eyes fell on them, momentarily raising the hair on the back of Axis' neck. Gently, he tugged on Lexia where her arm was hooked in his. She blinked and resurfaced from her fantasies to peer up at Axis.

The reckless butterfly.

Not that Axis could blame Lexia. Gauge was wearing a black crocodile skin blazer with an oxblood silk button-down, waistcoat, and tie. The oxblood lenses hid his blue eyes, no less penetrating from this distance. His cufflinks, buttons, hair beads, tie pin, and spectacle frames were all copper.

Were the accessories for his namesake, 'The Copper Count?' Or was it in defiance of his father's mistreatment? Would it be the same if Axis started smoking cigars? One day, the two misbegotten sons would sit down over a meal and share their scars—

Shit.

Axis caught himself staring as much as Lexia. When he glanced down at her, Lexia's eyes were still on Axis, but the hunger had grown into a gnawing starvation. He knew where she'd gone, and sometimes he wondered… Did Axis want to go there with Lexia?

"Prince. Heiress." A soft older voice snapped Axis out of his trailing thoughts. The voice belonged to the owner's husband. The elderly gentleman, shrunken from age, said, "Our apologies. As you know, we're a small establishment and have no need for reservations. While we can't offer you the usual table, we have one with a lovely view of the gardens."

Oh. Right.

They were here to eat dinner and make a public show of their unification. Axis would need to thank Gauge for making it a near-impossible task.

As if the Count could read the Prince's thoughts, Gauge nodded in their direction.

Axis would thank him properly, too.

"This way."

The Royal Couple followed with Rhyme in their wake. The bodyguard-spy had devoured the scene with entirely too much obvious scrutiny. He wasn't hiding his purpose any longer, and the marked pair would need to work harder to convince Rhyme and, by extension, Leon of their broken ties with Gauge.

Rumor had it that Axis, Tija, and Bolt arrived at the Copper Cathedral seven days ago with an ultimatum for Lexia and Gauge. In the standoff, Gauge chose Tija, and Axis agreed to take Lexia back after a period of bereavement—the seven days. Meanwhile, Bolt and Tija worked to negotiate affairs between the mines and the factories.

The papers called it 'Tarnished Love.' But there was nothing tarnished about Axis' relationship with Lexia. He wouldn't say she'd acted reasonably, but she'd acted perfectly as herself in the moment. He refused to find her at fault for it. As for Gauge...

How could anyone say 'no' to Lexia?

So here they were. Dancing to Gauge's music on the ballroom floor that was Winter. A waltz to Lya's requiem.

Even as privy to the plan as Axis was, he still didn't know how it would end. And there was something… exhilarating about it. The feeling was familiar. All the times Gauge had riled Axis up during a board meeting, the man's knowing smiles, and the chills during the few times the Count had revealed his eyes—

The thrill…

That's what had attracted Lexia.

The couple sat at a table in a bow window and held out their hands to one another automatically. Both showed off the other's timepieces on their wrists. Rhyme and the entire restaurant watched them order dinner, eat, and try to ignore Gauge's hearty laughter.

Axis tried his damnedest to sit closer to Lexia, pull her against his side, and sneak kisses on her neck and shoulder. But he was shaking, and she'd felt it. His heart beat so hard against his sternum, he thought it would break free of his ribcage. Had Gauge asked too much of Axis to overcome this anxiety?

Last week, at the top of the Cathedral, had been different. Axis had been desperate to reconnect with Lexia, and the people below were so far down he could barely make them out. Unfortunately, he recognized every face in the restaurant, and they watched with unveiled curiosity. Axis was doing his best.

And it was working.

Whispers circulated throughout the restaurant.

"The People's Prince. Do you see? He's marking his territory."

"Do you think Count Snow has noticed those two all over each other?"

"Dr. Tempest must be so relieved to have Prince Flicker back in the fold."

That was the hope.

When Gauge stood with his cane and helped Tija stand to make their way to the exit, the restaurant held a collective breath. Axis and Lexia whispered in each other's ear, but not really. It was to hide Lexia's eyes from roving over Gauge in that suit. Axis knew because he was doing the same.

But they couldn't miss it when Gauge passed by their table. The Count tipped his top hat to the Royal Couple on his way out, and the buzzing began.

What a relief.

Rhyme kept his eyes on Lexia and Axis as they left the restaurant. On the curb, Bolt waited in the car.

Axis nuzzled Lexia's neck, asking, "Do you want us to give you a lift?"

Lexia shook her head against Axis' collarbone and buried her face in his shoulder for a hug. She said, "You know me. I need the fresh air."

"Be careful."

"You, too. See you tomorrow."

Axis took a full step back to stop touching Lexia, saying, "Tomorrow then."

The love of his life smiled before turning and gliding down the cobbles. Rhyme pushed off the garden wall he'd been leaning against, gave a salute to Axis, and followed the beauty with her swaying white braid.

Without wasting more time, Axis slid into the backseat, asking Bolt, "Did you get everything you needed?"

"And more, sir. Also, you might want this. It came special delivery for you at Tempest Manor."

Axis' best friend handed him an envelope. It was from the playhouse. After reading it, Axis groaned incredulously and rolled his eyes.

"Seriously?"

"Aye, sir. Seriously."

"I never believed I was condemning the rest of the world to death, Lya."

"They were slated for starvation in a century or less. You couldn't save everyone even if you'd wanted to. Your choice spared Winter the loss, Little Snow. Freeze your heart to it and let it go."

Gauge was cold.

Even with Tija snuggled up to him in bed, he felt the ice in his soul. There was a tundra of permafrost in his conscience, but Lya had been right. He'd learned to live with it.

The warmth from his best friend's naked curves abated the chill, and Gauge snuggled Tija closer to him. She purred in her sleep and nuzzled against his bare chest. He peered down at where his oxblood gloves met her pale skin and ignored the soreness in his palm. It would heal.

The Copper Cathedral's clock tower chimed midnight.

"Tija, love, it's time," Gauge said as he gently shook her.

Depleted and sated, Tija rolled away from him and said, "Tell me how it goes."

Gauge smiled at her. She always was the last to rise. Only *she* could sleep through what had kept him awake and anxious. Anticipation fluttered in Gauge's chest as he walked naked across his room to the balcony door. There, a copper telescope waited. While Gauge resented all the gifts from his father, it seemed fitting to keep the last one Cam Snow had peered through.

The telescope was already pointed Southeast. As he looked through it, Gauge ignored the early spring air vying to match the cold on the outside with the frostbite on the inside. Some part of him took pleasure from being naked while on the balcony, searching for a sign from someone who would certainly mind his nudity.

Gauge smirked as he found the window he needed. Nestled among other apartments and townhouses on Flicker Avenue, Axis' Northwest facing window was dark. Once the clock tower finished chiming the twelfth hour, the light in the Prince's bedroom flashed.

Once.

Gauge waited with bated breath.

Five seconds passed.

Ten seconds…

The light flashed again.

All was going according to plan. While the Prince, the Heiress, and the Count distracted the bodyguard and the rest of Winter from their scheme, Bolt had opened a door for which they could enter and infiltrate. Not that Gauge could blame Sami. Bolt's salt and pepper hair and particular brand of charm would certainly appeal to many a lady in Winter. Moving on from the Heiress' bodyguard to the Prince's valet was another rung in the ladder. He was hoping she kept her bedroom ascension to herself.

No missives.

No couriers.

Axis, Lexia, and Gauge would have to trust each other to carry out their parts while coexisting in Winter's cozy community. Or claustrophobic community to Axis. Agoraphobic to Lexia.

How different they all were. The perfect marriage of abandon, calculation, and trepidation.

Gauge left the balcony, closed the door, and made his way through the sea of his and Tija's discarded clothes. He glanced down at her black croc-skin purse, a gift from him for tonight's affair. The lavender silk and nickel peeking through the top caught Gauge's eye.

Privacy was an understanding between Gauge and Tija. So he didn't pry, but he recognized the timepiece for what it was. Understated and beautiful—just like Tija.

Inspiration struck Gauge, and he went to the sitting room he'd converted into a closet. Coats, blazers, slacks, button-downs, waistcoats, ties, loafers, hats, and an assortment of accessories beckoned. He walked down the carefully coordinated and cataloged aisles until he found the suit he wanted to wear in the morning.

Gauge hoped it would make Tija smile, perhaps even take her breath away. He might live with the snow in his head, but at least he could give warmth to those he loved. Speaking of...

A knock sounded at the door.

While Gauge fancied himself an exhibitionist and his nudity had never bothered Jan in the past, the Count slipped into a robe before greeting the butler at the door. "Jan."

The old spy said, "Our guests have offered information in exchange for some accommodations. Namely, 'a pot to piss in.'"

Gauge couldn't contain his incredulous laughter, and after it escaped, he glanced over to find Tija still sound asleep in his bed. If the ice hurricanes finally brought the domes down around Winter, Tija would still sleep through it. With a smile on his face, Gauge followed Jan into the dungeon.

The female and male mercenary clung to each other for there was no fireplace or steam-powered heat generated this far beneath the Copper Cathedral. The hewn rock floor offered no warmth. Jan offered Gauge a handkerchief, and the Count accepted to spare at least one of his senses. They smelled of filth and the faint beginnings of rot.

The woman said, "Please, sir. We'll tell you everything we know about the doctor's dealings with Valve."

Finally.

Unfortunately, their current condition wasn't without some aversion. After all, what would Lexia think?

Gauge let out a sigh as he said, "Jan, get them a bed, two chamber pots, and a bath."

The butler's face fell. It's not that his expression was jovial before, but more that the lines of his face truly bowed under the weight of his disappointment.

For the second time tonight, Gauge had to fight not to laugh. He gave Jan a pat on the shoulder and said, "But you don't have to bring them fresh clothes."

Jan brightened instantly, and this time, Gauge laughed.

FIVE

Dazzling Snow

LEXIA GREETED THE MORNING WITH A SHOWER. The hot water revitalized her senses and prepared her for the work ahead. She dressed in a burgundy corset buckled over a loose white button-down, and made a messy bun of her white wavy hair with one gold butterfly pin. She tucked her white leggings into burgundy suede over-the-knee boots and completed the ensemble with Axis' burgundy and silver timepiece. He'd like the kohl around her eyes, but the burgundy lipstick always made the boy salivate.

The Royal Couple were public once again, and the people adored it. The servants living on Manor property had smiled and waved at Lexia as she'd walked home last night. Sami had even winked at her. This was a good sign.

It meant the plan was in motion, but Lexia took more from it than that. She'd missed the warmth of her childhood home. Unfortunately, the rose-colored glasses were clear now, and she couldn't forget the cool looks from those friendly faces only a day and a half ago.

Lexia kept this in mind as she made her way downstairs to the breakfast nook. Father was already waiting, reading the newspaper. It was easy to glimpse the headline before he could tuck it away.

Diamond Heiress, People's Prince, & Copper Count: Failed Throuple; Scorned Love Triangle.

There was a sketch of everyone from the restaurant last night beneath it.

"Good morning, father. What's on the agenda, today?" Lexia blew her bangs from her eyes before claiming a muffin she didn't really want to eat.

Leon smiled over his grapefruit, saying, "Well, I know Founding Season isn't over yet, but I thought we'd dive into some work today. How does that sound?"

Good.

Lexia smiled, and it was half-genuine. "Perfect."

For the next, Leon's smile faded, and he cleared his throat to say, "I've invited Ms. Tija to meet us at the office with Kol, our union representative."

Ah.

How would Leon's daughter respond to facing the woman Gauge had spurned her for?

Lexia let her eyes fall to her muffin as she pretended to eat. "Yes. We should sort out the best strategy to implement unions across the industries."

Leon brightened at his daughter's professionalism. "I thought so, too. You'll be happy to know I've invited Axis and Phoro along. You remember? The foreman of the Flicker wick's line?"

The smile returned to Lexia's lips, glowing into a beam—

"Count Snow might attend as well," Leon added, peering over his glasses. He said, "He'll bring Mrs. Tenz along."

Lexia wiped the smile from her face and replaced it with a neutral expression. Cool and collected, she said, "Of course, father. He should be there to support Mrs. Tenz in her first negotiation."

Curt. Respectable. The dutiful daughter ready to inherit the family business.

Leon gave that nod of approval Lexia was coming to suspect hid more than it said. Careful to fold the newspaper so it hid the front page, he returned to his morning routine.

Out of the corner of Lexia's eyes, she saw Sami leave her position at the stove in the kitchen to clear the breakfast table. The pretty kitchen hand with light brown hair had tailored her uniform to display her assets. Buxom was a gentle word for the woman's figure.

As Sami bent over to collect Leon's plate, Lexia, for the first time, observed her father as a widower. A man without ties but with needs as true as Lexia's and Axis'. He did not look up from his paper as he said, "Thank you, Sami."

"Sir. Miss."

Lexia met Sami's deep blue eyes before she left with their dishes. For one second, pity shone in them. Then Sami went about her chores leaving Lexia hopeful.

It was working—

Wait.

What did the back of the newspaper say?

Tarnished Love: An Operatic Epic.

Capitol Playhouse.

Were they serious??

Lexia had to fight an incredulous laugh. The premiere was two days away, and there was no way she would miss it. But how to convince Leon to let her go?

"Father, are there any events I should attend in an official capacity to represent the family?"

Lexia feigned innocence as Leon lifted his eyes from the paper. He folded it and set it aside with a considering look. "Now that you've mentioned it, there's an opera premiering this weekend."

Red flags waved and alarm bells rang in Lexia's mind. Leon had jumped to the conclusion too quickly. He was onto her. She said, "I was thinking more like a genus introduction? You know we're starting that new citrus orchard after Founding Season is over. I can take seedlings to the nurseries."

Delight sparkled in Leon's gray eyes. He said, "I believe that's a grand idea. You can begin the tour after we conduct this union business today. But I will have you attend the opera. I won't be able to make it, and someone should fill the Tempest's box."

Success—

"Of course, Rhyme will escort you."

Lexia didn't hesitate or show her disappointment. "Of course, father."

As if on cue, the bodyguard walked into the breakfast nook with a nod for Leon and a glance at Lexia. In good faith, she said, "I wouldn't dream of attending without him."

Lexia's eyes followed Rhyme as he strolled into the kitchen. Through the entryway, she watched him wrap his arms around Sami from behind where she was cleaning the dishes. She let him nuzzle his stubble against her neck, but there was something withdrawn about it.

It was working.

It gave Lexia hope which she carried with her the entire car ride to their offices down Tempest Boulevard. She stared out the window while Leon finished his paper and Rhyme drove. An air of tension stretched between them and tightened Lexia's shoulders.

Did father kill mother? Had Gauge asked too much of Lexia to sit beside a man they suspected of murder? And there were so many more questions without answers—

Axis.

The People's Prince stood on the curb with Bolt and Phoro. Rhyme pulled the car up, so all Axis had to do was open Lexia's door. She slid out of the backseat and into her fiance's arms.

As always for business, Axis had dressed professionally: a white three-piece suit accessorized with a little flame. One on his golden tie clip over a black tie. Two more flames on his golden cufflinks on his crisp white button-down. Another pinned to the golden band of his white fedora.

Axis squeezed the tension out of Lexia, and she would've begged for more if not for their audience.

Leon exited the car, saying, "Good morning, son. Are you excited for this next venture?"

Axis performed better than Lexia as he gave a hearty laugh. "Working during Founding Season? Of course. Why wouldn't I be excited?" Sarcasm dripped from his words, but Lexia knew better. He enjoyed getting things done.

Rhyme regarded it all coolly, but when Lexia glimpsed Bolt's jovial grin, she let the valet's good mood infect her. She held out her hand to him.

A charmer, Bolt brought Lexia's knuckles within a centimeter of his lips and said, "Ms. Tempest."

Axis nudged him. "Don't go stealing my girl."

A voice from down the street washed over Lexia and left her weak. "Oh, Ms. Tempest is far too good for that. Aren't you, dear lady?"

Lexia's breath caught in her throat, and her heart stopped.

Gauge.

No.

Too much was at stake. Lexia would not lose sight of their mission simply because Gauge showed up dressed like a colonel in a steampunk army parade.

The charcoal-gray militant coat went to Gauge's knees with the stiff collar just below his jaw. It blended well with his complexion, and the epaulets suited his boxer's shoulders. Shiny copper military buttons with a shooting star contrasting against the black silk shirt beneath. Gauge had tucked his charcoal trousers into polished knee-high boots. The Count even wore a peak hat brandishing a copper shooting star on top of his braids. A simple cane, charcoal gloves, and blue lenses completed the distracting uniform.

For the brief moment in which Lexia and Gauge's eyes met, she knew he was fully aware of the effect he had on her. But as quickly as they'd connected, he looked away to help Tija out of the backseat of his car.

Lexia lowered her eyes and tucked in closer to Axis, who defended her honor with more than a little censure. "I don't believe anyone invited your opinion on my fiance, Count Snow."

Gauge pulled Tija against his side and conceded to Axis with a bow of his head. "Quite right, *Master* Flicker. Pardon me for trying to add some levity to the situation."

"I believe there is a substantial amount of gravity between us."

Leon's word was final on the matter. As the two younger men glared at one another, the oldest one on the street stared at Gauge. The glare on Leon's glasses prevented Lexia from interpreting his expression, but something silent transpired between the Count and the doctor. They would have more to say on the subject later. For now…

Tija said, "Ms. Tempest, would you kindly escort us to your conference room where we can discuss the union agreements?" Tija maintained a professional air despite her pencil skirt ensemble perfectly matching Gauge's uniform. It was as much a united front as Lexia and Axis wearing each other's colors.

Phoro, Bolt, and Mrs. Tenz, who Gauge helped out of the car next, looked a little left out of the fashion show. Rhyme and Leon dressed appropriately, as usual, without flair or decoration. Their presence was simply enough.

Lexia gestured toward the door into the glass Victorian house. "If you'll please follow me."

Grace.

Poise.

Yes, Lexia could do this, but she couldn't help sparing a glance in Gauge's direction. She could feel his eyes on her, and they smoldered behind the blue lenses.

Soon.

Everything would come together, and so would they.

Axis watched Lexia, grateful she didn't say Gauge's name aloud this time. Even so, the thought of the Count had darkened her eyes with passion. It was a sight Axis would take in before Lexia went down on him. He glimpsed the expression as they sat down at the boardroom table.

Leon took one end, and Gauge sat at the other. Lexia sat on her father's right. Axis on Leon's left. The couple were across from each other. It was symbolic, but also strategic. This way, Axis could nudge her foot if needed.

Bolt sat on Axis' left, from there Phoro, then Mrs. Tenz on Gauge's left. Tija sat across from Mrs. Tenz on Gauge's right. Between Tija and Lexia sat Kol. Rhyme stood directly behind Axis, keeping his eyes front on Lexia.

This sent Axis' heart racing because everyone knew the reckless sprite couldn't school her face to save her life. Even now, Lexia kept her eyes locked on Axis as if afraid she might glance down at the end where Gauge was sitting like a military officer out of someone's uniform fantasy.

Oh, yes.

Axis had noticed the Count. It was hard not to stare when the Prince had become more aware of the other man's impeccable fashion sense. Bolt had even shaken his head incredulously at how ridiculously amped the outfits had gotten for today's events. A parade for the Founding Families—or what remained of them, anyway.

Sobered at the reminder of his orphaned status, Axis cleared his throat and said, "Let's begin." When both men at either end of the table gave Axis their attention, he continued, "Across the three domed sectors of Winter, we three industries employ approximately thirty thousand citizens each. With future expansions planned, we should consider the wellbeing of those employees moving into sector twelve. Here, we have a single representative from our respective silos and a respected liaison to speak on behalf of a hundred thousand people. Let's listen with reverence to this future, and how we may want society to transform beyond this moment. Because make no mistake, ladies and gentlemen..."

Axis felt his heart race as he met each pair of eyes on him. Leon nodded with approval, Bolt grinned, Phoro looked reverent, Gauge smirked, Tija beamed, and Mrs. Tenz dabbed the corners of her eyes with a handkerchief. Axis stopped when he met Lexia's eyes. Pride left her radiant as she gazed with warmth and love. He finished with a meaningful declaration. "We will change Winter forever."

When slow applause erupted, Axis snapped to the end of the table. Gauge clapped his gloved hands once. Twice. Then the Count said, "Very well spoken, young Master Flicker."

Axis didn't need to fake clenching his jaw at the moniker.

Gauge seemed to know this as his smirk crooked further. "With the tone so aptly set, let's get down to business. Foreman Phoro, as the party with the most urgent circumstances, would you care to state your demands first?"

Since Axis had last spoken to Phoro, the Flicker wick line foreman had engaged the rest of the factory leaders and returned with a longer list of demands than Axis had expected. The table listened respectfully as he relayed benefits, schedule changes, and education matters which had escaped Valve Flicker's sense of reason. The old Factory Master had certainly left a mess for Axis to clean up. Axis supposed he and Lexia had that in common. Perhaps even Gauge could join the club since he had to restore his family's name during Winter's formative years.

"Ms. Tempest."

When Gauge said her name, both Lexia and Axis seemed to snap out of their thoughts. Her startled, him annoyed. Now was the test of her composure. Axis watched as Lexia peered down the table with all eyes on her—specifically Leon and Rhyme's scrutiny.

Axis wanted to curse. It was necessary for the ruse, but he despaired the way Gauge kept testing Lexia. The Count stared down at her over his laced fingers. The Prince detected heat behind those blue lenses. Was Gauge undressing her in a fantasy as Axis had done only moments before? Was there any jealousy between them? Or more mutual curiosity—

"Yes, Count Snow?" Lexia regarded him with cool professionalism, and Axis' chest swelled.

Leon also seemed to approve.

Gauge pressed, "We're here to prevent a strike, but also to implement union models which you, yourself, constructed. Which approach do you think would best suit our situation with Mr. Phoro here?"

Lexia's eyes left Gauge's stare to meet Tija head on. Considering Winter thought the Count had discarded the Heiress for Tija, it was a bold choice. Lexia said, "Ms. Cloud, as liaison, would you agree the skilled and manual labor model would work best for the factory lines? It's the one I sent to you two weeks ago." Before the *affair*.

A smile pulled at the corner of Tija's lips before she said, "Oh, yes, Ms. Tempest. I think we'll find those models satisfy most of the demands we'll discover at this table today. Why don't we hear from Mr. Kol next? You're the foreman over the Tempest orchards, is that correct?"

Kol looked like a man who'd narrowly survived a duel earlier this month. Dark circles marred his complexion, similar in tone to Axis' tawny brown. If not for Lexia's intervention, he'd be a memory to his children rather than fighting for the rights of his coworkers and subordinates at this table.

Kol ducked his eyes at all the attention, but raised his voice to say, "Yes, Ms. Cloud. We are most happy at Tempest Crops, but we could better fulfill our duties with more amenities. Breaks and time off are rare occurrences..."

The foreman listed off demands of their own, and when he finished, Gauge peered down the table at Leon and said, "Well, I wasn't aware a day off was so uncommon for Tempest employees—"

"Neither was I." Lexia caught everyone's attention as she glared openly at her father.

A throat clear killed the tension, and Kol spoke up again to say, "I want to add, that if not for Ms. Tempest here, I wouldn't be with you fine people today. The Tempests are a wonderful family to work for. We only ask for a little more free time."

Gauge said, "You sound almost afraid of losing your job, Mr. Kol. Don't you worry. If there's any retaliation for your part in these negotiations today, Ms. Cloud will see to you."

Axis sighed. "Count Snow, with all due respect, your answer for every employee dispute can't be to hire our people out from under us."

"And just why not?"

"Because it's unethical and breaks the accords."

Gauge shrugged nonchalantly. "I can't be held responsible if you and Dr. Tempest can't control employee dissatisfaction."

Agitated, Axis leaned across the table and pointed at Gauge, saying, "If you didn't offer them such exorbitant sign-on bonuses, our employees might feel more inclined to discuss their 'dissatisfaction' with us instead of immediately jumping into bed with your copper and coal."

"Are they the only ones wanting to jump in bed with me—"

"Gentlemen!"

Axis wanted to wince at the firm reprimand in Lexia's voice. He and Gauge turned to her simultaneously, each chastened by her tone. Like a genuine leader, she stood at the table, fingertips on the mahogany top. Was she breathy? Something dark glimmered beneath the surface of her onyx eyes.

Lexia said, "None of the demands here today have been as unreasonable as your behavior just now."

Axis looked away to find Gauge doing the same. Admonished good and proper.

More than a little pride warmed Axis' heart as she continued with a glance at Leon. "Now, I don't know how you're accustomed to acting around my father, but *I* didn't invite everyone to the respected Tempest offices to host a circus. If we could please return to the topic of unions, I'd like to discuss with Ms. Cloud how my family can best accommodate Mr. Kol's accumulated demands in the fields. Perhaps, you two might be interested in how to do so in the mines and the factory lines. Yes?"

Gauge recovered quickly, and there was nearly too much passion in his response. "Yes, ma'am."

Axis fought not to roll his eyes at the other man as he said, "Yes, Ms. Tempest."

Rhyme and Bolt chuckled at the same time, making them peer at each other. When Leon patted Lexia's hand, she eased back into her seat and nodded down at the table toward Tija.

The union liaison took the cue and delved into the discussions with a fervor Tija was born to wield.

Meanwhile, Axis met Lexia's eyes. Black fire burned in them, and he knew she was fighting with everything in her not to share the look with Gauge. It wasn't hard to imagine what she was fantasizing just then, and Axis had to wonder, would it keep him awake tonight, too?

Gauge was so damned infuriating.

Gauge couldn't wait until this was all over because the second he was alone with Lexia, he planned to bend her over his knee and spank her ass until it turned bright yellow.

And Axis...

The young Master Flicker was lucky they'd had an audience today.

As Mrs. Tenz contributed to the union demands with admirable eloquence and sophistication, Gauge kept his eyes on Leon down at the end of the table.

"In the mines, I've experienced a sense of equality I couldn't find at Flicker's Factories during the previous Master's tenure. I'm proud of you, Prince Flicker, for meeting with us today with every intention of improving that situation," Mrs. Tenz said as she beamed down the table at Axis.

Gauge tried not to admire the way the younger man blushed at her praise. There was simply too much tension between all of them, and it wanted to erupt here at this table. Molten and explosive, the climax would make for an impressive show. But alas...

The good doctor said his first words since sitting down at the table. "More time off, mutual respect, and more promotion opportunities—These are such simple demands to accommodate that I'm ashamed we even required this meeting to air them between us. Mr. Phoro, Mrs.

Tenz, and Mr. Kol—Thank you for meeting with us today. While I'm unable to speak for the factories and the mines, I will say my daughter offers a brilliant strategy to rectify your grievances in a dignified and mutually beneficial manner. I will let her speak on behalf of Tempest Crops."

Gauge kept his brows from raising above his spectacles. It was an official handing off of the torch, and not one the Count had expected so soon considering Lexia's recent indiscretions. She took to it magnificently.

"Mr. Kol, we will work with Tija to dispense the new union model across our industry beginning with your orchards as a pilot run. If this seems reasonable to you, we can commence as soon as Founding Season ends."

Tija nodded with approval as Kol beamed, saying, "Yes, Ms. Tempest. We will be ready for you."

For the last decade, Lexia had worked as her father's understudy—A well-kept secret, hidden from Gauge. He understood why now. Her beauty surpassed any person living on Winter, and her spirit far outshone the wildest of creatures. Here, in an official capacity, she proved herself as a force to be reckoned with. Bold, elegant, and intelligent. Such a gorgeous trifecta that Leon had done well to hide.

From the moment Gauge had laid eyes on Lexia at the Founding Ball, they'd been bound to intersect. Maybe they would have sooner if they'd met in a boardroom on more professional terms. Or perhaps ran into each other at the playhouse. But there was something magical about their first encounter after ten years apart. Ten years to become their own person, separate from the influence of one another yet destined to meet again.

Then there was Axis.

All influence. Always with Lexia. The two were also destined for one another only for very different reasons. However, Gauge couldn't help wondering…

If the three of them had never met, would the attraction still be there?

As they glanced at one another across the table, disguised as celebratory nods and congratulations for a meeting well convened, Gauge was certain of it. He believed they were meant for this, and he knew this collision course which destiny had set them on would soon culminate. Consummate. And cement Winter with it.

Gauge said, "Of course, since the mines were already offering twice the time off, three times the promotion opportunities, and nothing but utter respect for our employees, we are equally eager to pilot Ms. Tempest's union models."

With the utmost subtlety, Axis scratched his brow with his middle finger as Tija shook her head incredulously. Bolt chuffed, Lexia hid a smile, and Leon said, "Yes. Well. My daughter and I have some business to attend at the nurseries. We'll see everyone out."

Spoil sport.

Eternity, for a decade Gauge was forced to put up with boring old men in the boardroom. It was exciting to see Axis free of his father's pervading shadow, and Gauge blamed Lexia for the Prince's good humor at this conference table. She shone like a beacon wherever she went, and the warmth was infectious. Important. Necessary.

With Leon shaking hands at the door, the group filed out of the boardroom. Gauge brought up the rear, following Tija's rather nice one out—

"Count Snow."

Gauge narrowed his eyes behind his glasses at Leon. "Yes?"

Leon asked, "Would you please stay a moment? I'd like a word with you."

There was no hiding their conspiratorial group exchanging concerned glances. Lexia, Axis, Tija, and Bolt peered nervously at the encounter, but truthfully, Gauge had expected it sooner. He took Tija's hand and slipped her an envelope while he kissed her fingers. After she nodded in confirmation, Gauge waved her and the rest of the group off, saying, "I'll be with you in a moment."

Once they left, Leon closed the door to the boardroom, locking himself and Gauge inside. The Count casually hopped his ass onto the tabletop and peered at his cane as he twirled it between his gloved fingers. He was surprised the doctor had waited this long for such a conversation.

Leon's voice shook with outrage as he said, "If duels to the death were still legal, I'd challenge you to one here and now."

Gauge raised his brows at the older man's audacity.

The doctor balled his hands into fists as he continued. "You disgraced my daughter and violated the good nature of our accords. I know what you hold over me, and I've never cared less than I did the moment my poor Lexia walked home in shame, despondent and heartbroken."

This was quite the convincing performance, and Gauge narrowed his eyes as Leon carried on with a straight spine despite his apparent loss of composure. As well as his ever-loving mind.

"Hereon, we will contend with you professionally, but don't you dare assume I will stand by and watch you instigate another disaster such as this last week. You upset my *home*, Gauge. The one threat you hold over me is my peace of mind where Lexia is concerned. Don't endanger it again."

Impressed, Gauge tipped his chin, saying, "Well, that was a very heartfelt speech from a father over the wellbeing of his daughter, but let me remind you, that while your precious butterfly was a guest in my home, I had every opportunity to damage your relationship with her irreparably. Yet you stand before me, her doting father, as if nothing had transpired. Consider yourself and your *home* lucky I have more grace than what you sit here accusing me of having. Believe me. I have no intention of harming your daughter, and I am certain she is no longer a danger to herself. Slaked as she is."

Gauge intended for the last to present a challenge. Leon could rise to the bait and begin a war. Or...

The good doctor closed his eyes and took a deep breath. When he exhaled, all the tension left his body with his breath. He loosened his fists and relaxed his shoulders. Leon opened his eyes to reveal steel behind his clear glasses as he said, "Good day, Count Snow." He didn't storm out. No, Dr. Tempest left with the regal carriage fitting of his station.

Disappointment and relief warred inside Gauge. He'd relished the idea of the conflict, but also felt relief for Lexia's sake. It was very possible Dr. Tempest's love for his daughter was genuine, but that made Leon all the more dangerous for what would come next.

After parting with the other families at their offices, Lexia and Leon made a tour of the nurseries. At each one, the dutiful daughter presented a new genus of citrus plant meant to withstand the less cultivated environment of sector twelve. It was a task she'd once enjoyed, but given the ambiguity of the situation, Lexia couldn't throw herself into the work as she'd done before.

Instead, she kept a close eye on Rhyme and Leon's interactions. How they murmured to one another in Lexia's peripheral vision. How the bodyguard followed her everywhere she went. It became so apparent that one child she'd helped sow a seed, asked, "Mister, do you follow Ms. Tempest to the bathroom?"

Rhyme had glared at the little boy until he'd wilted, and Lexia decided that was enough. After the third nursery, she said, "Father, I'm tired. May we please go home?" She'd almost said, 'go to the Manor,' but realized that wasn't very convincing for their cover story.

Leon generously agreed, and they arrived at Tempest Manor in time for dinner. There, Lexia played with her food, forcing herself to eat a bite or two while her father engaged her in small talk. "I hear Axis is attending the opera."

The mere mention of her fiancé's name brightened Lexia's demeanor. She said, "He's come a long way with his participation in public events."

Leon smiled. "He has." Then the lines around his eyes tightened into almost a wince as he said, "Some people credit Count Snow for the boost in Axis' confidence. What do you think, dear?"

It was true. Since Lexia had first encountered Gauge at the Founding Ball, Axis had come more out of his shell, but she was certain that's not what her father wanted to hear. So, she said, "I believe Axis is coming into his own with his father passing on."

There was that nod of approval again.

Lexia tired of the games. She dabbed her napkin to her lips, saying, "I'll need to excuse myself early tonight. Kol and Tija will meet us at the university bright and early to discuss educating more of our people in skilled positions." Expecting to be excused, she stood and waited for her father's response.

Leon peered up at her and said, "I trust you, Lexia. You may go on your own with Rhyme as your chaperon."

What a contradictory statement.

Even so, Lexia bowed her head. "Good evening, father."

"Good night, daughter."

Lexia glanced at the kitchens on her way out to find Rhyme snuggled up to Sami. At the Heiress' abrupt exit, he swiftly separated himself from the kitchen hand and followed Lexia to the stairs. She stopped at the bottom with her back to him.

This was ridiculous.

"Rhyme, I know you take the assignment of guarding me seriously, but I'm only on my way to my bedroom. Surely, I can go there on my own."

"A bedroom you regularly climb out of, and let's not play this game any longer. I've upgraded from your bodyguard to spy because you outran me once to the one place under the domes from which I had no jurisdiction to throw you over my shoulder and carry you back home."

Lexia spun on him, staring. Fuming.

Rhyme folded his arms across his considerable chest and leaned against the door frame. He crossed his good leg over his prosthetic as he casually assessed his charge. The bodyguard-turned-spy sounded as tired as Lexia felt as he said, "I don't want to do this, little Heiress, but you've left your father no choice. He cares about your welfare more than any parent I've ever met, and you continue to spit in his face. That's right. I said it. Don't recoil like some prim and proper privileged little saint. We all know what you were up to in the Copper Cathedral. Now, we can be grownups about it and move on. Let me do my job for a month or two without incident, and I'm sure your father will relinquish the reins a bit. But until then, stay out of mischief."

Oh, Lexia planned to get up to all kinds of mischief.

She contained the urge to stamp her foot and storm up the stairs. Lexia chose to glide up them instead with a bronzed shadow in her wake. When she closed the door in his face, it brought entirely too much satisfaction. She didn't need to hear his chuckle through the sturdy oak. The Heiress could feel it in her bones.

Alone at last.

Lexia sat down at her desk, took her papers from the drawers, and set upon them in a furious rush. The encryption she'd designed for her writing would fool her father and his spies. But she imagined Gauge or Axis could decipher it given enough time. The diagram on the wall drawn in makeup would only make sense to Lexia. Or perhaps... her mother.

With a heavy heart, Lexia peered at the picture of the picnic, lying frameless on her desk. She asked the empty room, "Mother, what would you want for me—"

A knock sounded on the door.

Lexia wasn't expecting anyone, but once she cleared her desk and hid the diagram, she called, "Come in."

Sami opened the door carrying a tray of tea. Lexia got up to help her bring it into the sitting room, not surprised by the woman's arrival. Lexia said, "Hello, Sami. What a pleasant surprise. Thank you for the tea."

The woman's cheeks flushed pink as she curtsied. "You're welcome, Ms. Tempest. I thought you could use the warmth."

By ducking her eyes, Lexia could appear distraught. "Thank you. You and I have spoken little since..." *The affair* hung in the air.

Sami nodded while anxiously wringing her hands. "Yes, well. My apologies for that. They make it difficult for us to talk to you."

Difficult.

"In what way?" Lexia sat down and gestured for Sami to sit beside her.

The kitchen hand took the invitation eagerly and said, "Rhyme. He said to treat you like you had a fever, and every night he says he has to watch you. That's why he can't stay—Oh, sorry."

Well, at least the constant surveillance was affecting Rhyme's love life as well. Lexia almost laughed at the notion. Instead, she took Sami's hand, asking, "What made you decide to risk speaking to me now?"

A beautiful smile blossomed on Sami's full lips as she said, "Another suitor. He was here just yesterday, and he reminded me of how important you are as a friend. I've missed our talks."

Bolt, what a charmer. Lexia shared the other woman's expression, and they spent the next ten minutes delving into gossip. All the while, the Heiress kept her secret hidden.

Lexia glanced at the picture on her desk. No one but their group could know.

Then Sami said, "After you left, Dr. Tempest went to visit your mother's grave."

"Excuse me?" Lexia blinked to hide her astonishment.

Sami nodded. "Right after you ran away that night, Rhyme gave me a kiss before he took Dr. Tempest out to the grove. Later, he told me the doctor wept for two hours in the snow. Oh, Lexia, he loves you so much. I know they're overbearing at times, but you didn't seem to mind it so much before you met the Count."

Lexia shook her head. She would not let Sami segue into that topic. With a wince, she touched her forehead, saying, "Forgive me, Sami. I feel a headache coming on." An utter lie. Lexia had never experienced a headache.

Unaware of this fact, Sami smiled and took up the tray of tea. "I'll just take this back to the kitchen before Rhyme comes knocking. Good night, Ms. Tempest."

"Good night, Sami."

Lexia waited for the door to close before locking it for the night. Not that it mattered much. Rhyme would certainly have a key. To be sure of no disturbances, Lexia turned down the lights in her room and wrote by the artificial moonlight. She needed another day or two to finish everything. Then, she would show it to Axis and Gauge.

In the meantime, the clock tower chimed twelve. Lexia went to her balcony, waited for the chiming to finish, and lit the exterior Flicker wick lamp. She stared at the Copper Cathedral high on its hill overlooking the city, turning down the lamp and waiting ten seconds before turning it on once more.

Gauge would see.

Axis would know.

Their plan was picking up momentum. Now to move on to the rest of the household.

Young Master Flicker,

I believe you owe me a dinner. I will collect on it tomorrow evening and not a moment later. We have much in the way of rehabilitation to discuss, and I grow weary of hosting my uninvited guests. As you write your R.S.V.P., please recall the dinner and my mercy were both your idea.

I expect you here no later than seven o'clock.

With highest regard,

Count Snow.

PostScript: I'm allergic to shellfish, so if your aim is to kill me, you'll have no better opportunity than tonight.

Axis laughed at the copper letter before he could stop himself. Before he'd left the offices on Tempest Boulevard, Tija had hugged him outside the conference room. It was startling, but welcome. She was a good friend despite all the drama between their group.

However, the embrace had served a dual purpose. When Axis finally sat down to relax for the night, he'd found an envelope in his jacket pocket.

A copper envelope.

As Axis peered down at it, his smile was incredulous; the ideas in his head were not. What should he cook for someone like Gauge? Someone who hadn't tasted actual food for a decade? Obviously, something without shellfish, which was, of course, Axis' favorite food.

The clock tower sounded the midnight hour. Axis went into his room and waited for the chiming to finish. Once done, he waited another sixty seconds before flicking the wicks on the lamps in his room. With the lights on, he imagined Gauge peering through the telescope at the window when an idea struck Axis...

It would take nerve. Confidence.

Axis stepped in front of the window. He licked his lips, slipped out of his jacket, and unbuttoned his shirt. Slowly, he stripped out of his shirt, bunching and stretching—exaggerating each step with his figure silhouetted against the curtain.

This was silly. Likely, Gauge had seen the signal and headed back to bed with Tija, but there was still a slight chance the Count was watching.

Which was why Axis slid his pants down and stood naked, framed in the window. He reached his arms out and stretched, turning to give the curtain his back. When he gave the curtain his profile again, Axis rubbed the back of his neck with both hands, contemplating what to do next.

Ridiculous.

Axis felt ridiculous as he trailed one hand down his chest, ribs, stomach, and hips. Before he lost the nerve, he teased himself for the sake of the picture he hoped to frame. It wasn't payback for Gauge sleeping with Axis' fiance, but it was vindictive in its own right.

With a foolish grin on his face, Axis turned off the light, climbed into bed, and went to sleep.

An urgent knock woke Axis from his sleep. It was still dark out as he slipped on pajama pants and answered his apartment door. Bolt stood outside in his pajamas with sleep in his eyes. Concern had aged his face. He held up a red envelope.

What fresh disaster had struck now?

Axis closed his eyes to steel himself for the news as he opened the missive—

No.

It wasn't a missive.

It was…

Valve Flicker
Born: 3410
Died: 3468
Aged: 58

Height: 6'1"

Weight: 22 Stones

Cause of Death: Chronic Obstructive Pulmonary Disease

Drugs Present:

- Acetaminophen

- Opiates

Axis skipped all the substances listed in the lab report until he came to something circled in blue ink.

Heavy Metals Present:

- Magnesium 25g

- Copper 210g

- Zinc 2.5g

Copper levels were elevated. Mostly present in the lungs. Likely due to unfiltered cigarettes, pipe tobacco, or cigars.

Copper...

"You killed him."

"You're in shock."

"No. Those fucking cigars. You may as well have killed him yourself."

Gauge.

Axis looked over the envelope, but there was no return address.

Bolt swallowed loud enough to interrupt the static silence in Axis' head. His best friend said, "Sir, you've turned pale. What does it say?"

The world spun—

No.

No fainting this time.

Axis plopped down on his couch and held his head in his hands. He closed his eyes. Deep breath. In through the nose. Out through the mouth. When next he opened his eyes, the world had gone still.

And so had Axis' heart.

Thawing Frost

GAUGE WANTED AXIS. GAUGE WANTED AXIS BENEATH HIM. The Count wanted the Prince beneath him with the Heiress beneath Axis.

Yes.

Only that would satisfy the searing need in Gauge's robust and creative imagination. He couldn't sleep last night for all the wild fantasies he'd come up with. He'd even shared a few with Tija, much to her snickering delight. When he'd told her of the peep show, she'd refused to believe Gauge. No way would the Prince, phobic of publicity, dare put on such a display.

Phobic or not—public or not—That was Axis' body in the window, and Gauge wanted to take a bite of it.

Tonight.

If the dinner went well, Gauge would see himself paying Axis back in spades. It's all he could think about as he stared out of his conservatory onto the Plaza below. People strolled through the gardens and skated on the frozen ponds—At their own risk.

Winter was thawing.

"We don't really discuss the prisoners in your dungeon. Are they still breathing?"

Tija's question brought Gauge back to reality. He glanced over at her where she sat at the conference table, elbow-deep in drafts of the union contracts. Work. Duty.

Gauge sighed as he returned to the task. He'd much rather spend the day contemplating if Axis and Gauge could explore their scars together. Instead, he sat across from Tija and answered her question. "Once they're done recovering from hypothermia, I'll interrogate them on Valve's engagement with Leon. Until I speak with Axis, I'll refrain from any decision as to what I'll do from there."

With her cerulean eyes on a benefits offer, Tija said, "So you are considering rehabilitation."

Gauge humphed. See the aforementioned arctic tundra where his conscience should be. However, the icy plateau was not so steep to ignore the opinions of others. Especially those he'd trusted with so much of his truth. Lexia and Axis were on their way to becoming his guiding light, and he wasn't even sure if they knew.

Tija smiled across the way, as if she knew exactly what Gauge was thinking. Before he could stop himself, he blurted, "I love you."

The smile broadened into a beautiful glow as Tija said, "I love you, too, old friend."

Gauge was relieved she'd taken it as he'd meant it, but it had occurred to him suddenly that he wasn't very vocal with his affection. He cared for Tija, Jan, Axis, and Lexia. Even Bolt counted as a friend more than an acquaintance at this stage in the game. Unlike his father, who'd been cold and cruel, Gauge wanted to show the people in his life how much he appreciated them.

Hence the dinner with Axis, and the surprise Gauge had in store tomorrow night for Lexia.

Jan walked in with the mail, saying, "Sir, I have your messages for this morning, and our uninvited guests are ready to speak with you."

"I appreciate you, Jan." Gauge meant every word. He tried to show it in his smile before the butler bowed and left the room. After which, Gauge filed through the stack of messages. At the sight of the burgundy envelope, he went lightheaded.

Rejection or acceptance.

It was probably the most important R.S.V.P. of Gauge's twenty-nine years.

Count Snow,
Prepare yourself for the meal of a lifetime. Shellfish, excluded.
Yours truly,
Master Flicker.

Heart racing. Breath captured.
This was it.

"Gauge, I don't think I've ever seen you turn that color before."

Tija's teasing snapped Gauge out of the enticing rush. He peered up and blinked at her, having forgotten she was in the room. In the time it took him to read it, she'd left the table and stood by his side. Heady and lightheaded, laughter burst from him. Even to his ears, it was bright and full of warmth.

Happiness.

Without a second thought, Gauge handed Tija the missive and enjoyed how her eyes widened at the sixteen words on the burgundy page. She beamed at him, saying, "This is fantastic! I'll make myself scarce for the night."

"I'm not certain that's necessary." Gauge ducked his eyes and turned away as his cheeks warmed.

Tija captured his face in her delicate, fair-complected hands and forced Gauge to look her in the eyes. She said, "No matter what you expect, the evening will go better if I'm elsewhere. Besides, I haven't been to my apartment in over a week. I'm sure my plants miss me."

Again, Gauge laughed. It was incredulous and light all at once. He pecked Tija a kiss. "Thank you."

The Founder of Winter. Count Snow. He was so fortunate in so many ways, and he wanted to show his gratitude. To his friends. His people. Sector twelve was an opportunity to demonstrate what he'd learned from Winter's growth. It wouldn't make up for his mistakes, but it would pave the way for benediction.

If someone like Axis could listen to Gauge's worst truths and still want his company, then this acknowledged all of his efforts to improve. To lead. And to find the worth he couldn't in his childhood.

"Tija, let's solve the issues with Flicker's factories first. They're the most pressing," Gauge offered for no reason whatsoever.

His liaison and best friend was not buying it, judging by the knowing smile on Tija's soft lips. Even so, she separated them and set about to work on Phoro's demands. Gauge joined her with renewed determination.

After some time, Tija peered out the window. There was a long pause before she asked, "Do you think they will strike, anyway? This runs deeper than a change of leadership. Some of these people were Valve's compatriots."

Gauge took off his glasses and rubbed his eyes with the back of his gloved hand. With a sigh, he said, "I know this is Axis' fight, but some part of me wants to take charge and threaten the bastards with the Wall."

The forlorn look on Tija's face lifted into a smile, which she turned and shone on Gauge. She shook her head incredulously, holding in laughter.

Gauge frowned and reseated his glasses. "What?"

Tija let out some laughter. "You." She said this as if it were obvious.

The frown deepened. "What do you mean, 'me?'"

"You get so cute when you're in love."

This knocked the wind from Gauge's lungs, and he raised his brows, blinking at her in baffled silence.

In love.

With Lexia *and* Axis?

What a concept.

<hr>

Lexia played the next chord and held it. The children joined in with their instruments, and she moved onto the next one. This way, she led them slowly through Winter's anthem. Once they'd gotten a feel for the notes, she increased the tempo. Their progress was exceeding Lexia's expectation, and she beamed while they played. They would be ready by Founding Day.

Sami stood by, watching her little girl on the oboe. Matori had come a long way on the woodwind instrument, especially for a ten-year-old with the attention span of a firefly. The little girl's father and Sami's husband hadn't believed the EMP would come. The day Winter was Founded, he'd been living his life outside the domes.

Was his death Gauge's responsibility or Lya's?

But Lexia knew what she really thought. Matori's father had decided to die on his own, despite Gauge's warnings. Was that cold of her? Cruel?

Whatever the case, Sami seemed happy now with her two suitors. Better off than being dead. And that was the last Lexia would let herself contemplate on Gauge's decision to only save three cities as a teenager posed with an impossible question. Later, she could deliberate on how to feel about her mother who'd posed the question.

Later.

When the music stopped, the parents who'd come to collect their children applauded. The kids squealed and beamed, jumping into their parents' comforting arms. Even Rhyme looked impressed as he slow-clapped with an approving smile.

Lexia mingled with the adults and tried to sustain her composure.

"Thank you, Heiress."

"It's so good to have you home."

"We knew you wouldn't stray far."

It took all of Lexia's restraint not to remind these people of how they'd treated her only a week ago, but that wouldn't accomplish anything. And their children didn't deserve the drama. So...

Gauge would be proud. Lexia played the part until only she and Rhyme remained in the music room. When she lowered the fallboard over the piano keys, her blood rushed fast and hot to her cheeks and other places. Would she ever look at a piano the same way again?

Rhyme spoiled the moment by saying, "When you make faces like that, I'm not sure how to describe them to your father. It's obvious what you're thinking about... But I do what I must."

Lexia bit her tongue and looked away. She refused to rise to the bait—To give Rhyme even an inch. Regal. Composed. Adults make decisions and must face the consequences, including judgment. And in this case, the scrutiny of an outspoken bodyguard with two keen eyes.

"Is something wrong, Lexia?"

She looked up to see her father had entered the room.

What timing.

Lexia faked a smile and said, "No. Just basking in the children's progress." At the unconvinced tightening of Leon's eyes, she pressed, "Is everything fine with you?"

As Leon came further into the room, he nodded at Rhyme. The bodyguard-turned-spy left the room on the signal, likely to find Sami. As Lexia steeled herself for whatever it was Leon wanted to say in private, her father tucked his hands into his pockets and walked over to the piano.

It was hard not to shiver at the chill traveling down her spine when Leon stared at the fallboard as if he knew.

Did he know?

"I can't tell you how happy I am that you're home, but I wanted to check in with you. To see how you're doing." When Leon looked at Lexia next, the shiver forced its way out. He said, "Please. Be honest with me."

Half-honesty. Lexia said, "I just want more freedom to move around on my own. Rhyme is suffocating me."

As if he'd expected it, Leon softened and gave her a paternal smile. "He's tenacious, isn't he? But you don't know how worried he was about his position here on the night you..."

Ran away and slept with Gauge? Escaped her gilded prison?

"Left."

It was too soon to press for independence, so Lexia blew her bangs out of her eyes and said, "I understand, father. But I'd like to revisit this. Soon—"

"Dr. Tempest."

The Manor butler stood in the doorway.

"Yes?"

The kindly older man looked from Leon to Lexia and back to his employer. "Prince Flicker is here to see Ms. Tempest."

Father didn't look surprised as he nodded. "Very good. Go on, sweetheart. He's waiting for you."

Lexia tried not to narrow her eyes in suspicion and eagerly left the room to find her fiance in the foyer.

Distraught.

Axis looked scooped out and hollow. There was no spark to those soft green eyes as they met Lexia's stare. Instead, his shoulders sagged, and his bones looked unable to hold the rest of him up.

Bolt stood beside his ward, despondent in his helplessness.

Lexia went to Axis, and in full view of everyone, embraced him tenderly. With a grateful look from Bolt, she nodded for the valet to head to the kitchen. Lexia wasn't sure what was wrong, but they would work through it. Axis leaned much of his weight on her, which was no insignificant amount, and she adjusted to shoulder him up the stairs to her room.

The need for privacy was unspoken, but nonetheless understood.

Slightly aware of Rhyme following them up, Lexia led Axis into her room and closed the door in the bodyguard's face. Keeping watch on her might not play out so well for him with Bolt and Sami alone downstairs.

Oh, what drama under this Manor's roof.

Lexia gently guided Axis down on her couch and sat beside him, brushing her fingers through his short, burgundy hair. She asked, "Do you want to tell me what's wrong?"

Axis wiped a hand down his face as if erasing all the bad in the world. He sounded haunted as he asked, "How did you really feel about Gauge dooming the rest of the planet to permanent Winter?"

This was unexpected, and Lexia didn't bother to school the shock on her face. Then she frowned as she considered her thoughts from earlier. She said, "It wasn't right for my mother to put him in that position."

"But she did. And he killed off most of the world's population out of spite. We forgave him instantly because of his age, but now…"

Lexia echoed Axis' words from almost a month ago. "'No man should have so much power.' But he did. Does. And Gauge has chosen to do the right thing with it since. I believe his conscience is broken, and he's looking to us for a new one. Don't you want to help build Winter's future together?"

Axis shut his eyes so tight it looked painful as he admitted, "I'm starting to doubt what that future means."

No.

Lexia wouldn't let him give up on this. Not now. Not when they were so close to everything.

"Axis, please tell me what made you change your mind."

No more secrets.

Axis handed the tox screen to Lexia without a word. Her eyes scanned over it, and he knew the moment she'd reached the same conclusion, because those thick white lashes of hers fluttered closed. However, he couldn't help but notice an absence of shock on her part.

With her eyes closed, Lexia whispered, "Why is everything so complicated?"

In a few hours, Axis would meet Gauge for dinner and cook for the man who'd killed his father. This went beyond complicated. He took her hands and said, "I don't know what to do with this. Just last week, you were here—In my position. Tell me, did it feel right to give into your impulses? To act without thinking?"

Axis could tell the direction of his thoughts had disturbed Lexia by the way she bit her lip and looked away. After some time to gather her thoughts, she said, "It felt dangerous. Not wrong, but not right. My mother called that 'gray.' Everything with Gauge is gray, Axis. He may have killed your father intentionally, but with all due respect, Valve was a bastard. And Gauge sat on a mountain of evidence to support the righteous death. But I know you. You're concerned with the imbalance of power. Although duels to the death were legal at the time of Valve's passing, I think we both know Gauge and your father stood an equal chance at a fair fight. So Gauge resorted to all that was left to him, and perhaps…"

Gauge had enjoyed the slow murder of Valve Flicker.

It hurt for Axis to let go of Lexia's hands and bury his face in his own, but he needed… What did he need—

Gentle arms embraced him and pulled him tight.

Lexia gave Axis exactly what he needed. She squeezed, and he wrapped his arms around her waist. The hug lasted a while—He lost count of how long and didn't care. They held each other in her black and white sitting room while the gray washed through his heart.

Once Axis drank from the well of Lexia's love, he opened his eyes and took in the room for the first time. Papers wadded up everywhere. Clothes strewn about. Makeup drawn on the walls.

Axis chuckled.

Lexia brightened at the sound and warmth infused her voice as she asked, "What's so funny?"

"Your chaotic way of living will fit in so well with my neat and orderly lifestyle."

They both laughed and separated from the hug to wipe tears from their eyes. Then this gorgeous sprite smiled with mischief on her supple lips. Lexia said, "I'm working on a surprise for our team. I can't wait to show it to you when it's ready."

Axis smiled—an unthinkable task after the last hour. "I look forward to it." A thought struck him and hurt his heart. He confessed, "I'm cooking for Gauge tonight."

Lexia's black eyes widened, turning the pearls into obsidian shards. She asked, "What will you do?"

So many things came to mind. Some white. Some black. Right. Wrong. Axis wasn't sure which he'd choose when the moment came. He said, "If someone asked me what I think of your impulsiveness, I'd say I believe your heart is always in the right place. And no matter how you get there, you always try to do what feels right. I know you said 'gray.' I know you said not right or wrong. But I believe it turned out right in the end."

As Axis spoke, Lexia searched his eyes, lips—Anything which might give away his intentions. She held her breath as she waited for the answer.

Axis leaned in and kissed her forehead, saying, "I promise to act on my impulses without thinking. I will try it your way."

This was neither concerning nor reassuring, and Lexia took it as such. Her brows crinkled into a beautiful frown, but she nodded her acceptance.

Would Axis arrest Gauge?

Would he cut off ties with him?

Could the Prince kill the Count—Disintegrate the last shred of trust between them and poison him?

Axis felt in his heart that Gauge had been wrong to take so much power into his hands and slowly, painfully execute Valve Flicker. To cast Walker, the man who'd attacked Tija, into the Wall of Pain. To nearly kill those mercenaries in his custody.

That's not mentioning the trillions who'd died on Winter's prior name.

No man should have so much power.

"Lexia, I need to prepare for the dinner, but before I go, I want to speak to your father."

The Heiress sighed as if she'd expected this. She took Axis' hand and kissed his palm, cupping it against her cheek as she peered into his eyes. Lexia asked, "Will I see you at the opera tomorrow?"

Axis tried to smile for her. "You can count on it."

They kissed, and it almost became more until Lexia broke it to say, "Promise me you'll kill Gauge quickly?"

If Axis went that route, then... "I promise to make it as quick as I can."

The heartache in Lexia's eyes was hard to swallow. She loved Gauge. She loved Axis. Her heart was big enough for both. Here she was on the verge of learning if her father had truly murdered her mother, and Lexia was spending her energy on comforting Axis in premeditation.

"I love you."

"I love you, too."

Axis left and nearly collided with Rhyme at Lexia's door. The presumptuous bodyguard was leaning back against the wall with his arms folded across his broad chest. He said, "Have a good evening, Prince Axis."

"That's Prince Flicker, Rhyme."

Something flashed in the man's eyes, but he hid it quickly.

Right at that moment, Sami escorted Bolt into the foyer. Her feminine laughter at something Axis' valet had said reached them all five stories up, and Rhyme did *not* look happy.

Before Axis descended the stairs, he said to Rhyme, "Enjoy your evening."

"You be careful out there, Prince *Flicker*."

There wasn't enough energy in Axis' body to waste on this man any further. He still had Leon to contend with and a dinner to prepare. He met Bolt at the bottom of the stairs and offered Sami a kind smile before she headed off to the kitchens. The woman was glowing, and Axis had to hand it to his valet. The man worked miracles fast.

Bolt beamed a little himself. Afterglow looked good on the middle-aged man. No doubt he was brimming with Manor gossip which Axis would pass on to Gauge later…

Later, if Axis didn't kill him.

With a sigh, he knocked on the study door.

"Come in."

Axis nodded for Bolt to stay outside as he entered the rosewood-paneled room. The aroma of leather-bound books and ink wells took

Axis straight back to his childhood. One of which he could barely look at now. He once reveled in the moments with the Tempests and ignored the abuse from his father. But now, it was all murky and tinged with unpleasantness.

Leon smiled with his usual warmth and gestured for Axis to have a seat, saying, "Hello, son. I was hoping to speak with you before you left."

Shattered on the inside, Axis sat across from the man who'd likely killed Lya Tempest and disguised her death as a tragic accident. Who'd lied to Lexia every day. Who'd lied to Axis' face only a week ago.

Exhausted, Axis cut straight to the chase. "Why did you send me that tox screen?"

Leon pressed his glasses higher on his nose before lacing his fingers together and resting them on his blotter. He took a moment to say, "I want to be transparent with the man who deserves to marry my daughter. You've been like a son to me your entire life, Axis. While I know Valve was not a model father figure, I believe he deserved due process. Would you disagree?"

No.

Axis didn't disagree.

A broken laugh left his throat before he could stop it. This was all so fucking convoluted. Incredulous, Axis asked, "What exactly was your plan? What did you hope I'd do with this information?"

As Leon stared across his desk into Axis' eyes, the answer hung heavily between them. So, the doctor knew the Prince would have the rare opportunity to kill the Count, and by sending this, he'd hope to accomplish exactly that.

Maybe Leon would get his wish.

Axis stood, buttoned his blazer, and bowed his head toward his future father-in-law. Not another word passed between them before Axis left the study and gestured for Bolt to follow. He glanced at Rhyme, who stood at Lexia's door on the fifth floor of the foyer. Axis felt for the woman trapped inside.

Groceries.

Shower.

Clothes.

Then Axis would arrive at the Copper Cathedral and prepare Gauge the meal of a lifetime.

Gauge had spent the last hour working with Tija to resolve the issues with Phoro's union demands, contemplating love and righteousness.

Could a man like Gauge earn the love of people like Lexia and Axis? And if he could, what would it take? More than he could afford? Or exactly everything he'd attained?

Inspired and restless, Gauge said, "If you'll excuse me, Tija. I believe I'll pay our uninvited guests a visit."

She surfaced from the sea of paperwork to come around the table and say, "I'll get to a stopping point here and head home. Oh, how will you pose this to the public? Your visit with the People's Prince?"

Tija asked all the right questions, but Gauge had thought of this when he'd sent Axis the invitation. He said, "This business with the mercenaries is all the cover I need. 'The Prince advocating for lenience on the convicts' sentences from the wicked Count who seeks to execute them.'"

After climbing on her tiptoes, Tija kissed Gauge's cheek and said, "The Prince and the Heiress are good for you. I'll see you tomorrow? I want all the gossip."

Gauge wrapped an arm around Tija and kissed her with gratitude on his lips. After he'd left her breathless, he promised, "All the gossip. Tomorrow." Wickedly, he turned on the heel of his shined boots and left her wanting more in the middle of the conservatory.

"Jan, with me."

The butler emerged from the shadows in the foyer to follow Gauge to the dungeon door in the kitchens. They made their way down the rock stairs to the cells. The smell had improved in the last day or two, and the prisoners were able to stand. With heavy bags under their weary eyes, they watched Gauge approach their cell.

"Good afternoon. I understand you're ready to speak to me."

The woman sagged, thinner than when she was first apprehended. She said, "Please. We weren't employed by Valve for long. He hired us here and there for intimidation, and we attended only a few meetings with him and the doctor."

When Jan suddenly shifted beside Gauge, the pair of mercenaries flinched. But the old butler was only grabbing a stool and setting it behind Gauge. The Count sat back on it, crossed his legs, and propped his cane in front of him. He asked, "Can you tell me anything I might find interesting? Like the nature of these meetings? What did they discuss? And was Lya Tempest ever mentioned?"

The woman glanced at the man, who caught the glance and wet his pale cracked lips to say, "Yes, actually. They mentioned her in the same breath as the domes. Specifically, the one over sector twelve."

Intrigued, Gauge leaned forward on the cane. "Tell me more."

"The old Master Flicker said he knew how it was constructed, and Dr. Tempest said he knew where to find the materials to replicate it. They would build a Winter of their own. One away from you."

Now there was a truly stimulating notion.

"Oh, really? Do go on."

———————————

"Father, I'd like to take Sami shopping."

Lexia stood in the door of Leon's study, where he'd just spoken to Axis. Where he kept a hidden portrait of her mother. And where he'd stolen the truth from Lexia and expected her to thank him for it.

The man who'd possibly murdered her mother beamed at her. "Of course, dear. Be sure to take Rhyme with you."

Lexia knew the protest was futile but expected as she said, "But, father. Isn't Sami escort enough?"

Gently, Leon shook his head and offered a compromise. "We'll discuss it more over dinner, but for now, they both go with you."

"Understood." Lexia left her father alone to his work as she went to the kitchens to snatch Sami from her duties.

Rhyme smirked, not smugly. Actually, the bastard always looked quite handsome for an older man. It occurred to Lexia that only a month ago, she'd mused to herself that she wasn't interested in older men. Then she went and slept with Gauge. Six years wasn't that much of an age gap, but still.

As the bodyguard followed Lexia across the house, she mused, "This isn't a date for you and Sami, you know?"

"I'll take any excuse to get out of this house at this point. You were easier to follow when you flitted about everywhere. It's been boring here in the Manor without you causing trouble."

It surprised Lexia to hear so much affection from Rhyme, and she almost said something to that effect when Sami turned the corner of the dining room.

"Hello, you two. I hear we're going shopping?"

Lexia would revisit this with Rhyme later. For now, she said, "That's right. While our seamstresses can work the most beautiful magic, they're busy on my dress. I don't want to bother them with an ensemble for tomorrow night. Besides, it's nice to support the local shops."

Sami beamed at Lexia, and Rhyme gave a conceding shrug. Then they were off.

On a walk, of course.

The beautiful kitchen hand had little respect for propriety in public. Sami had looped her arm through Rhyme's, and he acquiesced after many 'Pleases.' The trio practically skipped down Tempest Boulevard to the shops on Flicker Avenue.

Predictably, Lexia glanced down the row to Axis' apartment. It was late afternoon, and the lights were off. Maybe he was out shopping for the dinner. For the perfect way to kill Gauge—

"This! This is the outfit. Look at it, Ms. Tempest!"

Sami drew Lexia out of her reverie to gaze at a beautiful collection in a shop window. It was quite stunning, but it needed more flair. More gold. More black.

When Sami grabbed Lexia and pulled her into the store, it was enough. Lexia wanted to get lost in the fun of being outside with a friend and pretend everything was all right. Pretend that the divide had never happened, and that Axis wasn't about to poison Gauge.

Or fuck him.

Who knew what would happen?

Although Lexia would be lying if she thought she'd forgotten how preoccupied she was with the last notion earlier in the shower. The Heiress had never climaxed so hard on her own before the thought of the Prince and the Count together had occurred to her.

"Ms. Tempest, how lovely to see you out and among the people again."

Lexia turned from the clothing rack to find Tija standing behind her. They'd discussed how to act around one another in public, but Lexia didn't much like the indifferent persona. Instead, she followed her instincts by saying, "Hello, Ms. Cloud. It's good to be out of the house. I'd missed these shopping adventures."

Beside Lexia, Sami peered between the two before volunteering, "We're searching for an outfit for tomorrow's opera."

It was hard to notice Rhyme's eyes narrow at the encounter, so Lexia decided to keep it brief. She said, "I hope to see you there. You and the Count make an attractive pair. Excuse me."

For their audience's sake, Lexia ducked her eyes and rushed out of the store. It felt more natural to exude shame and embarrassment than to treat Tija badly. And it seemed to do the trick. Sami and Rhyme followed her out of the boutique without a backward glance at the blue-eyed brunette. There was no need to make a scene.

Only too late did Lexia realize where she'd run to.

The Copper Cathedral peered down at her from its perch on the hilltop. Snow Plaza shone with flaked mica in the cobbles, and it glistened under the glow of the Flicker wick lamps. A chime from the clock tower drew Lexia's eye higher to where Gauge's bedroom overlooked the capital city. From down here, she could barely make out the telescope perched on the balcony balustrade, and she imagined him peering into Axis' bedroom.

"Heiress, let's go back to the Manor."

Every impulse in Lexia's chemically charged brain fired. They said to run to the Wall of Pain and warn Gauge of Axis' predicament. To beg the Count to explain the situation to the Prince. The Heiress would advocate—referee, even. But...

Sami took Lexia by the hand and tugged for her to come along.

Back to prison.

"No."

Lexia said it out loud.

Rhyme stiffened and unfolded his arms, assuming a less relaxed stance. "Heiress?"

Sami's pretty face went drawn with concern.

Lexia was more than her instincts. She'd learned her lesson. Instead of demanding to go to the Copper Cathedral, she said, "There are a few things I want to pick up from my office if I am to work from home."

Rhyme glared at her for a moment, contemplating. Eventually, he said, "Fine by me. Lead the way."

The trio walked along Snow Plaza with its square shaped by gardens, ponds, and a hedge maze. Lexia didn't spare another glance at the copper-tipped structure. They walked in silence to the intersection where the street made a sharp angle onto Tempest Boulevard.

Lexia hated the pregnant silence. She blurted, "So, what do you think of the blazer, Sami?"

A smile tugged at the kitchen hand's lips at the mention of a more pleasant subject. Sami said, "The black silk? You could likely ask them to dip the lapels in gold…"

They carried on this way another block to Rhyme's quiet observation until they reached the office of Tempest Crops. The bodyguard and the fickle kitchen hand followed Lexia into her office, all made of rose-colored glass. There was a metaphor in there somewhere with its view of the Copper Cathedral on display.

It was still and quiet inside. The only sound was…

Drip.

Drip.

Lexia peered over at the leaky pipe—the one which had started it all—and wanted to laugh. Everything had gotten so absurd, but, as she claimed what she'd come for, Lexia knew it would come out gray in the end.

Please, Axis.

Don't kill Gauge.

SEVEN

Burning Flame

AXIS DIDN'T KNOW IF HE'D KILL GAUGE TONIGHT OR NOT. Even though Axis was an accomplished swordsman, he'd never killed anyone before. The notion didn't sit right in his chest and left a foul taste in his mouth.

Valve Flicker didn't warrant avenging, but should Gauge be allowed to kill without impunity?

Assassinations.

Public executions.

Silent metal casting—

Where did it end? And who was in the position to end it?

Axis.

It plagued him the entire afternoon he'd shopped for dinner. He breathed it in through the cedar-scented steam of his shower. The cold of it chilled him through the gilded buttons of his burgundy blazer. His plain, wine-colored two-piece suit reflected the surface of his thoughts. More toiled beneath his calm exterior.

"Bolt, I think I'll walk to the Copper Cathedral tonight."

Was that Axis' voice? It sounded remote even to his own ears. Or was his blood rushing that loudly through his body?

The valet stood in the door of his apartment with a confused frown. He pointed at the brimming bag of groceries in Axis' arms, saying, "Fine, but let me carry that."

When Bolt reached for the bag, Axis stepped back. "No, thank you, friend. I want to go on my own and clear my head."

Bolt's frown deepened as he searched Axis' eyes. After a long moment of consideration, the valet said, "Of course, sir. Send a courier should you need me."

To clear his friend's conscience, Axis patted Bolt on the shoulder, saying, "Don't worry. You look like you could use some rest after the afternoon you spent at Tempest Manor."

Bolt burst out in a masculine chuckle and raked a hand through his salt-and-pepper hair. "Thanks for the night off, boss. Try not to have too much fun tonight."

"Without you? I wouldn't dream of it." Axis gripped Bolt's shoulder one last time before heading out of their apartments onto Flicker Avenue.

The Flicker wick lamps lining the straight kept the dark off Axis' shoulders as he headed toward Snow Plaza. No concerns plagued him; no turmoil unfurled and beckoned him into the deep abyss growing in his mind. Instead, he passed his father's memorial with little more thought than how nice of an interment it was—Far better than Valve had earned.

Axis arrived at the steps to the Copper Cathedral as the clock tower chimed the seven o'clock hour. The Wall of Pain, with its faces locked in eternal horror, reminded the Prince of his mission. He didn't need to use the knocker—Jan opened the door and waved Axis inside.

"Welcome, Prince Flicker. The Count is expecting you in the courtyard."

Courtyard?

The butler didn't bother taking Axis' long coat, given how cold it must be in the gardens. When the older man led the way, Axis followed him to the heavy courtyard doors. He was not prepared for what awaited on the other side of them.

Lights twinkled along rows and rows of raised beds, statuary, and hedges. Each strand strung in the courtyard carried at least a hundred Flicker wicks. Ethereal and atmospheric, the sight left Axis speechless. In the center, flames danced in four tall cylinders surrounding a bistro set.

There stood Gauge. His black silk suit drank in the light and reflected the flames in shadow. It suited his rich complexion. Through clear lenses, the Prince could see the Count's blue eyes, where fire danced in hungry shivers.

After a silent second passed between them, the bold bastard smirked at Axis, swept his top hat off his loose braids, and bowed elegantly at the waist. Gauge said, "Good evening, Master Flicker. I see the table setting is to your liking."

With all the heat, Axis didn't need his coat. At Gauge's nod, Jan slipped the heavy garment off Axis' shoulders.

What wouldn't the Count do to make a statement?

Axis didn't have to fake his smile. "Hello, Gauge." It came out warmer than he'd meant. Warmer than he thought possible, though not hot enough to match the flames in the Count's eyes.

"Why, Axis… Are you sure you're safe without your chaperon?"

Safe?

No.

No one was safe with Gauge.

Axis shrugged and strode along the lit walkways to the courtyard's center with more confidence than he should feel. He said, "Safety is relative. The real question is, are you nervous yet, Count Snow? This is your first untested meal in a decade. Can you handle it?"

Without the slightest hint of the anxiety he must feel, Gauge said, "I can handle anything you want. Anytime. Anywhere."

It was too perfect for Axis to fight the grin blossoming on his face. How strange and natural the expression felt in the Count's company. Even after all these years of strife and tête-à-têtes. Respect made a world of difference, and even though Axis had once convinced himself he didn't *like* Gauge, he'd always respected the man.

Funny how fashion and a sense of humor could sway one from respect to… Interest. Curiosity.

Craving.

Axis repositioned the bag of groceries. "I'm up to the challenge. Are the kitchens through here?"

Humor flashed in Gauge's eyes, and he shook his head incredulously before nodding without a word.

Axis headed inside and set everything out. When Gauge followed him in, the Prince pointed a stern finger back out the door. "No. We made a deal. You don't watch me prepare this, and you don't test it. Consider this a leap of faith."

The tailored material of Gauge's blazer strained across his shoulders as he slipped his gloved hands in his pockets and considered Axis' words. The position shifted a bit and drew the Prince's focus to the cut of the Count's slacks.

Gauge hadn't bothered to wear undergarments.

A whistle snapped Axis' stare back to Gauge's clear glasses, and the eye contact stunned the Prince.

Knowing.

Confidence.

Sex.

All of it was in Gauge's infuriating and tantalizing cobalt gaze.

But there was also a hint of fear and a wince of pain. The lights...

More confounded than embarrassed, Axis gestured with a circling of his fingers for Gauge to turn around. The Prince chastised, "Out."

The Count chuckled and whistled on the way back out to the courtyard.

Confusion disturbed Axis' good mood as he set out the ingredients for the meal. Grilled mushrooms with potatoes boiled in butter and broth. There were two jars of stock.

One was chicken.

And one was lobster.

Which would Axis choose?

Three voices played in his head.

His own: *"Those fucking cigars. You may as well have killed him yourself."*

Gauge's voice: *"Just make sure Prince Axis knows if he needs anything, he shouldn't hesitate to call on me."*

And Lexia's reasoning: *"Everything with Gauge is gray, Axis. He may have killed your father intentionally, but with all due respect, Valve was a bastard. And Gauge sat on a mountain of evidence to support the righteous death. But I know you. You're concerned with the imbalance of power."*

Then the worst of Axis' conscience left him empty.

"Axis, you're better than me, and you always have been. I'm not long for this world, and I'll die with many regrets. This ice in your voice will make the top of that list. I'm sorry, son. Please, don't blind your old man."

Axis was capable of gray, but was he dark enough for murder?

For the rest of his life, Gauge would remember the look on Axis' face when he'd first walked into the courtyard. It held the same impact for the Count as the first time he'd laid eyes on Lexia when they were children and again when they were adults. Beauty in a smile; radiance in a gaze.

Gauge mused to himself as he strolled through the raised beds and brushed his gloved fingers along the hedges. He wished he could feel the prickle of their trimmed tufts, the fresh chill of the water in the fountains, and the softness of Axis' hair—All of it under the overly sensitized tips of Gauge's fingers. Between the slenderness of them.

Burgundy to obsidian.

Sunrise to dusk.

But Gauge was getting ahead of himself. First, he must contend with the meal. Truth be told, the thought of touching Axis proved pleasantly diverting compared to the mounting anxiety of the meal.

"It's the only way you'll ever truly find happiness. Trust someone completely."

Was Tija Gauge's guardian angel? Her voice played in his mind when he needed it most.

Trust Axis.

Appreciate this meal for the gift it was and then bask in the Prince for hours to come.

Heh. To come.

Gauge shook his head at his own immaturity. Axis and Lexia had a way of reducing him to a teenager. The teenager he never got to be.

The direction of Gauge's thoughts took him away from the enticing sexual fantasies to harsher planes in his memory scape. Raised away from other children. Forced to grow up ill and confined to a sickly body. Intelligent, but limited.

Hatred, blind and icy, froze Gauge's veins. One of the Count's greatest regrets in his life was that his father didn't die by his hand.

What would Axis think of that?

Gauge wanted to talk to the Prince about their childhoods away from Lexia's bright light. Into the shadows where their fathers lurked.

Did Axis hate Valve? Although Mrs. Tenz said the word 'abuse,' Gauge hadn't pried. He was morbidly curious about what 'abuse' had occurred.

How much were the Prince and the Count alike? Could they heal the scars of their childhood together? Surround themselves with Lexia's beacon and warm themselves in the butterfly's carnal flames?

Jan stepped out of the shadows into Gauge's path. The Count smiled for his butler, because while all things of his childhood left him cold, this old spy had remained, to this day, a bastion of constancy. Unfortunately, he was still wearing the same frown as when Gauge told him about tonight's dinner.

"Sir, you gave me permission to speak freely, and I employ it now to repeat my disapproval of the Flicker boy."

'Flicker boy' only made Jan sound ancient, but as Gauge looked his butler in those brown eyes, monoliths stirred.

Ancient was the right word.

Gauge patted Jan on the shoulder, saying, "Don't worry, old friend. I promise to eat tomorrow's breakfast without testing it—"

Jan startled. His eyes doubled in size, and his mouth fell open.

"—I owe you a debt of gratitude and not a small apology for these years of tolerating my mistrust. After tonight, that all changes."

After a second of wide blinks, Jan recovered himself. Now his frown held an edge of sadness. "But why tonight? Why Prince Flicker?"

It was a good question, and Gauge shrugged as he thought of the answer. "Because he's the one with the most motive to kill me."

This time, the butler didn't startle. No. Jan rolled his eyes and sighed, prompting a chuckle from Gauge.

"Very well, sir. But please—"

"Dinner is served."

Gauge turned away from Jan to see Axis sweeping his way from the kitchens with a tray. The covered plates added a certain dramatic flair, which the Count appreciated. His smirk said so.

Axis' answering grin lit the courtyard brighter than the flames. Sometime while cooking, he'd lost his blazer and rolled up the sleeves of his black button-down. It contrasted beautifully against his topaz skin.

Axis was far enough away not to hear Jan sigh again, and Gauge suppressed the urge to laugh this time. Instead, he crossed the courtyard with all the confidence in his glide. Let the light capture the ease of his movements—Not nearly as graceful as Axis' healthy, athletic frame, but one could still move like a panther even with a cane.

It proved a success as the grin slowly disappeared off Axis' face, replaced with...

Captivation.

But it was mixed with...

Contemplation.

Gauge stopped a hand's breadth away. With this smile, he wanted to convey trust, mutual attraction, and some measure of understanding. Since they were children, the Count and the Prince had been at odds. Adulthood had only brought the conflict to the boardroom, but it was Gauge's hope that the friction simply hid more.

This was their chance to explore it.

"Lexia knows we're having dinner without her tonight," Axis blurted.

Rather than letting the newsflash become awkward silence, Gauge mused, "Oh, how will our butterfly survive it? Tell me, when you informed Ms. Tempest of our meeting, did her chest flush bright yellow? You know? How it does when she—"

"You are a tyrant!" Axis plopped the covered plates on the table and sighed with exasperation. When he pinched the bridge of his nose, his shirt gaped at the buttons across his honed chest, revealing...

Enough.

Gauge rested both hands on the top of his cane and stamped it once to get Axis' attention. The taller man dropped his hand and peered into his host's glasses. Gauge said, "Axis, I may be a tyrant, but I'm *your* tyrant."

A change in the air between them rippled the cylindrical flames surrounding them. The current ebbed and flowed, taking and giving, asking and answering—

What was the question?

Axis broke the tension when he chuffed, turned his back on Gauge, and lifted the covers on the plates. The Count thought he heard the Prince mutter something like, "I'll show you a tyrant," before the younger man turned and ordered, "Sit."

Laughter erupted from Gauge, and Axis beamed with his own humor. The Count sat and busied himself with placing his napkin in his lap to hide the tremor in his hands. Nerves gnawed at his insides.

"Trust someone completely."

Although one to put off a climax, Gauge filled his fork full of potatoes and toasted it at Axis. The aroma of rosemary and butter elicited a growl from the Count's empty stomach, and he ate it completely before the Prince could return the toast.

When Axis' eyes narrowed in a harsh frown, Gauge knew something was wrong. And at the same time, he knew…

It was too late.

———————————

"Gauge Snow's vision will spare our city this electric devastation and see us flourish in a new future of steam-powered ingenuity. Valve Flicker and I back him despite the regulations which threaten to separate our growing community. We depend on each other and welcome anyone to challenge the facts. Our planet is due for a polar axis reversal, and it will reduce civilization to ruin. I trust our united triumvirate to see us through. I trust Gauge Snow. It's up to you to join us under the domes—To build the future. But I assure you, only Winter will remain."

"Father, what exactly happened to make you hate Count Snow?"

Leon, mid-sip, blinked over his soup spoon at his daughter.

It was too late for Lexia to regret her outburst, and her curiosity overrode her logic as she restated, "I can recall all the speeches you gave supporting him during the Founding of Winter, and it seems your discontent with him manifested only in recent years. Can you please share with me why that is?" She hoped the 'please' sweetened her tone and softened her purpose.

Truth be told, Lexia was looking for a distraction—Anything to get her mind off Axis and Gauge. Unfortunately, nothing seemed to take her mind far from the idea of her fiance murdering her lover. Prying into Leon's affairs would have to suffice.

The doctor set down his spoon, patted his napkin to his lips, and rested his arms on the table. Leon cleared his throat before saying, "I find this subject inappropriate in light of recent circumstances, but the answer is simple. I don't hate Gauge Snow. All in all, there's much to admire in the man, but some of his decisions—"

This implied the inclusion of Gauge and Lexia's affair.

"—Warrant some interrogation and, perhaps, merit some consequences."

How strange...

Lexia's father and Axis shared a similar opinion of Gauge. She only hoped Axis could see how much the Count was endeavoring to change since the three—Lexia, Gauge, and Axis—intertwined more and more. Tija and Bolt were a good influence, as well. Perhaps better so than Jan, who Lexia suspected of more than a few unscrupulous decisions of his own.

To disguise her earnestness as shame, Lexia looked down at her soup dish and frowned at the cooling liquid within. Her appetite was suffering under the stress, and she needed to keep her strength up to carry on with this ruse. She ate some in silence under Leon's watchful eyes. The sensation wasn't a chilling one. Even with all the strife between them, Lexia sensed the warmth of her father's affection and concern.

But how to reconcile it with everything at hand? That was the question.

Diversion.

Lexia needed a diversion.

She glimpsed Sami at work in the kitchen, providing a proper diversion. Lexia asked, "Where is Rhyme tonight?" Although she felt the relief of her bodyguard's absence, it was unnerving to wonder what he might be up to if not Sami's uniform.

Leon looked away as he took a drink of his wine and said, "Rhyme requested the night off. Weren't we just discussing how I don't provide my employees with enough vacation?"

Under the table, Lexia balled her Tempest linen napkin into her fists. Had Leon just lied to her? Turned her own crusade against her?

Lexia breathed deep of her troubles and released a sincere and heavy sigh. After which, she stood. "Father, if you'll excuse me. I wish to go up early tonight. You're the one who told me, 'There's nothing like a good night's sleep to prepare one for the next day ahead.'" She tossed her napkin on the table and left the dining room without another word.

Laughable.

As if Lexia could sleep on this precipice.

"Lexia?"

Without turning around, she stopped on the second flight of stairs.

Below, Leon said, "I know the situation is tense between us, and I am remiss at how our meal went. Please, let's start over tomorrow. We can begin everything anew after tonight."

After tonight…

There was the chill.

Lexia stared up at her bedroom door, ready to escape to the warmth of her writing. "Father, if I learn you sent Rhyme to spy on Axis and

Count Snow's meeting tonight, there will be no tomorrow. I will move in with Axis. Gauge will allow it—He owes me that much. You will never see me again except in passing. If you're so fortunate."

Impulse.

Control.

What a concept.

"My dear—My Lexia, I wish I were a better man. One who's brave enough to tell you everything, but there are some things which belong only to adults. To parents. You shouldn't know our entire lives. Especially that which is unpleasant to know. I ask for you to trust that this will all work out in the end."

Leon's plea rang true, but Lexia's heart was hardened by…

A soft cry.

A loud thud.

And then nothing.

Lexia let the sincere words fill the air as she finished the climb to her room. It hurt a part of her to close the door without a response, but she couldn't afford to give the little girl inside space in her mind. But Leon was right about one thing:

After tonight, nothing would be the same.

Please, Axis. Don't kill Gauge.

———————————————

A hot tear rolled down Axis' cheek as Gauge took a bite of the food the Prince had prepared for the Count. There'd been no hesitation on Gauge's part. He simply trusted Axis.

That made this next part even more painful to endure. By the tightness of Gauge's eyes, the Count knew it, too.

"You have too much power, Gauge. You wield it with less care than Lexia in some ways, and you refuse to see the vice it has on your heart in others. I can't love you if I can't forgive you, and I can't forgive you, if you can't see that you were wrong."

Gauge swallowed his first bite of untested food in over ten years too fast to have enjoyed it, and Axis' heart sank in time to it.

The enigmatic Count lost some of his sheen as confused terror clouded his eyes with a touch of grief. Through clear lenses, he searched Axis' eyes, and the Prince hoped the Count could see it—

No.

Axis *knew* when Gauge saw it. The Prince didn't have to toss the tox screen onto the table. Understanding dawned behind those glasses and replaced the cloud of confusion with desperation. The Count begged with his soul bare in his eyes. "Axis, please… I had to—"

"No. No, you didn't. Tell me you see that, Gauge." Axis stood, knocking his chair over, and gripped the metal table as he leaned forward to stare into Gauge's eyes. "Not for Winter or for Lexia—" He pounded a fist on his chest. "But for *my* sake! Tell me you see it!" The table trembled with Axis' sorrow.

Gauge started to say something, but seemed to think better of it and choked on his words. His eyes glistened with unshed tears before he looked away, defeated. Ashamed. Lost.

Axis cursed and shoved the table as he turned away. To hide from this—from all of it—the Prince shielded his eyes with his hand. A sob broke. With his back to Gauge, Axis said softly, "I've spent the last several hours thinking of reasons to kill you. Of a world without you in it. And I just... Can't." The torn Prince let his hand fall and shouted at the dome, "I won't! There will be no due process with you—I know it. You're the people's favorite, and my father was a bastard." He turned and beseeched Gauge. "Who *wouldn't* forgive you for his cold-blooded murder? But god damn it, he was still a human being. It wasn't righteous or the gray in between—Gauge, it was simply wrong."

Firelight encompassed Gauge in an ember halo, leaving him ethereal—untouchable—if not for the vulnerability spilling from his eyes. Despite the genuine display of emotion, Axis couldn't tell if the Count was crying because he'd *heard* the Prince's words—*felt* any remorse—or if he only regretted being caught. The questionable dichotomy left Axis heavy, and he walked back over to sink into the chair once more, staring out toward the gardens.

Nearby, a fountain trickled with the perfect amount of splash for serenity, the fire roared in the cylinders, and a chilly breeze rustled the hedges. Rosemary and expertly grilled meat scented the space between the pair of Founding royals. Winter's mettle—brittle and exposed.

Axis broke the silence between them. "I love your braids. Lexia's waves. I used to like my hair longer—Do you remember that?"

Gauge almost looked too stunned to afford the gentle nod he offered.

Axis said, "My father once tied me down and set the ends of my hair on fire with one of Snow's Finest. The other factory masters had watched and laughed." He raked shaking fingers through his hair and blew the air out of his cheeks. "I wish someone could tell me how to reconcile this mess."

A blunt chuckle broke Axis' melancholy, and he faced Gauge to find the other man with an ironic and sad smile. He was chuckling to himself, but it was a guttural, painful sound. It came from the darkest places in his soul. After smoothing a hand down his face and smearing the tears, Gauge said, "I don't think I'm in a position to offer you any advice on how to manage it, seeing as the only person who'd ever afforded me any wisdom told me to 'freeze my heart' to it. Given our current situation, I won't recommend Lya Tempest's method of coping." The smile disappeared, and Gauge's voice thickened with emotion. "I can't apologize enough that Valve used the means of his demise on you for torture—"

"He was my father, Gauge…"

Axis didn't like the effect his hollowed-out voice had on the Count, so he softened it as he said, "If anyone were to ask me what method of execution I'd choose for the old bastard, it would've been slow poisoning with those carcinogenic weapons. You gave him exactly the death he deserved. *After* a trial. No man should have so much power without council. The rest of Winter should have a say between innocence and guilt, rehabilitation and execution, life and death."

A long moment passed where Gauge peered at Axis, and the Prince wondered what the Count was thinking. All the cunning ways to salvage this without penalty to himself? Or was Gauge giving proper weight to Axis' dilemma?

As if Gauge had read Axis' mind, the Count stood. With inelegant and urgent tugs, the Count pulled off his gloves and held one hand out to Axis, saying, "Come with me, and I'll show you how much you've taught me."

Not words, but a gesture, perhaps?

Either way, Axis took Gauge's hand and noted the widening of the Count's eyes. Breathless, he said, "Your hands are rougher than I'd expected."

"And yours are impossibly soft." They were also paler than Gauge's face, but it seemed inappropriate for Axis to point that detail out. Instead, he gave his host's hand a gentle squeeze. "Show me what you've learned in a few short weeks."

Gauge shook his head. "No. From a lifetime of chasing you."

Shocked, Axis blinked at Gauge, who shied back from the boldness of his confession to say, "Never mind. Let's go."

Without another glance at Axis, the Count led the Prince into the kitchens and to a door hidden in an alcove. It was massive and made of iron-wrapped oak. It wasn't as intimidating as the Wall of Pain, yet it sent a chill down Axis' spine. He ignored the anxiety as he followed Gauge into the cold, dark cavern.

When Gauge flipped a switch, small Flicker wicks came to life and illuminated stirring shapes in the dark. One female. One male. They sat up on cots and peered up the hewn rock stairs at Axis and Gauge. After a moment of squinting in the dark, the Prince recognized the mercenaries last seen when Valve had died in the Count's foyer.

Only after Axis let out a sigh of relief did he realize he'd believed Gauge had executed them weeks ago. Rather, they were alive as the

Count had promised. Neglected? Yes. Traumatized? No doubt. But alive and in need of rehabilitation.

A burden lifted from Axis' soul as he looked toward the rock ceiling, closed his eyes, and swallowed those fears which had threatened to consume him. Gauge could change. There was hope.

As fresh tears spilled from Axis' eyes, only two words came to mind. "Thank you."

Gauge fought not to wince at the intensity of Axis' gratitude, all because he didn't execute the mercenaries. In recent weeks, the Heiress and the Prince were changing the dial on the Count's moral compass, but he still didn't fully understand. Hopefully, it was worth something that he *wanted* to understand.

It was wrong to kill the mercenaries after they'd pulled a gun on Gauge and Axis in the Count's own Cathedral. It was right to detain, re-educate, and provide them with an opportunity for redemption. That was the lesson.

Right?

As Axis lowered his eyes to meet Gauge's, he could see that yes, that was indeed the lesson. And the Count had passed. They could be friends again.

The callouses of Axis' hands left impressions on Gauge's over-sensitized nerves. Ones he would never forget, much like the silkiness of Lexia's hair and skin—Forever would it remain branded on his soul, but perhaps no longer out of his reach.

Axis stepped around Gauge to lead the Count by the hand down the stairs over to the cells. The People's Prince peered through the bars and asked in a gentle whisper, "Are you two all right?"

The male and female mercenary exchanged a look before the woman said, "We are better than we deserve. We see that now."

Gauge couldn't hear the sincerity in it, but supposed Axis did as he nodded his understanding. Then he did the most puzzling thing. The Prince asked, "What punishment do you think fits your crime of attempted murder?"

The man said, "Our time here seems fitting enough, but merc-ing is our way of life. And it has been since before the families Founded Winter. What else would you have us do?"

Was asking them to reform and rehabilitate a harsher punishment than confinement in the Wall of Pain? Was that why Axis insisted on it? For a human being to change their entire way of life for the betterment of the society—Was that more righteous?

Axis was still holding onto Gauge's hand as he stepped back and peered at the perimeter of the cells within the cavern. In only a single layer of clothing, Axis' breath puffed out of his lips. As it did with the prisoners, Gauge had to note. Their color looked a little bluish even, but at least Jan had hidden the torture instruments.

That was a plus.

Much like Lexia declaring duels were no longer to the death, Axis said, "We'll move you to the most basic apartments in sector ten. There, we'll provide you with the necessities while you attend courses at Tempest University to join one of the three industries. You can determine the path of your lives from here and make a positive impact on this small community in which we live, or you can falter, return to this dishonorable profession, and one day meet the other figures in the Wall of Pain. Do I make myself clear?"

Gauge stared at Axis in the dimly lit room and measured the man holding his hand. Gauge had never wondered why Winter's citizens had declared Axis 'the People's Prince.' However, it was in moments like these—quiet and unseen—in which the younger man truly shined.

Warmth stirred in Gauge's chest and attempted to thaw the cold within. Like Lexia's beautiful smile, Axis' charity and integrity could break through all this ice and leave a fire burning in his wake.

Did it matter at all that the man and the woman went to one knee and bowed their heads to Axis? Not to Gauge. They could choose to better themselves or not for all he cared. But it mattered to the Prince, and, therefore, mattered to the Count.

Axis faced Gauge and caught the older man staring. The younger tilted his head to the side before Gauge blinked and stopped his assessment by glancing at the future reformists. He said, "Very well. I'll arrange the course for your rehabilitation. You'll spend one last night down here to remind you of where you started. Thank the Prince for how far you may go."

"Thank you, Prince Flicker."

"My thanks, the People's Prince."

The scenery no longer suited Gauge's mood, so he tugged on Axis for the Prince to follow him back up the stairs. The cane tapping the rock steps and the flickering wicks were the only sounds as they entered the kitchens. Before the Count could turn the lights back down on the cells, Axis staved Gauge's hand and shook his head.

"Let them have some warmth, please."

Gauge couldn't help it. He smiled incredulously at the Prince and said, "Anything for you, your highness."

It was obvious Axis fought to keep a grin off his face, but it broke through anyway with an incredulous shake of his head. "You're such a pain in my ass, Gauge. Come on. Let's not waste a good meal."

Gently, Axis pulled Gauge back out to the courtyard where the wicks kept the glow soft and the fire cylinders kept the bistro set warm. They returned to their plates, and only then did their hands part. Mostly because Gauge wanted to devour every single thing on his plate.

Eternity.

When had he last *enjoyed* food? Also… "I must say, Axis, you could give my chefs some lessons." Gauge meant every word.

The Prince chuckled, saying, "I don't think you've ever eaten their food untainted, so I won't hold you to that compliment until otherwise."

Fair.

As always.

They ate together in silence, each of them taking in the view, tastes, and smells until a question occurred to Gauge. No, the question wasn't appropriate. But when had that ever stopped the Count? "So, we're not sleeping together tonight, are we?"

Axis laughed so hard that another tear fell out. "No, but not for the reasons you think." He reached over, pinched Gauge's chin, and made the other man raise his eyes to meet Axis' as he said, "When we meet in that arena, I want the entire night with you." He dropped his hand way too soon.

Well, wasn't that an enticing promise? Another question occurred to Gauge. "Can Lexia come?"

Again, Axis' chuckle was rich with humor and charm. "She has no problem doing that. At least not with me. I don't know about with you."

Laughter burst from Gauge, and he shook his head at the Prince's wit before assuring with all the confidence in the world, "Oh, believe me. That woman comes as much as she likes. Which, fortunately, is enough to write about."

"Amen."

"Amen."

A comfortable quiet settled over them. There was no need for more words as they finished their meal, hand-washed the dishes together—Axis scrubbed; re-gloved, Gauge rinsed and dried—and made their way to the grand foyer to part.

Axis said, "Next time, we'll dine over our success with Lexia in the middle."

It sounded more like a vow than a suggestion and more about the bedroom than dinner. Either way, Gauge was perfectly elated at the notion. "Assuming she survived without us tonight."

Something dark clouded Axis' eyes before his gaze flashed with intelligence. The Prince said, "I worry about how she's handling all of this."

Gauge gripped Axis by the shoulder, assuring, "She will conduct herself as only a sprite can. With the gracefulness of a butterfly, and the brightness of a diamond."

Without preamble, Axis gripped Gauge by the nape of his neck, pulled the Count against his hard chest, and kissed him. Magma rushed through Gauge's veins and threatened the frosted fortress in his chest. While his head and heart whispered caution, his libido screamed descriptive and enticing obscenities.

Axis must've felt where the blood had rushed to in Gauge's body, because he separated them with a knowing smirk.

There was…

Cruelty in there somewhere. A harder edge to those soft green eyes which implied merciless torture for hours upon end where the man would draw out every single syllable of his name from Gauge's lips.

Suddenly, Lexia's experience made more sense. And from that kiss, Gauge knew Lexia had been Axis' one and only. The younger man was in for quite the education, of which he was sure Axis was up to the challenge.

Up, indeed.

Breathier than he'd intended, Gauge said, "When this is all over…"

Axis' smirk crooked even further as he took a step back. He gave a conceding bow of his head. "When this is all over. Until then… Good night, Count Snow. Rest well."

Jan appeared from the shadows and opened the Wall of Pain for Axis to step through.

Speechless, Gauge watched the Prince leave while his brain misfired.

Fuck.

Say something witty.

Look at his ass in those slacks.

Nothing really helpful came to mind, so Gauge waved one gloved hand before climbing the stairs to his room alone—

No.

Gauge went to the balustrade and called, "Jan, please fetch me Ms. Cloud. I think she'll find the events of this evening most amusing."

Jan sighed heavily, less with disapproval than before and more with defeat. "Yes, sir."

EIGHT

Tarnished Love

LEXIA STAYED UP ALL NIGHT WRITING. She often held her pen still to stare out at the Copper Cathedral high on the hill. It was easy to make out the clock tower through the carefully manicured trees, almost as if Gauge had demanded the visibility of his citadel from all vantages. When it chimed midnight, Lexia had unfolded her long legs from her perch at her desk and signaled per protocol. There was no response, but she'd expected as much.

However...

Without word or signal from Gauge or Axis, Lexia fraught in her restlessness.

Had Axis killed Gauge? Or were they in bed together? What would either mean for her? For their crusade for the truth?

When light dawned on the horizon, Lexia showered and dressed in a hurry, eager to begin the day. She'd hear gossip about the Count and the Prince's meeting soon enough. Then later, Lexia would need to prepare for the opera. There was a full day ahead of her, and although she'd left things unpleasant with Leon last night, there was still a mission to complete.

Dressed in Axis' newest sweater and a pair of leather pants, Lexia headed down to the kitchens. It was still early, and the bakery smell of bread in the morning wafted throughout the house. Leon would wake to it in a half hour, leaving Lexia with time to find Sami. Surrounded by stuffed muffin tins, the kitchen hand was clearly the source of the wonderful aroma. The warmth of it suited her.

"Good morning, Sami."

The accomplished baker smiled and waved at a rack of cooled raspberry muffins. "Good morning, Ms. Tempest. I made your favorite."

Genuinely delighted, Lexia smiled as she took one. After a big bite and an unladylike swallow, she said, "You know you can call me by my name. We're friends."

Sami shook her head with a warm smile and wiped off the counter with a towel. "I'm afraid, in the house, it's still, 'Ms. Tempest.'" Then she leaned conspiratorially across the counter, whispering, "Are you excited for the opera tonight?"

Lexia's smile broadened into a grin as she said, "Absolutely. I wish you could come with me, but I think you're hoping for a certain visitor to come over while Rhyme is busy—"

"Shh! He hears everything in this Manor."

With a quirked brow, Lexia asked, *Everything?*

They snickered at the double meaning. Bolt was working wonders, and Lexia hoped his interest was at least partially genuine. She'd grown fond of Sami and perhaps forgiven the woman for her cold treatment toward Lexia during the worst of this drama. Was it truly the kitchen hand's fault if Leon had warned all the staff off from Lexia?

Unfortunately, the plan still relied on Sami. As the Manor's central hub, the kitchen lent itself toward all sorts of gossip. And Sami was easily the most valuable asset in the house. Once this was over, Lexia would guarantee the thirty-four-year-old's employment in whatever estate the Heiress and the Prince inhabited. Until then...

"Sami, I forgot to ask. What did you and Rhyme do on his night off?" Lexia didn't feel the least bit of remorse for asking the prying question she already suspected the answer to, but she needed something concrete to report back to Axis and Gauge.

Assuming Gauge was alive. Surely, she'd hear of his demise by now—

Sami turned back to the oven and checked the goods inside the steam-power appliance. Or maybe to duck her eyes away as she said, "Ahem. Well, it's none of my business what he does when I'm not around, is it? Or who else he might be seeing. Especially with me and Bolt—"

Sami stiffened and covered her mouth, peering around for any sign of the bodyguard.

Lexia smiled. "I think he's still sleeping whatever he got up to last night off. He wasn't at my door this morning, and while I don't mind the smell of his sandalwood aftershave, I have to admit, I don't miss it."

Sami turned all the way back around to face Lexia with a hopeful smile. "Or perhaps your father is finally listening to your good sense.

You're far too old for a babysitter *inside* the house. I agree that you need a bodyguard *outside*. Winter can be a wild place, you know?"

Gauge…

"Gauge, you feel too good to be wrong."

"But even now, I'm keeping secrets from you."

"I don't care. Just don't take your hands off me."

Axis…

"Are you afraid? I can feel your heart beating like a butterfly in a net. Do you want to feel free, Lexia?"

"I always feel free with you, Axis."

"No. You said 'warm' and 'safe.' Right now is about feeling free. You want a release, and I plan to give it to you. My way."

Lexia smiled. "You don't say."

Sami seemed to miss the dreamy expression on Lexia's face as she said, "But I did find the strangest thing…"

When the kitchen hand didn't finish describing her discovery, the Heiress gently pressed, "Oh?"

"I shine Rhyme's boots every morning first thing. He doesn't ask me to. I just like to do it. And do you know what I found with his shoes this morning?"

Eager to know, Lexia shook her head but said, "No, what?"

"Ice skates."

After breakfast, Lexia spent the rest of the day avoiding her father and waiting for news. When no word of Gauge's assassination came, she met Kol at the offices to work on union agreements. Between the man's bashful glances and blushing averted gazes, Lexia fought to get any work done. But eventually, the citrus union leader settled things for the afternoon. Just in time for Lexia to head home and prepare for the opera.

"Lexia."

Damn.

She'd almost made it up the stairs to her room. Lexia turned and faced Leon. "Yes, father?" Please, don't let him banish her from the opera. Not now. Not when she was so close to seeing her boys.

But Leon's smile was a kind one, his soft gray eyes once again filled with affectionate warmth. "I've asked Rhyme to give you some space tonight. He'll still guard the box, but not from inside as originally planned. I know it's not exactly what you wanted as far as independence, but it's an olive branch I'd like to extend."

If Rhyme hadn't been spying on Axis and Gauge last night, then Lexia's attack on Leon seemed unwarranted. Even though things between her father and mother were murky, she still didn't have concrete evidence of murder. Only an unhappy marriage. Even with tensions high between them, Lexia found it in her heart to wrap her arms around Leon and embrace him.

"Thank you."

Axis relived the kiss with Gauge while he showered, imagining the man's surprisingly soft hands tracing over his scars. Lexia ignored them for the most part, and Axis understood. But sometimes—every great once in a while—it felt like rejection. Like she didn't accept them as part of his reality because they were too ugly for her to think about.

But Gauge...

Axis imagined Gauge wouldn't shy away from them, and the Prince wanted to test this theory.

Unfortunately, it meant Axis' mind had strayed too far from the mission, and he kept having to remind himself of their quest.

The truth. Did Leon kill Lya? Or, more importantly, who was Lya Tempest in her heart?

After some time of rocking little Axis, Lya confessed, "I miss my family."

"But we're your family."

"Oh, sweet Axis. There is so much you don't understand."

"Lya... What didn't I understand?" Axis asked the foggy mirror before wiping away the steam and staring into the confusion in his eyes. "Why were you so unhappy, and why had we missed it?"

A knock from the exterior door made Axis slip on his fur-lined robe and answer it.

Bolt waited on the other side, and even Axis had to whistle, impressed. The valet wore a teal suit with black lapels and a black button-down. The jewel-toned color brought out the hazel flecks in his brown eyes, and the matching fedora suited his short-cut salt and pepper hair. Purpose hid behind his grin, but also... A touch of excitement.

With an answering grin, Axis asked, "Is all that for Sami?"

"Well, I thought I'd get your opinion first. Is it too much for a walk in the gardens?" Almost nervously, Bolt ran his hands down the lapels and straightened the bottom of his blazer.

Axis chuckled and patted Bolt on the shoulder, saying, "Not at all. It's perfect."

The valet blushed slightly before turning the subject onto Axis. "What about you? What will you wear to impress Ms. Tempest?"

Not just Lexia anymore.

No, now Axis was competing with Gauge in more than one arena.

It was enough to make the Prince smile as he stepped back to let Bolt inside. Axis said, "Actually, I was hoping to get your help."

"Help?" Bolt quirked a puzzled brow.

When Axis showed him the ensemble, the valet understood, saying, "We'd better get started. This'll take a while."

One hour before the premiere, Axis stood in front of the mirror, a little less certain than when they'd begun. He said, "I don't know about this."

Lexia's timepiece had inspired the outfit. The antique gold frock coat went to Axis' knees with black jacquard on the lapels. They matched the waistcoat cinched in the back with corset ties. A window cut out of the coat left the lacing on display, but tastefully hid the scars—Not enough to leave Axis confident, but enough for him to wear it for Gauge and Lexia. They'd equally appreciate the matching laces up the backs of his skin-tight black leather pants tucked into over-the-knee boots. He'd have to take the coat off for them to see the peeks of bare skin from his butt and thighs between the ties, and he knew if he'd leave the house dressed like this, he'd make a point of letting them see it.

In for a penny...

Bolt finished settling an antique gold crown on Axis' brow. When the Prince straightened to his full height and stared at himself in the mirror, the valet blew the air from his cheeks and said, "Sir, if I were ever into men, you'd be the one for me."

Laughter burst from Axis until he had to double over to catch his breath, hanging onto Bolt. The look on the valet's face was half-bewildered, half-serious. "I mean it. You're quite the handsome catch."

"It's—It's not that, Bolt," Axis finally said after regaining some of the air in his lungs and straightening. "I'm laughing because my life couldn't handle any further complications, but dressed like that, I'd make an exception for you, old friend."

They both chuckled a bit before Bolt patted Axis once on the back. "Ready, sir?"

After one last bolstering breath, Axis said into his reflection, "Ready as I'll ever be."

The ride to the playhouse passed in the blink of an eye, and Axis found himself sitting in the backseat at the red carpet with his palms sweaty and his face flushed to boiling.

What the fuck had he been thinking, letting his ass hang out like this? Of course the coat hid it, but now that he'd been bold enough to leave the apartment this way, what other choice did he have but to take it off at some point?

Oh, public phobia? Well, why not dress like a harlot for all the world to see—

Wait.

Did that make him a whore for Gauge—

Bolt opened the back door to let Axis out, and he just about fainted at all the lights flashing on his face. The air smelled of burning filament and body odor as the crowd pressed close to the car, despite the bouncers and velvet rope barricade. Copper glinted from the theater's entrance and blinded Axis with too much of everything—

A figure appeared in the silhouette of the blinding lights. Ample curves, legs for days, and voluminous wavy hair. When the lights turned onto Lexia, framed in the entryway, it gave Axis a reprieve, but also a chance to gaze at the stunning beauty further down the red carpet from him.

The Heiress' clothes matched the timepiece on her arm. A long burgundy blazer hugged her every curve, and it moved as if glued to her where it gaped open, unbuttoned with nothing beneath it. No top, corset, or bra. Simply white bare skin, exposing the flush of powder blue freckles across the swells of her tasteful cleavage, her toned stomach, and belly button. Like a second skin, black shorts protected the rest of her modesty, but only enough to give way to black fishnet stockings. Rather than wearing her trademark boots to cover her calves or thighs, Lexia displayed the length of her legs with a simple pair of spiked stiletto pumps. She stood taller than Axis in those. Her black and burgundy lipstick left him drooling.

Damn, Axis was one lucky man. Especially so, as Lexia glided down the red carpet and looped her arm through his. The burgundy angel asked in his ear, "Is this too much contact for you?" She gestured with a nod toward the cameras.

Lucky.

Axis whispered, "Hold me tight, woman, and I'll repay you later tonight."

Alongside Lexia's reassuring presence, Axis walked into the playhouse with more confidence than he really possessed. But it was enough, wasn't it? With her by his side, he could face anything.

Or so Axis thought.

They entered the theater's floor level with a crowd surrounding two figures in the center. One was a goddess in a lavender gown with a nickel zipper down the front. Tija's petite figure absolutely suited the transparent, skin-tight dress, and she glowed with her quiet confidence. The other figure…

Gauge stood at the front of the playhouse talking to Mrs. Tenz, her son, and Phoro—the Flicker wick foreman. The Count wore a lavender button-down so thin, the bright lights shone through it and silhouetted his arms, shoulders, chest, and waist. Equally transparent lavender slacks were only made appropriate for the silver silk lining, reminding Axis that Gauge didn't wear boxers or anything of the like.

Every ounce of the Count's body was more substantial and toned than the Prince had imagined, the result of hard work especially given Gauge's physical deficit. How much time had he spent on bulking out from the thin wiriness of his childhood and teenage years? And how had Axis not noticed until now?

Lexia's nudge and Tija's wave broke Axis from his reverie, and he realized Gauge was smirking at him from across the playhouse. Were

Axis' ears red? They felt pretty damned red. More like crispy. He buried his flushed face in Lexia's hair, pretending to whisper in her ear.

Rather than something suave, Axis said, "I can't believe I just did that."

Lexia giggled and said, "I can't believe he's actually wearing a timepiece."

That made Axis turn back, and, indeed, the Count wore a lavender and nickel timepiece.

Tija.

Was she wearing—

No.

With Lya's bones in it, Gauge's timepiece was surely in poor taste. Instead, she wore a massive corsage with a tiny replica of the clock tower in it. *That* was tasteful, and Axis couldn't help but nod his approval.

Mrs. Tenz and Phoro waved at Axis, signaling for him to come over, but as he glanced at Gauge, he knew he wasn't ready for this much publicity yet. Not to mention their mission. Axis murmured, "Lexia, please…"

The Heiress smiled and waved back to the others, while tugging the Prince toward the stairs to the playhouse balconies. Only as they approached the red carpet-lined steps did Axis notice Rhyme stood a more subtle distance from his charge. Perhaps things were looking up.

As Axis took one last glance over his shoulder in Gauge's direction, he caught a knowing gleam in the Count's persistent smirk.

Looking *way* up.

Damn it.

Axis came here with a mission, and when Lexia escorted the Prince to his box, he resigned himself to it. With the screen down on the balcony, Axis shook as he went to the banister, gave the theater his back, and shrugged out of the coat. He knew Lexia could see from her vantage point, because she let out a soft gasp. The hush of the crowd below also signaled success, but not as much…

With unsteady hands and a shaky inhale, Axis turned and faced the theater. Gauge had lowered his glasses, and his blue eyes smoldered like smoked cobalt glass as he peered over the rims at Axis. Hunger didn't cover it. Thirst couldn't describe the parched, sex-starved expression. Gauge stared as if he'd been deserted of touch for years and came across an oasis of sensation.

Lexia sounded equally ravenous. "Aren't you glad you didn't kill him?"

Yes.

Axis was.

Gauge wanted to slap himself. Or truly, he wanted Axis to slap him.

What in the hell were they doing playing these games amid their all-important mission?

Living.

That's what they were doing.

Tonight was for them—It was *their* story. Not the legacy of their parents, nor the constant apprehension of the future. Their interested and curious shared looks had inspired this opera, and Gauge would be damned if he didn't enjoy it.

Although the Count wanted nothing more than to march up those stairs and reward Axis' bravery, last night had been about the Prince. Tonight was about the Heiress, and, while Gauge was equally taken with Axis, he couldn't help but engrave on his memory the raw and delectable expression on the gorgeous sprite's delicate face.

Together, they would soon feast, but *after* Gauge gave Lexia what she needed.

"I've never seen three people look at each other the way you do."

Tija's soft confession brought Gauge's attention back to his date. Her smile was open and bright, not at all jealous or spiteful as she would have every right to feel. Rather, she looked happy for the trio. It was enough to make Gauge love her all the more. Perhaps, on some future night, the Count, the Heiress, and the Prince could invite Tija and upgrade their trio to a quartet.

Wasn't that a dream worth entertaining?

In the meantime...

"Ladies and gentlemen, please take your seats," a disembodied voice announced to the crowd.

Before Gauge escorted Tija to their theater balcony, he bowed to Mrs. Tenz, patted her son on the shoulder, and shook Phoro's hand. Once inside the box, Jan installed the screen for Tija and Gauge's privacy, but also because the butler knew of the Count's true intentions.

It took everything in Gauge to remain seated as the crowd settled. He glanced over at the Flicker's balcony. Axis sat up straight, and the daring outfit flaunted the strength of his honed body. Then Gauge peered across the theater at the Tempest's balcony. As expected, the doctor was absent—

Who'd want to watch an opera about their daughter getting railed by the planet's savior?

The privacy screen was raised, the drapes were open only a bit, and Gauge knew Lexia was behind all those barriers.

Was Rhyme with her?

Did it matter?

Gauge smirked to himself.

Tija laughed incredulously beside the Count, keeping her voice low as she leaned over to whisper, "You're on the prowl."

It wasn't a question as the curtain raised on Winter's stage.

Elated, Gauge kissed Tija's cheek and said, "I'll be back before the cast takes a bow."

"Take your time."

Tija slapped Gauge's ass as he made his way out of the box, and it left him smiling all the way around the theater to the opposite side. Jan followed discretely in his wake, aware of their destination. The anticipation left Gauge so ecstatic he didn't need his cane to walk, and instead, he twirled it all the way there.

Distracted with the stunning display on the stage, no one noticed Gauge stroll up to the Tempest's box. No one, but...

"Count Snow, may I ask where you think you're heading?"

Lexia's bodyguard had some big brass ones on him. It was almost enough to make Gauge like him.

Almost.

As cavalier as Gauge could manage with all the excitement, he stopped and peered over at Rhyme like he'd just noticed the bodyguard's existence. "Oh, hello, Rhyme. It's a lovely evening, isn't it?" Then he pressed toward the covered entrance to Lexia's balcony—

Faster than Gauge could move, Rhyme appeared in the way. It wasn't simply impressive for a man with a prosthetic. It was impressive for any mortal with a shadow.

Fortunately, Jan didn't have one.

The butler and the bodyguard squared off, face-to-face, suddenly existing in the same space at the same time. Warm brown eyes to cold dead ones, their glares would wilt any other opponent.

But Gauge knew something better than Rhyme could ever guess— Jan wouldn't hesitate.

The Count kept his voice low and felt the depth of it reverberate in chest as he said, "I have a matter to discuss with your ward—a professional one—but it requires privacy."

Rhyme didn't budge. Without taking his cautious eyes off Jan, he told Gauge, "Then you can make an appointment to meet Ms. Tempest at her family's offices."

Brave.

Gauge shook his head with an impressed smile, but alas... "I will see her. Now. So if you would please..."

When Gauge paused, the bodyguard hazarded a glance at the Count. "Move."

A full orchestra soared its sweeping score as an inaccurate depiction of Lexia's life from the past two months played out on the stage. Sure, the costume department had made a perfect replica of her gown from the Founding Ball, and the wigs were more or less convincing, but the dialog was so…

Cheesy.

Lexia kept snickering into her hand to stave herself from bursting out into laughter. Would it look good for the Heiress to guffaw at a play about her public sins? Well, that was probably more thought than the effort she wanted to put into it.

So, Lexia people-watched instead. It helped her measure the crowd's responses to her alleged infidelity and how best to address it. If at all. Axis had accepted her apology, and he was the only one who mattered—

A hand clasped around Lexia's mouth and snatched her wrist before she could retaliate with an elbow jab. Damn her for retiring the steam cannons after she banned duels to the death. Lexia's heart raced, pounding at her sternum. Frightful seconds passed before she recognized the frosted evergreen scent and realized the hand wore a soft leather glove.

Hot against her ear, Gauge whispered from behind, "Be still, butterfly. It's only me."

Every muscle in Lexia's body relaxed at the reassuring depth of his voice. Despite that, he stayed out of sight and continued to restrain her. A little spike of adrenaline made her heart skip a beat.

What was the Count doing in her box? Why would he risk their mission—

Gauge swept Lexia's hair off her shoulder and pressed his soft lips against the sensitive bend of her neck. He purred against her skin,

"Our handsome Prince has made great strides, and I'll take some credit for that. But…" Then came another kiss on her neck. "There are some experiences he hasn't been able to give you, and I'm here to rectify that." On the last, he sucked her earlobe in between his teeth and nibbled, breathing against her.

When Gauge released Lexia's wrist, she reached behind her and ran her fingers through his braids, loosening them from their twisted plaits. Meanwhile, Gauge bit the glove off his free hand and traced slender pianist fingers down the line of Lexia's lapels at her collarbone, chest, and lingered between her breasts before continuing lower. He circled her belly button with a masculine chuckle at her ticklish inhale.

Sweet as vermilion, Gauge said, "I'll ask you once. Do you want this?"

Lexia answered the only ways available to her. The only answer she knew with all her heart. She nodded and parted her thighs in the seat.

There was no hesitation when Gauge reached the top of Lexia's shorts. He slipped his hand inside, quick as he liked—the same way the Count approached everything else in his life. He claimed it.

Lexia arched her hips to Gauge's fingers and moaned against the gloved hand on her mouth. If not for that, the next row of seats on either side would hear her satisfied sounds.

"That's what you like. Held down, caught in my net. All the while, no one knows what you do inside—"

Gauge emphasized the word with the action.

"—Spread your wings for me, Lexia. Let me take you higher."

Wanton, the Heiress did as the Count asked, giving into every impulse.

Free.

The opera went on for two hours, and Gauge never once asked for anything in return. Anything aside from Lexia's abandon, and she gave it willingly. He kissed her freckled temple before vanishing when the cast came out for their final bow. Lexia floated adrift on an ecstatic cloud, trembling in her soaked seat.

As the playhouse's audience stood for the ovation, Lexia tried to put her stilettos under her and failed twice. She couldn't wait to tell Axis—

Where the hell was Rhyme? And how had Gauge gotten by her shadow?

With the bodyguard gone, now was the time. Axis would have to wait.

Lexia slipped on her long black coat and lifted the hood with every intention of blending in with the crowd as people milled out of the theater. She glanced down at the bodies below. "Hmm… Not so easy like this," she said, before removing her heels. "Much better."

A few people, notably Mrs. Tenz, recognized Lexia as she shifted into the crowd, but after a polite nod toward the kind forewoman, the Heiress became an anonymous figure beneath her hood. Lexia hoped Axis wouldn't miss her as she made her way to Tempest Boulevard.

Maybe there was something in the office which could help their mission.

As Lexia strolled unescorted down the cobbled way, she kept her eyes sharp. People parted into groups or pairs, leaving the theater and heading home for the night. To cozy up and gossip about what Lexia could only presume were astounding performances.

Someone bumped into Lexia, musing, "I wouldn't mind spending the night with *that* Count."

"You mean you wouldn't want to spend the night with the real one?"

"Oh, no way. Count Snow would ruin me for other men."

Completely unaware of how right they were, the pair of ladies giggled drunkenly off to the side as Lexia came to the city block with her family's offices. Although made of glass, the Tempest office facility blended in with the trees and gardens like an organic shell—Shiny and holding something more within.

With her personal key, Lexia slipped inside and considered a cover story as she made her way up the glass stairs to her father's offices. The top floor, reserved for executives, boasted the most beautiful views, second only to the Copper Cathedral. Vistas stretched beyond the main grounds before aligning in rowed acres. They belonged to Tempest Crops from here to dome's edge.

Despite everything, Lexia still loved the view from her office.

No one had a better vantage point than her father next door. Leon had left the conference room adjacent to his personal office unlocked. With a quiet prayer to her mother, Lexia tested the doctor's door, and it opened.

There was nothing atypical inside. A filing cabinet, some chairs, and a desk. This desk was the same as the one in his study, and if Lexia would hazard a guess...

The spring-loaded mechanism gave just as the one in Tempest Manor, and the bottom drawer came unlocked. Lexia couldn't conceal her intentions now—No cover story would save her. If she was caught snooping at Leon's desk, it was all over.

But was it worth it?

Inside the drawer, Lexia found the same file system as the one in her father's study. Identical down to the document with Gauge's and Lya's names. But the typed page wasn't about her mother's murder.

Lexia bit her lip and frowned.

It was about the domes.

For the second time tonight, Axis asked himself what the hell he thought he was doing. He waited in the conference room as people milled out of the theater. Gauge would chat with the playhouse troupe, delight them with his presence, and compliment their performances. Soak up all the attention Axis couldn't bear.

Afterward, the Count and his escort would follow the red carpet to the street. Perhaps they would stop off somewhere for a nightcap and some public displays of affection. Or maybe take a stroll to Snow Plaza for a night of breaking the pre-marital laws.

Either way, there was one thing Axis knew for certain—The red carpet had to pass by this room before it exited the theater.

Like clockwork, Gauge came strolling down the hall with Tija on his arm. Even with the cane, there was a slight gait to his step, which Axis knew meant the Count had exceeded his physical limitations for the day.

Well, surely spending two hours in Lexia's theater box would do that to a man.

As if Axis hadn't seen Gauge sneaking around the third floor? How much Gauge had flaunted his conquest had left Axis rolling his eyes but also…

A little jealous.

Of Lexia.

Of Gauge.

But mostly of the adrenaline from the complete abandon between the two. Axis wanted—for once—to let everything go and give in without a single thought for who might see, or laugh, or torment him.

So here Axis was. Waiting on deliverance.

As Gauge stepped by the conference room, Axis darted out, grabbed the Count, and threw the shorter man into the room. All while managing a quick finger to his lips and a, "Shh," at Tija. She grinned her approval at the Prince before the transaction completed and kindly left them to it.

"What the fuck are you thinking, *Master* Flicker?"

While Gauge's words sounded rife with disapproval, a smirk tugged at his lips. He knew exactly what Axis was thinking. But…

Once again, the Prince floundered as his insecurities rose like a tide and threatened to drown him in anxiety—

Gauge cursed before he gripped Axis by his tie and brought their lips together. The Count's kiss was almost as soft as his touch, and just as demanding. It stole the Prince's breath away and left him holding the other man for harbor in this storm.

Before Axis knew it, Gauge had backed them against the conference table, where the Count sat on the edge and let the Prince stand between his spread legs. With Axis' skin-tight pants and Gauge's gauzy slacks, there was no doubting their need for one another, however…

Axis parted their kiss to breathe two words across Gauge's lips. "Not yet."

The Count looked cute when he pouted. 'No' was obviously something he'd heard very little since Founding Day. "And just why the hell not?!"

Axis couldn't control his chuckle any more than the tremor in his rigid body as he forced a step away from Gauge. He said, "We need to focus. I only wanted to warn you about seeing Lexia in public."

The wicked smirk finally appeared as Gauge asked, "So you caught me ruining her panties? If you're a good Prince, maybe she'll let you choke on them later—"

Without a thought for his next actions, the Prince lifted the Count's hand, removed the glove, and sucked the taste of Lexia from one talented finger then the next. He never took his eyes off Gauge, and the response was worth it. The other man's eyes fluttered closed, and he took a steadying breath.

Then Axis lowered Gauge's hand and reapplied the glove. Before the Count could open his eyes and find his footing on this plane once again, Axis changed the subject. "How did you manage to get by our tenacious Rhyme?"

Gauge blew the air out of his cheeks as if the shift in gears was almost too much for him. He took off his glasses and cleaned them, avoiding eye contact as he said, "I told him Bolt was screwing Sami as we spoke, and if he hurried, he might get lucky and make it into a threesome."

Axis' jaw dropped to the floor before he could help it. When he found his senses, he frowned. "Are you insane?! You'll blow our cover! And what about Bolt? Rhyme will kill him—"

"Relax. Duels aren't to the death anymore, and I get bored without trouble to make." Gauge winked as if that would fix everything, and it annoyed Axis that it worked. Gauge said, "Besides, I trust your refined valet to charm his way out of any situation, as well as any secrets from that attractive kitchen hand. It'll all work out."

Axis pinched the bridge of his nose and counted to ten before asking, "But at what cost?"

"A few gray hairs in Rhyme's rugged, ginger stubble?"

"See? When I call you a 'tyrant,' this is what I'm talking about. You've been a brat since we were kids—"

Gauge gripped Axis' laced ass cheek and stared into the Prince's eyes as he said, "Remember whose tyrant you're addressing, your highness. Now fuck me or fight me. Either way, we don't have long before someone notices us missing—"

Before Gauge could spout another infuriating word, Axis twisted the Count's arm around his back and shoved him face first onto the conference table. He ground his hips against Gauge's ass, bent over him, and said against his ear, "I promised you an entire night, remember? When this is over—And only if we *all* make it out alive. Don't endanger my friend again."

"On my vow, I'll *try* to contain myself." Then the cheeky Count shifted his ass against Axis and said, "You know? This whole dominating thing really works for you. Perhaps you should try it on Lexia sometime—"

The last thing Axis heard as he walked out of the conference room, without another word, was Gauge's knowing laughter.

No.

Not the last thing.

Soft, almost too soft for Axis to hear, Gauge said four words which melted the Prince's heart and soothed any lingering agitation.

"Thank you, your highness."

NINE

Diamond Truth

"Mrs. Tempest, why do you entertain my father's stories? *There are no such other worlds.*"

"Oh, but there are, Little Snow. Exactly as he describes them and so many more."

Sometimes Gauge wondered if he remembered Lexia's mother—Winter's Diamond—with fondness or fear. Reverence or fear. Hidden inside his vault, he sat with his ankles crossed on a tufted leather ottoman. As he drank bourbon from a crystal tumbler, he stared at the macabre timepiece with reverence and fear.

What a woman.

And yet...

Lexia had far surpassed her predecessor. There was no substitute for genuine kindness and mirth. The girl exuded radiance and love with every breath from her pale, freckled chest.

Not sadness and foreboding.

No.

Lexia was less of a Diamond, more of a Pearl. A luminous ornament on Winter's crown. But who wore it? The Count or the Prince?

Gauge chuckled at his own musings as he tossed back the last of his drink. He uncrossed his legs and used his cane to spring up from the sofa. It took two steps to cross the room and touch the faceted amber jewel inside the copper watch.

It was almost time.

Although his joints creaked, Gauge stretched his limbs out and groaned with a satisfied sigh. Everything was exceeding his expectations thus far. Only…

At midnight last night, Lexia failed to give her signal. And even though Gauge had enjoyed Axis stripping in the window, the darkness from Tempest Manor had distracted the Count from indulging too much in the Prince's show.

Lexia—the wild card—could make or break Gauge's machinations with so much as a word. Spoken to the right person at the right time, she held all the power in this stratagem, and the Count doubted the Heiress even knew it.

Which was why the journey to Tempest Manor was necessary this afternoon. The lack of a signal required investigation, and he'd sent a coded message to Axis saying as much with the morning courier.

Young *Master* Flicker,

Your presence is requested at Tempest Manor this afternoon to discuss Ms. Cloud's proposal to address all the trouble brewing in

Flicker's Factories. Dr. Tempest and his protégé may have some guidance to offer, and we can't afford another Walker incident on our hands, now can we? The Wall looks mighty full.

Should you choose to join us, we can cover your part in the Founding Day ceremony.

Count Snow.

They could kill three birds with one Pearl. Until then…

A knock came from outside the vault, and Gauge stepped out to find Jan waiting as expected. The old butler said, "Sir, Mr. Bolt has arrived, and lunch is arranged in the dining hall."

Right on time.

Gauge smiled. "Thank you, Jan."

There was a change in the older man's serious expression. A warmth in the lines around his eyes, which Gauge found endearing. He couldn't help but recall the look on Jan's face when Gauge first ate a bite of his breakfast without testing it only two days ago.

Astonished and grateful.

Happy.

Gauge patted the butler on the shoulder before heading down the spiral stairs to greet Bolt in the foyer. He held out a gloved hand for the other man to shake, saying, "Thank you so much for joining me on such short notice."

Axis' valet beamed. "Well, when one receives a copper envelope, they R.S.V.P. immediately." Then a puzzled frown furrowed his arched brows. "Although I still don't see why I couldn't tell Prince Flicker about this. I'm not sure I'm entirely comfortable with it."

Gauge gave a sweeping gesture with his cane toward the dining room. "Let's discuss it over lunch." He assessed the older man's response through black lenses and grinned when Bolt headed in that direction. Gauge continued, "I want to learn about your progress without distracting Axis from his primary concerns at the factories."

Bolt seemed to appreciate this with an approving nod, saying, "I understand. Kitchen gossip may not amount to much compared to Phoro's strides with the other line foremen. Which has been little progress, I'm sad to say."

That's right. Valve's cancer had metastasized and spread throughout the factories until most of middle management had become infected and agreed to strike. Poor Axis. It was such a mess to clean up while mourning. Despite the lack of love lost between the Prince and the old Factory Master, Gauge understood better than anyone the relationship between victim and long-term abuser.

Complicated didn't begin to cover it.

But all that aside, Gauge and Bolt strolled into the dining room with Jan in their wake. Although the cautious butler had learned to accept Axis, Jan was still the most weary of the Prince's camp. Including 'Mr. Bolt.'

Gauge sat at the head of the table where the place setting put Bolt on his right. The older gentleman said, "I suppose you're most interested—"

"One moment." Gauge held up a gloved finger, dug a fork into some mashed sweet potatoes, and took an untested bite with a moan. Buttery and slightly sweet, he relished in the pure flavor of it. Oh, how he'd missed food.

Bolt watched, half-amused, and made Gauge a little self-aware of how he must look to an outsider. It was enough to make him laugh. "Sorry, friend. Tell me all about the gossip at Tempest Manor."

They ate as Gauge learned from Bolt about the comings and goings, the happenings, and relationships in Tempest Manor. Leon kept Lexia locked in her room with Rhyme at the door mostly, which the Count had suspected and truly…

Hated.

What was Leon playing at? It made no sense to further wedge the divide between father and daughter. And Lexia was performing admirably for tolerating the isolation—

"And ever since, Dr. Tempest has been visiting the late Mrs. Tempest's tomb. Sami says he goes there to beg Mrs. Tempest's ghost for advice to reach young Ms. Tempest."

Now that was interesting.

Gauge asked, "Does he go inside?"

Bolt blinked for a second at the specificity before rubbing his smoothly shaven jaw. "You know? Come to think of it. Sami said they could *hear* him weeping and pleading, but she said nothing about actually seeing the doctor. That the mountain of flowers he brings spills out from the inside—So, yes. I reckon so."

That checked out with the mercenaries' intel, further conflating the evidence of Leon's involvement in some secret city plans outside of Winter's sectors.

Gauge peered at the stained glass butterfly and clicked his tongue in deep thought. "Huh… Interesting…"

"What is, sir?"

The Count had forgotten his guest momentarily and shook his head to bring him back to the moment. He said, "It's nothing we can't work through. Will you be joining us at Tempest Manor this afternoon?"

Bolt patted his mouth with his napkin, nodding. "Oh, yes. Prince Flicker wouldn't miss it. I must say, all this time with you and Lexia has done worlds of good for his self-esteem. Thank you."

There were those two words again.

Gauge couldn't wait to hear them from Lexia and Axis in the bedroom.

It all came down to the domes.

Lexia took another long draw of the whiskey Sami had brought with her the night before. Apparently, Rhyme had arrived at Sami's cottage last night in the middle of the kitchen hand's date with Bolt. Sami had resorted to shoving the poor valet out of a window while soothing the bodyguard's righteous insecurities. Then, sometime around two in the morning, Sami arrived at Lexia's room with alcohol and tears.

Sami was still passed out on Lexia's couch now as dawn broke on the horizon. Meanwhile, Lexia sat in her fishnets and blazer, drowning away her mascara into the whiskey. She tried hard not to compare the shade of it to the color of her mother's bones in Gauge's timepiece—

Gauge.

Count *fucking* Snow.

Lexia took another draw and ignored how heavy her hair felt all messed on her head. Last night was a blur, not only because she was blind drunk, but because she couldn't recall the walk back from the Tempest office complex to the Manor. All Lexia could remember was the shock to her system and then Sami appearing at her door. But wasn't there—

Gray eyes flashed so fast in Lexia's vision that it made her stumble over on her way to the en suite.

"Fuck."

There was no taking the clothes off. Lexia turned on the taps, heard the hiss from the pipes, and stepped into the spray before the steam started. She didn't scream when the cold water poured over her. Instead, the inheritor to Winter's cursed Diamond closed her eyes and parted her lips, soaking it in.

Try not to think.

Try not to cry.

Nothing made sense anymore.

How could Lexia trust anyone when the truth was only half-told? And when the unknown poised her on the brink of oblivion?

That's what Lexia sought as she took another drink, diluted by the shower's water spilling into her mouth. When the blazer and fishnets became too heavy, saturated as they were, Lexia finally peeled them off of her. They landed on the tile floor with a wet 'splat.' The sound satisfied something in Lexia as the rainy scent of her conditioning oils detangled her hair. The white waves needed it as much as she had pulled on her roots throughout the night.

The alcohol barely touched the sorrow and confusion. It only seemed to make Lexia more aware of how much it took to get her drunk. Or sick. Or injured.

Perhaps she should jump off the roof and see if anything broke—

"Ms. Tempest?"

Ah… Sami was awake.

Antithesis to her thoughts, Lexia called, "I'm fine. Get some rest. I'll cover for you." She would, too.

A broken heart earned a day off. Although, according to Sami, Rhyme had been gentle in his questioning. Not accusing or angry. Just…

Hurt.

Lexia suspected Gauge at the heart of it—At the heart of everything.

The sigh which came out of her lips was sucked directly from her soul, where it hurt to carry her heavy bones out of the shower and into the closet.

Clothes.

Mundane and necessary, Lexia took no joy in dressing today. She could barely find the energy to comb out her hair and apply the minimum amount of makeup to hide the dark circles and puffiness of her eyes. Once the hangover kicked in, she'd wished for Gauge's shaded spectacles, but until then…

One foot. Then the next.

Try to walk without falling over.

In the only flats Lexia owned, she stumbled into her desk with a giggle choked on a hiccup. The first tear threatened to fall.

No.

Lexia would sober up and deal with this like an adult. She'd face her father and approach her tasks with intelligence and patience. Then, when the opportunity finally presented itself, she would confront Gauge.

Perhaps she'd consult with Axis first, but either way, she would try to control her impulsiveness as not to endanger their mission.

The truth looked murky from here, but that was nothing new to Lexia after the last two months.

One drunken night wouldn't change that.

Lexia unlocked the drawer in her desk and peered at the encrypted writing inside. She'd find the truth.

Half an hour later, Lexia sat across the breakfast table from Leon. He was reading the morning paper, per usual, which headlined favoring reviews of last night's opera. The one Lexia had been too distracted by Gauge's fingers to watch.

Please don't ask about it.

Please don't ask—

"How is Axis?"

Lexia kept her sigh of relief to herself, saying, "He's lovely, as usual, father."

The familiar tone of the endearment brought a smile to Leon's lips as he flicked the paper to continue reading it. All was fine—

Rhyme stomped into the breakfast nook with his heavy boots, looking...

Was there any word better than 'stricken?'

The bodyguard leaned down on his prosthetic to mutter in Dr. Tempest's ear, "Flicker and Snow are here. Do you want me to turn them away?"

Leon shook his head with a glance at Lexia before saying, "No. Axis is always welcome. Show them to the parlor."

Lexia noted the lack of 'Gauge' in that sentiment and tried not to take a deep breath to steel herself. Or at least not an obvious one.

Why would Gauge come here—

Oh.

No.

Lexia had forgotten the signal last night—She'd been so distraught. The thought of facing Gauge at this very moment turned her stomach while the thought of seeking council in Axis' arms lifted her spirits. The dichotomy squeezed her heart.

If only Lexia hadn't read the document last night.

"Mommy, I'm afraid of the ice hurricanes."

"Don't worry, darling. I'll be here to protect you."

"Forever and ever?"

"For always and Eternity."

If only Lexia hadn't learned that Gauge had used her mother's bones to build the domes.

Axis smiled at Tija as her car pulled into Tempest Manor. Unlike Gauge and Axis, the daring brunette had driven herself. As a man proud of his physical accomplishments, Axis admired Tija for a skill he'd yet to learn.

Bolt helped her out of her car while Axis said, "I didn't know you drove, Ms. Cloud."

"I like to ride, too, Prince Flicker." Tija said with a blushing smile and a wink in Gauge's direction. Axis' cheeks burned as she continued,

"But enough about me. Today is about you and the Founding Families. We will clear the legacy your father left behind and arrive at this year's Founding Day with renewed hope. Work will start again, and together we can ensure the future is as beautiful as your betrothed, dear Prince."

In an act counter to his public phobia, Axis pulled Tija in for a hug despite Gauge, Bolt, and the Tempest servants looking on. Axis squeezed her a bit for his own comfort. When he released Tija and saw the shock on her face, Axis ruffled her hair with a chuckle. "Don't look so surprised. You're a good friend, and I should show it more often."

"Hey! What about me?" The pout wasn't on Bolt's face, but it came through the petulance in his voice.

Axis said with a sigh, "If I must..." Roughly, he wrangled Bolt in for a hug, which turned into a headlock as the two competed in a wrestling match on the Tempests' porch.

"It warms my heart to see all of you so fond of one another."

Leon's voice sucked the playfulness out of the moment. Axis released Bolt and straightened to face his fiancé's father. Off to the side, with Tija on his arm, Gauge frowned behind his dark lenses. While Axis glanced at the Count, the frown deepened, prompting the Prince to turn around and see...

Lexia looked terrible.

Behind her father, the Heiress was nursing a powerful hangover with pale yellow bruises under her eyes. Dressed in the most comfortable clothes she owned, Lexia still made for a vision, but Axis wanted to draw her into his arms and offer her comfort.

What had happened? Is this why Gauge had wanted this meeting today?

The Count said, "Good afternoon, Dr. Tempest. I know this is impromptu of me, but I was having lunch and thought, 'Let's solve young Master Flicker's dilemma today. Once and for all.' What say you and Ms. Tempest?"

Leon stepped to the side, leaving Lexia more visible, saying, "As you can see, my daughter isn't feeling well. Perhaps we should reconvene at another time—"

"No, father. We can help Axis." Lexia swayed a bit before embracing the door frame with unsteady earnestness.

Did she just hiccup?

Axis hadn't heard Lexia make that sound since they were eighteen.

"Lexia Alya Tempest, what do you think your father would say if he'd been the one to catch you and Axis down here in the cellar together?"

Good and caught, a drunken Axis held a drunken Lexia in his arms. Why not embrace the moment with a little humor? He offered, "You drank the wrong vintage?"

Lexia snorted as she giggled into Axis' shoulder while Mrs. Tempest shook her head incredulously until she burst out into a fit of bright laughter.

It was a moment Axis had often looked back on with fondness, and he found he still could, despite the melodrama surrounding Mrs. Tempest's death. In all honesty, whether the woman wanted to die or Leon had murdered her in cold-blood, Axis took some comfort in seeing Lya's good nature in Lexia's laughter.

Far from laughing, the drunken Heiress gestured for them to come inside, saying, "We can discuss it over tea."

Tea would do her some good, so Axis hurried across the portico to his fiance's side, and gently took her by the elbow. He muttered, "Are you all right?" He wasn't used to leaning down to her ear unless they were naked. Was she really wearing flats?

Lexia gave over to Axis to keep her balance as they headed for the veranda. She answered his question with one of her own. "Can you help me talk to Gauge away from my father? I have something important to ask him."

Axis couldn't contain a worried frown, but nodded. "I'll do my best."

Sami hurried by with a tray of tea toward the back gardens. She set up the massive bistro set quickly as the party arrived. Axis glanced over at Bolt, who kept his eyes forward with Rhyme in tow behind Leon. The kitchen hand curtsied, dismissing herself without a word.

Axis held out a chair for Lexia, who took it. When the Prince sat on her right, the doctor sat on her left, insulating her from the Count. Smug and infuriating as ever, Gauge sat across from them with a smirk. He knew exactly the game Leon was playing, and Axis wanted to roll his eyes at how much amusement Gauge took from it. This was serious, but the Count treated everything like a game.

Not the one to play referee, Bolt looked uncomfortable sitting between Gauge and Axis. Meanwhile, Tija took the seat between Leon and Gauge, always comfortable with any situation.

Lexia reached under the table and took Axis' hand while she kept her eyes down on the wrought-iron and glass tabletop.

It gave the Prince the courage to address the people at the table. "Thank you for sitting down with me today. I know we've been discussing these matters with our union leaders present, but I disdain putting Phoro in the same position repeatedly to advocate on my behalf. So here it is. I need to replace a good two-thirds of my middle management staff, and I'm looking to do it after tomorrow. We all know why Count Snow... " Axis nodded toward Gauge as he said, "Placed Founding Day two days before Founding Season's end. Tomorrow is a day of triumph and celebration." For once, Axis felt this was true. "Then we need two days to recover from the festivities before returning to work as usual."

There was a long pause where Axis met everyone in the eyes. After which, he said, "But for Flicker's Factories, and for all of Winter, there will be no 'as usual.' We are opening a new sector—a new era—and it requires change for what's to come. My line workers have leveraged many accusations against the men and women loyal to my father. As an advocate for the people, I think it's time to move past copper casting and into due process. Let them face their alleged crimes among their peers and see if we can find a better justice than pain. No, they don't deserve to work in management ever again—no matter how thorough their rehabilitation. They were trusted with positions of power once, and it has proven too much for them to manage. Instead, let them learn from their mistakes and work under penalty in the most mundane of our industries. Do any of you have any feedback you wish to share?"

Everyone looked at Tija. As union liaison, and the one with the most experience on the lines, her opinion mattered above all. She smiled and said, "'A better justice than pain.' I think we should use that motto to lead your new crusade. We'll enlist the union forepeople to recommend the best for promotion to the new ranks—Count Snow, do you have any suggestions on how we should arrest the current perpetrators?"

Gauge stared at Axis for many moments. There was no way to tell his expression behind those dark-tinted lenses—No way to know what was on the Count's mind. For all Axis knew, the man was doodling dinosaurs in his head or...

Last night in the window came to mind. When Axis finished his... performance, there'd been a flash of light from the Cathedral's copper eaves. Had that been a glint from Gauge's telescope? Or a trick of Axis' imagination?

Axis nearly slapped himself.

Was that even an appropriate notion to have right at this moment? On the verge of a campaign with his fiance exhausted and drunk beside him?

The smirk which spread across Gauge's lips implied he knew every single thought which had just crossed Axis' mind, and the Count was enjoying the Prince's discomfort. Gauge stopped staring at Axis and turned his spectacles onto Bolt before he asked, "What say you, Mr. Bolt? Do you think you and Mr. Phoro can assist my guard in identifying and arresting these offenders?"

Axis could see Bolt restrain himself from smiling. The jovial valet would especially struggle to hide his camaraderie from Leon and Rhyme, but it was necessary. He said, "Yes, Count Snow. We'd be glad to."

Gauge grinned and stamped his cane. "It's all settled then. Dr. Tempest, how about we draw up some warrants and—"

"Actually..."

Everyone at the table peered over at Lexia. The open regard in Leon's eyes threw Axis off kilter. There was love for his daughter. Love and respect. Even though she was attending a work meeting blatantly drunk, he still gave Lexia the space to soar on her own.

Lexia took that space to say, "I would like Gauge, Axis, and I to draw up the warrants together. We can use your study, father."

While Axis was privy to Lexia's suggestion, Gauge's brows went up over the rim of his glasses. Leon frowned before clarifying, "Alone?"

Lexia leaned over and whispered to her father loud enough for only Axis to overhear. "Please let me confront this in the comfort of my home. I'll never be able to mature from my mistakes otherwise."

That did it.

Leon looked convinced and kissed Lexia on the crown. No matter how this played out—the doctor as a murderer or not—Lexia accepting the gesture had taken a piece of her soul. It was in her eyes as she turned back to face Axis and Gauge.

"You two... With me."

With so little life to her, it was strange to hear Lexia say something she would've been happy to say only a day ago. What had taken the luster out of their pearl? Was it the same as what had threatened to take the life out of Winter? The Diamond's death?

Axis stood, clenched his jaw, and followed his fair butterfly into the Manor. Snow trailed in his wake.

———————————

Gauge tapped his cane along the parquet flooring through the halls of Tempest Manor.

Alone with Lexia and Axis.

It was their first time together since they'd initiated their plans, and many, many spectacular events had taken place since then. What new and wondrous circumstance would see them to this moment?

Well...

Perhaps 'wondrous' wasn't the right word.

The slump to Lexia's normally elegant and straight shoulders as she led them into her father's study didn't bode well for this encounter. The situation only worsened as she collapsed gracefully into an armchair. It wasn't that she took a seat, but the *way* she curled into it.

When the Heiress pulled her knees to her chest and stared into the fire burning under its mantle—the flames in her black eyes and the waves of her hair in a mess—all of it...

"Lya, are you certain?"

Mrs. Tempest stared into the fireplace in Gauge's library and sighed. "Little Snow, I've never been more certain of anything. Take from me what you need."

Without turning away from the flames, she held out a hand and pointed a finger.

Gauge raised his sword and brought it back down—

"Is something wrong?"

Oh, nothing really. It's just Lexia sat in exactly the same way as her mother had the last time Gauge had encountered Winter's Diamond. The night before Lya Tempest's death.

Spooked, Gauge startled from the memory at the softness in Lexia's voice. There was a drag at the end, as if it had taken a good deal of energy for her to even speak. It worried Axis, judging by the frown he shot Gauge over her head.

What the fuck was happening?

Lexia said, "I'll cut straight to the chase, and Axis, please step in if you feel I'm being too impulsive or if perhaps my drunken state impairs my judgment, but Gauge, I believe you owe me an explanation."

Axis and Gauge exchanged a confused glance, but the Count suspected... "Is this about the domes?"

Lexia confirmed his suspicions by staring off, blowing the bangs from her face, and giving a heavy nod.

Gauge noted Axis' knees were so well-oiled that when he crouched beside Lexia, nothing in the athletic Prince's body popped or creaked. However, when Gauge did the same...

Crack.

Groan.

The Count would need help standing back up, but it was worth meeting Lexia's eyes and forcing her to look at him. He asked, "What do you think you know?"

She didn't hesitate or preamble it. Raw and impulsive as she was. "You used my mother's bones to build Winter. My father knew, and it put him in a terrible position. Gauge..." Lexia finally *saw* Gauge. Her voice trembled, and a tear rolled down her cheek as she asked, "How is this possible? What was she—What am I?"

With a burst of unexpected energy, Lexia hopped out of her chair, forcing a spike of adrenaline which brought Gauge standing before her as she glared up at him. "Did you use her?! Were you planning to use me?!" So much shaking fury and unbridled passion. All of it was directed into the fire reflected in her dark eyes, the tremor of her chin, and the soft ire in her voice. On the brink of heartache, Lexia warned, "No more of your half-truths, Gauge. Tell me all of it this time, or I swear I'll—"

Lexia raised her hand to slap Gauge, and Axis wouldn't get to her in time. Cane in hand, the Count clasped the Heiress's wrist, gripped her by the nape, and with little thought other than wanting to taste her wrath, Gauge kissed Lexia before Axis could circle around her waist and pull her away.

Swept up in the rush, Lexia forced Gauge back against Leon's desk until the Count sat upon it. Consumed by the scent of summer rain from her hair cascading over him, Gauge moaned into the Heiress' mouth. She was on him quickly, straddling him on the edge of her father's desk, and he was ready to let her mount him. They'd delve into Lexia's paternal issues while Gauge delved into her—

"Ahem."

Axis stood off to the side with his arms folded. He gave an incredulous shake of his head.

Lexia stiffened and broke their kiss. Sat up on Leon's desk, hard and ready for action, Gauge had to stifle a ridiculous laugh. This was sex with a sprite—wild and all-encompassing. They were about to fuck in view of Lya's covered portrait without a care for the people awaiting them outside.

Gauge loved it. He kissed Lexia's freckled temple and straightened her gently, saying, "I *do* owe you an explanation. Both of you, but much like Jan's story, it's not mine to tell. It's your mother's tale."

Lexia.

Pouted.

It was unintentional, and that made it even more endearing. Confusion was breaking Lexia's heart further, and that wasn't what Gauge wanted. He bit off a glove to nudge her under the chin with a knuckle. When another tear spilled from her lashes, Axis came over and wrapped an arm around Lexia's side. Gauge slipped off the other glove and took both of them by the hand.

"I promise, I intend to give you every bit of the truth once I understand it all myself. It's complicated and not very pretty. Much of it depends on the information we gather *together*." As Gauge said the last, he gave their hands a gentle shake. "Lexia, Axis and I know how hard it is to be disillusioned about your parents. We don't enjoy seeing you suffer this way. Please trust me."

Axis surprised Gauge by saying, "I trust you," without hesitation.

Lexia peered up at Axis before separating herself to stand on her own—Unsuccessfully. The drunken beauty stumbled a bit and sighed heavily, as if that were the last straw. "This is... asking a lot. I can trust you, but I don't know how much longer I can continue without information vital to my identity." She placed a hand over her heart, saying, "To my *soul*."

When Lexia's voice shook on a sob, Gauge lost his composure. "C'mere."

At the same time, Axis said, "I got you."

Both men went in at the same time to circle their arms around their butterfly sprite—Gauge's arms around her waist, and Axis' around her shoulders. It didn't take long for Lexia to cling to them for stability and strength. They would give her all of it—every last drop—if it meant ending her tears—

Axis' arm shifted and slipped around Gauge's shoulders. It was so unexpected that the Count stiffened at first, but it quickly passed. With a soft squeeze, Gauge opened wider and hugged Axis by the waist. The three held each other in the storm.

Shelter.

Home.

Love.

There was nowhere Gauge would rather be.

After some coaching and assurance from Lexia's boys, she emerged from her father's study with handwritten warrants. They weren't named, but each one bore a signature from the Founding Families. She carried them out onto the veranda and handed the important documents over to Bolt.

Axis' valet faced Lexia with an honorific smile. The consideration for which he held the responsibility thickened Bolt's voice as he said, "Thank you for trusting me with this."

Meanwhile, Leon and Rhyme watched the demonstration with inscrutable expressions. Lexia tried to assess them in her peripheral vision, but there was no way to tell if Leon was wondering about the conversation which had taken place in his study.

Did he suspect a conspiracy—

No. Truthfully.

How could he not?

Lexia's father was a man of intelligence and composure. Even in the less pleasant memories seeping through the cracks of Lexia's consciousness, Leon had never lost his patience with Lya in their arguments. It was always mother who stormed off or clicked her tongue. Stamped her foot—

Honestly, Lexia couldn't doubt where she'd gotten her personality from. However, the Heiress didn't understand one important thing about Winter's Diamond.

Why had Lya wanted to leave her daughter so badly?

Lexia almost sighed as she slumped back into her bistro chair. She was frankly too drunk for all of this right now. Gauge had promised her the truth—

"When?"

The entire cast of eyes fell on Lexia, and she realized she'd asked aloud. Too late to undo it, the Heiress met the Count's tinted glasses and repeated the question. "When?"

Evidently, the look in Lexia's eyes was enough for Gauge and the Prince to discern what she'd meant. Axis peered at Gauge as well, expecting an answer. Tija and Bolt glanced between the trio, while Leon and Rhyme stared on.

Gauge smirked for show and held out his hand for Tija to take it and stand from her chair. He said, "Founding Day, Ms. Tempest. We'll reconvene on the matter tomorrow. When else?"

Axis actually—

Truthfully—

Rolled his gorgeous green eyes almost right out of his head.

Of course, Gauge would make a show of it. Lexia's life—all of their lives—were a soap opera to him. But the promise in his devilish smirk…

It was entirely too sexy to resist.

Lexia looked away to hide the flush of her cheeks and the fantasy in her eyes.

Damn him.

Wait…

Did Axis just do the same thing for the same reason?

Oh, now Lexia's face burned like a sun.

"When will you pursue the culprits?" Leon asked, and the weight in his voice said he knew he was interrupting something between the throuple. Interrupting something he didn't approve of.

They were *not* doing the best job concealing themselves.

Too busy exchanging exasperated glances between Gauge, Axis, and Lexia, Bolt couldn't answer.

So Tija said, "What better day than Founding Day. Mr. Bolt and Winter's guards will make the arrests tomorrow, and I'll work with Prince Flicker to arrange their path to rehabilitation thanks to Count Snow's generous contribution. We will see them become better citizens of Winter."

A thought entered Lexia's head, and it made her frown.

Leon voiced it, "And if they don't adhere to your 'rehabilitation path?'"

A heavy silence blanketed the moment. Over the last week, Lexia had given this thought much consideration. At what point was a criminal irredeemable? For instance, if a man murdered his wife, should they offer him a path to righteousness? And if not, what should they do with him?

"Exile."

Once again, all the faces at the table turned and peered at Lexia. The intensity, especially in Leon's soft gray eyes—like stone in the sunlight—begged her to elaborate.

Lexia said, "If they refuse rehabilitation—If they never learn from their mistakes and attempt to better themselves, then what other choice do we have? Winter operates on limited resources, and there isn't room for non-contributors."

Gauge lowered his glasses to show Lexia the respect in his eyes. Tija displayed a sad, but understanding smile. With his arms folded perpetually in bodyguard pose, Rhyme looked at Lexia as if seeing the adult in her for the first time. The reverence in Bolt's eyes said he agreed, yet glanced over at his Prince. Axis frowned, but eventually gave a heavy tip of his chin.

Lexia stared at her father, who nodded once in approval. He couldn't understand—could never know—she was referring to him. But she wanted to make herself very clear. If Leon was responsible for Lya's death, then...

"We exile them to a world as cold as their hearts."

TEN

Founding Day

AXIS WOKE EARLIER THAN USUAL TO MUSIC, STIRRING NAKED IN HIS SLEEP. Loud and celebratory, the brass marching band announced the opening of Founding Day. The notes of Winter's anthem boasted promise and lauded their savior, Axis' newest lover.

That's right.

Although they'd yet to sleep together, not a night went by where Axis didn't treat Gauge to a show and himself to an orgasm with the Count's name from his lips. Lexia's, too. He couldn't wait to feel them both together once they buried all this 'bones and domes,' 'murder and redemption' mess.

Drama followed Snow wherever he went, but Axis found himself more comfortable outside the darker-complected man's limelight. To be the shelter Gauge sought when the curtain fell, summer rain and smoking cedar mingling over Axis' imagination—

Axis finished again first thing before committing to his morning routine. He couldn't remember this much solo action since the early days of his and Lexia's relationship. Seventeen, eighteen—On the cusp of adulthood and swept away in teenage romance, the Prince had spent plenty of hours alone with fantasies of his Heiress soon come to light.

That's how it felt now with the Count. Fresh and exciting, a layer of danger and mystery all wrapped into a silken three-piece behind tinted lenses.

Hot.

Damn.

Axis could barely focus on his push-ups for the blood rushing low. It made him grin into the floor as he kept up with his usual pace. The following shower was cold to help with the hypertension and flush—

A knock from the door asked Axis to climb into a pair of pajamas, throw on a robe, and answer it to Bolt in the doorway. The valet grinned knowingly before stepping aside to reveal Lexia further down the foyer's hallway. She stood there, panting from a run. A sheen of sweat decorated her efforts down those toned arms and her bare stomach. Her hair, tied back from her face, left her eyes clear—Wild and demanding.

Lexia *wanted* Axis, and something told him it was for the same reason he couldn't tear from his own thoughts. At his nod, she ran over and jumped into his arms. Bolt chuckled on his way to his apartment, leaving the couple to it.

There were no words. Just each other. And maybe… one more participant in spirit.

After a few hours, a shower together, and breakfast, Lexia left. They didn't need to say anything with the anticipatory electricity crackling between them. So much rode on today, and there was no better event for unveiling the truth.

Founding Day.

The anniversary of the EMP, which had devastated all but Winter, thanks to Gauge.

No.

Thanks to Lya.

To say Axis had wondered about the exchange between Lexia and Gauge—the one about Lya's bones—was an understatement. But he trusted the Count to get everything out in the open. It was all a matter of timing with that enigmatic and infuriating tyrant.

But first…

Axis met Bolt in the foyer, both of them dressed in their morning suits—plain but stylish two-pieces. They would save the pomp and circumstance for the evening. Right now, it was all about the factories. They arrived to a crowd waiting outside the Factory Master's offices—Axis really needed to think of a better title.

Factory Captain?

President didn't quite work since he wasn't elected, and Factory Facilitator was a mouthful.

"Sir, are you sure you're ready for this?"

Axis looked outside at the expectant faces and nodded. With Lexia and Gauge in his corner, he could withstand anything. "I am."

Bolt grinned and said, "Damn right you are," before exiting the car and opening the back door for Axis.

The Prince unfolded to a pressing crowd. Winter's guard, Gauge's personal well-dressed army, held the people back while others stood at attention, steam cannons and shackles in hand. Their pristine matte-black uniforms, both functional and stylish, commanded authority and more than a few nervous glances.

Axis had better attend to his audience before some kind of riot broke loose. He held up his hands and lowered them to induce a hush, which actually worked. They waited for their appointed Prince's speech to begin.

Factory Boss?

No.

Axis said, "While I'm happy to see our family all gathered here, I'm sad to see you at work during your Season off. We still have three days left, and today, of all days, should be spent with friends in good cheer. Yet we find ourselves outside our place of business, wondering what's next for Flicker's Factories."

A flare of anxiety pulsed through Axis as soon as he realized how many people he'd captivated. For one second, all the faces blended into one, and the sky spun—

A small hand on Axis' back steadied him while taking him by surprise. He turned to find Tija there with Bolt, Phoro, Kol, and Mrs. Tenz. Mrs. Tenz's son waved from the street beyond. The familiar warmth exuding from Axis' friends suffused him with the courage to continue.

Axis gestured toward the team who'd lead the triumvirate's industries into sector twelve—into Winter's future—saying, "Let me introduce you to the next wave in organization and project management. Ms. Tija Cloud, our liaison with Snow Mines and Tempest Crops, worked alongside past and current forepeople to create a union model which will see us into a brighter tomorrow."

Some people reacted with smiles and approving nods. But others...

"With all due respect—"

There was no respect in the foreman's tone.

"—Not all of us *want* unions. Some of us like how things are."

Another, a woman Axis recognized immediately as one of Valve's favorites, spoke up. "We should respect your father's wishes and stay the course rather than making rash decisions in the face of desperation. Right?" She elbowed one of her linemen, who shrunk away from her and nodded in fear.

On Axis' right side, Bolt said, "Pryl Mont, as it so happens, we are concerned with you specifically. As well as..." The valet listed another name and read the warrant. And another. And another. People in the crowd spread away from the accused as Bolt continued, "We hereby apprehend you for interrogation of crimes against your employees—"

Pryl scoffed, "What crimes?"

Another voice Axis couldn't forget from his childhood barked, "On what grounds?"

Axis had known this confrontation was coming. He'd shored himself enough to say, "Based on accusations levied against you by your subordinates through an archive of personnel complaints and grievances. Ones which my father ignored for his favoritism of you. Ones which I will now address with more than a little of my own biases. So, I've set myself aside and asked for a trial amongst your peers to judge your actions. Until then, Winter's guard will escort you to temporary lodgings. Do you understand?"

"Boy, remember that I know you—*very* well—and you don't have this in you." While the man said one thing, Axis heard another. A ghost—A wraith—he thought Lexia's love had long since exorcised.

"Be still, you little brat. I'm not done yet."

As Axis gripped his fists tight enough at his side to pierce his palms, he knew then some scars would never heal. No matter how much love he'd receive from those who cared for him. Tears threatened to squeeze from his closed eyes—

The same small comforting hand from earlier circled around his fist.

Tija.

Axis opened his eyes to look down at the bright blue sympathy reflecting on him. She shook her head and moved Axis behind her. With no hesitation, the gorgeous brunette physically removed the Prince from his trauma, and addressed the situation with all the sovereign authority of Winter's Countess. "Mr. Bolt, guards, please apprehend the accused and place them in Count Snow's custody."

Winter's military presence surged through the crowd with swift efficiency, shackling wrists and forced to wrestle some to the ground. No bones were broken. No blood was shed. Bolt stayed behind as the guards escorted the offenders to the Copper Cathedral. With their mouths gagged, the bastards tried to have a last word, completely unaware that if it weren't for Axis, they'd be in the Wall of Pain by now.

The remaining factory employees peered at Axis with apprehension, and that's the last thing he wanted. He said, "I've heard you out, and we will hear them out as well. As Ms. Tempest recently declared duels are no longer to death, I have denounced quiet executions. Now, alleged criminals will face due process and you…" He made a sweeping gesture at the crowd, saying, "You will determine their guilt or innocence. Not to face liquid copper, but rehabilitation. Believe me when I say, Winter's future is bright and fair. And I want all of you alongside me as we take the first steps toward it. Please reconsider the planned strikes and listen to Mr. Phoro's proposal for our new factory organization. The Flicker name is no longer 'Master' to you."

A woman in the back called, "But what will we call you then?"

"Prince Flicker hardly seems appropriate on the lines," another employee said.

Murmurs followed.

Axis looked at Tija for help, but she shook her head with a gentle smile which said this was all him. Bolt nudged Axis, and he faced his valet, who smiled in a way to instill confidence in the Prince. They trusted him with this.

What word said 'participant' and 'guardian?' What word implied Axis worked alongside his people without lording over them? This was an organized collaboration, not a slave line.

When it came to Axis, he couldn't help but smile.

"Call me 'Factory Caretaker.'"

The people cheered.

Affectionately known as 'Snow Day,' Founding Day was Gauge's favorite day of the year, and this one would prove more spectacular and transformative than any in the last ten years. Everything must align perfectly to fit the Count's careful preparations. The lighting, music, and colors would set the mood. A visual display beyond that which Winter had ever experienced would set the tone. By tomorrow, nothing would be the same.

Gauge lingered a little longer in his closet, taking a meticulous approach to the day's ensembles. Jan joined him in the clothing suite, arms wide for suit jackets, waistcoats, slacks, and accessories—All of which Winter had yet to see. It seemed every year the Count pestered his tailors earlier and earlier until this last year he all but started the very day the ninth Founding Season had ended.

After all, it wasn't often a man celebrated a decade of power and prestige, and Gauge was so fortunate as to reach his thirties in such a position. And the new friends and relationships he'd cemented over the last few months made him feel all the more rich and privileged.

Yes.

The Decennial Founding Day was already the pinnacle of Gauge's lifetime, and its peak would only rise higher the later they went into the night until it culminated—hopefully—with Lexia, Axis, and Gauge consummating their newfound futures together.

But enough with the hype.

Gauge asked Jan, "When will Tija be joining us?"

Despite the heavy fabrics loaded onto his arms, the butler answered with ease and poise. "Ms. Cloud will arrive at noon."

"Good. And is the adrenaline ready?"

Jan didn't need to roll his eyes or sigh for Gauge to hear the exasperation in the older man's voice as he said, "Yes, sir. But if I may? Why do you insist on risking yourself by delivering the information in person?"

There was no keeping the mischievous grin off Gauge's face. True, it was ridiculous to keep stirring the pot and making trouble, but goodness was it ever fun. He said, "If I can't see Leon's reaction in real time—to hear the man's response in person—then what is the point of all this? Life is for living, Jan. You, of all people, should understand that by now."

A little chastened, the old spy straightened his spine to his full height until Jan almost towered over Gauge. It was something the Count hadn't seen since his childhood. Jan asked, "What would I do if something were to happen to you? Something I couldn't prevent?"

Silence. Only the exchange of air from their lungs filled the room of draped garments and belted accessories with sound—

No.

Above their breath, Gauge distinctly heard the flow of blood in his veins and the beat of his heart. He'd been reaching for a tie when Jan had asked the impossible-to-answer question, and as the words washed over Gauge, he let the tie fall to the ground. He turned, afraid to move too fast and ruin the moment. It was a slow alignment until he faced the butler, who peered at him through brown eyes. No longer glass or frosted over with ice, there was a clarity to Jan's expression.

Whatever had led the old spy to the Snow family was all Jan meant to do with the rest of his life. And without Gauge…

No more words.

Or time wasted.

Gauge threw his arms around Jan, and the butler dropped all the carefully arranged fabrics to embrace his ward. This was not a father and son relationship. It was something deeper. There were no familial ties to keep Jan with Gauge, and no income to obligate the butler to serve his charge. Jan had declined it long ago. Instead, there was a profound sense of responsibility and care.

Jan loved Gauge, and the feeling was mutual.

The Count asked against his best friend's shoulder, "Where would *I* be without you?"

Gauge had never heard Jan's stern voice so soft as he said, "One day, we'll see. It's my hope that Ms. Cloud, Ms. Tempest, and I suppose the Flicker boy will be there for you."

The constant disdain for Axis made Gauge laugh and pat Jan's back. "I love you, old man."

A clearing of Jan's throat and some flustered noises equated to, "Same. Or me, too," between them. It was the most Gauge would get out of the old spy, and it was more than enough.

Two hours later, Gauge sat in a chair, letting the stylists work their magic for the afternoon's events. That's where Tija found him, walking into the fitting room with a garment bag of her own.

"Well, I must say, Count Snow. Eye kohl suits you more than anyone woman I've ever met."

As the smoked black ring around Tija's large eyes emphasized the striking blue of them against her pale complexion, Gauge would have to disagree. He said, "Not so much when looking at you, my dear. You're a vision."

There was the girlish blush Gauge appreciated so much. No matter how often he'd seen Tija stripped bare, he could always elicit a kiss of pink to her cheeks, and he reveled in it.

The blush transformed into a sweet smile as Tija said, "I've just come from Flicker's Factories."

Gauge couldn't help straightening in his seat at the mention of Axis. A smirk even tugged at his lips while the stylists swept his micro-braids back from his face. "How did it go?" There was more concern in his voice than he'd intended, but well… There was no helping his worry for the younger man's affairs.

"We've arrested the accused and enacted the unions. At Mr. Phoro's last determination, all the lines agreed to trial them until the next Founding Season where auditors, such as myself, will revisit the negotiations."

Gauge slapped his thigh and laughed. "Damn. That is exciting news. Are the prisoners already in their new apartments?"

Tija beamed back at him, saying, "Yes. We skipped the cells and went straight to them, much to Jan's disappointment, I'm sure. They'll begin their new menial positions anonymously in two days once work picks back up again. Five days on the lines, in the mines, or in the fields, and two days' rest while on lock down in their new homes. Until they stand trial, of course."

"Of course." Gauge still didn't quite understand the entire 'due process' business, but he would leave that up to Axis. Instead, the Count changed the subject back to more exciting news. "And how is the People's Prince handling all of this? Well, I hope?"

Again, Tija's smile lit up the room as she said, "Excellent. Truly extraordinary. Axis is really coming into his own since his father passed, and I couldn't be more elated with his progress." A slightly humorous lilt changed her expression from one of elation to silent laughter. "He's chosen a new name for the Factory Mastership."

Gauge quirked a brow. "Oh, is that so?"

A little giggle escaped Tija before she said, "Factory Caretaker."

Nothing could stop Gauge from pinching the bridge of his nose and sighing. "Of course he would call himself that. What a champion of the people."

There was no cure for cheesiness.

"Factory Caretaker?"

Lexia couldn't keep the laughter from escaping with the name on her lips. Oh, sweet Axis. The smile which faced her in the mirror shone with all her love for him as she pinned her hair this way and that.

Sitting on the couch in Lexia's sitting room, Sami went on to say, "And Bolt escorted the prisoners to their holding quarters. I'm so proud of him for how he handled everything. There's not a smug or spiteful bone in his body."

His rather 'stout' and 'capable' body, if any of Sami's smut talk wasn't exaggerated. These chat sessions were becoming a twice daily occurrence in which Lexia badly wanted to share her own stories of Gauge and Axis, but still had to maintain the ruse. Maybe one day, she and Sami could become genuine friends. Until then...

"Sami, do you want to use my room to prepare for your night off? If Rhyme will let you, that is."

The kitchen hand seemed to spend more time with Lexia lately than the ruggedly handsome bodyguard. And it showed. Rhyme's demeanor had come across gruffer than usual when Lexia had left her father for breakfast this morning. He'd caught her alone in the hallway.

"We both know what happened at the opera the other night," Rhyme had said with all the warmth of a snowman.

Lexia had faced him, sober and sure. "Whatever may have happened, you can't report to my father because you abandoned your post."

With a sigh, Rhyme had raked a hand through his thick red hair, saying, "Ain't that a bitch?" Then he'd softened unexpectedly and let his entire body fall into a relaxed posture—almost saddened by the weight of his older bones. "Your father only wants what's best for you, and he doesn't believe Count Snow falls into that category. Can't you see that?"

Even though Lexia hadn't dignified Rhyme's observations or his sentiments with a response, she'd thought of it throughout the morning as all of Winter prepared for Founding Day.

Sami interrupted Lexia's recollection by saying, "I can bring Matori, and we can prepare together. Do you think the children are ready?"

The thought of the children, so eager and dedicated to their parts, was enough to make Lexia smile. She said, "As much as any children's choir can be."

"They'll be fantastic. You've worked so hard with Matori, and she's excited to meet Count Snow."

Ah. The segue.

Here and there during their conversations, Sami tried to steer their talk onto Gauge. She was curious, as naturally anyone would be, but Lexia couldn't trust that Sami's intentions were harmless. Yes, Bolt had done a wonderful job dividing the kitchen hand's loyalties, but Rhyme was still a distracting temptation toward the opposing side.

Lexia deftly steered the topic back onto the night. "Remember, all the children are wearing blue and white. It's an honor to celebrate the Founding of Winter." So said the anthem, but Lexia knew how she wanted to celebrate.

Blue, black, burgundy, and gold interlaced.

All night or forever.

Forever would be nice.

Hours of interrupted gossip later, Lexia stood in front of her floor-to-ceiling mirror, adjusting any flaws in her layered ensemble. Whatever her bones were made of—in all the ways they were useful to Winter—Lexia was blessed with a straight back, petite shoulders, and long legs. Her posture and carriage reflected a life of privilege, with very little in the way of worries or anxieties.

Lexia kept reminding herself of this as she tried to push aside any current concerns to enjoy the evening. The first layer of clothes consisted of a long burgundy coat belted and strapped at the waist with a black leather underbust corset. Through the slits of the coat, one could make out black leather and tall boots, but that was all. The coat and corset credited great emphasis to her breasts while leaving much to the imagination. Let people wonder what was beneath.

The fluffy waves of Lexia's white hair gave her even more height, pinned back to leave her face free, aside from a well-placed tendril here and there. Gold glitter, dusted across her eyelids, dripped onto her thickly coated lashes, and black kohl shaped her eyes in stark contrast to her fair complexion. More molten gold melted into black lipliner for a decadent kiss. There'd be no sneaking around with Gauge with this makeup, but Axis wasn't off limits.

Lexia's reflection smiled at her and promised an enticing evening.

Sami stepped out of the sitting room with her daughter dressed in a matching white leotard and a blue skirt. They looked like a pair of ballerinas in silk slippers. Mother held a pair of ice skates in her hand, and daughter held a matching miniature set.

Matori said, "I didn't get to skate before, so this will be my first time. Ms. Tempest, will I fall down?"

Nothing—no worry or concern in the world—could keep Lexia from smiling at the little girl. "Yes, but you know what?"

"What?"

"You'll get right back up." Of that, Lexia was certain.

As Matori and Sami's faces blossomed into brilliant smiles, the marching band came around the bend of Flicker Avenue and Tempest Boulevard. The skilled musicians would make their way down the Myrtle-lined street to Snow Plaza, where the festivities would begin.

It was time.

Butterflies fluttered in Lexia's stomach as they peered outside. It was funny how in the last ten years, she'd avoided the Founding Day gatherings, and how it had taken only one presumptuous copper invitation two months ago to change all that. To change their lives.

A knock sounded from the door, and Sami answered it after Lexia's nod. Rhyme's voice carried from the fifth floor landing as he said, "Dr. Tempest is waiting to leave. He wants to know if Ms. Tempest is joining—You… you look stunning, Sami."

The drop of Rhyme's professional tone and the genuine warmth in his voice took Lexia by surprise. It especially resonated as little Matori squeezed between her mother's thigh and the doorway, asking, "Me, too? Me, too?"

Rhyme groaned, and his prosthetic squeaked when he went to pick the little girl up. "Absolutely, sweet pea." From the sitting room, Lexia watched him boop Matori on the nose and say, "You're the spitting image of your mother. Radiant."

Even Lexia blushed. It was too sweet a moment for her to eavesdrop on, but considering all the moments Rhyme had made himself privy to her in life lately, the eavesdropping carried on.

The bodyguard said, "The other kiddos are waiting on you downstairs. Do you want to walk with them?"

"Mother, can I?"

"Of course, baby. See you there, Ms. Tempest." Sami waved as she took her daughter and left Lexia alone with Rhyme.

His eyes barely shifted as he checked out Lexia's coat. There was nothing scathing in the look, only a cursory examination. Rhyme said, "Your father is downstairs and waiting to see if you'll be joining us on the walk to the Copper Cathedral."

There was so much tension in the air, Lexia could glide across it. Truths left up in the air, and questions left unanswered. But Gauge had promised.

Tonight, he'd reveal everything.

Lexia beamed and took Rhyme by the arm, a gesture he narrowed his eyes at. It was easy enough to ignore as she led them to the stairs. Leon peered up at the landing with so much and nothing in his eyes.

Everything waited for them outside.

"Shall we, gentlemen?"

Lexia followed them out to the growing parade and joined the dusking night. Flicker wick lanterns and Myrtle petals floated by, and her spirits soared along with them—

An explosion sounded, followed by a whistle in the sky. Then...

Bright white sparks fanned out toward the dome. They reflected off the metallic surface of the Copper Cathedral's eaves and set it alight. Another explosion sounded with the same whistle, and blue sparks fizzled and twirled in the sky.

The sight took Lexia's breath away as the faint smell of sulfur reached them all the way down Tempest Boulevard. More followed suit in the shape of diamonds and stars, and she took them as a love letter straight to her heart.

"Gauge."

Rhyme muttered, "The Count's outdone himself."

Lexia kept the next to herself.

Just you wait.

On their walk to Snow Plaza, Axis paused at his father's memorial. Bolt also peered up at it, reflecting the colorful blasts from above in his brown eyes. They could hear the band make its way down Tempest Boulevard from here, and Axis knew Lexia must be on her way to the Copper Cathedral by now.

It was all merging here.

Tonight.

Against the chill of the waning day, Axis popped the golden jacquard collar on his black duster. Bolt, dressed in a burgundy and silver tuxedo, accompanied him down Flicker Avenue. People milled in a mass toward the source of sulfur and light, huddling against the cold Winter's night.

The music led them down the cobbled street, masking the creak of Axis' clothes beneath the long coat. He smiled to himself as he recalled the lengths to which it had taken him and Bolt to fit the Prince into the ensemble. Maybe Gauge would actually eat his heart out.

Set on the only hill in Winter, the Copper Cathedral glittered from the sparks in the twilight sky. Shining into a mirror below, the flaming display spiraled down toward a frosty sheet formed right in front of Snow Plaza. Manufactured ice.

People hurried to strap into their skates and slip onto the ice, where skaters in skimpy outfits synchronized their swan's dance into a show.

Their leotards and skirts matched tonight's theme: blue and white. Axis marveled at their athleticism and grace, while also promising himself to master the art.

Later.

Fire features and bodies warmed the setting to a comfortable temperature, fueled by the promise of later tonight. Tomorrow guaranteed a new beginning and a continuation of Winter's Verse, but until then, many would seek a lover or two to finish this year with a bang.

Boom!

A rocket exploded above in a dancing shower of glitz and sulfur. The biggest yet to cease the music and hush the crowd. Sparks zigged above the clock tower where onlookers gazed at the dome above. Thanking Winter. Thanking Gauge. And unknowingly thanking Lya Tempest.

"Axis? Axis, dear, are you crying?"

Tucked away in the closet beneath the servant's stairs of Tempest Manor, Axis thought he'd hidden himself well enough this time. He stifled his next sniffle and wiped his tears on the back of his chubby hand, turning his face away from the fair beauty.

But Lexia's mother would have none of that. Lya settled under the stairs and folded her knees to her chest beside him. They waited there a moment in silence before she said, "I came here to cry. Not to intrude on your tears, sweet child."

"You cry here, too?"

Axis would never forget the haunted look in the woman's black eyes. So similar to Lexia's, only far less expressive. Not today. Today, a great sadness welled in those inky pools. A tear spilled down her cheek and meant to fall from her chin, but Axis caught it with a soft gasp.

It was the second time he'd seen Lya cry, and Axis remembered her reason from the last time. Instead of asking, he sidled up beside her and nestled against her ribs. His best friend's mother said nothing as she wrapped an arm around him and squeezed. They cried together in silence.

Axis hated his family, and Lya missed hers—whoever and wherever they were. Neither could do much about the other, so sorrow they shared—

"Axis? Mommy? Are you in there?"

Lexia.

She sounded close. Maybe outside the closet door.

Axis took as much comfort from the little girl's proximity as from her mother's arms. He peered up at Lya, who glanced down at him. She asked, "Shall we?"

When they smiled together, Axis knew sorrow wasn't all they shared. They both loved Lexia with all their hearts.

Lya squeezed him one more time and made him promise, "Protect her?"

"Always."

Always and from whatever would come next.

Winter cheered when Gauge's silhouette stepped through the Wall of Pain and onto the raised veranda of the Copper Cathedral's entrance. He wouldn't start with the rousing speeches until the Founding Families joined him for the spectacle. Like years past, Axis represented the Flicker family. Unlike years past, he would do so without Valve. Silence resettled among the people, softening the moment and acknowledging the loss, as he climbed the stairs to join Gauge.

In another change for this year's event, Leon climbed the opposite stairs with Lexia in tow. Rhyme followed behind, dressed a little too practically compared to everyone else. And in a brown coat at that. No blue or white in sight.

That brought Axis' attention to Dr. Tempest. He wore a plain white tuxedo with elements of gold to represent their family's colors. Leon regarded Axis with kind eyes and a reassuring nod as if he understood this was the moment Axis officially inherited his father's position as head of Flicker's Factories and the second Founding Family of Winter.

Lexia, looking down-right edible in that coat, offered Axis a smile so similar to her father's that it puzzled the Prince. How could Leon be vile enough to murder his wife when he was full of the same warm nature as his daughter? Tonight would finally yield those answers.

Hopefully.

Lights projected onto the raised entrance, nearly blinding Axis to the crowd, although he could make out Mrs. Tenz, her son, Phoro, Bolt, and Kol in the front. As Axis neared center stage, Tija waved at Axis. Her glittering blue gown hugged her figure until it spilled out behind her in a white train which led all the way back to the copper doors.

And finally...

This close, Axis could see Gauge, and the Count took the Prince's breath away.

Diamonds sparkled along the man's black clothes and top hat. A massive gem dazzled Axis from atop Gauge's functional yet ornate cane. The knee-length suit coat hid most of the outfit aside from shimmering slacks tucked into what must be thigh-high black boots. Copper ribbon decorated Gauge's mass of micro-braids, half up, half down, and tied back from his face.

And that's all Axis could see because the Count had hidden most of his face behind a mask of black silk and diamonds. It shielded his eyes. A veil flowed from it to loosely cover his nose and mouth. Like the man himself, it was beautiful, enigmatic, and downright infuriating.

"Gauge."

Beside Axis, Bolt gave an incredulous shake of his head. "Does that man know what limits are?"

Axis couldn't wait to find out.

Sex.

Adrenaline.

Little compared to moments like this when all of Winter peered up at Gauge, waiting for his words, his soul. 'Intoxicating' didn't begin to cover it. He was sharing the stage with two people who'd threatened or tried to kill him in the last two months, and one whose idea of intimacy had changed the course of his life.

Every single heartbeat paused, waiting for the Count to speak.

"Winter."

There was no hesitation—The crowd roared with a deafening raucous at one single word. But it wasn't just any word. Since they'd renamed their planet and outlawed their origins, 'Winter' was synonymous with 'survivor,' 'perseverance,' and that which would always remain. While the icy hurricanes outside had claimed their vast planet, the people standing here today thrived thanks to the careful planning and dedication of the families standing on these steps.

And Gauge would never let them forget it.

Another firework soared into the sky and exploded in sparks of white and blue. Intentionally, Gauge wore black for more than one reason, but mostly to stand out amongst his own people. Vanity, all that.

The Count gripped the balustrade with gloved hands, leaned forward, and said, "In the last ten years, we've established a community—a civilization—when we were told repeatedly this was not possible. Yet here we stand, sheltered by our combined ingenuity and strength, with many stories to share and many more to write. Only during Founding Season should we look back, and tomorrow we will look forward. But today, we celebrate the present moment in which we stand together and revel in our fortunate trust. Enjoy the festivities and theatrics. There is so much more to come."

On cue, a trail of Flicker wick torches lit one-by-one down a line on either side of the Copper Cathedral. They illuminated feats of steam-powered innovation and engineering—Rides, slides, and aisles of food climbed high in two towers flanking Gauge's home. The torches lit basins of oils which wrapped around the tiered structures until the heights nearly matched those of the copper gables.

Snow Plaza was open for Founding Day.

This was only the beginning.

After spreading his arms wide, Gauge said, "Enjoy yourselves! Enjoy the moment! Winter, you've earned it."

Cue the orchestras followed by the smell of searing meats and the whirring of exhilarating machinery. Like a river surging through rapids, the people of Winter flowed around the Copper Cathedral into the mirroring mazes of delight. They cheered and hollered with excitement—more music to Gauge's ears than the rousing brass marching band leading the way.

The Count turned his back on the lights and faced the doctor, the Prince, and the Heiress, saying, "You'll have your turn for speeches later. I promise." He winked at Tija for good measure.

The beautiful brunette beamed. These were the surprises she knew were in store. Gauge couldn't wait to show her the ones she had no idea were coming.

Looking rather dashing in his simple tuxedo, Leon spoke first. "Congratulations on another year in Winter, Count Snow."

Axis, inciting much of Gauge's curiosity about what creaked under his coat, said, "Yes. Congratulations to us all. We've held Winter together for ten years, and tonight culminates a decade of our families' accomplishments."

"So it does." Leon sounded... on the fence to Gauge. There was something entirely too neutral to his tone and his smile. He looked certain that no matter how tonight turned out, he would maintain a steady course. The doctor asked, "I assume you're paying these people to work on their one night off?"

Gauge couldn't wait to test the man's stable foundation as he said, "All the entertainment and food vendors are volunteers working on revolving shifts so that no one misses out."

With a little curtsy, Tija bowed her head toward Lexia. "Welcome, Ms. Tempest, to your first Founding Day. What do you make it of it so far?"

The burgundy of Lexia's coat emphasized the liquid gold painted on her full and inviting lips. All colors suited the fair-complected Heiress, but the Count couldn't help thinking she needed a little more copper in her life. In response to Tija's kind words, Lexia stepped across the veranda, took the brunette by the hands, and gave her one long look down her dress and up.

There was kindness, appreciation, and something… darker in Lexia's eyes—A heat perhaps too familiar for their audience. The wild sprite, with no sense of appropriate timing, said, "Nothing here made it more worth it than the sight of you in this dress."

Tija.

Blushed.

Full red from her cheeks to the tops of her breasts, and Lexia's answering smile was almost wicked—

No.

Most certainly wicked, while keeping in mind her father's presence.

There was a sadistic streak in this one—planting impossible notions of the potential between the two women in the heads of all the men present.

Whatever Lexia was thinking, Gauge wanted more of it in the bedroom.

And poor Axis.

The 'Flicker boy' drooled at the pair of gorgeous ladies admiring one another. Rhyme and Bolt looked uncomfortably anywhere but at Lexia and Tija. Gauge had to practice all his self-control and discipline not to act on a dream too far out of reach—Lexia, Axis, Tija, and Gauge together.

Wild sprite, indeed.

It was Leon who further singularized the moment by saying, "Lexia, I'm giving Rhyme the night off."

Everyone peeled their eyes off the two ladies to peer at the doctor.

He continued, "I trust you'll keep our arrangement in mind as you enjoy yourself tonight. You're as much responsible for Winter's happiness as anyone else on this veranda. Remember that."

With a sweep of his long white coat, Leon took the stairs down into the milling crowd. He couldn't quite disappear into it—There was too much distinction in the straightness of his shoulders. He followed the current toward one exciting tower to the side.

Interesting.

Rhyme stood there, probably all too aware he didn't belong among the faces on the veranda. He peered at each of them through narrowed eyes before shaking his ginger head incredulously and exiting the stage. Hopefully, in search of that lovely kitchen hand, which obviously disappointed Bolt by the sudden slump of the valet's shoulders.

Gauge faced his friends—Bolt, Tija, Jan, Axis, and Lexia—asking, "Are you ready to rattle some foundations?"

Tija smiled, aware of the call back to her earlier comments about Lexia changing Gauge's life. Funny how true that had turned out. Tija took Bolt by the arm and left for the festivities. The valet bowed before escorting her to their respective duties.

Jan melted into the shadows, literally disappearing from view off to utilize his best abilities.

That left the Prince, the Heiress, and the Count on the stage. Some onlookers would mark this moment later in a great epic, but no one could know what Gauge had planned.

"I'll see you two later tonight. We have a promise to keep."

ELEVEN

Golden Butterfly

To enact their plan, Lexia let Axis lead her away from Gauge. She almost blew the Count a kiss, but decided against it. While her father might have been sincere when he sent Rhyme off to play in the theme park, there was too much at stake to risk a kiss.

Impulse control.

It was against Lexia's very nature, but she could say with reverence that Gauge and Axis were excellent influences on the professional side of her personality.

Axis leaned down to nuzzle Lexia's cheek as they walked in her father's footsteps. Hot against her ear, he said, "It's hard to walk away, isn't it?"

Lexia couldn't resist looking over her shoulder where Gauge still watched them leave. Softly, she said, "Yes, it is."

The thick crowd couldn't afford to give the Prince and the Heiress a wide berth. Instead, children ran about with sparklers and zippy noises, fish in bowls, and sticky prizes. Parents let their kids scamper as they held hands down the main thoroughfare of glowing fire, meaty smoke, and excited cries.

Like a train, a car spiraled along tracks carrying passengers up high into the air and dropping them down in a thrilling loop. Swings twirled on a mechanized merry-go-round, heralding delighted cheers from above. Then there were tunnels where lovers sat close before disappearing into a heady dim filled with flowers and soft ambiance. Ice dancers and fire breathers offered demonstrations of spectacular wonder, and everyone waited in line to take lessons.

The Founding Day Carnival and Theme Park was a success, and the perfect distraction for whatever reason Gauge had asked Lexia and Axis to stay behind and follow her father. What was the Count up to? And how would it bring Lexia closer to the truth about her parents?

Axis hugged Lexia closer as they trailed behind Leon some thirty people back. The good doctor was making his way toward the ice arenas, where injuries were sure to happen. He smiled here and waved there, stopped to taste some squid on a stick, and won a game for a little girl with tears in her eyes.

It all reminded Lexia of growing up in the Manor, warm and safe. Tucked into bed and sang to sleep. Kissed when scraped and tutted when bruised. But always, she'd been encouraged to keep climbing those trees and playing in fountains. Never once did she feel threatened by her father—Something neither Axis nor Gauge could say. Something

Lexia would fix if she could. To have a father like Leon was a privilege, a blessing, but…

How could Lexia reconcile all this? The gaps, the holes—The utter issues with control. Mother had wanted to leave for a reason. Perhaps their daughter had never gotten a true taste of the bitterness before now, but it was here. And it soured her ability to enjoy the evening—

Axis pulled Lexia in for a surprise hug and whispered, "I'm here. Talk to me, butterfly. Are you nervous?"

Lexia kept her eyes on her father, but gave into Axis' strength and protection, saying, "I just want to know. How? Why?"

Axis kissed her cheek. "I meant about the children."

Oh.

Of course.

Lexia laughed. She had forgotten. She'd let her personal drama consume her for a bit. Meanwhile, Leon bent down to check on a little kid who'd fallen on the ice. For all his faults, he *did* care about Winter.

Let it go for now.

Lexia leaned back to let Axis see the love in her eyes and said, "The children will do their best. I've nothing to be nervous about." It wasn't true, but…

Where was her father?

"Axis."

The Prince took Lexia's meaning and glanced over where Leon had just been standing. He was gone. Vanished in a brief respite between the couple. They whirled this way and that, searching for him and no longer trying to hide it.

Leon was nowhere to be seen—

A wave captured Lexia's attention, and she narrowed her eyes as she glimpsed its source. Rhyme waved from a perch above. Sami and Matori were with him, the little girl eating spun sugar at his side. When their eyes met, the bodyguard gave Lexia a suspicious salute before he shoved his hands into his pockets, turned, and walked with the mother and daughter pair toward the amphitheater.

Lexia breathed, "I think something has gone horribly wrong."

Axis took her by the hand, saying, "There's only one way to find out."

They walked together up one level of the theme park. Gauge had situated the amphitheater in the center of the tier. The Prince and the Heiress made their way through the massive crowd gathered in the semicircle. On the stage in its center, a conductor and a choir director arranged Winter's children in rows.

The anthem.

Axis squeezed Lexia's hand and gestured her toward the outer rim. There, Tija and Bolt stood in the back. Neither looked happy with them all gathered in the same spot. They'd been led here not by Gauge, but by their alleged enemy.

"Ladies and gentlemen, please join us for Winter's Anthem, performed by the ambassadors of our future."

Matori wiggled in the front and waved at Rhyme, who threw a daisy onto the stage prematurely. It made the little girl sway in her spot and beam at the crowd as the music started. With great patience, the conductor led the children's orchestra into the quiet opening before it swept into the first verse.

Despite the present danger, Lexia's heart soared at the gentle command the children held over their audience. They sang with all their hearts, and nothing could take away the pride she felt in the moment until the very last note.

"And Snow will protect Winter/May it never thaw."

No one could hear the crowd cheer over the explosion and whistle from above. Louder and booming, the concussion of it sent Lexia and Axis low. The sparks illuminated a shape in the sky against the domes.

Beside Lexia, Axis gasped, "What in Eternity am I looking at?"

To answer his question, enormous Flicker wicks fueled spotlights which shone onto the smoky clouds above. It was a balloon—no, some kind of aircraft. All too reminiscent and yet completely different from anything in Lexia's early memory. It wasn't fueled by solar panels or electricity drops, but by steam-powered propellers. She didn't need to ask where it had come from. The blue and white silk of its hull gave it away.

And that's when Gauge's face appeared across the sky.

Across the canvas of the magnificent flying machine, Gauge addressed the people of Winter, and Axis thought he'd seen it all. Gauge's head was bowed with both hands on his bejeweled cane. His sparkling top hat hid his face from the camera. Behind him, rosewood paneling surrounded by black, gold, blue, and burgundy drapes set the scene. It was dramatic and perfectly him.

The Prince had the wherewithal to spare a glance at Lexia, who gazed up with her mouth open, stunned. Wonder suited her, from the slight smile of her lips to the dazzling shine in her black eyes. Oh, yes, Gauge had had an influence on the couple for sure.

Only after sense had returned to Axis did he think to question where in the hell the Count was projecting from. The 'how' was already asked by the gasping crowd. Even Rhyme's eyes went wide, and the bodyguard gave a little shake of his head in disbelief before blinking in momentary shock at the sight.

Gauge had that effect on people.

Axis grinned.

With his voice silky and rich, the Copper Count said, "Winter, apologies for interrupting your good time."

Off to the side, a woman fainted, and her friends rushed to help her. The scene tore Lexia and Axis' attention away from Gauge momentarily, after which the Heiress gave the most feminine and prideful giggle the Prince had ever heard. It said, 'This is a man I've known intimately, and, yes, the fainting is warranted.'

Axis chuckled incredulously.

Gauge continued, "I have a few… revelations I'd like to make. What you're about to witness will shock you and change Winter forever. Know that I come to you as a leader—a pillar of our community—but not all pillars are constructed to withstand the test of time. We've recently lost one. For Valve Flicker, let's have another moment of silence."

As all of Winter went quiet, an emotion—powerful and provocative—blossomed in Axis' chest. He only recognized it for the familiar sensation of Lexia at his side.

Love.

Axis loved Gauge.

Then the Count straightened and lifted his head. Gone was the mask, and with no glasses, Gauge's blue eyes were piercing amid his deep complexion. The dark melt of his skin was made even more striking by swirls of body paint. On his cheeks, outlining his eyes, lips, and jaw—all of it gold, black, burgundy, and blue.

The melding of their colors in the exotic filigree didn't stop at the Count's jaw. It went down his chin, over his surprisingly honed chest, taut stomach, and toned arms, which belonged on a boxer. Where it disappeared into Gauge's belt line only enticed Axis' curiosity as to where else the Count had decorated on his body. The glittering combat pants tucked into knee-high boots gave nothing away.

Less silken, more aggressive, Gauge said, "Not only were they not all meant to stand forever, many were built with flaws. Faults, cracks, and weak foundations which may have destabilized Winter, but no longer. Tonight, as we usher in a new era of Flicker, Tempest, and Snow, we tend to the carbon left in our wake."

Video played on the screen, much as it had when Gauge offered Lexia and Axis his confession from the palm of his hand. Was that how—

Lexia sniffled beside Axis as sweet moments with Lya when they were children flashed on the aircraft's hull. Laughter, gentle chiding, and tears. So Axis wasn't the only one who'd encountered Mrs. Tempest's loneliness from their childhood. Then, the scenes began to include Leon like a shadow, looming in a mirror. The longer the video played, the more sorrowful or cold Lya looked, until the state of her unhappiness became clear as well as the culprit responsible.

Allegedly.

Axis split his attention between the show and the woman on his arm. Lexia, enraptured, stared up at the sky with tears springing from her eyes. Her makeup didn't budge, but he wiped them away regardless, prompting the Heiress to snuggle in closer against the Prince.

The Count carried on.

"Winter's Diamond, flawless and ethereal, suffered at the hands of one such pillar. All along, Dr. Leon Tempest has served our beautiful cities as a physician, an educator, and the cultivator of our crops—But how did he serve as husband and father? When we peel back the saintly veneer, is there a savior or a savage in our midst?"

There.

The footage from that night in Tempest Cemetery played, and Winter witnessed the footage Gauge possessed of Lya's death.

Shaken, Lexia looked away.

All around, people gasped, horrified, with hands clasped over their mouths. Many cried out and balked. One vomited off to the side. The conductor on stage tried to shield the children. Many parents went to retrieve them. As Sami rushed to Matori from Rhyme's side, the bodyguard glared across the audience at Axis, aware now of the Prince's involvement.

Tija looked pale, and Bolt let her lean on him for support. So this was a truth even she didn't know.

Gauge said, "We speak of due process and rehabilitation, of justice and tribulations, so here I present you, Winter, with the most difficult case of all. What should we do with Leon Tempest?"

When Axis had proposed a 'trial amongst their peers,' this wasn't exactly what he'd had in mind.

Gauge hoped Lexia and Axis kept their faith in him a little while longer as the crowd began to chant, "Wall. Of. Pain. Wall. Of. Pain."

The gondola hovered close enough to the Copper Cathedral for the Count to make out the words. People were dangerous. He knew better than anyone. After his father's indiscretions had ruined the family name and outcast Gauge as a disreputable scientist, he knew full well how mob-mentality worked. That's not what he wanted here. He wanted to reveal the truth and pave the way for Lexia to usurp her father's title as head of the Tempest Family.

This was a task weeks in the making, and not to mention, a nice slice out of Gauge's hand. Yet here they were, and there was no backing down now. He tucked his cane into the bend of his arm and held up his ungloved, painted hands to placate the crowd through the projection, saying, "Now, now. That's not the way we want to move forward, is it? End Founding Season with an execution and pave the way to sector twelve in Leon's blood? No. We'll do this Ms. Tempest and Prince Flicker's way. Your new Factory Caretaker—"

It took everything in Gauge not to chuckle.

"—Wants Winter to embrace retribution through the proper channels, and I tend to agree with him for most cases. But for this particular set of circumstances, I think we should embrace the butterfly's grace. Exile, not execution. What say you, Winter? For all the good doctor has treated the rest of the population with warmth and kindness—for all of his contributions to our glorious survival—shall we cast him out into the hurricanes of ice, and let them decide his fate rather than subject him to the fires of smelted copper?"

As the people howled their approval, Gauge hoped the plan would work as he'd expected.

Please.

Let him get this right.

"What about a defense, Gauge Snow? Or do we not wish to hear the accused out?"

Gauge was simultaneously relieved and chilled by the voice from behind, and he closed his eyes to feel both. He knew Leon's words had carried through the projector's microphone at the hush of Winter. Everything was falling into place.

How the good doctor had managed to find his way inside of Gauge's zeppelin? The Count may never know. But here they both were with far more left to say.

Slowly, Gauge turned and faced the man he'd once considered a friend. The spotlights below cast Leon in a silhouette of a tall man, with a dancer's figure in a long coat. Outlined in shadow, glasses and the popped collar of his coat cut a sinister demeanor from such an inviting individual.

A long, long time ago, before Lya Tempest had come to the Count, Leon was a man to revere. To aspire to impress. To make proud.

Gauge asked, "Do you have something to say for yourself? For your daughter? Will you tell the truth now, Dr. Tempest, while all of Winter waits to hear?"

With more confidence than Leon should have at this very moment, he pointed at Gauge and said, "Let's talk about what's on your wrist first."

Gauge stepped to the side so the projector would keep both him and Dr. Tempest in frame. Then he held up his hand for Winter to see. The ornate timepiece of copper featured the amber diamond most prominently on his wrist. "A parting gift from Winter's diamond."

Leon lowered his hand and took a step forward until the interior lights illuminated his face. He was not as fair as Lexia, but lighter than Axis. The sandy brown of his hair had given way to a few gray streaks some years back, and it suited the older man's status. His gray eyes were famously soothing and kind.

But not tonight.

Tonight, they chilled Gauge to the bone.

In a tone the Count had never heard from the doctor before, Leon said, "It's what you would take from my daughter. It's what you would keep from Winter. The secret of Lya's bones. I'm not the only one with confessions to make, *Gauge.*"

Pure.

Disappointment.

Not wrath or fear, even.

No.

Leon Tempest said the Count's name with utter regret, as if Gauge had let down all the older man's expectations. It was a familiar tone— One Gauge had heard many times from his father and from disapproving male figures in his field. Never had he thought he'd hear it again and actually care.

But Gauge did.

Despite what he knew and/or suspected of Leon, hearing a man he'd once respected talk to him in such a manner had cut Gauge to the quick.

The Count swallowed an overwhelming need to apologize and atone. Instead, he narrowed his eyes at Lexia's father. "So… I suppose the question is, 'Which one of us goes first?'"

"I want you to tell Lexia the truth. Tell her your side of things—all of it this time—and then I'll tell mine."

With a nod, Gauge peered into the camera and said, "The domes of Winter are a gift from our Diamond. We made them together with the regenerative properties of her bones." He didn't want to pause too long for fear of Lexia's reaction to this news, so he faced the camera head on.

Lexia, hear me out.

"In your mother's desperation to protect us from the oncoming storm, she came to me with a plan. Whatever she was—whatever you are—held a marvel of medical wonder and genetic engineering. Indestructible. The restorative properties allowed for infinite possibilities, and so she gave me access to a stockpile she'd gathered for I don't know how long—"

Gauge waved Leon off before he could interrupt and said, "I mean that honestly. Lya Tempest had been preparing for untold years. Decades—possibly centuries—even. I never knew her actual age, but I know it far surpassed any lifespan on our planet. She taught me how to mold the glass and manufacture the domes. Your father believes I intended to use you in the way he believes I used her, but there was no manipulation—no schemes. That's the truth of it, Ms. Tempest—Dear Lexia."

Then Gauge turned and gave his full attention to Dr. Tempest. "What I don't know is how you were involved in Lya's plan or why you caused her such unhappiness. But I *did* learn some interesting facts from sources all across Winter. You, and someone who shall remain anonymous out of respect, conspired against our way of living. Your cabal devised a way to replicate the domes and deigned to build your own sector outside of Winter's dominion. On my planet. What do you have to say for yourself?"

During Gauge's confession, Leon's expression went from disdain to remote. Unreadable. When Gauge finished, the older man said, "No more of this, Gauge. I want to speak to my daughter. Take us down."

Gauge took a step back and knocked on the door behind him without taking his eyes off Leon. When Jan called from inside the cockpit, the Count ordered, "The clock tower, if you would be so kind."

"Yes, sir."

As the zeppelin descended and the lights grew brighter, Gauge kept his eyes on the doctor. Tonight's preparations had taken a toll on Gauge, and he leaned on his cane more for genuine support than the drama. If this got ugly, he'd need adrenaline to survive, and that was assuming the doctor knew nothing of his own physical capacity. For all Gauge knew, Leon was an expert duelist, and something told the Count a duel tonight wouldn't stop at first blood.

Once the gondola alighted at the top of the clock tower, Leon looked into the camera—right into Lexia's soul—and confessed, "It's true. I am the reason that Lya is only bones."

Now they were getting somewhere.

Nothing mattered.

Not the stares as Lexia ran down the thoroughfare. Nor the tears which were scalding her cheeks. Not even Tija's orders to stave the guards as their team rushed into the Cathedral's foyer. Nothing would stop Lexia from reaching the top of the clock tower and confronting her father.

Lexia ran up the stairs of the Copper Cathedral with Axis, Tija, and Bolt in her wake. Somewhere behind them, Rhyme brought up the tail of this parade. But she didn't care.

Wind blasting from the aircraft's propellers blew Lexia's hair back as she made it onto the roof. Axis stayed in stride and stood with her to watch the machine alight. He took her hand—the one bearing his timepiece—with the one bearing hers. They would face this together.

Stairs unfolded from a gondola beneath the balloon, and Jan walked out to anchor the machine to the balustrade. With their eyes on each other, Leon and Gauge walked out next, not giving the other one an opportunity to make a move. The tension made Lexia's ears want to pop.

Did she believe Gauge's story? Yes. Did she understand why he'd kept some of it to himself until now? Also, yes. He'd clearly wanted Leon to tell her before this big confrontation, and yet...

Here they were.

And Lexia was ready to kill Leon. "I challenge you to a duel." No hesitation. No thought. Only wild impulse. She wanted to kill her father for killing her mother, and now she would see this through.

Just for tonight, Lexia would go against her own declaration. For Lya. For Winter. And for their future.

Lexia spared a glance at Axis, who stared down at her with his jaw clenched. He clearly didn't like this, but after a moment of silence, he nodded. Lexia stepped forward to face her father.

Gauge stepped aside with Jan and Tija, who'd only just now made it up the stairs. Bolt stayed back with Rhyme, ready to apprehend the bodyguard if necessary.

Only Leon stayed in the center with Lexia. Father peered at daughter with nothing in his eyes, unarmed. But Lexia wasn't...

She brushed her arms against her dual hip holsters and considered this moment with a heavy heart. Could she murder her father while he had no way of defending himself? No weapon to draw?

A soft cry.

A loud thud.

And then nothing.

Yes, Lexia could.

When the Heiress let her resolve show in her eyes, the doctor said, "I accept your challenge."

A nightmare come true, Lexia turned her back and listened for Leon's steps as he crossed the roof. When he put his back to hers, the warmth reminded her of every hug, every kiss on her hair, and every tuck into bed. It broke her heart. Unbidden, fresh tears burned her eyes, and she swiped them and her makeup on the back of her hand.

It was time to grow up.

Lexia took the first step forward, away from Leon, and counted, "One." The next, "Two."

Leon walked away, saying in tandem, "Three. Four. Five."

"Six. Seven. Eight."

Winter counted, "Nine. Ten."

Lexia turned, drew both steam cannons, and fired. One in the middle, and one at the top. It took a few seconds for the vapor to dissipate, and in those moments, she held her breath.

Waiting...

The steam cleared, and Leon stood twenty paces away with two holes in him. One in his heart, and one between the eyes. The second shot had split his glasses in two.

Wait...

Stood.

Leon was still standing.

Hyper-focused, Lexia could only see him—Not the surrounding people, but she heard a chorus of gasps which left her dizzy. Or maybe it was the adrenaline?

Either way, the aircraft spun in time to the ticking of the clock tower's hand, and Lexia fell to her knees. She went face-first onto the tiled surface of the roof's veranda—

Warm arms encircled Lexia and kept her from falling to the ground. The body which saved her was strong, and she breathed deep expecting cedar. Instead, she smelled...

Vanilla.

"Father?"

Leon's voice was soft and sad. "Are you vindicated? Is your mother's memory avenged by this shot in my chest? The one in my head is for lying to you."

Stunned, Lexia lifted her head stiltedly and stared at her father in shock.

White skin.

White hair.

And black hollows for eyes.

"Lexia, please don't leave me, too."

Axis gaped. Openly and without restraint. There was no keeping his mouth shut or stopping his eyes from widening.

What.

Was.

Happening?

Gauge looked equally perplexed, but more suspicious than the rest of the faces on the balcony—

No, wait.

Rhyme didn't look surprised at all. Of course, he wouldn't. He'd probably known the truth all along.

Leon cradled Lexia in his arms with his bizarre eyes soft upon hers. She searched them and reached out to touch his hair—The same color as her own. Gone were the lines aging his eyes and mouth. They were replaced by an ethereal youth, reminding Axis of Lya entirely.

The world didn't make sense anymore. And yet...

It made perfect sense.

Whatever Lya had been—Whatever Lexia was... Leon also was.

Angels? Aliens?

Soft as they were, Leon's words still made it to Axis' ears. "My butterfly. My sweet daughter, please forgive me."

Lexia's voice sounded broken as she asked, "Why—Why would you keep this from me?"

"We don't belong here, and I feared if you knew, it would drive you mad as it did your mother."

Axis burned to know the answer to the question Lexia asked next. "What are we?"

Leon tucked an errant strand of Lexia's hair behind her ear as he said, "We are Aegis, and we are far from home." After he spoke, he flicked— actually popped—the bullet from between his eyes, and the slug went bouncing away. The one in Leon's chest fell out when he expanded his ribs on a deep inhale. Yellow blood seeped from each wound.

Gauge made a cutting gesture at his neck, and Jan pressed buttons on a device. From there, the projection stopped playing on the aircraft's canvas, leaving Lexia and Leon to their conversation in private. It raised some questions for Axis.

How much of this had Gauge suspected? For how long? Had he expected this outcome between Leon and Lexia? What about Lya's death?

But Axis didn't want to interrupt the moment to ask. No one did. Everyone watched father embrace daughter and kiss the top of her head.

"I'm so sorry."

Lexia gripped Leon's coat, begging, "Tell me. I can't keep this up anymore. Tell me everything, father, or you really won't ever see me again."

Leon looked over his shoulder and said, "Gauge…"

The Count walked to the pair on their knees and held out his hand, the one with the timepiece. The doctor peered up at Gauge with an accusation in his eyes, but the Count appeared unaffected. He let Leon take the timepiece off his wrist, and in challenge, Gauge leaned down to kiss Lexia on her freckled temple. She soaked the affection in with her eyes closed and lingered against Gauge.

It was enough to make Axis cross the roof and stand at Gauge's side. The Prince took the Count's hand and took the Heiress' petite fingers. They were together, and they were with her.

Lexia smiled with tears in her eyes before she faced Leon again. After a nod from her, the doctor touched the amber jewel, and the world as Axis knew it melted away.

Sensation—the silk of skin, the smell of vanilla, and the bright burning of flames—poured into Axis as a hand slipped into his. He turned and faced Lexia—

No.

Not Lexia.

Lya Tempest stood beside Axis, naked and alive.

She held onto his hand as a ship plummeted through the black of space, the clouds of planetary atmosphere, and into the fertile dirt of an unknown world. All the while, Axis only felt relief at the sight of her smile. War had forced them from their home, but this would not end their race. They would see each other through this adversity and all the others to follow.

These were Leon's feelings, and Axis felt them with the foreigner.

Their ship burrowed deep, forming a crater and tunneling into the planet's mantle. Created for terraforming, it was rich in ore, bacteria, and gas. These released upon the forming planet and restructured it to something suitable for habitation. Meanwhile, Lexia and Leon lived beneath the surface for what felt like eons and not enough time at all.

"Tomorrow, let us see what we have created."

"Let creation have more time, Lya."

"No. Tomorrow..."

There was a *need* in her voice, bordering on sorrow, and for the first time Leon wondered...

Was it so bad living together on their own?

"I should have seen it then."

Axis startled from the trance as Leon emerged at the edge of the scenery. He was wearing the long white coat and tuxedo from Founding Day, and his figure stood out in slow motion against the memories fast-forwarding at high speed. Their emergence, the discovery of civilizations, and the advancement of technology played in the background as Leon told his Verse in Winter's song.

"You can't understand the world from which we hail—Limitless and multitudinal. Our people, infinite.

"*Were* infinite."

Faces flashed, all of them with white hair and white skin, some completely indefinable from the others. Aside from their eyes. Every pupil was different. Lya turned and faced Axis then as the images of her people soared by. Her pupils were the closest to what Axis understood as natural to humans.

Mrs. Tempest, as Axis knew her, took his hand, and smiled at him with the same sad expression she'd shown him in the closet all those years ago. Just as she did then, Lya said, "Protect her…"

The figure of her vanished like the steam from Lexia's cannons, and in her place, the Heiress stood. She held Axis' hand, and at the tug of his other, Axis turned and found Gauge. The three of them stood in a space where memories and lifetimes unfolded all around them.

Outside of their trio, Leon said, "Lya's only mission—to return home—had consumed her to the point of loathing her existence." He met Lexia's eyes to say, "All of it, except for you. *You* were her everything, Lexia. You were her butterfly. Free and unburdened by our history and the truth which Lya couldn't escape…

"We would never return home."

Axis pulled Lexia snug against him and brought Gauge closer until they pressed into Axis' chest. There, he circled their waists and cinched their trio together for support. He did this to prepare Lexia for a hard truth.

Axis said, "I knew Lya was unhappy. I glimpsed her crying more than once as a child."

"As did I," Gauge confessed.

Lexia peered between them with a frown and took a shaky breath before meeting her father's eyes again. "How did she die?"

Leon shook his head and lifted Gauge's timepiece between them. He stared at the stone in its center, saying, "Your mother's not dead, dear. Lya is waiting to go home. This precious diamond preserves her consciousness, her essence, if you will. With the right technology, we could resurrect her, but I am limited by the stagnation of this planet's advancement."

Lexia, Axis, and Gauge peered at the stone. The Heiress let out a soft sob before reaching for the timepiece. Leon let her have it, and Lexia held it in her hands like the treasure it was.

Axis kissed her cheek while Leon asked Gauge, "How long have you known?"

"I first suspected when Lya offered me her bones, but there's still much I don't understand."

Leon gave a bow of his head. "Ask."

Gauge glanced at Axis and Lexia. Overwhelmed, the Heiress opened her mouth, closed it, and shook her head. Unable to form words.

Axis understood. He had so many more questions—An entire world to explore, but right now he couldn't organize a single thought.

Gauge could. "Why did Lya help me form Winter? Your spouse kept her reasoning as much a secret from me as from the rest of the world."

Leon said, "Winter's prior civilization had lost interest in the stars. Only men like Cam Snow sought planets beyond this one. Lya led him to our ship."

One puzzle piece clicked into place for Axis. He breathed, "Ignis Crater."

Leon nodded.

As Gauge helped Lexia strap his timepiece onto her wrist, she said, "So, she hoped Cam would garner enough of a following to explore the galaxy."

Axis leaned forward to help Lexia slip out of her coat for them to better fasten it onto her forearm. Leon finally made a facial expression by frowning at her ensemble. A burgundy bustier over a blue poet's blouse. Someone, likely Sami, had painted Lexia's pants on—literally. The liquid black vinyl had hardened from a gel applied thinly against her skin.

Axis knew Gauge's interest was piqued—inappropriate as the timing was—by the press of the other man's arousal against Axis' thigh.

Time and place.

But, also.

Damn…

"Gauge…"

The Count looked up at his name and met Leon's stare head on. He took a step back from Lexia with a wide split to adjust himself in a way Axis found obvious, but hopefully Lexia's father didn't notice. "Yes, doctor?"

Leon asked, "What is your interest in my daughter? If not for her bones, then…"

"I love Lexia, and I love Axis."

The confession came bold and forthright. No hesitation or confusion. It burned in Axis' heart, and the flames reflected in Lexia's black eyes. They stared across the ethereal space at their lover.

Gauge went back to the couple and reached out his hands. They took what he offered, and Axis indulged in the softness. The Count continued, "I want to unite our triumvirate, truly. Not for Winter's sake, but for ours. I know what you think of me, Dr. Tempest, but your wife was ill and came to me for help. How could you believe I should say, 'no?' Instead, imagine the sorrow in Lya's eyes as she asked me to chip her away. Imagine the sorrow in my heart. She was my friend."

Leon looked away.

Axis hated himself for asking this, but he needed to say something. "Why did Lya fake her death, and why did you let Gauge blackmail you all this time?"

"I know how it looked—How Lya wanted it to look. Even such a being as I am, I didn't want to risk exposure to our enemies. They'd monitored this planet until recently. I'd say they stopped about a decade ago, which barely constitutes a heartbeat to me. We can disguise ourselves, but Lya couldn't bear it any longer. I begged her to find roots here, but she still sought Cam Snow and you, Gauge. We tried for a family, but it wasn't enough to hold her sanity together. She needed a way to anchor me to our mission—To Winter and to Snow."

With Axis' timepiece on one wrist and Gauge's on the other, Lexia stood between her partners and said, "You didn't drive mother to kill herself."

Leon gestured at Gauge, saying, "I thought it was his doing, but I've seen the truth. And now you, Gauge, have returned Lya to her family."

Axis peered down at the timepiece on Lexia's wrist as the others did simultaneously. The faces and places stopped playing around them, turned into darkness with a spotlight shone on their center stage. The Prince asked an obvious but pertinent question, "Where do we go from here?"

Gauge placed one hand on Lexia's shoulder and wrapped the other around Axis, trembling from the day's exertion and his weakness. It made Axis return the embrace and support the Count as best he could. Lexia peered at her father from between them, and Axis kissed the top of her head, prepared to face the future with them.

Leon took in the symbolism and said, "My butterfly, my sweet daughter. You've grown into a beautiful and capable young woman with your mother's spirit and on the path to my wisdom—I ask you. How do you want this to end?"

Axis watched Lexia peer down at her mother's diamond in Gauge's timepiece and smile.

"Happily ever after."

TWELVE

Copper Union

THE TRUTH WAS OUT.

Finally.

As the scene returned to Copper Cathedral, Gauge felt a weight lift off his shoulders. Relief freed a promise left unfulfilled in his soul, knowing he'd finally done the right thing. And his efforts weren't without reward.

Lya was alive, held all this time inside the stone on Gauge's timepiece. Axis and Lexia wanted Gauge and accepted his understanding of love. And Leon was still a man to impress and to make proud.

Winter was free to move forward with all the best in tow.

Gauge squeezed his hand closed, soaking in the sharp pain from the wound in his palm. While Jan had disparaged cutting out the projection device, exploiting the technology had proven satisfactory.

Below, Winter awaited the final determination of Leon's confession, and Gauge hated to keep an audience waiting.

He brought Lexia's delicate hand to his lips and kissed her knuckles. Then he did the same to Axis' larger, much stronger fingers, loaded with potential.

Gauge had to fight to keep a smirk off his face as he stepped back from them and gestured for Jan to reengage the feed. Once his face appeared on the Zeppelin's envelope, he took off his top hat and made a sweeping bow. His people cheered at the return of their show.

With the Heiress and the Prince behind the Count, Gauge straightened and said, "The triumvirate of Founding Families invites you to welcome the future with sector twelve's groundbreaking in two days' time. We aren't complete without you, the good people of Winter. Our three industries—agriculture, mining, and manufacturing—will usher in an age of exploration as we see to the stars for Winter's Diamond. In the meantime, we'll leave you to speculate on the rest of the story. Enjoy the festivities."

The music began again, and people returned to their lines. Din replaced the silence as the crowd below chatted about the night's events. This was a story for the ages.

High heels clicking across the tiled veranda brought Gauge back around. Lexia crossed the roof to her father and opened her arms. Leon took what she offered, closing his eyes in gratitude and soaking in his daughter's affection.

Softly, but loud enough for Gauge to hear, she said, "I'm sorry mother left us both."

"I'm sorry I kept so much from you." Leon opened his eyes and looked at Gauge, saying, "I suppose I should thank you."

Axis jumped on it. "Yes, you should."

Gauge suppressed a chuckle. His new guardian would need reining in for diplomacy's sake. Actually, the idea of reins sounded delectable—

"Thank you, Gauge," Lexia said before stepping back from her father. She squeezed Leon's shoulders with her back to Gauge, but he was certain she gave the doctor a look.

With a little reluctance and a lot of encouragement, Leon managed to say, "Yes. Thank you, but I'm still uncertain of your motivations."

Bolt groaned. "For crying out loud. The man reunited your broken family and strengthened Winter's Founding Families. He secured a future for Ms. Tempest and Prince Flicker to lead, and you're still doubting him?"

Gauge didn't fight the grin this time. There was so much to like about Axis' valet.

Rhyme said on his master's behalf, "Because the Count is holding back, aren't you?"

Well…

As everyone's eyes fell on Gauge, he wondered how far tonight's revelations and confessions should go. 'Ulterior Motive' was the Count's middle name, and in the spirit of honesty, he said, "There's no point in hiding it." He twirled his cane, emphasizing a creak and crack from his shoulder's ball and socket joint. He narrowed his sensitive eyes against the migraine building from all the spotlights against his weak corneas. With a limp, he took a step forward before buckling to one knee. Axis and Tija rushed to his side as he said with a grunt, "I could benefit from the medical technology your people must possess. I'm nearly thirty now, and I don't want to spend another decade of my life condemned to this."

Leon cocked his head to the side, considering. "Did it ever occur to you to ask? I am a doctor, after all."

Laughter, bitter and sudden, left Gauge's lungs on a harsh whoosh as Axis helped him stand. With a few creaks from beneath his coat, the Prince threw one of the Count's arms over his shoulders, and the younger man's warm proximity revived Gauge with a flush.

In his defense, Tija reminded Leon, "You could've offered."

Rhyme clicked his tongue with a gruff, "Yeah. Right. Offer medical treatment to the bastard blackmailing you about your wife's self-induced coma—"

The bodyguard stopped breathing mid-sentence, stiffening with his good instincts. Jan was behind him, having emerged from the shadows with a sword pointed at the base of Rhyme's skull. One good thrust, and poof! No more 'bastard' this and 'blackmailer' that.

But Gauge didn't want the night to end in bloodshed. Besides, Rhyme had a point. "At ease, Jan."

The butler nodded before backing into the shadows and melting away.

Lexia said, "One day, he'll have to teach me how to do that."

All around, Jan's voice echoed, "Anytime, Ms. Tempest."

A chill shot down Gauge's spine, reminding him that his butler was a man to fear. Perhaps the others felt the same as they'd all fallen silent, staring at where the old spy had just been standing.

Leon interrupted the moment to say, "You can relax, Rhyme. I believe the Count and I want the same outcome. A happily ever after."

Gauge met Leon's black hollows across the rooftop and watched them turn back into gray. Gone was the chin-length white hair, now sandy brown with a touch of silver. The signs of graceful aging returned to his face. It was eerie, but also fascinating.

What wonders the Aegis could bring.

Leon said, "Gauge, you help keep my daughter safe, and I will do everything in my power to ensure you all have a long and healthy life. One of youth and vitality with endless adventures and mysteries." He watched his daughter return to Axis' arms and added, "Of friendship and love." The last, he said while peering at Gauge's timepiece on Lexia's wrist.

Axis asked an excellent question. "What about the war with your people? Your enemies?"

Lexia asked, "And how do we resurrect mother?"

"That's easy." The couple glanced at Gauge as he continued, "The Ignis Crater."

Leon nodded.

Tija guessed, "It's your ship."

Bolt muttered something about finding intelligent women attractive, and that girlish blush kissed Tija's cheeks. If Gauge wasn't careful, Rhyme wouldn't be the only one with a partner charmed out from under him.

Lexia held up the timepiece on her wrist. "Can we? Please?" Her voice broke on the last, wrenching Gauge's heart.

At Leon's gentle silence, Axis kissed Lexia's freckled temple and whispered, "It's not time yet."

Gauge assured, "But it will be. Sooner rather than later."

Leon said, "Yes. I'll receive word when the war ends, and then we can return home. Everyone on this roof can come with us. We could encompass all of Winter, should it come to that."

A softness settled in the quiet moment between them, with so much to anticipate in the future—

Wind, cold and slicing, blew across the roof and chilled Gauge's shirtless body to the bone. He couldn't control the shiver, which Axis felt as indicated by his sudden laughter. He shifted his purchase on Gauge around the waist, asking, "Was it worth the fashion statement?"

"To see the look on your face? Hell. Yes."

Lexia laughed for the first time in a long time before pegging Axis with a flirtatious smile. "Your turn."

Tija said, "Yes, I'm sure we're all dying to know what's creaking under there."

Bolt burst out in bright laughter as Rhyme rolled his eyes in disgust. Leon shook his head incredulously. But Gauge was with the ladies.

"Let's have it, your highness."

The big boy scout blushed like one of Gauge's tomatoes before unbuttoning his coat and rolling his shoulders out of the sleeves.

Leon swiped a hand down his face, hiding his eyes. Rhyme pinched the bridge of his nose. Tija blushed and looked away.

Bolt chuckled knowingly. Lexia's eyes filled with heat.

And Gauge's mouth fell open.

"Oh, my."

____

Lexia wanted Axis to take a bite out of her while he was dressed in all that leather. A suede cerulean knight's tunic went to his knees where it gave way to hip-high soft black leather boots and… that was all. Axis wasn't wearing pants or undergarments beneath the tunic, and the slits up the sides gaped here and there to show topaz pelvic bones and butt cheeks, toned and inviting. The splits in Axis' sleeves displayed the bunch of his biceps and the comforting bulk of his shoulder caps. Gold filigree, uncannily similar to Gauge's body paint, decorated the tunic and the inner lining of Axis' coat.

A white knight.

Lexia's hero—Now Gauge's, too.

The People's Prince.

All the leather materials squeaked as Axis shifted his weight from one boot to the other. With one hand on a hip and the other fingering the hilt of his signature sword on his belt, well…

Axis could rescue Lexia anytime. Right here in front of everyone, for all she cared—

"Psst."

Lexia hated to tear her eyes off Axis to glance over at Rhyme. The bodyguard tapped the corner of his mouth and whispered, "You're drooling."

Bolt chuckled.

Gauge blindly patted at Lexia's arm, turning her attention back to him. The Count hadn't peeled his unblinking eyes off the Prince, and he said, "Tell me I'm not dreaming."

Tija and Lexia laughed, but it was Leon who said, "You're not, but I wished I were unconscious."

Axis smiled, and it took Lexia back to their teen years—boyish and sheepish. Uncertain and a little shy. But damn was it sexy.

"Ahem."

Everyone turned and looked over at Tija, who gestured toward the surrounding carnival. She said, "The night continues without us, and we've plenty of work ahead. Let's conclude this drama, then turn in for some much needed rest." The last, she emphasized toward Gauge's cane, which he leaned on with most of his weight.

Lexia took the hint. "There are still more questions without answers. What caused the electromagnetic pulse?"

Leon said, "Gauge's discovery was accurate. In the crater's sediment, you can measure the frequency of a recurring pulse, but did Lya ever tell you the truth as to the why of it, Count Snow?"

Gauge shook his head, his braids swaying with the motion. "I always assumed it's what attracted your ship to our planet in the first place."

Before Leon could answer, Lexia asked, "Was it her doing?" There was no keeping the apprehension from wavering in her voice.

Leon sighed. "No, dear. But in some ways, yes. In our escape from home, our ship sustained damage. The terraforming went wrong. Upon initialization, it reversed the planet's magnetic poles and set loose the hurricanes of ice. They eventually became a torrential downpour, which resulted in a planet lush with life for millions of years. But then it happened again. And again. All while we lived beneath it, waiting for the reversal to stabilize.

"It never did. Not completely, but before too long, civilization started. Your mother couldn't resist leaving the security of our ship to exist amongst others as we'd once done among our people. Even while knowing these new humans would ultimately face another polar axis."

Lexia said, "I want to know so much… About our people and where we're from… Our enemies."

Axis must've heard the sorrow in her voice, because he crossed the space to put an arm around her once more. Everything felt heavy, and the Heiress could do with some rest. Hopefully, in the Prince's arms. The Count's, too.

Gauge said the next as if he'd already guessed the answer, "I want to know why you're visiting Lya's tomb when you know it's empty."

Leon shoved his hands in his coat and looked up toward the domes. "Do you have enough material to make the dome over sector twelve?"

The group peered over at Gauge, who said, "No."

Leon said to the amber shield, "You do now."

Tija asked, "So you no longer wish to build a civilization away from Winter?"

Bolt added, "You want to stay, even with Count Snow's hold on this place?"

Rhyme humphed, but Leon peered between Axis, Gauge, and Lexia. When her father's gaze settled on his daughter, he paid close attention to both timepieces. A hopeful smile spread across Leon's lips. "I don't think that will be an issue any longer."

Hope for the future blossomed in Lexia's chest.

"I'm going home with my father tonight."

Axis wasn't disappointed by Lexia's announcement. Father and daughter had much to discuss, and everyone looked a little tired. Especially Gauge, who kept sneaking glimpses of Axis' thigh. Every discrete glance only confirmed what the Prince had only hoped.

The Count had enjoyed the peep shows, after all.

Throughout the night, the heat between the trio could melt the storms raging outside, but the exhaustion could also leave them all in a week-long coma. There was so much to digest and so much to consider with very little time to sort it all out.

Two days.

In two days, they'd break ground in a new sector and mantle it with a dome made of Leon's bones.

Could the evening get more bizarre—

"Welp..."

The group turned to find Rhyme heading for the stairs, which went back inside the Cathedral. After capturing their attention, he said, "I have a date to finish, and a Tunnel of Love to ride."

The double entendre was not lost on Axis, and it made him spare a glance over at Bolt. The valet had grown close to Sami over the last two weeks, and Axis wondered if Bolt would want to continue the relationship now that the mission was over. Judging by the slight frown on Bolt's face, it was obvious he'd take offense to losing her.

"Bolt..." Rhyme's gruff voice speaking the other man's name brought a puzzled frown to all their faces. Even more so once he said, "Maybe you can watch Matori while I take a turn, and you can ride with Sami while I watch Matori after we finish."

Axis' mouth fell open.

Again.

Beside him, Lexia beamed, and beyond her, Gauge grinned. Her expression was hopeful, while the Count's was knowing. Smug even.

Had the Count suspected Rhyme knew about Bolt's affair all along? Had he predicted this outcome?

Infuriating Tyrant.

After Bolt shook the shock off his face, he crossed the roof in a hurry, saying, "Yeah. That sounds fine to me, but why don't I get to go first, and you can go after?"

Rhyme laughed on the way down the stairs. It was rich and gravelly, filled with a warmth Axis hadn't credited to the bodyguard since this entire mission had started. Rhyme said, "You should consider yourself lucky that you're alive."

Even as Bolt took the steps down, he swallowed loud enough for Axis to hear. "You're right. I'm glad you're not a sore loser."

Rhyme laughed again as he disappeared through the doorway with Bolt eagerly in his wake.

Lexia tugging on Axis' hand brought him back around to her. She smiled, saying, "We should take a turn."

Tija agreed. "We should all enjoy the carnival. I think we've earned it."

Gauge cozied up beside Tija, and she snuggled against his weaker side on instinct. The little movements between them, and the way Gauge subconsciously leaned on her, told the story of their friendship. Axis would like to learn more.

The Count said, "We should all have a go on every ride. Doctor?"

Leon stopped staring at the airship to glance over at Gauge, who asked the doctor, "Will you be joining us?"

Dr. Tempest returned his sight back to the machine, asking, "How much did you pay attention to your father's lessons, Count Snow?"

Gauge's bittersweet smile stirred Axis. Not his libido, but that deep-rooted need in him to protect the people he loved from harm.

Funny.

Two months ago, Gauge riled Axis to no end. Many times, the Prince had thought of challenging the Count to a non-lethal duel. But that was always the answer, wasn't it? He wanted to fight with Gauge, not against him. To challenge the Count, but never to kill him. To be the 'no man,' when so many yeses surrounded them.

Stoke the fire.

Fan the flames.

And now Axis would die to reverse all the pain in Gauge's smile.

The Count said, "You killed him, didn't you?"

Leon said nothing.

Axis and Lexia both played tennis with their eyes, glancing between Gauge and Leon, waiting.

Tija stared at the machine with Gauge, calm in a way which said she was used to the drama in Gauge's life. But also in a way which said she didn't mind if Leon had been the one to end Cam Snow's life.

While Axis hadn't heard Tija's story—A story Gauge had politely left to mystery for Tija's privacy—Axis could guess it now. He recognized the expression of one who'd suffered abuse at the subject of the current conversation. The expression of one who'd attended that tormentor's funeral with so much conflict and pain.

No.

Axis would never need to ask about Tija and Cam Snow. It was in the oceanic depths of her eyes.

But what about the doctor and the professor?

Lexia asked a question which thickened her voice with emotion. "Was mother having an affair with him?"

Leon shook his head, saying, "In an eternity as long as ours, the word 'affair' doesn't apply. Many admirers came and went, but none with such means as Snow to reach the stars. False hope is dangerous. In this way, he posed a threat to your mother's sanity. But no, I didn't kill him. He'd regrettably put your mother in the position to do so."

Axis asked, "How?" before the answer dawned on him. He looked over at Gauge, who said nothing. Only stared at the machine.

"My father loved everything about this other world he was so fascinated with, but my favorites come from the era of this machine. The Zeppelin."

Leon said, "When the time comes, Gauge, I'll ensure you're alive to see this world. All of you."

Tija cut through the tension with sweet sadness in her voice. "In the meantime, that rollercoaster looks exciting and more deserving of our attention than the subject at hand."

Axis squeezed Lexia against his side. "Do you want to join me for the Tunnel of Love?"

She grinned. "I'm flying the Zeppelin."

Gauge called, "Jan?"

The butler's voice permeated the space from all angles once again. "Yes, sir?"

"Do you mind showing Ms. Tempest how to pilot our machine?"

Jan stepped out of the shadows of the spotlights right next to Lexia with a bow. "It would be my pleasure, miss."

Gauge loved the way the Heiress beamed as she followed Jan inside the Zeppelin. Axis made to join her, but Gauge cut in, "Actually, *your* highness, it would do me great pleasure if you would join me on a ride. Might I steal him for a bit, Lexia?"

It hurt a little the way the other two glanced at the cane, then back at Gauge's face.

For fuck's sake.

Yes, Gauge was exhausted, but he'd be damned if he let it stop him from having a good time. He held out the crook of his elbow for Axis to take it. On the other side of him, Tija smiled and shifted so that Gauge had to support himself more. His bones creaked with the effort, but eventually, Tija separated herself entirely to switch places with Axis.

The ladies would take lessons on the Zeppelin, while Gauge and Axis had a talk.

Leon could do whatever the hell he wanted, as long as he made good on his promise.

Youth and vitality.

Soon.

The soon-to-be-thirty bachelor grinned at the Prince as Axis took the Count's arm. Wearily, the younger man asked, "Which ride?"

Gauge chuckled. "You'll see." He waved at the girls. "Bon voyage, ladies!"

They snickered and climbed the gangplank onto the Zeppelin while Jan looked entirely too pleased. Leon stayed on the roof, watching the airship lift away while Gauge escorted Axis down the stairs, away from his white-haired, long-legged safety net.

How delicious.

They discussed plans for sector twelve on their way back down to the carnival. Gauge noted how adorable Axis acted without his chaperon, nervous like a caged tiger, but it was the Count's ultimate goal to put the Prince at ease. So when they approached the very ride Rhyme and Bolt had discussed, Gauge shot Axis a warm smile. One which conveyed the meaning at the core of the gesture.

The Tunnel of Love.

A crowd trailed behind them, following the Count and the Prince with whispers and speculation. All of it melted away as Axis approached the next velvet-lined carriage and held it open for Gauge to slide in. The people gawking didn't matter—All that mattered was the comfortable silence which settled between the two men as the carriage slipped into the dimly lit corridor. It smelled heady of flowers, and the gentle water flowing alongside them relaxed Gauge as much as easing into the seat.

Admittedly, he'd need a soak and some morphine before sleep tonight, and his disappointment tasted as bitter as his poison test kit. All night, Gauge had anticipated spending the late hours with Lexia and Axis in bed together, but with him sore and her going back to the Manor, the opportunity had slipped away—

"Tomorrow."

Gauge blinked and looked over at Axis, who'd broken the silence. The Prince said, "We'll have dinner at the Copper Cathedral—you, me, and Lexia. Tomorrow."

As a man of influence, Gauge never needed to hide his reactions or school his face. He enjoyed doing so to withhold himself and maintain mystery. But with Axis, no.

Gauge beamed.

Axis' smile crooked into a smirk, and the confidence looked good on the Prince. "No more pouting on this ride with me, then?"

That got a laugh out of Gauge. "Was it that obvious?"

Axis chuckled incredulously. "Only to anyone who's sat across from you in a boardroom for the last ten years."

Their laughter died down into the hush of water streaming alongside them. Gauge wasn't a fan of the quiet, so he asked, "Did you ever imagine anything like this? All those hours shouting at each other."

Axis tipped his head to the side, thinking. Eventually, he said, "No, not really, but I'm pretty dense when it comes to flirting."

Gauge blurted out another laugh.

"No seriously. You should ask Lexia about it sometime. She tried for an entire year to seduce me, and I was completely oblivious until I found her naked in my bed one afternoon. Even then, I'd snatched my robe for her before it finally dawned on me."

By the time Axis finished, Gauge's sides were sore, and his grin was so wide that it hurt his jaw. The thought of Lexia frustrated during their teenage years with her long legs bare to Axis in bed and the Prince not catching on almost did Gauge in. Tears spilled from his sore eyes, and he appreciated the low lighting without his glasses.

Which led to a great segue for…

Gauge reached into the pocket of his combat pants and held out a wrapped gift box for Axis. It was about the size of the Prince's fist. Soft green eyes searched Gauge's blue ones, and the Count said, "In case I've been too subtle…"

Axis opened the box and peered down at the solid object inside.

Gauge elaborated, "I figured Lexia would appreciate the pain, but you? Not so much. So to prepare yourself, you'll want to use this throughout the day tomorrow."

Axis' white knight blush was charming and sped up the rhythm of Gauge's heart. Then the Prince laughed in a way which made the damned thing melt, saying, "I don't think I'll be asking Bolt to help me with this."

"Heh. I'm sure Lexia would be more than happy to. Will you be staying at the Manor tonight?"

Gently, Axis took Gauge's hand and traced around the stitches from where Jan had cut out the projection device. Brown skin to blue-black. The Prince said, "Yes. I think Lexia needs me, and it will help us both heal. Gauge?"

With every indention from Axis' fingerprints on Gauge's palm, the Count's breath quickened. He breathed, "Yes?"

Axis stopped and asked, "Will you break your pre-marital laws? Will we spend tomorrow night together?"

Gauge took Axis by the chin and lifted his jaw until the younger man met his eyes. He vowed, "I will end them tonight if that's what you want."

Axis nodded, breaking eye contact to glance down at Gauge's lips. He licked his own as if suddenly parched, and that was enough.

Gauge kissed Axis under the soft glow of the Flicker wicks. The warmth of cedar overwhelmed the scent of tulips blooming in the snow, and Gauge deepened the kiss with a flick of his tongue.

Permission.

Consent.

That virtue mattered to Gauge and to Axis, so when the Prince gave it, the Count's chest swelled with gratitude and pride. They didn't even notice the change in lighting.

"See, Ms. Cloud. I told you the boys were getting along famously."

Lexia.

Axis broke the kiss at the sound of her voice and blinked wide green eyes at Gauge. They hadn't noticed the sharp inhales all around, nor the gasps from the crowd. The ride was over, and their secret was out.

Tija and Lexia stood on the berth, arm-in-arm. The ladies exchanged knowing glances with more than a little flirtation between them. All the while, Axis held Gauge's hand in his suede lap—More than a little enticed by their sudden audience.

Delicious, indeed.

Now Lexia wanted Axis to take a bite out of Gauge. The fantasy left her skin flushed and her breathing erratic. The timing wasn't right tonight, but tomorrow…

Oh, yes.

Tomorrow held promise.

"Ms. Tempest, how did you find the Zeppelin?" Gauge asked as Axis helped him out of the carriage.

Lexia couldn't help the silly grin on her face as she said, "Quite splendid, dear Count. I should like another lesson soon."

Tija nodded. "We could both use further instruction."

Axis caught on and blushed.

But Gauge rolled with it. "Very well. Would you like to join us tomorrow, then?"

"Tomorrow," Lexia and Axis said in unison.

With radiance and grace, Tija separated herself from Lexia and took the arm Gauge was offering her. "Until then, we should enjoy the rides. Ms. Tempest. Prince Flicker. Have a good rest of your evening."

It was obvious to Lexia now the way Gauge leaned against Tija, and she was happy for both of them to have such an understanding.

Sure, there was a kindred spirit between Gauge and Lexia—Gray and exquisite. But nothing like the easiness between her and Axis, like between Gauge and Tija. That came from years together.

Lexia certainly looked forward to finding it with Gauge. She said, "Good night, Ms. Cloud. Count Snow, we'll see you tomorrow."

Gauge waved without looking back as Tija led him toward the Copper Cathedral's entrance. Lexia hoped he didn't feel too left out of the party, and to ensure he didn't miss anything, she said to Axis, "We should head back to the Manor, my handsome Prince."

Axis flashed Lexia a hopeful smile, and goosebumps rose on his skin in excitement.

Tonight was for the long-standing relationships. The comfortable, easy lovemaking. Fresh exploration could wait on some rest—

Oh.

Lexia tried to take Axis' hand, but he was secreting something into his pocket. He leaned against her and whispered, "A gift from Gauge. I'm sure you'll appreciate it—"

"We'll have to walk home."

With a slight start, Lexia turned to find her father waiting for them. He'd disappeared while she was on the Zeppelin. Then his words sunk in, and she raised a questioning brow.

With a soft smile barely on his lips, Lexia's father pointed toward the ice rink.

Bolt and Sami stood at the wall, little Matori in tow. She glided easily across the ice, not at all worried about falling anymore, but what did that have to do with the car—

Another 'oh.'

Bolt and Sami were helping Rhyme onto the ice. For the first time in Lexia's recollection, the bodyguard seemed uneasy but determined, nonetheless. She recalled Sami mentioning the ice skates.

As Rhyme scooted onto the rink, it was obvious he'd been practicing. He glided toward Matori and took her offered hand. Slow and steady, finding their footing together, they skated toward the far end while Bolt and Sami followed in their wake.

Axis glowed beside Lexia, and the sentiment was contagious. She took his arm and held out her hand to take her father's. He accepted, and Lexia teased, "Are you sure you can handle the long walk home, old man?"

"Twice, I have walked across this planet and many others like it."

In wonder, Lexia breathed, "Tell me. Tell me everything."

Axis, Lexia, and Leon walked home in companionable silence after Leon declared they'd all had enough revelations for one evening. They arrived at Tempest Manor with Lexia tired of her heels and ready for a shower. She couldn't wait to wash off the PVC paint poured onto her legs and strip Axis of his courageous ensemble. But first…

"Father, I know it wasn't easy arriving at this point," Lexia said, standing at the bottom of the stairs. "But I'm thankful we made it here. I believe mother would also be grateful the truth was out."

Leon sighed and opened his arms.

Like a little girl in braids, Lexia ran into her father's embrace and squeezed.

He said, "You have unimaginable strength and grace, just like your mother. Now get some rest. We can talk more over breakfast."

Breakfast.

Home.

Family.

Only a few hours ago, this place and what it represented had felt foreign to Lexia. Like a prison, but now she understood. And like Leon, she didn't want to let it go.

"Good night, father."

"Good night, daughter mine." Against Lexia's shoulder, Leon nodded at Axis, "Son."

With more warmth than usual, Axis said, "Good night, Leon."

Lexia took Axis by the hand and led him upstairs. Once inside her room, she locked the door and leaned her forehead against it.

What a day…

Deep breath in.

Long breath out.

Lexia's bangs blew from the rush of the exhale, and she sighed to relieve some tension in her shoulders—

"Lexia, will you help me with this?"

The Heiress turned and faced her Prince, ready for some rest and relaxation after a long night in bed together—

What in the world was Axis holding in that box? Was that…

A second wind brought a grin to Lexia's face. She felt her cheeks flush yellow, but on her stilettos, she glided over to her lover and helped Axis with this fresh surprise.

Oh, what adventures tomorrow would bring.

THIRTEEN

Little Death

L EXIA WOKE THE NEXT MORNING WITH A SONG IN HER HEAD. It was one her mother used to sing her to sleep when father worked late at the university. As a young girl, Lexia hadn't understood the words, nor had she heard anyone else sing or play it. Now she understood everything.

Loss is a beginning/

Sleep: a renewal for Spring/

Tomorrow waits for me/

When Winter ends, I'll see my family.

Alone in bed, Lexia shed a tear—

No.

Not alone.

The inheritor to Winter's Diamond peered down at the heavy timepieces on her wrists. But it was a comforting weight. A reminder of those who loved Lexia and kept her safe. Gauge and Axis. Lya. Leon.

A sparkle captivated Lexia. It was from the round-cut amber bones. More family than Winter awaited Lexia somewhere, and today she awakened ready to find them. To explore the stars.

Lexia rose out of bed, showered, and dressed—Yes, with Gauge and Axis in mind. Tonight, they would share each other, but today, she would spend time with her father.

What to wear?

A tight white button-up shirt accentuated Lexia's breasts, something Axis would appreciate. The puffy sleeves, buttons undone, and belted waist added even more of a flirtatious flair. The shirt was long enough to cover her butt, which she fitted in tight cobalt leggings. Lexia paired the ensemble with black over-the-knee boots, tight to her calves. The stilettos exaggerated the length of her legs, something Gauge would appreciate. She braided her hair with burgundy ribbon woven throughout, complimenting both partners in a swirl of color, while the gold glitter on her cheekbones stayed true to her signature look.

Lexia couldn't wait to see it all on the floor of Gauge's bedroom in a pile of discarded clothes. She went to leave the room, ready for breakfast, when a thought occurred to her. The Heiress went to her desk and retrieved the pile of encoded papers from the locked drawer. The document bulked out her folio, but it would do nicely. With the stack hugged to her chest, Lexia lowered the sheet on the wall, revealing the diagram she'd drawn in kohl.

The sketch was complete now—The story made whole. And Lexia couldn't wait to share it with Winter.

Words reached her at the bottom of the stairs, and she paused rather than turning the corner to the breakfast nook.

"So, Dr. Tempest, when you say you can encompass all of Winter on your homeworld, what do you mean?" Axis sounded genuinely curious.

Leon took a moment, presumably to finish chewing, before saying, "Imagine a sphere filled with a million Winters. Now imagine a second one. They comprise what I call home."

Lexia blinked, trying to fathom it. To someone from a place like that, Winter must feel claustrophobic.

Mother...

Vice versa, the idea of a world so vast left Lexia a little anxious. Winter was home. She'd been younger when the electromagnetic pulse had consumed the planet in ice, and she'd been raised with solid truth.

All the people of Winter had held faith in each other, and they'd survived polar Armageddon because of it. But what would happen if they ever went to Lexia's homeworld? Would they scatter and lose the bond which held them together? How was that better—

"Don't worry about it for now, son. We'll cross that bridge when we come to it—All of us." Leon may as well have read Lexia's mind.

Live for the moment; worry about the rest later—Lexia's motto for all things 'life.' She turned the corner and smiled for the men gathered at the breakfast nook. Leon sat at the head of the table, and Axis sat on his left. Rhyme stood behind the master of the house, leaned against the wall with his arms crossed. He glanced over Lexia's outfit when she entered the room and rolled his eyes with an incredulous shake of his head.

The fact that Rhyme didn't approve of Lexia's clothes made her beam all the more, and she greeted, "Good morning, gentlemen. Fine day, isn't it?"

Axis chuckled into his oats.

Leon snapped his paper and lifted it in a way which hid his reaction. "Good morning, my dear. Grapefruit?" He indicated the other half on the table from his breakfast.

Lexia winked at Axis as she said, "I'm afraid I'll need more calories than that."

Rhyme dropped his arms, uncrossed his ankles, and quit the room with a hearty clearing of his throat. Lexia followed him with her peripheral vision. His boots stomped into the kitchen and stopped at Sami's station, where Bolt was helping the kitchen hand stir a pot of porridge.

The trio acted as one. Bolt dished up a bowl while Rhyme kissed Sami's shoulder. When Bolt handed Rhyme the porridge, Axis' valet leaned down and kissed Sami's other shoulder before the bodyguard left the kitchen to return to the breakfast nook.

With a satisfied smirk, Rhyme handed Lexia the breakfast bowl.

It looked like they could *all* use the calories.

"Lexia?"

The Heiress stopped staring at the bodyguard with a silly grin on her face and faced her father. "Yes, sir?"

Warm light suffused the gray in Leon's eyes, lighting them up so the hollows behind them silhouetted his alien disguise for a heartbeat. It made Lexia's grin soften into a smile, and she asked again, "Yes, father?"

Beside Leon, Axis peeled a banana, peering between father and daughter with all his faith restored. It was written all over his sweet smile before he took a bite of the potassium-loaded fruit.

Leon cleared his throat to say, "I'd like for you to venture out to the Copper Cathedral this afternoon with a handful of volunteers. I'm sure Count Snow's people will need a great deal of help to clean up after last night's carnival."

Lexia was torn. On the one hand, this would give her a wonderful excuse to arrive early for her plans with Gauge, but on the other hand…

"What about the rest of Founding Season…" Lexia snapped her fingers when an idea struck her. "I can offer the volunteers vacation for the first week of on-season."

Behind Leon, Rhyme gave an approving dip of his head, while Axis beamed at his fiance. Leon's chest swelled as he said, "Agreed." He looked over at his future son-in-law around his newspaper, asking, "What about you? Do you have any volunteers looking to ease into the next work season?"

Lexia almost clapped with giddiness—her father was being so accommodating—that was until Axis shook his head. She pouted as the Prince finished a sip of his orange juice and said, "I need to meet Tija, Mrs. Tenz, and Phoro at the factories. Kol's bringing his family. We're preparing to launch the union models at the groundbreaking, and we need everything to run smoothly."

With a slump of her shoulders, Lexia plopped ungracefully on her father's right and doodled in her porridge with her spoon—

"But I'll be along shortly with a cleanup crew of my own."

Lexia's eyes met Axis', where he smirked at her. But it wasn't his usual boyish grin—

No.

There was a glint there. It reminded Lexia of his voice a few days ago when Axis had taken pleasure from causing her pain during their lovemaking. The Prince had enjoyed the Heiress' torment then, as he was enjoying postponing her release now.

Lexia.

Couldn't.

Breathe.

Axis turned his smirk down into his second bowl of oats. He wanted it to be obvious he was also storing carbs for later today as he said, "Wait for me before you begin, would you?"

Unable to form words, Lexia nodded.

Axis met her eyes as he bit into a strawberry, red juice dripping down his chin. He licked it from the corner of his full and soft mouth—

"Ms. Tempest, you look lovely this morning," Sami said as she came to collect the empty dishes.

It was enough to break the spell, and only then did Lexia realize her father and Rhyme were trying really hard to blend in with the furniture. Embarrassment boiled in Lexia's alien blood. Flushed from head to toe, she snatched her manuscript folio, and fled the breakfast nook—

Oh, wait.

She popped her head back into the room long enough to say, "Thank you, Sami. You have a lovely day."

Rhyme's irritating laughter followed Lexia out of the Manor.

"Bolt, I promise. This is the last outfit I'll ask you to help me with."

"Sir, you are an honorable man, and that makes you an abysmal liar."

After a snap here and a buckle there, Bolt added, "I'm not sure how you expect Ms. Tempest to get you out of this thing."

Axis chuckled and said, "With help."

With a pat on Axis' back, Bolt said, "I think I liked you better when you were shy."

The Prince turned and faced his valet, and Bolt turned red as a beet. He scratched the back of his neck in an awkward gesture as he said, "On second thought, I believe Count Snow may have been the best cure for your confidence issue."

Axis grinned and slipped into his new cobalt frock coat with black and gold jacquard on the lapels. "I'll take it." He patted Bolt on the bicep, saying, "Come on, old friend. Let's head to the factory now."

"You know? I'm not sad Sami volunteered to clean up around the Copper Cathedral. At least I'll have some company while you three sully the Count's expensive sheets," Bolt mused as he went to the driver's seat of the car.

Axis paused before sliding into the backseat, asking, "Do you suppose they're made of copper, too?"

Bolt shot Axis a flat, incredulous look, rolled his eyes, and got behind the wheel. "Yup. I definitely preferred you as a contradicting wallflower."

The Prince laughed all the way down Flicker Avenue.

Tija, Mrs. Tenz, Kol, and Phoro waited outside the factories, and Axis practically left the car before Bolt put it in park, eager as he was to move on from this afternoon to the evening.

"Hello and thank you for joining me here at the end of Founding Season. Your dedication will not go unrewarded."

Tija beamed and reached up on tiptoe to kiss Axis' cheek. Mrs. Tenz did the same, much to the Prince's blushing surprise.

Phoro said, "I'll settle for a handshake, Prince Flicker," while the quiet Kol simply nodded.

Axis clapped his hands and chafed them together. "Is everyone ready for the groundbreaking?"

Tija laughed.

Mrs. Tenz snickered.

Phoro shook his head, incredulous.

And Kol blinked a few big ones at the Prince.

"What?" Axis glanced at each of them.

Bolt looked equally confused before Tija nudged Axis and said, "Don't you think you should head over to the Copper Cathedral and help clean up after the carnival?" Her knowing smile made Axis want to look away.

Unfortunately, that put him face-to-face with Mrs. Tenz, who beamed up at the Prince. "Live in the moment, Prince Flicker, and the moment is waiting for you at Snow Plaza."

Phoro assured, "We have everything under control here. You've worked hard to reunite the lines and repair the damage left by your father's legacy."

"Take a break," Kol finished. "Ms. Tempest deserves your unfettered attention."

Their shared knowledge of how Axis wanted to spend his night brought a burn to his cheeks and a rise in his blood pressure. He closed his eyes to the sudden familiar panic—

No.

Not now.

A gentle hand on his back, small and kind, soothed Axis before Tija's sweet voice further combated the anxiety. "We can never let go of the past, not completely. That's our curse."

Axis opened his eyes to meet Tija's blue ones, filled with the same compassion in her voice as she said, "But at least in Gauge's arms, we can forget it for a little while. Embrace what the future has to offer, Prince Axis."

Tija *understood*.

Even with their audience, Axis asked, "What about you?"

Her laughter charmed the last of the fear out of him as Tija assured, "One day, absolutely, but you should celebrate as a power throuple before we get into the complications of anything more."

Axis thought about all those mouths and limbs, and laughter erupted from him. "I could see that being complicated." But it was certainly a very enticing complication.

A sudden and sharp swat to his ass made Axis laugh harder as Tija waved the sting from her hands. She said, "Head on to the Cathedral now. We'll be ready for groundbreaking in two days. You'd better not surface until then, am I clear?"

"Yes, ma'am."

With winks and smiles all around, Axis slid back into the car and waved to the people in his life. It was fine that they knew his desires and intentions, because theirs were in the best place. As for anyone else? Well, Axis couldn't give a damn what anyone else thought of him.

Live in the moment and forget the rest.

At least for tonight.

Jan had informed Gauge of Lexia's arrival in time for the Count to sit down at his grand piano for a few chords. But as the lovely Heiress glided into the conservatory, Gauge decided a little more finger work would do. From the stilettos to the braids, everything about Lexia Tempest screamed 'fuck me,' and Gauge intended to do just that.

But not before Axis arrived.

No.

They would start this threesome the right way—Together.

So even though the long-legged temptress sauntered her way over to the piano with a light trace of her fingers across the glossy casing, Gauge took a page from Axis' book and clenched his jaw tight.

Nope.

Lexia would not win this battle of wills—

The siren slid onto the bench next to Gauge, and he'd be damned for giving Lexia the space to do so. Sweetly, her soft fingers joined his gloveless ones in the melody on the higher keys—light to his darkness. Flirting in song, wordlessly.

Well, until Gauge snatched Lexia by the waist and lifted her ass onto his lap. She gave an excited, "Yip!" But the Count remained true to the Prince. No other touching. Not even a kiss on those inviting, naked lips. Rather, the Heiress joined him once more in the tune. It proved a challenge at this angle, but that was something Lexia would never shy away from—

Lexia's blouse gaped a bit, revealing her bare breasts beneath and driving Gauge mad. She knew now that he was well and truly affected beneath her leggings. To drive the point home, Lexia parted her thighs slightly and twisted her hips against Gauge, eliciting an involuntary groan.

Maybe three more seconds of this, and Gauge might buckle.

Lexia's fingers moved onto his, playing with his naked hands in tandem. She could predict the notes which Gauge played from the heart, further proving their undeniable compatibility. Somehow, this turned him on more than the way she parted her lips on a gasp—

Three.

Two.

"Prince Flicker has arrived, sir."

"For god's sake, send him in, Jan." Gauge didn't mind that he sounded as desperate as he felt, because Lexia rewarded him with a knowing smile which suited her bedroom eyes.

Axis walked into the room with a big grin on his face. It was so open and honest that it took Gauge's breath away. Lexia's sudden inhale told the Count the effect was contagious.

Before Jan left the room, Axis said, "I'm grateful you two didn't start without me," and Gauge's heart expanded. His brave knight had come so far. Once a display of affection so public would've sent the poor Prince into hiding, but now…

Axis shrugged out of his frock coat and dropped it on the floor.

Every single bit of material on Axis' athletic frame was snapped or buckled together in a mishmash of leather and silk, which left everything and nothing to the imagination. Snap button fastening tightened a corset around the Prince's billowing shirt, which, itself, was buckled at the seams. The same fastening lined his pants all the way down to his calf-high boots. Every seam revealed toned muscle.

Easily, the Count and the Heiress could unwrap their Prince like a present, and Axis beamed as if their shock was the response he'd hoped to see.

Wearing yesterday's stubble, Gauge felt under-dressed. He thought they'd be naked in no time, so he hadn't bothered to dress for the occasion. Instead, the Count had showered and slipped into a casual button-down and houndstooth trousers. He hadn't even bothered to button the shirt, which likely only enhanced the sensation of Lexia's silky hair against his bare chest as she sat in his lap.

Gauge hadn't thought the whole 'sit in his lap' move entirely through. Back to Axis' fantastic outfit, the Count found enough breath to say, "I've been thoroughly upstaged."

Lexia swung one leg high, almost up to their faces, before hopping out of Gauge's lap with an excited cry and running into Axis' arms. He lifted her and swung her around—

Wait a minute.

There was no ass to those pants.

Gauge damned near fell out. Until…

What was he seeing on the Prince's topaz skin? Small mounds of circular flesh peppered his cheeks here and there—

Scar tissue.

Burn scars, to be specific.

The Count swallowed hard before he could squeeze out, "Axis…"

The Prince's face fell, and he lowered the Heiress slowly, a puzzled frown forming on her lips. She asked, "What's wrong?"

But Axis looked as if he knew, and he shut down.

"No." Gauge rushed across the room as fast as his limp would let him. He took Axis' face between his glove-free hands and forced the Prince to make eye contact. The Count begged, "Please forgive me."

Axis touched Gauge's hands, and a tear spilled from burgundy lashes. "I already have."

The Prince captured the Count's lips and slipped his fingers into Gauge's braids. Axis' short hair felt surprisingly spiky to Gauge's gloveless hands, making it a completely unique experience to Lexia's silky tresses. Both felt stimulating and enticed Gauge to explore further.

Live in the moment.

The Count reached out, and the Heiress brought his sensitive fingers to her lips. She kissed the swirls of his fingerprints, then around the cut in his palm, until he cradled her cheek.

Axis broke the kiss to pull Lexia between them, her back to his front. Shorter than both men, but tall enough to maintain eye contact with Gauge, Lexia kissed the Count's bare collarbone, chest, neck—All the while, the Prince kissed one of her shoulders, while Gauge nibbled her earlobe.

Sighs and gasps abound.

Gauge went to put his hands around Axis' waist, and the Prince reached for the Count's nape—

"Ow! My nose!"

Truly, the Heiress' button nose had poked Gauge in the chest, and she snorted in her giggles. Lexia complained, "You're both too solid for this."

Gauge chuckled, only to hear the sound echo from Axis' throat.

Lexia gave an incredulous sigh. "Boys…"

"Just you wait, sweet butterfly. I have so much more in store for you."

Lexia's heart skipped a beat while staring into Gauge's naked eyes. A devil hid behind all that blue ocean and churned beneath the surface with a punishing ebb and flow she couldn't wait to experience. Meanwhile, Axis' chest against Lexia's back comforted her with all the familiar touches and scents—He knew her body better than anyone. And he knew exactly where to press his lips, slip his tongue, or simply breathe against Lexia's skin to resuscitate her frozen pulse.

Someone get her a fan. It was too hot in here.

Almost as if Gauge had heard Lexia's thoughts, he took her hand and pulled her with him. In a reassuring grip, Axis took her other, and they left the conservatory together. Thirteen stories seemed like a lot to climb, but it went by in a blur following the Count's ass up the stairs. No, it wasn't as captivating as Axis' bare cheeks in that enticing puzzle of leather and silk, but Gauge kept fit. The power in his gait only added to the signature sway of his hips.

They arrived in a heady haze—Axis breathing heavily behind Lexia, not because of the exertion but because of the effort to resist. At the top, he gave in and pulled Lexia into his powerful arms for a kiss. Poised on the landing, just one misstep away from a long and painful tumble, the Prince arched the Heiress' back over the brink. Dizzy, her blood rushed in two separate directions, leaving her drunk on his kiss.

With Lexia's eyes closed, she couldn't see what Gauge was doing to Axis, but she heard the whisper of skin-on-skin friction. She moaned against her lover's lips before separating them to see.

The Count was kissing the Prince's shoulder where a seam had left it bare. He circled the soft press of his lips around one of Axis' scars until he stroked his tongue along the diameter of it.

Axis' eyes rolled back, and his lashes closed on a flutter which matched his breath. All the while, Lexia could fall at any moment if her Prince didn't maintain his purchase. She wrapped one leg around Axis' trunk of a leg and gasped when Gauge lifted it higher until she squeezed against Axis' hip.

Hard to soft.

Eager to ready.

Lexia had to swallow twice before she could say, "Take me to the bedroom."

Gauge pressed against Axis' ass, grinding the Prince's hips into the Heiress' thin leggings and the slip of material she barely considered panties. With their gasps, the Count assured, "You're not in charge here anymore, sprite. Just hold on tight and enjoy the ride."

Literally.

Lexia wrapped her other leg around Axis' hips and locked her stilettos against his bare cheeks. She encircled his neck to keep from falling down the stairs, and the Prince didn't even need to flex to sustain them. He could make love to her right there, and she wouldn't care—

A snapping of fingers brought the engaged couple back to reality. Gauge waited at the door to his room with a sly smile that said he wouldn't mind watching. Still, he nodded for them to join him inside.

With no effort at all, Axis swung Lexia around the landing and toward the bedroom. She let out a little, "Woo!" from the rush of movement and giggled as she buried her face in her lover's neck and kissed the sensitive skin there.

Axis practically purred against Lexia as they made their way to Gauge's obscenely enormous bed. Truly, one could have an eight-person orgy here without feeling compressed. Eager and excited, the Prince sat down on the edge of the bed, and the Heiress sat astride him, tracing her fingers along the buckled seam which revealed his chest. Gazing into the love raw in his eyes, she sucked in her bottom lip and circled her hips—

Metal clanking brought them both around.

Gauge leaned against one gigantic bedpost holding…

When Lexia beamed at the shackles in his hand, Gauge said, "Your highness, would you care to repay our sprite for her indiscretions in this Cathedral?"

Too excited, the words didn't sink in, and Lexia only panted at the devilish smirk on Gauge's lips. She didn't hear Axis agree. She just knew that suddenly she was flipped onto her back on the silk sheets, wrists pinned by a lover who'd never gotten aggressive with her before.

But dear Eternity...

The smile on Axis' face was so foreign, so punishing, so...

Delicious.

Lexia spread her legs to his hips—

No.

She couldn't

Axis kept them pinned closed with the exquisite weight of his heavy thighs. The metallic clank of the shackles came closer as Gauge appeared over the Prince's shoulders. He dangled them with a little shake before taking one of Lexia's wrists and clasping the copper around them.

Lexia's heart raced, and the urge to struggle made her wiggle beneath Axis and withhold her other hand from Gauge—but he didn't take it immediately.

No.

The Prince lifted the Heiress around the small of her back and sat her up against a bedpost. Then the Count shackled the other wrist behind her back, behind the post. She tugged, unable to move or to reach. With a little inelegant effort, she managed to tuck her legs beneath her for the sake of comfort. All the while, the men sat back, out of reach.

Lexia pouted. "No fair."

Gauge chuckled while saying, "Oh, I believe we've yet to ante up. For several days, you had me all to yourself."

He turned on his knees and faced Axis. The Count ran his fingers through the Prince's short hair, and when Axis kissed the wound on

Gauge's palm, the sharp and painful inhale brought a flutter to Lexia's pulse. Her heart stopped altogether when Axis opened his eyes and shot her a dark look over Gauge's hand.

"Now it's my turn."

Axis gripped Gauge behind the nape and brought the Count forcefully against his lips. Brown fingers swept over black skin as the Prince explored Gauge's bare chest. The latter wasted no time in gripping Axis' naked ass, pressing their hips together.

Meanwhile, Lexia stared, unblinking and unbreathing.

What a moment to live for.

Axis enjoyed the taste of Gauge almost as much as the pout on Lexia's lips. He hated to admit it, but some part of him—some dark part he'd likely inherited from his father—took pleasure and satisfaction from touching the Count outside of the Heiress' reach. There was a measure of comfort in the fire in Lexia's black eyes as she watched. Axis glimpsed it as he broke the kiss, tilted Gauge's head back, and sucked on the other man's Adam's apple. She didn't know she was doing it, but with each press of their lips on each other, with each exploring caress, Lexia's breathing quickened and her thighs spread a little more.

Almost as if Gauge knew Axis' attention was more focused on Lexia, the Count gripped the Prince's hips and forced them closer. They met eyes, and need shone in Gauge's blue stare. Axis smirked into the next kiss.

Maybe he took dark delight in antagonizing them both, and maybe…
that wasn't so bad. The rewards certainly seemed worth it.

To extend the gratification, Axis laid down, stretched out on his
front, peered over his shoulder at Gauge, saying, "I put your gift to
good use." He rocked his hips from side to side, and a bell rang to prove
his point. "Care to do the honors?"

The Count's eyes darkened to storm clouds, but he shook his head
and said, "Not so fast."

Across the bed, Lexia gave a soft whimper as Gauge unsnapped
the back of Axis' corset, one button at a time. The Prince sighed and
rested the side of his face on his folded arms, watching the Count
undress him slowly. He closed his eyes as Gauge untucked Axis' loose
shirt from the back of his patchwork pants.

A hand, impossibly soft and warm, slipped under the material and
lifted it higher until cool air kissed Axis' bare back. Someone hissed
on an inhale, and Axis opened his eyes to see the same expression on
both Gauge and Lexia's faces.

Starved.

They shared a heartbeat, and it feasted on the sight of Axis' skin.
But while there was hurt in Lexia's eyes at the Prince's worst secret,
there was something softer in the Count's stare.

Understanding.

Respect.

Love.

While Axis watched, Gauge leaned forward and kissed the mound
of scar tissue which made up the Prince's back—A long history of thin

belts, spiky whips, and Flicker wick flames had ruined this landscape of Axis' finely honed muscle. A body forged not from vanity or athleticism, but from necessity and self-preservation.

Axis was the protector—the defender—because no one had been there to protect or defend him.

He blinked once.

Twice.

Before Axis knew it, he'd squeezed his eyes shut as tears, hot and plump, sprung from a well hidden deep within him. Lexia loved him— He *knew* it for certain. But she'd never been able to understand or even face this part of him.

Gauge touched every mound, kissed every groove, and accepted every centimeter of Axis' ugliness with reverence and empathy.

There was a pause where Gauge's lips hovered just above Axis' skin. He felt the Count breathing there, warm and reassuring. It prompted Axis to open his eyes once more.

There were tears in Gauge's eyes. Lexia's, too.

Overwhelmed and ready to welcome this emotion between them, Axis confessed with all his soul, "I love you, Gauge."

A smile spread across Gauge's lips before it crooked into a smirk. With a strangled laugh, he said, "Professing your love already? Your highness, we've barely begun."

Lexia let a giggle escape.

And Axis rolled his eyes incredulously. "You Tyrant. Get on with it, then. I've heard so much about your brand of lovemaking—"

"Fucking," Lexia corrected.

"—Show me what you're made of, Count Snow."

There was no time to react—no time to stop Gauge—before the Count pulled the toy free of Axis. The Prince let out a hard cry followed by a moan at the sudden sensation, enticed by the hollow left behind which begged to be filled once more. And it was.

Gauge explored Axis with his fingers as he prompted the Prince to turn on his side. There, the Count unsnapped the fastenings of the front of Axis' pants, releasing him. Gauge's lips were indeed as soft as his hands, but also wildly more experienced at coaxing pleasure from Axis.

That was no insult to Lexia. In the corner of Axis' eyes, he watched her scissoring her legs for friction, and his heart expanded at her secondhand excitement. The woman could draw climax after climax from her lover any hour of any day, but Gauge knew where to lick, to tease, and when to incite release.

Panting and biting his lip, Axis gripped Gauge by the braids and held on as the Count was quick to the finish line, eager to move forward to more unclaimed territory. Dirty and yet pure in the desirous expression, Gauge cleaned up his mouth with his fingers and sucked on the tip of one with a delighted smile.

"You taste like snow, your highness."

Axis rose onto his knees, reached out, and said, "I want to know what you taste like, tyrant—"

"No." Gauge gently laid Axis onto his back, saying, "We waste too much time, and I'm afraid our butterfly has no more patience to exercise. I'll unwrap the rest of our present and take you now, unless you'd rather—"

"Have me now, Gauge. I've never been more ready for you."

With an aggravating and self-assured chuckle, Gauge spread Axis' legs and began unbuckling and unsnapping the last of which held his clothes together. Axis went to help by stripping the material from the sleeves of his arms, but Gauge stopped him.

"No, leave those. I quite like the way they frame you."

That wink meant the world to Axis as Gauge stripped the Prince bare from the waist down. Naked beneath another man, the Prince tried to position himself best for the Count, and the more experienced of the two leaned forward until his lips brushed Axis' ear, saying, "I got you."

No anxiety.

No fear.

There was only a deep inhale followed by a soft cry, matched by Lexia's voice as Gauge claimed Axis. It was clear from the beginning that the Count wasn't a man to prolong pleasure, and the Prince looked forward to educating his new lover in patience, but not before an exquisite orgasm rocked his foundation.

Lexia found release at the same time, or so Axis could assume. Before he could bask in the afterglow, he was on all fours, rushing to the other side of the bed with Gauge in tow.

There was a loud crack, followed by a sudden thunderous snap.

Panting, both men looked over to the source at the corner of the bed. Lexia stood before them while the pillar of a bedpost fell back behind her. Her hair had fallen from its plaited braids and haloed her in wild white waves.

A bedroom angel—

No.

Not an angel.

Lexia held up her copper chains and snapped them apart.

The devil was indeed in Gauge's bed, but not within the Count. This devil had wings, and they were in the shape of a gilded butterfly.

Lexia had stripped herself of her leggings and dropped what remained of her black panties on the bed. Her shirt kept her decent, but the short length of it left her bare legs on display. The buttons were gone, and the silk fell off to one side with the tops of her breasts kissing the air.

The Heiress stood over the Count and the Prince, hands on her hips and fire in her eyes.

"Both of you take me. Now."

Apparently, the Aegis possessed unimaginable strength.

Gauge couldn't help but grin up at Lexia, demanding they fuck her after taking each other with her just out of arm's reach. She looked feral with the fireplace roaring behind her, silhouetting her wild hair and demanding stance.

"Damn, I love you, woman."

The words came to Gauge easily and made him grin even broader as he held his arms out to Lexia. With so little hesitation as to make the Count chuckle, the Heiress fell into his embrace and pulled Axis into joining it. Rushed kisses and exploring caresses followed. Both men entered her with fingers first, ready and eager on a gasp and a cry.

Lexia arched between them, and Gauge took point, teasing what her breasts offered before lowering Axis onto his back. The Prince—mercifully—followed the Count's lead without question or awkward discussion. This allowed Gauge to easily position Lexia over Axis, where the two met hip to hip with brief resistance.

Gauge wondered if Lexia had ever been this ready before today as Axis' eyes rolled back with a moan. Yes, they moved together in a concert so beautiful, Gauge wanted to play the score with his fingers alone. Alas, that's not what the butterfly had demanded of her lovers.

So Gauge took Lexia as well.

Axis on bottom, Lexia in the middle, and Gauge on top against the Heiress' elegantly arched back.

'Decadent' was the only word to describe it—

No.

'Indulgent' worked best.

There was nothing like a well-matched threesome, and Gauge had only experienced one other in his life. This moment with this pair topped it beyond reality. Lexia and Axis' familiarity with one other combined with their fresh wonder for Gauge left them in a symphony of stunning sensation and a marriage of melodic moans all in simultaneous satisfaction.

Together.

Apart.

Sighs.

Cries.

Gasps.

And more gasps came, as Gauge circled Lexia's neck with his fist from behind. Axis drank from her lips, stealing her breath in a kiss. Together, they drowned her in ecstasy and pain, lust and punishment.

Just the way the Heiress liked it.

Wanted it.

Had craved it for so long that Gauge felt it in Lexia's release, and the intensity of it brought his own—Brought Axis with them.

Hours passed this way.

Days could go by if they wanted.

No one would care if they missed the launch of the new sector by a week—

Well. No one but Gauge.

As much as he could lose himself in Lexia and Axis forever, he put Winter first.

After their third meal in bed together, second shower, and god knew how many orgasms—or hours for that matter—the throuple lay in bed together, fully sated.

No. Not true.

They'd never be truly satiated of one another, and perhaps that's what would make this relationship stand up to Lexia's eternities.

But that was a thought for another time.

Right now, Gauge simply luxuriated in their shared breathing. Chest rising and falling in love and warmth. They'd made a cozy nest of sheets and pillows in front of the fire and rested on one another.

Naked.

Glorious.

Happy.

Then Lexia interrupted the moment—as a butterfly would—with a sudden, "Oh, yeah!"

With energy Gauge couldn't fathom from where she stored it, the long-legged beauty hopped out of her perch on his lap and rushed over to the long-forgotten pile of her things. A little frown of curiosity formed on Axis' face, and both men exchanged an interested glance as Lexia hurried back across the room with her folio, of all things.

"I remembered!" Excitedly, she held it out to them like a kitten presenting a dead mouse. So cute and full of enthusiasm. But also a little skepticism. As if she hadn't trusted her human to hunt this down on his own.

Axis took it first and held it out to Gauge. The Count smiled and opened it between them, both peering over the documents stored inside like two lovers reading together on a picnic.

Both frowned.

The words written in gold and black ink made no sense.

Well, not at first.

The longer Gauge narrowed his sore eyes at it, the more the words fell into a pattern—A code. It was encrypted.

The Count spared a glance at the Heiress, who smiled, proud of her innovation, as the story started to calibrate.

A long time ago, two angels fell from heaven, safe in their warm embrace. For eons, they stayed this way until the most beautiful angel could no longer take the solitude and broke free from the confines of their isolation. She gifted the world with her elegance and grace.

But this still couldn't make the beautiful angel happy.

Nor could a loving miniature of herself.

So the angel fashioned a world which would keep her daughter safe.

That's where the story changed from a prequel to the events of the last two months. From Axis failing to propose to Lexia in that restaurant, to her meeting Gauge as adults, and the beginning of their affair—but it wasn't all one-sided. This compendium of events and evidence forged the entire story in a gilded casing of love and fortitude.

Lexia said, "This is Winter's Verse."

Axis smiled and asked, "When did you find the time to write all this? To piece it together?"

But Gauge knew the answer. "You started when you were trapped inside the Manor for a week on your own. Like your mother, you found a way to cope."

With a sad smile, Lexia reached out and cupped a cheek on each man, saying, "But unlike her, I have you two. Intimately. Completely. I don't need to hide from either of you, and I know you'll help me finish the story. Together."

Gauge echoed her smile and tucked a wild tendril of hair behind her ear. "I know it upheaved your entire existence, but I'm happy we met again."

"Me, too," Axis said before kissing Lexia on the cheek.

Then the Heiress said something which reached the Count's core.

"*Winter* is happy we three met again."

Yes.

It was.

FOURTEEN

Platinum Winter

On the first day of work season, Lexia snuggled her ass against the front of Axis' hips, naked in bed. Comfy and happy. With a little stretch forward, she kissed Gauge's shoulder, squeezed between them as she was. Unfortunately, both men ran hot, and at least one of them snored.

"I need a cold shower," Lexia said before springing from their nest.

The sound of their male laughter followed her naked jaunt to the en suite. As the cool water washed away hours of gray, Lexia reflected on the past two months. So many ups and downs. Rights and wrongs. But from all of it, she took away the comfort of sleeping for the first time in Axis' arms. Gauge's, too. It was perfect, and everything was wonderful.

The boys hadn't joined Lexia for the shower, choosing instead to indulge one another to a couple's rinse while she dressed. She knew exactly which clothes from Gauge's closet she wanted to steal: the steampunk colonel coat. She paired it with some tights which employees from Tempest Manor had delivered during the last two days. With long legs as blue as her freckles in the black coat with copper buttons, Lexia felt like part of Winter's defenses. It was fitting with the domes and all. Both timepieces and some heavy eye kohl finished the look.

Lexia's men traded places with her in the closet before she'd dressed—Gauge had led Axis inside while saying, "I finally get you out of the closet, your highness, and now I'm leading you right back in."

Axis had laughed a boyish chuckle. It was one Lexia hadn't heard since the first night he realized she wanted to make love to him.

Long, long ago.

The People's Prince had pulled back the sheets on the Heiress' naked body, asleep in his bed, freaked, and reached for a robe to cover her before the big boy scout had gotten the hint. To think, it had taken them six years for them to sleep in a bed together overnight. Finally.

Lexia smiled at the nest over in front of the fire. At a whistle from the closet, she turned back around and stopped breathing. When had Gauge gotten Axis' measurements? Or found the time to commission all of this?

Both men stood in their matching suits—The Prince in cobalt and the Count in burgundy. The knee-length coats were solid, but the waistcoats beneath sported a black and gold swirl, mixing the colors. Silk solid-black button-down shirts with black ties formed the next layer closest to their contrasting skin—a cravat for Axis and a bow tie for Gauge. Each wore metal hardware befitting their crests displayed on the buttons, silver flames and copper comets, respectively.

Axis must've enjoyed Lexia's reaction, whatever was on her face with her mouth slightly apart, because his lips blossomed into a beautiful grin. A little shy, completely masculine, and all Axis.

Gauge smirked and said, "We were hoping you might like to dress our hair?" He twisted one of his braids for emphasis.

Lexia was ready for them to go at it again, but there wasn't time for them to have sex, shower, and get ready once more—So tonight, they'd celebrate another triumph. Until then, braids, hair gel, and guy liner.

As a preteen, Lexia had attended the groundbreaking for Winter's first dome. It had been an awe-inspiring and terrifying experience. One built entirely on faith. Faith in the belief the world would end and faith in the people who'd come together to survive it.

Now here they were, expanding for those very people. Under her family's bones, no less.

From Gauge's room, they took the stairs down to find Jan standing at the bottom in the foyer. He bowed before saying, "Ms. Tempest, you're a vision, as always."

Lexia didn't hesitate to ask, "Jan, will you tell me your story? It's the only piece I'm missing from my Verse." She hugged the thick folio to her chest.

The butler straightened with a glint in his cold brown eyes and nodded. "Of course. On our way to the train, if you don't mind?"

Axis and Gauge held out the crook of their arms, wearing varying degrees of humor on their faces. One astonished by Lexia's audacity.

The other, amused by it. Both men admired her, but both for different reasons.

It warmed Lexia's heart as she accepted their arms and followed Jan out to the veranda. There, the rear of the Copper Cathedral enjoyed the sight of the Ignis Crater. The Aegis ship, buried deep within, sat waiting for a signal. One which may never come.

Jan said, "Once upon a time, there lived a boy in a school for young men, a good distance from where we stand now. This boy suffered, as many men do. But unlike most men, he didn't suffer alone—"

The train whistle blew, and Lexia beamed at the copper rail car which pulled up to the veranda. She glanced up at Gauge, and he peered back down with a cocky grin. He said, "Yeah. The ladies love it."

"Oh, I'm sure," Axis said, rolling his eyes.

Lexia muttered to herself, "You loved his train last night—"

"What was that?"

"Nothing."

Gauge burst into laughter as they boarded the train. He led them to what practically qualified as a throne in the car's center, saying, "Be sure to strap in."

Lexia smiled sweetly at Axis, all innocence. The Prince shook his head at the Heiress, incredulous, as they strapped into the banquet on the side of the elegant silk and velvet car. Blue, black, and white wrapped in a copper casing which suited Gauge's motif, but the stained glass butterfly above the kitchenette puzzled Lexia.

"Gauge, why—"

The train took off faster than any ride Lexia had ever taken. It threw her into Axis, and then the tunnel opened up to the bare tracks. They helixed immediately, climbing upward and looping upside-down before descending sharply into another tunnel.

Lexia blinked, grateful to her Aegis genes for preventing whiplash.

Snickering brought her back around to the here and now. Axis stared at Lexia, laughing against the back of his hand.

"And what is so funny, my loving fiance?"

Axis couldn't say anything, so Gauge said, "Your hair."

Oh, no!

Lexia retrieved a mirror from her folio and gaped at the sight in its reflection. All those careful pins in her braids couldn't defy gravity. While peering at herself, the Heiress blew the air from her cheeks, fluffing her once-perfect bangs.

Gauge smiled, his braids still fastened like the man contained his own center of gravity, saying, "You still look lovely. Is this your first time on a train?"

Lexia sighed. "I don't get out much. But that will all change now." At the last, her frown transformed into a bright smile. "Thank you, Gauge. For everything."

Before Gauge could respond, Jan said, "We're approaching sector twelve."

Axis sat forward, peering through the port windows. Lexia unbuckled and turned around to look through the one on the wall behind them. Gauge didn't bother to look at all.

And why would he?

There was only Winter outside.

Not even the mass of bodies at the carnival matched the one waiting outside the railcar. Or maybe it only looked sizable because the miniature dome containing them was so small. To begin work, Gauge had erected the structure which would expand as they worked on the city, thanks to Leon's contributions.

There was more of a crowd than Axis had ever seen at any event. Either way, the Prince felt the familiar sensation of light-headedness and the first rush of adrenaline.

Lexia's warm slender fingers laced with Axis' more calloused hands, and he squeezed her for support. Behind them, Gauge's employees unbuckled and moved about, preparing to depart, but Axis was struggling to practice his breathing exercises. So great was the crush beyond the copper barrier.

Another hand, softer even than Lexia's, slipped through Axis' free fingers. He looked down at the intertwining of topaz and obsidian. The Count had taken his gloves off to hold the Prince's hand and risked over sensitization so early in the day.

Axis met Gauge's eyes and tried to convey the significance of the gesture in them—

Fuck it.

"I love you, Gauge."

Even though Gauge was the more experienced man, he reached up and brushed an errant strand of Axis' short hair from his brow, saying, "I love that you say it first. It takes away any fear of rejection for me."

Lexia watched the interaction, sitting still beside them until now. She said, "I love you both, and I have no fears or doubts that we will see this future thrive together. We will see Winter into the Aegis homeworld, and I will never leave your side."

Axis swallowed and said, "Nor I."

Gauge nodded without anxiety or ulterior motivation in his expression. Only naked trust dawned in his eyes like a sunrise on the ocean. This was it.

This was home.

A knock sounded from the carriage door, and Jan said, "It's Dr. Tempest and the others. They await your presence, sirs. Miss."

Axis squeezed both their hands and led them to stand. "Let's welcome tomorrow, together."

Gauge went first through the door with his hand out for Leon to shake. "Good morning, doctor. It's one hell of a day to begin a new city, wouldn't you say?"

Axis almost laughed, recalling the first time he'd had to face Dr. Tempest after Lexia's father had learned of their affair.

Meek.

Shy.

And a little ashamed of taking Lexia's virginity.

But not Gauge. The Count grinned in Leon's face and gestured for Lexia to step out of the train behind him, saying, "My dear." Twice the mischievous devil, he did the same with Axis. "Dear Prince."

Rhyme humphed, turned away, and scratched the ginger beard forming on his face.

A voice sprung up from behind Leon, feminine and approving. "Well, I see you three are in good spirits for our groundbreaking."

Leon stepped aside to let Tija in view. Short and curvaceous in that mini dress and faux-fur wrap, she glowed like a wet dream. "Are you sure you're prepared to build foundations, not rattle them?"

Lexia flushed yellow beside Axis, and he pulled her close to hide his response against the side of her neck, saying, "If I don't feel embarrassed, there's no reason for you to feel it."

With a slight startle at the realization, Lexia met Axis' eyes and beamed at whatever she found there. Confidence. Self-assurance. Or happiness.

Either way, the three of them—the Heiress, the Count, and the Prince—shared the same triumphant grin. Not only had they experienced the most amazing thirty-six hours in bed together, they'd united their triumvirate in a way never—hopefully—a way never done before, but they were also proud of it.

Tija held her arms wide, and all three of them joined in the embrace. The four hugged in the circle of a throng held back by Winter's militia while Leon and Rhyme watched on, quietly observing.

When another voice broke through the din of curious whispers and inappropriate shouts, Axis grinned even broader—an improbable feat. Bolt asked, "Will the three of you be exchanging vows, then?"

Axis glanced at Gauge, who glanced at Lexia. She smiled with entirely too much wickedness—

"No."

They all turned and faced Leon, who said, "Prince Axis had to overcome an immense trial to win my daughter's hand. Count Snow, other than spending one day without boasting or preening, I haven't thought of your trial yet. But mark my words, it will test you."

Axis smirked, but Gauge stamped his cane, saying, "I accept whatever it may be."

Lexia and Tija both gasped, eyes wide and hands cupped over their mouths.

But not Axis. Nothing was outside of Gauge's reach, and if he and Lexia wanted to marry—Axis wouldn't stand in the way—

Wait...

Why was Gauge looking at Axis like that?

Axis' mouth fell open as he pointed at himself. Then he gestured a pendulum between him and Lexia. Astonished at the realization, he asked, "Marry *both* of us?"

The confidence in Gauge's blue blazing eyes flickered a bit, fading as he said, "If you'll have me—"

Axis and Lexia answered at the same time.

"Yes."

It was impulsive and too soon in their relationship, but was it?

Axis, Gauge, and Lexia had been headed for this collision, this inevitable triangulation, all their lives. The nature of it—platonic or romantic—changed little about the rest of their lives leading Winter. A three-way union solidified Winter and made for a brilliant political maneuver here on the brink of space exploration. The brink of a new sector.

Whether it was Lexia's free spirit or Gauge's flair for the dramatic or Axis' head for business—the marriage worked for them.

So as Gauge peered at them wide-eyed with his mouth open—a rare sight, indeed—Axis nodded firmly.

He said, "Yes, Gauge. Absolutely. Let the three of us marry. Today."

Tija threw her arms around Lexia and Gauge before roping Axis in for a hug. The girls hopped up and down in delight, but the Count separated them. The shock left him staring into the Prince's eyes. Only after a moment did Axis see the shininess of them, and by then a tear spilled forth.

Gauge choked out, "Truly?"

Lexia answered with what Axis had wanted to say, "You pick the venue, and we'll be there."

Despite the gasps and cheers from the crowd, Winter melted away, leaving one copper monument and one wild beauty. A fire sparked in Axis' heart, and the icy grip of fear in his chest finally let go. Happiness was here—right at Axis' fingertips. He only needed to reach out and...

The Prince cupped the Count's well-cut jaw, brought their lips together, and the only other thing that mattered was Lexia's soft, approving smile.

Love lived outside of fear, and now, so did Axis.

———————————

Gauge swallowed a whimper against Axis' lips to the sound of Lexia's sweet sniffles. These people loved him enough to accept his off-the-cuff and rather impulsive proposal. Sure, the Copper Count had given thought to a glorious marriage ceremony of epic proportions between the People's Prince and the crop Heiress, but never once did he see himself as one of the grooms.

Well, until about five seconds ago.

Now, it's all Gauge could see.

Was the same day short notice? Perhaps for some, but not for Gauge. Winter would make it happen if only to cement their saga as a power throuple.

Yes.

Gauge broke the kiss to stare into Axis' eyes, breathless as the Prince was. Blindly, the Count reached out his gloved hands, and Lexia took one. Tija took the other. He said, "On my honor, Dr. Tempest, I will endure whatever trial you should demand to prove myself worthy of your daughter's cherished hand."

Leon sounded remote again, and a sideways glance in his direction showed the doctor in full Aegis regalia. Fascinated, Gauge was desperate to know everything about Lexia's natural born people, but that would come later. For now, he waited for the doctor's blessing.

Leon said, "It must be a private event."

Tija, Bolt, Axis, Lexia, and even Jan and Rhyme whirled on the doctor.

Gauge was the only one with his back to him, and he lowered his head with an ironic smile.

Of course...

His sole weakness.

Anonymity.

And for such a spectacular affair to go unwitnessed by all of Winter?

"Leon Tempest, you are a cruel negotiator, but I accept your terms—"

Tija gasped again—The woman who knew Gauge best.

"—However," the Count said as he turned and faced the doctor. "I request no less than ten guests."

Leon conceded with a bow of his head. "Done."

Gauge faced his fiances once more, asking, "Lexia? Axis? Will you marry me in that cozy restaurant you love so much?"

Somewhere in the crowd, an older voice cheered, "We'll guarantee your favorite table this time!"

People laughed, and it was filled with hope and affection. Gauge loved to hear it.

Lexia and Axis exchanged a look before both beamed and threw their arms around Gauge with a resounding, "Yes!"

Loud enough for the Count to hear, Tija said to Bolt, "Are you prepared to get them dressed for this?"

The valet chuckled, "Certainly not. And I thought opening this city would constitute as work for today."

Oh, right.

The groundbreaking.

Gauge raised his cane and encompassed the crowd with his gesture. "Ladies and gentlemen and those who identify otherwise of Winter. Welcome to this auspicious event—The Founding of sector twelve!"

He paused to let the cheers soar and waited for them to lessen before saying, "To memorialize this ambitious event—not to mention the latest in news and gossip for our ardent city—I have decided to extend off-season by one additional week. The only work today will be between me and this shovel."

An employee handed Gauge a steel shovel with a copper handle encrusted with gems from his mine. He took it with his gloved hand and held it out to Axis and Lexia. Taking the hint, the two cozied in beside him. Together, all three of them thrust the spade into the ground, lifted a few grams of dirt, and shoveled it aside.

Even Rhyme clapped.

Outside, the ice hurricanes raged on, but inside…

Massive pyres lit on cue, illuminating the small entry dome from outside. One after the other, they blazed on and on as far as anyone could see, shining light on the amber bubble above and beyond. It was impossible to conceive—vast and enormous, stretching out and out to shelter all of sector twelve's supposedly brand new, unexplored landscape.

Gauge smirked as people stared in silence. Even Tija gazed in wonder at the Count's secret accomplishments. He could taste the intensity, so palpable and decadent.

So when Gauge spoke next, everyone in the near vicinity startled at the sudden noise bursting the tension. He said, "Welcome to Winter's Spring."

Not only had Lexia's mother donated enough of her bones to supply this venture, but she'd taught Gauge how to replicate it within the mines. What would Winter do with the hoard Leon had recently contributed?

Well, what *couldn't* they do with it?

After all...

What was Winter without Summer?

Gauge returned to the Copper Cathedral with Jan and Tija. Bolt and Axis had gone their way, and Lexia had left with her father, Sami, and Rhyme to collect her dress. When the seamstresses confirmed it was ready, Gauge offered them a raise to come work for him. Leon had objected, and Axis' nose had almost bled.

No, the Count wasn't done being a tyrant simply because he was marrying the people's appointed champion. He would forever try to swindle employees out from under the Tempest and Flicker empires, and there wasn't a damned thing they could do about it.

But that's not what this moment was about.

"Thank you, Tija... Your advice ultimately changed my life."

The lovely and rightful Countess of Winter had helped Gauge into a special tux for the wedding. Now she was weaving white ribbons through larger plaits made from his micro braids. He met her eyes in the mirror, a darker blue than his own, and basked in the glow from her red-painted smile.

"Axis will love the flames," Tija said without making a fuss of Gauge's acknowledgments.

Instead, she referred to the blue fire painted along the Count's skin. It was visible through the sheer material of the black tuxedo. As was the stained glass butterfly marked on his back. This wasn't the time to hold back, even without the benefit of all of Winter's eyes on them.

No one had said anything about the reception being private.

Gauge smirked at his own musings, and Tija adjusted the fallen strap of her bra back onto her shoulder. Heat licked at the Count's libido as he considered the easy and comforting sex between him and his long-term partner. A loving spouse if ever there was one—More so, since Tija didn't seem to mind he was marrying two other people tonight.

"We should Saint you."

Tija laughed. She didn't need the joke explained. Rather, she kept it going. "Next, you'll have my virginity restored."

Gauge chuckled, reached for Tija's hand, and placed a tender kiss on it, saying, "Anything for you."

"Besides, once the honeymoon is over, I fully intend to join you three." Her wink in their reflection meant the world to him. Then she said, "Lexia told me about the shackles."

Still proud of the imagination of it, Gauge beamed. "It was a task to restrain someone so wild, but a joy to watch her squirm."

Tija leaned forward and pressed her lips against Gauge's ear to say, "We plan to repay you in kind."

Thump-thump.

Silence.

Thump-thump.

Gauge's heart actually skipped a beat.

This day was the rest of Lexia's life.

The Heiress fluffed her completed gown; the skirt was slitted on both sides. A corset-tie bodice with a sweetheart neckline and a window of missing fabric showed off her blue-freckled breasts and bellybutton. Short petal sleeves gave way to full-arm gloves. All of it was matte black—Only the corset ties were laces of gold. Sami had braided Lexia's white wavy hair with gold and black ribbon. After Sami applied black to Lexia's eyelids and lips, the Heiress painted a gold stripe down the middle of both. Gold lacing tied black stiletto pumps all the way up Lexia's legs, visible through the slits.

Axis' burgundy and silver timepiece and Gauge's blue and copper timepiece completed the ensemble—Winter's Diamond at a high shine.

Was it macabre?

A little. But every sector of the city—including the new one—owed their structure to Lya's bones, and well...

She deserved to be at Lexia's wedding.

A knock sounded at the door, and Lexia knew before Sami answered it that Rhyme stood on the other side. He said through the crack, "Dr. Tempest is ready downstairs."

Lexia beamed while Sami rushed over and gave a few last-minute touches to their hair. The kitchen hand called, "Matori, you can come out now."

"I don't wanna."

"Young lady..."

Lexia laughed. "Come on, Matori. How can you be my flower girl if you hide in the restroom all night?"

The little girl opened the door and stepped out into the room in a cute slip dress. She looked adorable with that churlish pout, asking, "But what if I wanted to wear a tuxedo like Prince Axis?"

Sami put a finger to her lips. "Shh. Don't go sounding ungrateful."

Lexia didn't want to undermine the other woman's mothering skills, so instead, she asked, "How about you change into whatever you like for the reception? I hear the ice dancers will be in the rink all night."

Matori lit up. "Really? Will Rhyme and Bolt come?"

Oh, wasn't that adorable?

Sami blushed at the mention of her suitors, but as Lexia was about to marry two men in her life, she grinned, saying, "Of course! But only if you hurry."

Matori skipped to the door and reached for the knob before turning back. "Mother, what are we waiting for?!"

Sami gave Lexia an apologetic look, but the Heiress would have none of it. She said, "I hope to have ten just like her."

After taking one look at Lexia in her dress, Leon had insisted they drive—not walk—to the little restaurant. Churlish and pouting, the Heiress sat in the car and stared through the window as Winter passed them by. Were all fathers so uncompromising?

But no. That wasn't fair.

Leon was a good… Aegis? Man? Person… And he only wanted to keep her dress a surprise. Plus, what must this be like? Giving his daughter away to two men? One he adored and the other he'd tried to have assassinated recently.

Lexia smiled at the glass. It was a good thing Gauge liked the drama of it all and forgave easily.

"Your mother would be thrilled."

Breath caught in Lexia's throat, and she almost choked on a sob as she turned to face her father.

Leon said, "She always liked Gauge, and I believe everyone appreciates Axis. They both meet in the middle with you, and I think it's a lovely marriage of your personalities and politics, even without the ceremony."

Lexia couldn't form words, so she reached out and touched Leon's hand. He took hers on the seat between them. They didn't talk the rest of the way; they just sat in comfortable silence until Rhyme announced their arrival.

Not that it was necessary.

Lexia couldn't believe that only two months ago, she'd walked into this teeny place in the hopes Axis would propose to her. Now she was marrying both the Prince and the Count in it. A journey marked by her newly published manuscript. It was already converted into a play for tonight's reception. The people of Winter sang it on Lexia's arrival.

True, Leon had called for a private gathering, but even Gauge's militia couldn't keep Winter from lining the entrance of the cobblestone streets. Unlike the opera, there was no red carpet or flashing lights.

An old couple owned the restaurant, and they waited at the curb while Rhyme, Sami, and Matori opened the car door for Leon and Lexia to exit. The doctor had given Lexia his coat, and she used it to shield most everything she could on the quick jaunt into the restaurant's foyer.

The wife of the old pair said, "Prince Axis has already arrived. We've secreted him off in one of the back rooms. We'll take you upstairs. The Count is on his way."

Lexia's heart pounded in her chest, and butterflies danced in her stomach.

This was it.

The Heiress would marry the Prince and the Count tonight.

Sami made a squeeing sound before rushing Lexia toward the stairs, saying, "Hurry, miss! We need to finish preparing you—"

"Wait…" Lexia stopped and turned around to face her father.

Leon searched her eyes before opening his arms, and the little girl in Lexia rushed into them. He kissed her braided hair and said, "I'll give you away whenever you're ready."

"Thank you, father. I know at times I'm a brat—"

Rhyme chuckled practically on cue.

"—But I'm always grateful for everything you've done for me and for Axis. And now I know you've done so much for mother and Winter. More than I could imagine. Thank you."

Leon sighed, saying, "Oh, daughter mine. I can't wait to show you the rest."

As the doctor mentioned stories yet told, Lexia suddenly remembered…

Jan hadn't finished his tale. The little sneak.

Lexia beamed. Meaning for both Jan and for her father, she said, "I'd love to hear it sometime."

This day was the rest of Axis' life.

The Prince paced the small back room from potato to cheese wheel back to potato again. He knew Bolt, leaned casually against the door, never took his eyes off his ward, back and forth. Back and forth.

No less than ten.

Kol, Phoro, Mrs. Tenz, her son, Matori, Sami, Bolt, Rhyme, Tija, and Jan. And obviously Leon made eleven—

Were Axis' palms sweating?

"Sit down, man. You're ruining the Brie."

The Prince stopped, hand on his hip pushing back his jacket, while the other pinched the bridge of his nose. He said, "I promise, it's not an issue with the publicity of it."

Bolt folded his arms, saying, "Well, let's hope not. Not only are there only two handfuls of people out there, but also, once you went assless in public, I figured you were kinda over it."

Axis dropped the hand at his brow and looked up toward the ceiling, seeking...

Guidance?

Council?

No.

With a little more heartache than Axis would like to admit, it suddenly hit him all at once that he had no family to support him. Yes, of course, there was Bolt and Leon—But no one of his own. While Gauge was in a similar situation, he didn't seem to mind. But Axis had always wanted a family like the Tempest's, shadowed as it was.

The Prince confessed, "I just wish…" When the thought struck him, he had to say aloud, "I just wish my father were here to see me marry Count Snow."

Bolt burst into a fit of chuckles, and Axis laughed along with him at the irony. The wedding would probably have sent Valve into the ground more quickly than the damned copper-lined cigars.

Axis met the warm brown of Bolt's eyes, saying, "Damn, this has been a wild ride."

"You're telling me. I was single last week, and now I'm sharing a partner with the top duelist in the capital."

A knock sounded and Bolt said, "Speak of the devil," as he opened the door a crack.

Rhyme's gravelly voice came through the door. "They're ready."

Axis let out a rush of air and straightened the leather lapels of his burgundy three-piece. Meant for his wedding to Lexia, it sported a gold waistcoat, but the plain blue strip of silk around his neck, Axis had added for Gauge. No, the Prince would never appreciate breath play the way Lexia did, but it seemed like a nice touch to cement their throupling.

Bolt opened the door wide, asking, "Are you ready, groom?"

The Prince ran a hand over his hair and rushed to meet his best man. Axis' palms weren't sweaty, and once he took a deep, steadying breath, he found his center. Axis said, "Yes. Yes, I am," and meant it.

As primary groom, he went to the altar made of the host's podium. The husband who owned the restaurant stood there as the officiator. Rhyme stood on Lexia's side with Sami. The kitchen hand waved at

Bolt, and when the valet blew her a kiss, she blushed while Rhyme shook his head.

No one knew any shame here.

Bolt walked at Axis' side, 'giving the Prince away' of sorts. They stood to the left of the podium, waiting. There was no need to fidget or loosen the silk around Axis' neck. Lexia was his 'meant-to-be,' and Gauge was everything the Prince dared to dream of but never to speak of.

No marriage was more perfect, and Axis didn't need a parental figure to tell him so.

"Psst."

Axis blinked before seeking the source of the sound. It was Mrs. Tenz, sitting down in Axis' third of the space. She and her son waved, and feeling giddy in the moment, Axis waved back like a goof. He was grinning ear-to-ear before he knew it.

Phoro caught his eye, too, from the Flicker section. He looked happy to be there. Kol waved from the Tempest side. Everyone present—few in number, but big in heart—shared the same expression of benevolence and pride.

Only happiness resided within this simple venue, and Axis couldn't wait—

A chime sounded.

Just the tiniest bell, and Axis knew before the music started, that Gauge was walking down the aisle first. The Count appeared at the end of the room with Tija on his arm. She walked alongside him down the way, while Axis took in the sight of Gauge. The blue flames thrilled Axis, but the teeny shorts protecting his 'modesty' should nullify the arrangement with Leon the second the doctor laid eyes on the secondary groom.

Axis almost rolled his eyes at his tyrant, but that would mean taking them off of Gauge—And that wasn't happening.

Well, not until the Flicker wicks along the stairs lit up the banister on the second floor.

Lexia…

Axis couldn't breathe.

Both men stopped and stared up at the butterfly—the literal butterfly—at the top of the stairs. Lexia stood there in a dress, a shock of its own, but this one fluttered with wings from her back. Small gemstones glittered as she took the first step down, with Leon at her side.

With her hair pulled back, there was no competing with Lexia's smile. She brought Gauge and Axis together, and she shone with the victory of it brighter than any diamond in the night sky.

No one needed to say anything as all the guests watched the throuple come together in the center of the restaurant. The old couple beamed with pride and secondhand elation. When Lexia stood between Axis and Gauge, Leon gave her a kiss on the cheek, nodded to both men, and left to sit with the rest of the guests on Lexia's side.

Axis opened his mouth to tell them how beautiful they were when Matori ran into the space, rushing to throw flowers at their feet and all around. She gave a little twirl before flipping the entire basket upside in the air and dousing herself in black, burgundy, and blue rose petals.

Sami sighed. Rhyme and Bolt chuckled simultaneously before glaring at one another across the venue, but Gauge's reaction stole Axis' heart.

Even more so.

The Count swung the little girl up in his arms and chafed his nose against hers. Matori giggled and blushed before squirming to set back down and run into her mother's arms. She whispered, "Mommy, he's more handsome in person."

More chuckles abounded, and Gauge's eyes were alight with sweet humor when he turned back and faced Lexia and Axis.

Axis blurted it again, and would likely never restrain himself from saying it. "I love you."

Lexia beamed. "Ditto."

Gauge grinned. "Then all that's left is 'I do.'"

Axis almost choked on a tear as Lexia held out both arms. The gentlemen placed one hand on each timepiece and held onto each other's free hand together.

The old husband acting as officiator said, "In Winter's Eternity, time stops for you. You belong to one another once the second hand ceases."

Axis pressed the button on his timepiece, and Gauge pressed the one on his. Both watches stopped ticking.

Six o-three.

When the officiator announced the time of marriage, the throuple said the most important words in Winter.

"Until Eternity takes me, I'm yours."

The old wife said, "Excuse me," before opening the door and repeating the time to the people waiting outside. The most deafening roar, even louder than the announcement of the carnival, sounded from outside the restaurant.

Winter celebrated tonight, and everyone knew...

So would Axis, Lexia, and Gauge.

Epilogue

AFTER A DIVINE MEAL AT THE MODEST RESTAURANT, THE THROUPLE MADE THEIR WAY TO THE THEATER—RED CARPET STYLE. So infatuated as they were with each other, it had taken them a while to exit the car and make the formal appearance. Flashing cameras likely captured at least one or two photos of them half-naked through the windows, but as long as Axis and Lexia didn't mind, Gauge couldn't care less.

Once inside, they went to the stage and gave speeches. It turned into a long night of song and dance, play acting, ice skating in the rink transported within, and flaming acrobatics above.

Winter had never been so drunk.

So ecstatic.

And neither had Gauge.

The Copper Count, the People's Prince, and the crop Heiress luxuriated in good company and fun. They snuck off many times throughout the night together or in pairs. Gauge spent almost an equal amount of time with Tija, thanking her dressed and naked for her devotion and admiring her many pleasant attributes.

Thoroughly.

Everything seemed perfect until a bright spark of electricity split the room. Beyond it, Gauge glimpsed the improbable—

No.

The impossible.

A world of purples—all varying shades from marbled floor, to columned walls, and distant ceilings.

Through it, a woman stepped into the aisle which split the theater in two.

Blond, short—

That's all Gauge made out before another one stepped through.

Black hair at the roots and white at the ends.

White…

The blond said to the other woman, "C'mon, Rayne, we only get a few hours with each other a week, and I've missed you—"

"Sagan, where are we?"

The woman with black and white hair peered around the people in the theater as the blond finally turned around and blinked.

"Uhm… Huh…"

Gauge threw back his champagne, took Axis' glass from beside him, downed it, and Lexia's wine on top of it. He needed the boost as he straightened his lapels and took point. He walked down the aisle, happy to hear his spouses' steps in tow.

Winter remained divided across the room, mid-drink, mid-bite, or mid-fuck.

Honestly, who knew what time or even what day it was? And Gauge was exhausted to his marrow, but he'd be damned if the festivities ended because of uninvited magical guests.

No.

Not magic.

Gauge was a scientist at his core, and he knew spatial displacement travel when he saw it, but the how of it...

Well...

That's why Gauge approached the newcomers and said, "Welcome, ladies, to our wedding. I have questions."

The blond, named Sagan, broke into a warm smile and held out her hand. "Hi, I'm Sagan. This is my girlfriend, Rayne. We didn't mean to interrupt, but I was looking for somewhere specific."

Gauge laughed, incredulous, but shook her hand to return the friendly gesture. With gloved fingers, he gently cupped her tiny tan hand between both of his. "Ms. Sagan, you and your partner are free to ask any questions you like as long as I can ask mine. Starting with, 'how did you get here?'"

Sagan eased her hand out of Gauge's, and he dropped them at his side carefully to show he meant no harm. The girl tapped her two index fingers together, abashed. "Well, you see? We've been missing a planet for a few months, and I was wondering if this is Monarch 2?"

Ah.

At the gasps in the crowd, Gauge wanted to sigh.

Even Lexia placed a hand on the Count's shoulder. "Gauge?"

Axis said, "I can't believe it. They've only been here five seconds, and we have to arrest them."

Sagan's eyes widened, but Rayne's reaction caught Gauge's attention. She didn't react at all. To none of it. The woman looked perfectly comfortable despite all the shocked and offended faces surrounding them. She said, "You told us we were free to ask any question."

Gauge *did* sigh this time, saying, "Any question, but that one."

Someone drunkenly shouted, "Arrest them!"

Another slurred as they said, "They said the one ultimate sin."

"Wait!"

Gauge was afraid to take his eyes off this Rayne figure, glowing as she was, to look over at Leon parting the crowd.

Lexia looked a question at her father as he approached Gauge's side, repeating, "Wait."

Gauge held up his hand, and the crowd stopped inching forward.

Leon dropped the disguise, and Rayne and Sagan both stared at him with wide eyes. The blond breathed, "Another Aegis."

Rayne said, "Are you related to One, Zero, or Three Two Four?"

In response, Leon muttered, "Thank Eternity. No. I'm not related to our maker." He turned and faced Gauge, gesturing at the young women. "This is it. This is the signal."

Gauge swallowed.

Lexia took a tentative step forward, Axis at her side, and only then did Rayne and Sagan seem to notice her.

The short blond girl paled as if she'd seen a ghost and fell a little against Rayne's side. "Rayne, am I seeing things?"

"No," Rayne said before holding up her palm. A projection appeared in her hand, and everyone but Gauge, Lexia, and Axis took a step back.

Sagan said into the device, "Lucas, are you decent?"

A man—another Aegis said, "That depends—"

This Lucas in the projection stopped speaking and stared at Lexia. When the doctor stepped into frame, Lucas took one look at Leon and said, "Leonidas. You survived."

Leonidas…

Like the king in Cam Snow's stories?

Gauge stared upside Leon's head, waiting for the doctor to deign a response. Unconcerned with Gauge's incredulity, Leon said, "I did. And what of the war? Our people?"

"My friend, come home. We have much to discuss."

The projection ended, and the two women blinked a bit, peering around the room once more.

Leon asked, "Count Snow, do you recall the vow I made to you?"

Eternal youth.

Vitality.

Gauge asked, "How could I forget?"

Leon turned, and, for the first time in a long time, smiled at the Count. "Consider it fulfilled."

Lexia took Gauge's hand, the one which stung from a projection device. It was very much like Rayne's device which Jan had cut from his hand. And Axis placed a hand on Gauge's shoulder.

But all the Count could think through the sag of his spine and the ache behind his glasses—

This was it.

This day truly was the rest of Gauge's life.

Author's Note

If this is your first introduction to my universe, welcome. I hope you read the Vast Collective Series to learn more about Sagan and Rayne.

If you're not new, welcome back. You might know that I took a break from writing after *Polar Axis*. I hope by the time you're reading this, I've already written my sixteenth book, but there's a chance I'm still working on it. If that's the case, keep in touch using my website.

I promise. I'm not finished yet.

nicolehayeswriter.com/

You can find the entire series on Amazon by scanning the QR code below.